FATHERS AND SONS

THE AUTHOR ON THE NOVEL

CONTEMPORARY REACTIONS

ESSAYS IN CRITICISM

A NORTON CRITICAL EDITION

IVAN TURGENEV

FATHERS AND SONS

THE AUTHOR ON THE NOVEL

CONTEMPORARY REACTIONS

ESSAYS IN CRITICISM

Edited with a substantially new translation by

RALPH E. MATLAW
UNIVERSITY OF CHICAGO

W · W · NORTON & COMPANY · INC · *New York*

Library of Congress Catalog Card No. 66-11789

ISBN 0 393 04285 5 Cloth Edition

ISBN 0 393 09652 1 Paper Edition

PRINTED IN THE UNITED STATES OF AMERICA

1 2 3 4 5 6 7 8 9 0

Contents

The Contemporary Reaction

Essays in Criticism

Preface

Translating Turgenev's novel poses many problems, beginning with the title. The literal translation is *Fathers and Children.* But "sons" in English better implies the notion of spiritual and intellectual generations conveyed by the Russian *deti.* It is almost impossible to reproduce the rich yet firm texture of the prose. At the same time Turgenev is distinctly old-fashioned, so that a new translation into contemporary English would distort the work. The solution adopted was to use the translation made by Constance Garnett at the turn of the century, which has a comparable quaint but dated charm, and to revise it with three aims in mind: first, to correct many errors and omissions that were the results of the text Mrs. Garnett used, the rapidity of her work, and occasional misinterpretation; second, to change some of the locutions that are too outmoded or too British into others that are less distracting and more comprehensible to the reader; and third, to recast sentence structure when Mrs. Garnett followed the Russian too closely, to the detriment of English style.

No book published in Russia has ever aroused a critical storm as violent and acrimonious as that around *Fathers and Sons.* The controversy is not yet over. Folejewski shows how it has flared up in a new form in the Soviet Union, and in various ways it engages the attention of all who write on Turgenev, so that it becomes a central problem for those who study Russian intellectual life in the second half of the nineteenth century (see Mathewson's eloquent statement on the plight of the writer in meeting the demands of the Russian reading public). The background material is vast, and in one sense necessary only to the specialist, since the novel itself dramatizes the issues so well. The bibliography offers some possibilities for exploring the historical background. In the notes to the text I have indicated some of Turgenev's specific jibes at certain contemporary ideas, and I have grouped a considerable amount of the background material under the heading "The Contemporary Reception," where the reader may follow these ideas and trace the attempts to justify or condemn Turgenev's work by the most important writers of his day. Turgenev's own involvement and defense of his intentions occupied him for the remainder of his life and embittered and angered him. The excerpts from his correspondence and his own defense of the novel reprinted here indicate this but also show his concern for revising the work to increase its clarity and its artistic polish.

To the western reader many of these problems do not seem so significant nor even entirely germane to the novel. Writers like Prosper Mérimée and Henry James were happy to pay tribute to Turgenev as a fellow artist—he is, after all, the most European of all nineteenth-century Russian writers in form and subject. But the vast literature on Turgenev has dealt comparatively little with those aspects of his work. I have tried to indicate in my own essay why this occurred, though the other essays published here fortunately prove that I am wrong.

Still, an overwhelming proportion of criticism on *Fathers and Sons* deals with its main figure and turns into Bazarov criticism instead. This is entirely understandable since Bazarov so thoroughly dominates the novel, but such criticism has a disturbing tendency to turn into psychological or socio-political speculation on that personage at the expense of literary analysis of a character in a novel. There has been no way of avoiding such material, the more so as it would have falsified the historical significance of the novel if it had been omitted. It is particularly evident in Turgenev's letters and Pisarev's article, and to a lesser extent in Strakhov's more balanced review of the book, Garnett's article, and the second part of my own piece. For matters of craft and composition, the reader may refer to Freeborn's analysis of the structure, to Justus's treatment of nature as a thematic device as well as a descriptive one in the novel, to Pustovoyt's discussion of various stylistic features and compositional devices characteristic of Turgenev, and to Hindus's analysis of the function of a particular scene.

The first four Essays in Criticism are so arranged that the reader with little or no background may obtain a fairly complete picture of Turgenev, his art, and the particular historical and aesthetic problems of *Fathers and Sons.* Mirsky's is a concise summary of Turgenev's life and art, Yarmolinsky's of the circumstances attendant upon the publication of the novel. Wellek has given some of the background of the critical controversy that raged around the novel but points to and emphasizes the more permanent features of the book. My own essay considers a broader spectrum of Turgenev's attitudes and literary predilections before embarking on a brief discussion of his novel. The reader may refer to it for a summary of critical attitudes toward Turgenev as well as for the principles, stated or implied, that guided the selection of other materials.

There has been no attempt made to make the transliteration of names consistent in the entire volume. Since the names are readily identifiable this should present no problem. In the text and in the translations prepared for this edition, the *a* or *aya* at the end of family names in the feminine has properly been omitted, so that Anna Sergeevna's last name is Odinstov, and I have bitten my thumb at the "emancipated lady" and left her as Kukshin. No accentuation has been provided for the Russian names, nor have I followed the practice of indicating the possible implications of the names. Yet I cannot refrain from pointing out that the hero's name —Bazarov—is among the most appropriate ever devised, for it contains and symbolizes those ideas bruited during the 1860's in the intellectual marketplace.

Ralph E. Matlaw

The Text of
Fathers and Sons

The Translation by Constance Garnett,
Revised by Ralph E. Matlaw

Fathers and Sons

Dedicated to the memory of
VISSARION GRIGOR'EVICH BELINSKY [1]

I

"Well, Peter, not in sight yet?" was the question asked on May 20th, 1859,[2] by a gentleman a little over forty, in a dusty coat and checked trousers, who came out hatless to the low porch of the posting station at S——. He was addressing his servant, a chubby young fellow, with whitish down on his chin, and little lack-lustre eyes.

The servant, in whom everything—the turquoise ring in his ear, the pomaded streaky hair, and the civility of his movements—indicated a man of the new, improved generation, glanced condescendingly along the road, and replied:

"No, sir; definitely not in sight."

"Not in sight?" repeated his master.

"Not in sight," responded the man a second time.

His master sighed and sat down on a little bench. We will introduce him to the reader while he sits, his feet tucked under him, gazing thoughtfully round.

His name is Nikolai Petrovich Kirsanov. He had twelve miles from the posting station, a fine property of two hundred souls, or, as he expressed it—since he had arranged the division of his land with the peasants, and started a "farm"—of nearly five thousand acres.[3] His father, a general who had fought in 1812, a half-edu-

1. Belinsky (1811-48), the most gifted critic Russia produced in the nineteenth century, was the idol of young liberals in the 1830's and 1840's. He enthusiastically reviewed Turgenev's early work. The dedication thus immediately implies a work dedicated to the highest ideals of liberal or progressive thought. See Turgenev's letter to A. V. Toporov, November 25 (December 8), 1882.

2. The novel is deliberately set before the liberation of the serfs, which took place February 19, 1861 (old style). The Julian calendar, used in Russia until 1917, was twelve days behind the Gregorian calendar in use in the West. February 19 was therefore March 3 new style.

3. Kirsanov's action marks him as a liberal landowner, choosing to ameliorate the serfs' lot on his own initiative. He had substituted quitrent (obrok)—a fixed sum of money to be paid annually by each peasant—for the indentured service—*barshchina* (In France *corvée*)—the owner could demand from his serfs. The quitrent required far less of the serfs' time. Kirsanov has also divided his property into that part reserved for his own and those plots farmed by the serfs to provide their own food and earn their quitrent.

cated, coarse, but not ill-natured man, a typical Russian, had drudged all his life, first in command of a brigade, then of a division; and constantly lived in the provinces where, by virtue of his rank, he played a fairly important part. Nikolai Petrovich was born in the south of Russia like his elder brother, Pavel, of whom more hereafter. He was educated at home till he was fourteen, surrounded by cheap tutors, free-and-easy but toadying adjutants, and other regimental and staff people. His mother, one of the Kolyazin family, as a girl called *Agathe*, but as a general's wife Agafokleya Kuzminishna Kirsanov, was one of those "lady commandants." She wore sumptuous caps and rustling silk dresses; in church she was the first to advance to the cross; she talked a great deal in a loud voice, let her children kiss her hand in the morning, and gave them her blessing at night—in fact, she got everything out of life she could. Nikolai Petrovich, as a general's son—though so far from being distinguished by courage that he even deserved to be called a little coward—was intended, like his brother Pavel, to enter the army; but he broke his leg on the very day when the news of his orders arrived, and, after being in bed two months, retained a slight limp to the end of his life. His father gave him up as a bad job, and let him go into the civil service. He took him to Petersburg as soon as he was eighteen, and placed him in the university. His brother happened about the same time to be made an officer in the Guards. The young men started living together in one set of rooms, under the remote supervision of a cousin on their mother's side, Ilya Kolyazin, an official of high rank. Their father returned to his division and his wife, and only rarely sent his sons large quarto sheets of grey paper, scrawled over in a bold clerkly hand. The bottom of these quarto sheets were adorned by the words, "Peater Kirsanof, Major-General," [4] enclosed carefully in scroll-work. In 1835 Nikolai Petrovich was graduated from the university, and in the same year General Kirsanov was put on the retired list after an unsuccessful review, and came to Petersburg with his wife to live. He was about to take a house near the Taurus Garden and had joined the English club, but he died suddenly of a stroke. Agafokleya Kuzminishna soon followed him; she could not accustom herself to the dull life in the capital; she was consumed by the boredom of existence in retirement. Meanwhile Nikolai Petrovich had already, in his parents' lifetime and to their no slight chagrin, had time to fall in love with the daughter of his landlord, a petty official, Prepolovensky. She was pretty, and, as it is called, an "advanced" girl; she used to read serious articles in the "Science" sections of the journals. He married her as soon as the term of mourning was over; and leaving the civil service in

4. A phonetic transcription that indicates the general is not too literate.

which his father had by favor procured him a post, was perfectly blissful with his Masha, first in a country villa near the Forestry Institute, afterwards in town in a pretty little flat with a clean staircase and a rather chilly drawing-room; and then in the country, where he settled finally, and where in a short time a son, Arkady, was born to him. The young couple lived very happily and peacefully; they were scarcely ever apart; they read together, sang and played duets together on the piano; she tended her flowers and looked after the poultry-yard; he sometimes went hunting, and busied himself with the estate, while Arkady grew and grew in the same happy and peaceful way. Ten years passed like a dream. In 1847 Kirsanov's wife died. He almost succumbed to this blow; in a few weeks his hair was grey; he was getting ready to go abroad, if possible to distract his mind . . . but then came the year 1848.[5] He returned willy-nilly to the country, and, after a rather prolonged period of inactivity, occupied himself with the reorganisation of his estate. In 1855 he brought his son to the university; he spent three winters with him in Petersburg, hardly going out anywhere, and trying to make acquaintance with Arkady's young companions. The last winter he had not been able to go, and here we see him in the May of 1859, already quite grey, stoutish, and rather bent, waiting for his son, who had just taken his degree, as once he had taken it himself.

The servant, from a feeling of propriety, and perhaps, too, not anxious to remain under the master's eye, had gone to the gate, and was smoking a pipe. Nikolai Petrovich bent his head, and began staring at the crumbling steps; a big mottled chicken walked sedately towards him, treading firmly with its great yellow legs; a muddy cat gave him an unfriendly look, curled up coyly on the railing. The sun was scorching; from the half-dark passage of the posting station came an odor of hot rye-bread. Nikolai Petrovich fell to dreaming. "My son . . . a graduate . . . Arkasha . . ." were the ideas that continually came round again and again in his head; he tried to think of something else, and again the same thoughts returned. He remembered his dead wife. . . . "She did not live to see it!" he murmured sadly. A plump, blue-grey pigeon flew into the road, and hurriedly went to drink from a puddle near the well. Nikolai Petrovich began looking at it, but his ear had already caught the sound of approaching wheels.

"It sounds as if they're coming, sir," announced the servant, popping in from the gateway.

Nikolai Petrovich jumped up, and fixed his eyes on the road. A carriage with three posting-horses harnessed abreast appeared; in

5. The revolution of 1848 initiated the most reactionary phase of Nicholas I's reign. It became practically impossible for Russians to travel abroad.

the carriage he caught a glimpse of the blue band of a student's cap, the familiar outline of a dear face.

"Arkasha! Arkasha!" shouted Kirsanov, and he ran waving his hands. . . . A few instants later, his lips were pressed to the beardless, dusty, sunburnt cheek of the youthful graduate.

II

"Let me shake myself first, daddy," said Arkady, in a voice hoarse from travelling, but cheerful and youthful, as he gaily responded to his father's caresses; "I am covering you with dust."

"Never mind, never mind," repeated Nikolai Petrovich, smiling tenderly, and twice he struck the collar of his son's cloak and his own great-coat with his hand. "Let me have a look at you; let me have a look at you," he added, moving back from him, but immediately he went with hurried steps towards the yard of the station, calling, "This way, this way; and horses at once."

Nikolai Petrovich seemed far more excited than his son; he seemed a little confused, a little timid. Arkady stopped him.

"Daddy," he said, "let me introduce you to my good friend, Bazarov, about whom I have so often written to you. He has been so kind as to promise to stay with us."

Nikolai Petrovich turned around quickly, and going up to a tall man in a long, loose, rough coat with tassels, who had only just got out of the carriage, he warmly pressed the bare red hand, which the latter did not at once hold out to him.

"I am heartily glad," he began, "and very grateful for your kind intention of visiting us. . . . May I know your name and patronymic." [6]

"Evgeny Vassilyev," answered Bazarov, in a lazy but manly voice; and turning back the collar of his rough coat, he showed Nikolai Petrovich his whole face. It was long and lean, with a broad forehead, a nose flat at the base and sharp at the tip, large greenish eyes, and drooping side whiskers of a sandy color; it was animated by a tranquil smile, and showed self-confidence and intelligence.

"I hope, dear Evgeny Vassilyich, it won't be boring for you with us," continued Nikolai Petrovich.

Bazarov's thin lips moved just perceptibly, though he made no reply, but merely took off his cap. His long, thick dark-blond hair

6. The patronymic is formed by adding the appropriate suffix to one's father's given name, and Russians normally address each other by name and patronymic rather than as Mr. or Mrs. plus family name. In speaking to close friends, children, or inferiors the patronymic is usually omitted. Bazarov gives the short popular form of his patronymic, thereby exaggerating his lower origin. The use of the family name alone, particularly for female characters, as later in this book, and without Mr., Miss, or Mrs. can convey various shades of characters' (or author's) behavior and attitudes.

did not hide the prominent bumps of his large skull.

"Well, Arkady," Nikolai Petrovich began again, turning to his son, "shall the horses be put to at once, or would you like to rest?"

"We will rest at home, daddy; tell them to harness the horses."

"At once, at once," his father assented. "Hey, Peter, do you hear? Get things ready, my good boy; look sharp."

Peter, who as a modernised servant had not kissed the young master's hand, but only bowed to him from a distance, again vanished through the gateway.

"I came here with the carriage, but there are three horses for your coach too," said Nikolai Petrovich fussily, while Arkady drank some water from an iron dipper brought him by the woman in charge of the station, and Bazarov lit a pipe and went up to the driver, who was taking out the horses; "there are only two seats in the carriage, and I don't know how your friend . . ."

"He will go in the coach," interposed Arkady in an undertone. "You must not stand on ceremony with him, please. He's a splendid fellow, so simple—you will see."

Nikolai Petrovich's coachman brought the horses round.

"Come, hurry up, bushy beard!" said Bazarov, addressing the driver.

"Do you hear, Mityukha," put in another driver, standing by with his hands thrust behind him into the opening of his sheepskin coat, "what the gentleman called you? It's bushy beard you are too."

Mityukha only gave a jog to his hat and pulled the reins off the heated shaft-horse.

"Look sharp, look sharp, lads, lend a hand," cried Nikolai Petrovich; "there'd be something to drink our health with!"

In a few minutes the horses were harnessed; the father and son were installed in the carriage; Peter climbed up on to the box; Bazarov jumped into the coach, and nestled his head down into the leather cushion; and both the vehicles rolled away.

III

"So here you are, a graduate at last, and come home again," said Nikolai Petrovich, touching Arkady now on the shoulder, now on the knee. "At last!"

"And how is uncle, quite well?" asked Arkady who, in spite of the genuine, almost childish delight filling his heart, wanted as soon as possible to turn the conversation from the emotional to a commonplace channel.

"Quite well. He was thinking of coming with me to meet you, but for some reason or other he gave up the idea."

"And how long have you been waiting for me?" inquired Arkady.

"Oh, about five hours."

"Dear old dad!"

Arkady turned round quickly to his father, and resoundingly kissed him on the cheek. Nikolai Petrovich gave vent to a low chuckle.

"I have got such a capital horse for you!" he began. "You will see. And your room has been freshly papered."

"And is there a room for Bazarov?"

"We will find one for him too."

"Please, dad, be nice to him. I can't tell you how I prize his friendship."

"Have you made friends with him lately?"

"Yes, quite lately."

"Ah, that's how it is I did not see him last winter. What does he study?"

"His chief subject is the natural sciences. But he knows everything. Next year he wants to take his M. D."

"Ah! he's in the medical faculty," observed Nikolai Petrovich, and he was silent for a little. "Peter," he went on, stretching out his hand, "aren't those our peasants driving along?"

Peter looked where his master was pointing. Several carts harnessed with unbridled horses were moving rapidly along a narrow by-road. In each cart there were one or at most two peasants in sheepskin coats, unbuttoned.

"Yes, sir," replied Peter.

"Where are they going,—to the town?"

"To the town, I suppose. To the pot-house [7]," he added contemptuously, turning slightly towards the coachman, as though appealing to him. But the latter did not stir a muscle; he was a man of the old stamp, and did not share the modern views of the younger generation.

"I have had a lot of bother with the peasants this year," pursued Nikolai Petrovich, turning to his son. "They won't pay their rent. What is one to do?"

"But are you satisfied with your hired laborers?"

"Yes," said Nikolai Petrovich between his teeth. "They are being set against me, that's the mischief; and they don't do their best as yet. They spoil the tools. But they have tilled the land pretty fairly. When things have settled down a bit, it will be all right. Do you take an interest in farming now?"

"You've no shade; that's a pity," remarked Arkady, without answering the last question.

"I have had a great awning put up on the north side over the

7. The pot-house (*kabak*) was a kind of small inn or hut, something like a bar, where peasants would go to drink.

balcony," observed Nikolai Petrovich; "now we can even have dinner in the open air."

"It'll be rather too like a summer villa. . . . Still, that's all nonsense. But what air there is here! How delicious it smells! Really I fancy there's nowhere such fragrance in the world as in these regions! And the sky, too."

Arkady suddenly stopped short, cast a stealthy look behind him, and said no more.

"Of course," observed Nikolai Petrovich, "you were born here, and so everything is bound to strike you in a special——"

"Come, dad, it makes no difference where a man is born."

"Still——"

"No; it makes absolutely no difference."

Nikolai Petrovich gave a sidelong glance at his son, and the carriage went on half-a-mile further before the conversation was renewed between them.

"I don't recollect whether I wrote to you," began Nikolai Petrovich, "your old nurse, Egorovna, is dead."

"Really? Poor thing! Is Prokofich still living?"

"Yes, and not a bit changed. Grumbles as much as ever. In fact, you won't find many changes in Marino."

"Have you still the same bailiff?"

"Well, to be sure, there is a change there. I decided not to keep about me any freed serfs who had been house servants, or, at least, not to intrust them with duties of any responsibility." (Arkady glanced towards Peter.) "*Il est libre, en effet,*" [8] observed Nikolai Petrovich in an undertone; "but, you see, he's only a valet. Now I have a bailiff, a townsman; he seems a practical fellow. I pay him two hundred and fifty rubles a year. But," added Nikolai Petrovich, rubbing his forehead and eyebrows with his hand, which was always an indication with him of inward embarrassment, "I told you just now that you would not find changes at Marino. . . . That's not quite correct. I think it my duty to prepare you, even though . . ."

He hesitated for an instant, and then went on in French.

"A severe moralist would regard my openness as improper; but, in the first place, it can't be concealed, and secondly, you are aware I have always had special ideas as regards the relation of father and son. Though, of course, you would be right in blaming me. At my age . . . In short . . . that . . . that girl, about whom you have probably heard already . . ."

"Fenichka?" asked Arkady easily.

Nikolai Petrovich blushed. "Don't mention her name aloud, please. . . . Well . . . she is living with me now. I have installed her

8. "He is free, actually."

in the house . . . there were two little rooms there. But that can all be changed."

"Goodness, daddy, what for?"

"Your friend is going to stay with us . . . it would be awkward . . ."

"Please, don't be uneasy on Bazarov's account. He's above all that."

"Well, but you, too," added Nikolai Petrovich. "The little lodge is so horrid—that's the worst of it."

"Goodness, dad," interposed Arkady, "it's as if you were apologising; I wonder you're not ashamed."

"Of course, I ought to be ashamed," answered Nikolai Petrovich, blushing more and more.

"Nonsense, dad, nonsense; please don't!" Arkady smiled affectionately. "What a thing to apologise for!" he thought to himself, and his heart was filled with a feeling of condescending tenderness for his kind, soft-hearted father, mixed with a sense of a certain secret superiority. "Please stop," he repeated once more, instinctively revelling in a consciousness of his own advanced and emancipated condition.

Nikolai Petrovich glanced at him from under the fingers of the hand with which he was still rubbing his forehead, and there was a pang in his heart. . . . But at once he blamed himself for it.

"Here are our fields at last," he said, after a long silence.

"And that in front is our forest, isn't it?" asked Arkady.

"Yes. Only I have sold the timber. This year they will cut it down."

"Why did you sell it?"

"The money was needed; besides, that land is to go to the peasants."

"Who don't pay you their quitrent?"

"That's their affair; besides, they will pay it some day."

"I am sorry about the forest," observed Arkady, and he began to look about him.

The country through which they were driving could not be called picturesque. Fields upon fields stretched all along to the very horizon, now sloping gently upwards, then dropping down again; here and there groves were to be seen, and winding ravines, planted with low, scanty bushes, recalling vividly the representation of them on the old-fashioned maps of Catherine's time. They came upon little streams too with hollow banks; and tiny lakes with narrow dykes; and little villages, with low hovels under dark and often tumble-down thatch roofs, and slanting barns with walls woven of brushwood and gaping doorways beside neglected threshing-floors; and churches, some brick-built, with stucco peeling off in patches, others wooden, with crosses fallen askew, and overgrown graveyards. Slowly Arkady's heart sank. To complete the picture, the peasants they met were all in tatters and on the sorriest little nags; the willows, with their trunks stripped of bark, and broken branches, stood like ragged beggars along the roadside; lean and shaggy cows looking pinched by hunger, were greedily tearing at the grass along the ditches. They looked as though they had just been snatched out of the murderous clutches of some threatening monster; and the piteous state of the weak, starved beasts in the midst of the lovely spring day, called up, like a white phantom, the endless, comfortless winter, with its storms, and frosts, and snows. . . . "No," thought Arkady, "this is not rich land; it does not impress one by prosperity or industriousness; it can't, it can't go on like this, reforms are absolutely necessary . . . but how is one to carry them out, how is one to begin?"

Such were Arkady's reflections; . . . but even as he reflected, the spring regained its sway. Everything around shone golden green, everything—trees, bushes, grass—glistened and stirred gently in wide waves under the soft breath of the warm wind; from all sides flooded the endless trilling music of the larks; the peewits were calling as they hovered over the low-lying meadows, or noiselessly ran over the tussocks of grass; the rooks strutted among the half-grown short spring-corn, standing out black against its tender green; they disappeared in the already whitening rye, only from time to time their heads peeped out amid its grey waves. Arkady gazed and gazed, and his reflections grew slowly fainter and passed away. . . . He flung off his coat and turned to his father, with a face so bright and boyish, that the latter gave him another hug.

"We're not far off now," remarked Nikolai Petrovich; "we have only to get us this hill, and the house will be in sight. We shall get on together splendidly, Arkasha; you shall help me in farming the estate, if it isn't a bore to you. We must draw close to one another now, and learn to know each other thoroughly, mustn't we?"

"Of course," said Arkady; "but what an exquisite day it is to-day!"

"To welcome you, my dear boy. Yes, it's spring in its full loveliness. Though I agree with Pushkin—do you remember in *Evgeny Onegin*—

'To me how sad thy coming is,
Spring, spring, the time of love!
What . . .' [9]

"Arkady!" called Bazarov's voice from the coach, "send me a match; I've nothing to light my pipe with."

9. Pushkin's "novel in verse" (1823–31) is the classic of Russian literature, and Pushkin is its greatest poet.

Nikolai Petrovich stopped, while Arkady, who had begun listening to him with some surprise, though with sympathy, too, made haste to pull a silver matchbox out of his pocket and sent it to Bazarov by Peter.

"Will you have a cigar?" shouted Bazarov again.

"Thanks," answered Arkady.

Peter returned to the carriage, and handed him with the matchbox a thick black cigar, which Arkady began to smoke promptly, diffusing about him such a strong and pungent odour of cheap tobacco, that Nikolai Petrovich, a life-long nonsmoker, was forced to turn away his head, as imperceptibly as he could for fear of wounding his son.

A quarter of an hour later, the two carriages drew up before the steps of a new wooden house, painted grey, with a red iron roof. This was Marino, also known as New-Wick, or, as the peasants had nicknamed it, Landless Farm.

IV

No crowd of house-serfs ran out on to the steps to meet the masters; only a little girl of twelve appeared alone. After her there came out of the house a young lad, very like Peter, dressed in a coat of grey livery, with white armorial buttons, the servant of Pavel Petrovich Kirsanov. Without speaking, he opened the door of the carriage, and unbuttoned the apron of the coach. Nikolai Petrovich with his son and Bazarov walked through a dark and almost empty hall, from behind the door of which they caught a glimpse of a young woman's face, into a drawing-room furnished in the latest style.

"Here we are at home," said Nikolai Petrovich, taking off his cap, and shaking back his hair. "The main thing now is to have supper and rest."

"A meal would not come amiss, certainly," observed Bazarov, stretching, and he dropped on to a sofa.

"Yes, yes, let us have supper, supper directly." Nikolai Petrovich, with no apparent reason, stamped his foot. "And here just at the right moment comes Prokofich."

A man about sixty entered, white-haired, thin, and swarthy, in a brown dress-coat with brass buttons, and a pink neckerchief. He grinned, went up to kiss Arkady's hand, and bowing to the guest, retreated to the door, and put his hands behind him.

"Here he is, Prokofich," began Nikolai Petrovich; "he's come back to us at last. . . . Well, how does he look to you?"

"As well as could be, sir," said the old man, and was grinning again, but he quickly knitted his bushy brows. "You wish supper to be served?" he said impressively.

"Yes, yes, please. But won't you like to go to your room first, Evgeny Vassilyich?"

"No, thanks; no reason to. Only give orders for my little box to be taken there, and this garment, too," he added, taking off his frieze overcoat.

"Certainly. Prokofich, take the gentleman's coat." (Prokofich, with an air of perplexity, picked up Bazarov's "garment" in both hands, and holding it high above his head, retreated on tiptoe.) "And you, Arkady, are you going to your room for a minute?"

"Yes, I must wash," answered Arkady, and was just moving towards the door, but at that instant there came into the drawing-room a man of medium height, dressed in a dark English suit, a fashionable low cravat, and patent leather shoes, Pavel Petrovich Kirsanov. He looked about forty-five: his close-cropped, grey hair shone with a dark lustre, like new silver; his face, yellow but free from wrinkles, was exceptionally regular and pure in line, as though carved by a light and delicate chisel, and showed traces of remarkable beauty; specially fine were his shining, black, almond-shaped eyes. The whole figure of Arkady's uncle, with its elegant and aristocratic cast, had preserved the gracefulness of youth and that air of striving upwards, away from earth, which for the most part is lost after a man's twenties.

Pavel Petrovich took out of his trouser pocket his beautiful hand with its long pink nails, a hand which seemed still more beautiful against the snowy whiteness of the cuff, buttoned with a single, big opal, and gave it to his nephew. After a preliminary handshake in the European style, he kissed him thrice after the Russian fashion, that is to say, he touched his cheek three times with his perfumed moustaches, and said "Welcome."

Nikolai Petrovich presented him to Bazarov; Pavel Petrovich greeted him with a slight inclination of his supple figure, and a slight smile, but he did not give him his hand, and even put it back into his pocket.

"I had begun to think you were not coming to-day," he began in a musical voice, rocking gently and with a shrug of the shoulders, as he showed his splendid white teeth. "Did anything happen on the road?"

"Nothing happened," answered Arkady; "we were rather slow. But we're as hungry as wolves now. Hurry up Prokofich, dad; and I'll be back directly."

"Stay, I'm coming with you," cried Bazarov, pulling himself up suddenly from the sofa. Both the young men went out.

"Who is that?" asked Pavel Petrovich.

"A friend of Arkasha's; according to him a very clever fellow."

"Is he going to stay with us?"

"Yes."

"That unkempt creature?"

"Why, yes."

Pavel Petrovich drummed with his finger-nails on the table. "I fancy Arkady *s'est dégourdi,"* [1] he remarked. "I'm glad he has come back."

At supper there was little conversation. Bazarov especially said nothing, but he ate a great deal. Nikolai Petrovich related various incidents in what he called his career as a farmer, talked about the impending government measures, about committees, deputations' [2] the need for introducing machinery, etc. Pavel Petrovich paced slowly up and down the dining-room (he never ate supper), sometimes sipping from a glass of red wine, and less often uttering some remark or rather exclamation, such as "Ah! aha! hm!" Arkady told some news from Petersburg, but he was conscious of a little awkwardness, that awkwardness which usually overtakes a youth when he has just ceased to be a child and has come back to a place where they are accustomed to regard him and treat him as a child. He made his sentences quite unnecessarily long, avoided the word "daddy," and even sometimes replaced it by the word "father," mumbled, it is true, between his teeth; with an exaggerated carelessness he poured into his glass far more wine than he really wanted, and drank it all off. Prokofich did not take his eyes off him, and kept chewing his lips. After supper they all separated at once.

"Your uncle's a queer fish," Bazarov said to Arkady, as he sat in his dressing-gown by his bedside, smoking a short pipe. "Only fancy such style in the country! His nails, his nails—you could send them to an exhibition!"

"Why, of course, you don't know," replied Arkady. "He was a great swell in his own day, you know. I will tell you his story one day. He was very handsome, you know, used to turn all the women's heads."

"Oh, that's it, is it? So he keeps it up in the memory of the past. It's a pity there's no one for him to fascinate here, though. I kept staring at his exquisite collars. They're like marble, and his chin's shaved simply to perfection. Come, Arkady Nikolaich, isn't that ridiculous?"

"Perhaps it is; but he's a splendid man, really."

"An antique survival! But your father's a capital fellow. He wastes his time reading poetry, and doesn't know much about farming, but he's a good-hearted fellow."

"My father has a heart of gold."

1. "has become more easy going."

2. Created and headed by Alexander II for considering problems of the emancipation of the serfs.

"Did you notice how shy he is?"

Arkady shook his head as though he himself were not shy.

"It's something astonishing," pursued Bazarov, "these elderly romantics! They develop their nervous systems to the breaking point . . . so balance is lost. But good-night. In my room there's an English washstand, but the door won't fasten. Anyway, that ought to be encouraged—an English washstand stands for progress!"

Bazarov went away, and a sense of great happiness came over Arkady. Sweet it is to fall asleep in one's own home, in the familiar bed, under the quilt worked by loving hands, perhaps a dear nurse's hands, those kind, tender, untiring hands. Arkady remembered Egorovna, and sighed and wished her peace in heaven. . . . For himself he made no prayer.

Both he and Bazarov were soon asleep, but others in the house were awake long after. His son's return had agitated Nikolai Petrovich. He lay down in bed, but did not put out the candles, and his head propped on his hand, he fell into deep thought. His brother was sitting long after midnight in his study, in a wide Hambs armchair before the fireplace, on which there smouldered some faintly glowing embers. Pavel Petrovich was not undressed, only red Chinese slippers without heels had replaced the patent leather shoes on his feet. He held in his hand the latest issue of *Galignani*,[3] but he was not reading; he gazed fixedly into the grate, where a bluish flame flickered, dying down, then flaring up again. . . . God knows where his thoughts were rambling, but they were not rambling in the past only; the expression of his face was concentrated and surly, which is not the way when a man is absorbed solely in recollections. And in a small back room there sat on a large chest a young woman in a blue dressing jacket with a white kerchief thrown over her dark hair, Fenichka. She was half listening, half dozing, and often looked across towards the open door through which a child's crib was visible, and the regular breathing of a sleeping baby could be heard.

V

The next morning Bazarov woke up earlier than any one and went out of the house. "Oh, my!" he thought, looking about him, "the little place isn't much to boast of!" When Nikolai Petrovich had divided the land with his peasants, he had had to build his new manor-house on the acres of perfectly flat and barren land. He had built a house, offices, and farm buildings, laid out a garden, dug a pond, and sunk two wells; but the young trees had not done well, very little water had collected in the pond, and that in the wells tasted brackish. Only one arbor of lilac and acacia had

3. A daily newspaper, *Galignani's Messenger,* published in English in Paris.

grown fairly well; they sometimes had tea and dinner in it. In a few minutes Bazarov had traversed all the little paths of the garden; he went into the cattle-yard and the stable, routed out two farm-boys, with whom he made friends at once, and set off with them to a small swamp about a mile from the house to look for frogs.

"What do you want frogs for, sir?" one of the boys asked him.

"I'll tell you what for," answered Bazarov, who possessed the special faculty of inspiring confidence in people of a lower class, though he never tried to win them, and behaved very casually with them; "I shall cut the frog open, and see what's going on in his inside, and then, as you and I are much the same as frogs, only that we walk on legs, I shall know what's going on inside us, too."

"And what do you want to know that for?"

"So as not to make a mistake, if you're taken ill, and I have to cure you."

"Are you a doctor, then?"

"Yes."

"Vaska, do you hear, the gentleman says you and I are the same as frogs—that's funny!"

"I'm afraid of frogs," observed Vaska, a boy of seven, with a head as white as flax, and bare feet, dressed in a grey smock with a stand-up collar.

"What is there to be afraid of? Do they bite?"

"There, get into the water, philosophers," said Bazarov.

Meanwhile Nikolai Petrovich, too, had waked up, and gone in to see Arkady, whom he found dressed. The father and son went out on to the terrace under the shelter of the awning; near the balustrade, on the table, among great bunches of lilac, the samovar was already boiling. A little girl came up, the same who had been the first to meet them at the steps on their arrival the evening before. In a shrill voice she said—

"Fedosya Nikolaevna is not quite well; she cannot come; she gave orders to ask you, will you please to pour out tea yourself, or should she send Dunyasha?"

"I will pour out myself, myself," interposed Nikolai Petrovich hurriedly. "Arkady, how do you take your tea, with cream, or with lemon?"

"With cream," answered Arkady; and after a brief silence, he uttered interrogatively, "Daddy?"

Nikolai Petrovich in confusion looked at his son.

"Well?" he said.

Arkady dropped his eyes.

"Forgive me, dad, if my question seems unsuitable to you," he began, "but you yourself, by your openness yesterday, encourage me to be open . . . you will not be angry . . .?"

"Go on."

"You give me confidence to ask you. . . . Isn't the reason Fen . . . isn't the reason she will not come here to pour out tea, because I'm here?"

Nikolai Petrovich turned slightly away.

"Perhaps," he said, at last, "she supposes . . . she is ashamed."

Arkady turned a rapid glance on his father.

"She has no need to be ashamed. In the first place, you are aware of my views" (it was very sweet to Arkady to utter that word); "and, secondly, could I be willing to hamper your life, your habits, in the least thing? Besides, I am sure you could not make a bad choice; if you have allowed her to live under the same roof with you, she must be worthy of it; in any case, a son cannot judge his father,—least of all, I, and least of all such a father who, like you, has never hampered my liberty in anything."

Arkady's voice had been shaky at the beginning; he felt himself magnanimous, though at the same time he realised he was delivering something like a lecture to his father; but the sound of one's own voice has a powerful effect on any man, and Arkady brought out his last words resolutely, even with emphasis.

"Thanks, Arkasha," said Nikolai Petrovich thickly, and his fingers again strayed over his eyebrows and forehead. "Your suppositions are just in fact. Of course, if this girl had not deserved. . . . It is not a frivolous caprice. It's not easy for me to talk to you about this; but you will understand that it is difficult for her to come here, in your presence, especially the first day of your return."

"In that case I will go to her," cried Arkady, with a fresh rush of magnanimous feeling, and he jumped up from his seat. "I will explain to her that she has no need to be ashamed before me."

Nikolai Petrovich, too, got up.

"Arkady," he began, "be so good . . . how can . . . there . . . I have not told you yet . . ."

But Arkady no longer listened to him, and dashed away from the terrace. Nikolai Petrovich looked after him, and sank into his chair overcome by confusion. His heart began to throb. Did he at that moment realise the inevitable strangeness of the future relations between him and his son? Was he conscious that Arkady would perhaps have shown him more respect if he had never touched on this subject at all? Did he reproach himself for weakness?—it is hard to say; all these feelings were within him, but in the state of sensations—and vague sensations—while the flush did not leave his face, and his heart throbbed.

There was the sound of hurrying footsteps, and Arkady came

on to the terrace. "We have made friends, dad!" he cried, with an expression of a kind of affectionate and good-natured triumph on his face. "Fedosya Nikolaevna is really not quite well to-day, and she will come a little later. But why didn't you tell me I had a brother? I should have kissed him last night, as I have kissed him just now."

Nikolai Petrovich tried to articulate something, tried to get up and open his arms. Arkady flung himself on his neck.

"What's this, embracing again?" sounded the voice of Pavel Petrovich behind them.

Father and son were equally rejoiced at his appearance at that instant; there are touching positions, from which one nevertheless longs to escape as soon as possible.

"Why should you be surprised at that?" said Nikolai Petrovich gaily. "Think what ages I have been waiting for Arkasha. I've not had time to get a good look at him since yesterday."

"I'm not at all surprised," observed Pavel Petrovich; "I feel not indisposed to embrace him myself."

Arkady went up to his uncle, and again felt on his cheeks the touch of his perfumed moustache. Pavel Petrovich sat down to the table. He wore an elegant morning suit in the English style, and a gay little fez on his head. This fez and the carelessly tied little cravat carried a suggestion of the freedom of country life, but the stiff collars of his shirt—not white, it is true, but striped, as is correct in morning dress—stood up as inexorably as ever against his well-shaved chin.

"Where's your new friend?" he asked Arkady.

"He's not in the house; he usually gets up early and goes off somewhere. The main thing is, we mustn't pay any attention to him; he doesn't like ceremony."

"Yes, that's obvious." Pavel Petrovich began deliberately spreading butter on his bread. "Is he going to stay long with us?"

"Perhaps. He came here on the way to his father's."

"And where does his father live?"

"In our province, sixty-five miles from here. He has a small property there. He was formerly an army doctor."

"Tut, tut, tut! To be sure, I kept asking myself, 'Where have I heard that name, Bazarov?' Nikolai, do you remember in our father's division there was a surgeon Bazarov?"

"I believe there was."

"Yes, yes, to be sure. So that surgeon was his father. Hm!" Pavel Petrovich twitched his moustaches. "Well, and what precisely is Mr. Bazarov himself?" he asked, deliberately.

"What is Bazarov?" Arkady smiled. "Would you like me, uncle, to tell you what he really is?"

"If you will be so good, nephew."

"He's a nihilist."

"How?" inquired Nikolai Petrovich, while Pavel Petrovich lifted a knife in the air with a small piece of butter on its tip, and remained motionless.

"He's a nihilist," repeated Arkady.

"A nihilist," said Nikolai Petrovich. "That's from the Latin, *nihil, nothing,* as far as I can judge; the word must mean a man who . . . who accepts nothing?"

"Say, 'who respects nothing,' " put in Pavel Petrovich, and he set to work on the butter again.

"Who regards everything from the critical point of view," observed Arkady.

"Isn't that just the same thing?" inquired Pavel Petrovich.

"No, it's not the same thing. A nihilist is a man who does not bow down before any authority, who does not take any principle on faith, whatever reverence that principle may be enshrined in."

"Well, and is that good?" interrupted Pavel Petrovich.

"That depends, uncle. Some people it will do good to, but some people will suffer for it."

"Indeed. Well, I see it's not in our line. We are old-fashioned people; we imagine that without *principes,* (Pavel Petrovich pronounced the word softly, in the French way; Arkady, on the other hand, pronounced it harshly, "*pryntsip,*" emphasizing the first syllable), without *principes* taken as you say on faith, there's no taking a step, no breathing. *Vous avez changé tout cela.*[4] God give you good health and the rank of a general, while we will be content to look on and admire, worthy . . . what was it?"

"Nihilists," Arkady said, speaking very distinctly.

"Yes. There used to be Hegelists, and now there are nihilists. We shall see how you will exist in a void, in a vacuum; and now please ring, brother Nikolai Petrovich; it's time I had my cocoa."

Nikolai Petrovich rang the bell and called "Dunyasha!" But instead of Dunyasha, Fenichka herself came on to the terrace. She was a young woman about three-and-twenty, all soft and white, with dark hair and eyes, red, childishly pouting lips, and little delicate hands. She wore a neat print dress; a new blue kerchief lay lightly on her round shoulders. She carried a large cup of cocoa, and setting it down before Pavel Petrovich, she was overwhelmed with confusion; the hot blood rushed in a wave of crimson under the delicate skin of her pretty face. She dropped her eyes, and stood at the table, leaning a little on the very tips of her fingers. It seemed as though she were ashamed of having come in, and at the same time felt that she had a right to come.

4. "You've changed all that."

Pavel Petrovich knitted his brows severely while Nikolai Petrovich looked embarrassed.

"Good morning, Fenichka," he muttered through his teeth.

"Good morning to you," she replied in a voice not loud but resonant, and with a sidelong glance at Arkady, who gave her a friendly smile, she went gently away. She walked with a slightly rolling gait, but even that suited her.

For some minutes silence reigned on the terrace. Pavel Petrovich sipped his cocoa; suddenly he raised his head. "Here is Sir Nihilist coming to honor us," he said in an undertone.

Bazarov was in fact approaching through the garden, stepping over the flower-beds. His linen coat and trousers were besmeared with mud; clinging marsh weed was twined round the crown of his old round hat; in his right hand he held a small bag; in the bag something alive was moving. He quickly drew near the terrace, and said with a nod, "Good morning, gentlemen; sorry I was late for tea; I'll be back directly; I must just put these captives away."

"What have you there—leeches?" asked Pavel Petrovich.

"No, frogs."

"Do you eat them—or breed them?"

"For experiment," said Bazarov indifferently, and he went off into the house.

"So he's going to cut them up," observed Pavel Petrovich. "He has no faith in *principes,* but he has faith in frogs."

Arkady looked compassionately at his uncle; Nikolai Petrovich shrugged his shoulders stealthily. Pavel Petrovich himself felt that his witticism was unsuccessful, and began to talk about husbandry and the new bailiff, who had come to him the evening before to complain that a laborer, Foma, "was deboshed," and quite unmanageable. "He's such an Æsop," he said among other things; "in all places he had protested himself a worthless fellow; he's not a man to keep his place; he'll walk off in a huff like a fool."

VI

Bazarov came back, sat down to the table, and began hastily drinking tea. The two brothers looked at him in silence, while Arkady stealthily watched first his father and then his uncle.

"Did you walk far from here?" Nikolai Petrovich asked at last.

"Where you've a little swamp near the aspen grove. I started some half-dozen snipe; you might slaughter them, Arkady."

"Aren't you a hunter?"

"No."

"Is your special study physics?" Pavel Petrovich in his turn inquired.

"Physics, yes; and the natural sciences in general."

"They say the Teutons have lately had great success in that line."

"Yes; the Germans are our teachers in it," Bazarov answered carelessly.

Pavel Petrovich had used the word "Teutons" instead of Germans, with ironical intention; no one noticed it, however.

"Have you such a high opinion of the Germans?" said Pavel Petrovich, with exaggerated courtesy. He was beginning to feel a secret irritation. His aristocratic nature was revolted by Bazarov's absolute nonchalance. This surgeon's son was not only unintimidated, he even gave abrupt and indifferent answers, and in the tone of his voice there was something coarse, almost insolent.

"The scientists there are a clever lot."

"Quite so. But you probably have a less flattering opinion of Russian scientists?"

"Very likely."

"That's very praiseworthy self-abnegation," Pavel Petrovich declared, drawing himself up, and throwing his head back. "But did not Arkady Nikolaich tell us just now that you recognize no authorities? Don't you believe in them?"

"But why should I accept them? And what is there to believe in? They talk sense, I agree, that's all."

"And do all Germans talk sense?" uttered Pavel Petrovich, and his face assumed an expression as detached, and remote, as if he had withdrawn to some cloudy height.

"Not all," replied Bazarov, with a short yawn. He obviously did not care to continue the discussion.

Pavel Petrovich glanced at Arkady, as he wanted to say to him, "Your friend's polite, I must say." "For my own part," he began again, not without some effort, "I am so unregenerate as not to like Germans. I won't even mention Russian Germans; we all know what sort of creatures they are. But even German Germans are not to my liking. In former days there were some here and there; they had—well, Schiller, to be sure, *Goetthe* . . . my brother —he takes a particularly favorable view of those two . . . But now they are all some sort of chemists and materialists. . . ."

"A good chemist is twenty times as useful as any poet," broke in Bazarov.

"Oh, indeed," commented Pavel Petrovich, and, as though falling asleep, he barely raised his eyebrows. "You don't recognize art then, I suppose?"

"The art of making money or of 'shrink hemorrhoids'!" cried Bazarov, with a contemptuous laugh.

"Indeed, sir indeed. You are pleased to jest, I see. You reject everything, then? Granted. That means you believe only in science?"

"I have already informed you that I believe in nothing; and what is science—science in the abstract? There are sciences, as there are trades and vocations; but abstract science doesn't exist at all."

"Very good. Well, and do you maintain the same negative attitude in regard to the other conventions accepted as social customs?"

"What is this, an examination?" asked Bazarov.

Pavel Petrovich turned slightly pale. . . . Nikolai Petrovich thought it his duty to interrupt the conversation.

"We will discuss this subject in greater detail some day, my dear Evgeny Vassilyich; we will get to know your views, and express our own. For my part I am very glad you are studying the natural sciences. I have heard that Liebig has made some wonderful discoveries in soil fertilization. You can be of assistance to me in my agricultural work; you can give me some useful advice."

"I am at your service, Nikolai Petrovich; but Liebig is far beyond our heads! You have to learn the alphabet and then begin to read, but we haven't started our ABC's yet."

"You certainly are a nihilist, I see," thought Nikolai Petrovich. "Still, you will allow me to apply to you on occasion," he added aloud. "And now, brother, I think it's time for us to have a talk with the bailiff."

Pavel Petrovich rose from his chair.

"Yes," he said, without looking at any one; "it's a misfortune to live five years in the country like this, far from mighty intellects! You turn into a fool directly. You try not to forget what you've been taught, but there—poof!—it turns out that it's all rubbish, and you're told that sensible men have nothing more to do with such foolishness, and that you, if you please, are an antiquated old fogey. What's to be done? Young people, of course, are cleverer than we are!"

Pavel Petrovich turned slowly on his heels, and slowly left. Nikolai Petrovich went after him.

"Is he always like that?" Bazarov coolly asked Arkady, as soon as the door had closed behind the two brothers.

"Listen, Evgeny, you really were too sharp with him," remarked Arkady. "You offended him."

"Yes, I'll pamper them, these provincial aristocrats! Why, that's all vanity, dandy habits, fatuity. He should have continued his career in Petersburg, if that's his bent. But there, enough of him! I've found a rather rare species of a water-beetle, *Dytiscus marginatus*, do you know it? I will show you."

"I promised to tell you his story," began Arkady.

"The story of the beetle?"

"Come, don't, Evgeny. The story of my uncle. You will see he's not the sort of man you fancy. He deserves pity rather than ridicule."

"I don't dispute it; but why are you so concerned about him?"

"One ought to be just, Evgeny."

"How does that follow?"

"No; listen . . ."

And Arkady told him his uncle's story. The reader will find it in the following chapter.

VII

Pavel Petrovich Kirsanov was educated first at home, like his younger brother, and afterwards in the Corps of Pages. From childhood he was distinguished by remarkable good looks; moreover he was self-confident, somewhat ironical, and amusingly caustic; he could not fail to please. As soon as he received his commission as an officer, he began to be seen everywhere. He was much admired in society, and he indulged himself, played the fool, even gave himself airs, but that too was attractive in him. Women went mad about him; men called him a fop, and were secretly jealous of him. He lived, as has been related already, in an apartment with his brother, whom he loved sincerely, though he was not at all like him. Nikolai Petrovich was a little lame, he had small, pleasant rather melancholy features, small, black eyes, and thin, soft hair; he enjoyed loafing, but he also enjoyed reading, and was timid in society. Pavel Petrovich did not spend a single evening at home, prided himself on his audacity and agility (he was just making gymnastics fashionable among young men in society), and had read in all five or six French books. At twenty-eight he was already a captain; a brilliant career awaited him. Suddenly everything changed.

At that time, there was occasionally seen in Petersburg society a woman who has even not been forgotten today, Princess R——. She had a well-educated, well-bred, but rather stupid husband, and no children. She used to go abroad suddenly and suddenly to return to Russia, and in general led an eccentric life. She had the reputation of being a frivolous coquette, abandoned herself eagerly to every sort of pleasure, danced to exhaustion, laughed and jested with young men, whom she received in the dim light of her drawing-room before dinner; while at night she wept and prayed, found no peace anywhere, and often paced her room till morning, wringing her hands in anguish, or sat, pale and cold, reading the Psalms. Day came, and she was again transformed into a grand lady; again she went out, laughed, chattered, and simply flung herself headlong into anything which could afford her the slightest distraction. She had a wonderful figure, her hair, gold-colored and heavy as gold, fell below her knees, but no one would have called her a beauty; in her whole face the only good point was her eyes, and not even the eyes themselves—they were grey, and not large—but their glance was swift and deep, unconcerned to the point of audacity, and pensive to the point of dejection—an enigmatic glance. Something extraordinary shone in them, even while her tongue babbled the emptiest of inanities. She dressed exquisitely. Pavel Petrovich met her at a ball, danced the mazurka with her, in the course of which she did not utter a single sensible word, and fell passionately in love with her. Being accustomed to make conquests, in this instance, too, he soon attained his object, but his easy success did not damp his ardor. On the contrary, he was still more agonizingly, closely attached to this woman, in whom, even when she surrendered herself completely, there always seemed something still to remain mysterious and unattainable, which none could penetrate. What was hidden in that soul—God knows! It seemed as though she were in power of mysterious forces, incomprehensible even to herself; they seemed to play on her at will; her limited intellect could not master their caprices. Her whole behavior presented a series of inconsistencies; she wrote the only letters which could have awakened her husband's just suspicions to a man who was almost a stranger to her; while her love always had an element of melancholy; she ceased to laugh and to jest with the man she chose, she listened to him, and gazed at him with a look of bewilderment. Sometimes, for the most part suddenly, this bewilderment passed into chill horror; her face assumed a wild, death-like expression; she locked herself up in her bedroom, and her maid, by listening at the keyhole, could hear her smothered sobs. More than once, as he went home after a tender meeting, Kirsanov felt within him that heartrending, bitter vexation which follows definite failure.

"What more do I want?" he asked himself, while his heart was heavy. He once gave her a ring with a sphinx engraved on the stone.

"What's that?" she asked; "a sphinx?"

"Yes," he answered, "and that sphinx is you."

"I?" she asked, and slowly raising her enigmatical glance upon him. "Do you know that's awfully flattering?" she added with a meaningless smile, while her eyes still kept the same strange look.

Pavel Petrovich suffered even while Princess R—— loved him; but when she cooled toward him, and that happened rather quickly, he almost went out of his mind. He was on the rack, and he was jealous; he gave her no peace, followed her about everywhere; she grew sick of his persistent pursuit, and went abroad. He resigned his commission in spite of the entreaties of his friends and the exhortations of his superiors, and followed the princess; he spent four years in foreign lands, sometimes pursuing her, at others intentionally losing sight of her. He was ashamed of himself, he was disgusted with his own lack of spirit . . . but nothing availed. Her image, that incomprehensible, almost meaningless, but bewitching image, was deeply rooted in his heart. At Baden he once more regained his old footing with her; it seemed as though she had never loved him so passionately . . . but in a month it was all over: the flame flickered up for the last time and went out forever. Foreseeing inevitable separation, he at least wanted to remain her friend, as though friendship with such a woman were possible. . . . She secretly left Baden, and from that time steadily avoided Kirsanov. He returned to Russia, and tried to take up the threads of his former life again; but he could not get back into the former groove. He wandered from place to place like a man possessed; he still went into society; he still retained the habits of a man of the world; he could boast of two or three fresh conquests; but he no longer expected anything special of himself or of others, and he undertook nothing. He aged and his hair turned grey; to spend his evening at the club, in jaded boredom, and to argue in bachelor society became a necessity for him—a bad sign, as we all know. He did not even think of marriage, of course. Ten years passed in this way; they passed by colorless and fruitless—and quickly, fearfully quickly. Nowhere does time fly past as in Russia; in prison they say it flies even faster. One day at dinner at the club, Pavel Petrovich heard of the Princess R——'s death. She had died at Paris in a state bordering on insanity. He rose from the table, and a long time he paced about the rooms of the club, or stood stockstill near the card-players, but he did not go home earlier than usual. Some time later he received a packet addressed to him; it contained the ring he had given the princess. She had drawn lines in the shape of a cross over the sphinx and sent him word that the solution of the enigma was the cross.

This happened at the beginning of the year 1848, at the very time when Nikolai Petrovich came to Petersburg, after the loss of his wife. Pavel Petrovich had scarcely seen his brother since the latter had settled in the country; the marriage of Nikolai Petrovich had coincided with the very first days of Pavel Petrovich's acquaintance with the princess. When he came back from abroad, he had gone to him with the intention of staying with him a couple of months, to enjoy gazing at his happiness, but he had only succeeded in standing a week of it. The difference in the positions of the two brothers was too great. In 1848, this difference had grown less; Nikolai Petrovich had lost his wife, Pavel Petrovich had lost him memories; after the death of the princess he tried not to think of her. But to Nikolai, there remained the sense of a well-spent life, his son was growing up under his eyes; Pavel, on the contrary, a lonely bachelor, was entering upon that indefinite twilight period of regrets that are akin to hopes, and hopes that are akin to regrets, when youth is over, while old age has not yet come.

This time was harder for Pavel Petrovich than for any other man; in losing his past, he lost everything.

"I will not invite you to Marino now," Nikolai Petrovich said to him one day, (he had called his property by that name in honor of his wife Mary); "you were bored there even when my wife was alive, and now I think you would simply languish away."

"I was stupid and fidgety then," answered Pavel Petrovich; "since then I have grown quieter, if not wiser. On the contrary, now, if you will let me, I am ready to settle with you for good."

Instead of answering Nikolai Petrovich embraced him; but a year and a half passed after this conversation, before Pavel Petrovich made up his mind to carry out his intention. When he once settled in the country, however, he did not leave it, even during the three winters which Nikolai Petrovich spent in Petersburg with his son. He began to read, chiefly English; in general he arranged his whole life in the English style, rarely saw the neighbors, and only went out to the election of marshals, where he was generally silent, only occasionally annoying and alarming land-owners of the old school by his liberal sallies, and not associating with the representatives of the younger generation. Both the latter and the former considered him "stuck up"; and both parties respected him for his fine aristocratic manners; for the rumors of his conquests; for the fact that he was very well dressed and always stayed in the best room in the best hotel; for the fact that he generally dined well, and had once even dined with Wellington at Louis Philippe's table; for the fact that he always took everywhere with him a real silver dressing-case and a portable bath; for the fact that he always smelt of some unusual, amazingly "aristocratic" scent; for the fact that he played whist in masterly fashion, and always lost; and lastly, they respected him also for his incorruptible honesty. Ladies considered him enchantingly romantic, but he did not cultivate ladies' acquaintance. . . .

"So you see, Evgeny," observed Arkady, as he finished his

story, "how unjustly you judge my uncle! To say nothing of his having more than once helped my father out of difficulties, given him all his money—the property, perhaps you don't know, wasn't divided—he's glad to help any one, among other things he always sticks up for the peasants; it's true, when he talks to them he frowns and sniffs eau de cologne. . . ."

"His nerves, no doubt," put in Bazarov.

Perhaps; but his heart is very good. And he's far from being stupid. What useful advice he has given me, especially . . . especially in regard to relations with women."

"Aha! a scalded dog fears cold water, we know that!"

"In short," continued Arkady, "he's profoundly unhappy, believe me; it's a sin to despise him."

"But who does despise him?" retorted Bazarov. "Still, I must say that a man who stakes his whole life on one card—a woman's love—and when that card fails, turns sour, and lets himself go till he's fit for nothing, is not a man, but a male. You say he's unhappy; you know best; but he hasn't got rid of all his fads. I'm convinced that he seriously considers himself worthwhile because he reads that wretched *Galignani*, and once a month saves a peasant from a flogging."

"But remember his education, the age in which he grew up," observed Arkady.

"Education?" broke in Bazarov. "Every man must educate himself, just as I've done, for instance. . . . And as for the age, why should I depend on it? Let it rather depend on me. No, my dear fellow, that's all shallowness, dissoluteness! And what about all these mysterious relations between a man and woman? We physiologists know what these relations are. Study the anatomy of the eye a bit; where does the enigmatical glance you talk about come in there? That's all romanticism, nonsense, rot, artiness.[5] We'd better go and look at the beetle."

And the two friends went off to Bazarov's room, which was already pervaded by a sort of medico-surgical odor mingled with the smell of cheap tobacco.

VIII

Pavel Petrovich did not stay long at his brother's interview with his bailiff, a tall, thin man with a sweet consumptive voice and knavish eyes, who to all Nikolai Petrovich's remarks answered,

5. Bazarov echoes N. A. Dobrolyubov (1836–61), a radical critic after whom he is in part drawn. The radical, or civic, critics flourished in the middle of the nineteenth century. Their primary interest in literature was its social and political content, its expression of progressive ideas, and its reflection of "reality." They became spokesmen for a particular kind of political opinion, called by some "liberal," since under tsarist censorship it was easier to discusss politics under the guise of literary criticism than in its purer state.

"Certainly, sir, of course, sir" and tried to make the peasants out to be thieves and drunkards. The estate had only recently been put on to the new reformed system, and the new mechanism, creaking like an ungreased wheel, cracking like homemade furniture of unseasoned wood. Nikolai Petrovich did not lose heart, but he often sighed and sank into thought; he felt that things could not go on without money, and his money was almost all gone. Arkady had spoken the truth; Pavel Petrovich had more than once helped his brother; more than once, seeing him struggling and cudgelling his brains, at a loss which way to turn, Pavel Petrovich moved deliberately to the window and thrusting his hands into his pockets, muttered between his teeth, "*mais je puis vous donner de l'argent,*" [6] and gave him money; but to-day he had none himself, and he preferred to withdraw. The petty details of agricultural management depressed him; besides, it constantly struck him that Nikolai Petrovich, for all his zeal and industry, did not set about things in the right way, though he would not have been able to point out precisely where Nikolai Petrovich's mistake lay. "My brother's not practical enough," he reasoned to himself; "they cheat him." Nikolai Petrovich, on the other hand, had the highest opinion of Pavel Petrovich's practical ability, and always asked his advice. "I'm a soft, weak fellow, I've spent my life in the country," he used to say; "while you haven't seen so much of the world for nothing, you see through people; you have an eagle eye." In answer to which Pavel Petrovich would only turn away, but did not contradict his brother.

Leaving Nikolai Petrovich in his study, he walked along the corridor which separated the front part of the house from the back; when he had reached a low door, he stopped in hesitation, then pulling his moustaches, he knocked at it.

"Who's there? Come in," sounded Fenichka's voice.

"It is I," said Pavel Petrovich, and he opened the door.

Fenichka jumped up from the chair on which she was sitting with her baby, and giving him into the arms of a girl who at once carried him out of the room, she hastily straightened her kerchief.

"Pardon me, if I disturbed you," began Pavel Petrovich, without looking at her; "I only wanted to ask you . . . they are sending into the town to-day, I think . . . please order some green tea for me."

"Certainly," answered Fenichka; "how much do you want to buy?"

"Oh, half a pound will be enough, I imagine. You have made

6. "But I can give you money."

a change here, I see," he added, with a rapid glance round him, which glided over Fenichka's face too. "The curtains here," he explained, seeing she did not understand him.

"Oh, yes, the curtains; Nikolai Petrovich was so good as to give them to me; but they have been put up a long while now."

"Yes, and it's a long while since I have been to see you. It is very pleasant here now."

"Thanks to Nikolai Petrovich's kindness," murmured Fenichka.

"Are you more comfortable here than in the little lodge you used to have?" inquired Pavel Petrovich, politely, but without the slightest smile.

"Certainly, it's better, sir."

"Who has been put in your place now?"

"The laundry-maids are there now."

"Ah!"

Pavel Petrovich fell silent. "Now he will go," thought Fenichka; but he did not go, and she stood before him motionless, hesitatingly moving her fingers.

"Why did you send your little one away?" said Pavel Petrovich at last. "I like children; do let me see him."

Fenichka blushed all over with confusion and delight. She was afraid of Pavel Petrovich; he scarcely ever spoke to her.

"Dunyasha," she called: "will you bring Mitya, please." (Fenichka did not treat any one in the house familiarly.) "But wait a minute, I have to put something on him," Fenichka moved towards the door.

"That doesn't matter," remarked Pavel Petrovich.

"I will be back directly," answered Fenichka, and she went out quickly.

Pavel Petrovich was left alone, and this time he looked round with special attention. The small low-pitched room in which he found himself was very clean and snug. It smelt of the freshly painted floor and of camomile and hydromel. Along the walls stood chairs with lyre-shaped backs, bought by the late general on his campaign in Poland; in one corner was a little bedstead under a muslin canopy beside an iron-clamped chest with a rounded lid. In the opposite corner a little lamp was burning before a big dark image of St. Nikolai the wonder-worker; a tiny porcelain egg hung by a red ribbon from the protruding gold halo down to the saint's breast; by the windows there were glass jars of last year's jam carefully tied down, shining green; on their paper covers Fenichka herself had written in big letters "Gusberry"; Nikolai Petrovich was particularly fond of that preserve. A cage with a bobtailed siskin hung on a long cord from the ceiling; the bird was constantly chirping and hopping about, the cage was constantly shaking and swinging, while hempseeds fell with a light tap on to the floor. On the wall, between two windows, above a small chest of drawers, hung some rather bad photographs of Nikolai Petrovich in various attitudes, taken by an itinerant photographer; there also hung a photograph of Fenichka herself, which was an absolute failure; it was an eyeless face wearing a forced smile, in a dark frame, nothing more could be made out; while above Fenichka, General Ermolov, in a Circassian cloak, scowled menacingly at the Caucasian mountains in the distance, from beneath a little pincushion which fell right on to his brows.

Five minutes passed; bustling and whispering could be heard in the next room. Pavel Petrovich took up a greasy book from the chest of drawers, an odd volume of Masalsky's *Musketeers*, and turned over a few pages. . . . The door opened, and Fenichka came in with Mitya in her arms. She had put on him a little red smock with an embroidered collar, had combed his hair and washed his face; he was breathing heavily, his whole body working, and his little hands waving in the air, as is the way with all healthy babies; but his elegant smock obviously impressed him: an expression of pleasure was reflected in every part of his chubby little figure. Fenichka had put her own hair in order, too, and had arranged her kerchief better; but she might well have remained as she was. And really is there anything in the world more captivating than a beautiful young mother with a healthy baby in her arms?

"What a roly-poly!" said Pavel Petrovich graciously and he tickled Mitya's little double chin with the tip of the long nail of his forefinger. The baby stared at the siskin, and chuckled.

"That's uncle," said Fenichka, bending her face down to him and lightly bouncing him, while Dunyasha quietly set in the window a smouldering incense cone putting a half-penny under it.

"How many months old is he?" asked Pavel Petrovich.

"Six months; it will soon be seven, on the eleventh."

"Isn't it eight, Fedosya Nikolaevna?" put in Dunyasha, with some timidity.

"No, seven; what an idea!" The baby chuckled again, stared at the chest, and suddenly caught hold of his mother's nose and mouth with all his five little fingers. "Saucy mite," said Fenichka, not drawing her face away.

"He resembles my brother," observed Pavel Petrovich.

"Who else should he be like?" thought Fenichka.

"Yes," continued Pavel Petrovich, as though speaking to himself; "there's an unmistakable likeness." He looked attentively, almost mournfully, at Fenichka.

"That's uncle," she repeated, in a whisper this time.

"Ah! Pavel! so this is where you are!" Nikolai Petrovich's voice was suddenly heard.

Pavel Petrovich turned hurriedly round and frowned; but his brother looked at him with such delight, such gratitude that he could not help responding to his smile.

"You've a splendid little fellow," he said, and looking at his watch. "I came in here to speak about some tea."

And, assuming an expression of indifference, Pavel Petrovich went out of the room.

"Did he come of himself?" Nikolai Petrovich asked Fenichka.

"Yes, sir; he knocked and came in."

"Well, and has Arkasha been in to see you again?"

"No. Hadn't I better move into the lodge, Nikolai Petrovich?"

"Why so?"

"I wonder whether it wouldn't be best just for the first."

"N—no," Nikolai Petrovich brought out hesitatingly, rubbing his forehead. "We ought to have done it before. . . . How are you, fatty?" he said, suddenly brightening, and going up to the baby, he kissed him on the cheek; then he bent a little and pressed his lips to Fenichka's hand, which lay white as milk upon Mitya's little red smock.

"Nikolai Petrovich! what are you doing?" she whispered, dropping her eyes, then slowly raised them. Very charming was the expression of her eyes when she looked up as it were from under her brows, and smiled tenderly and a little foolishly.

Nikolai Petrovich had made Fenichka's acquaintance in the following manner. He had once happened three years before to stay a night at an inn in a remote district town. He was agreeably struck by the cleanness of the room assigned to him, the freshness of the bed-linen. Surely the woman of the house must be a German, was the idea that occurred to him; but she proved to be a Russian, a woman of about fifty, neatly dressed, with a pleasant, clever face and discreet speech. He entered into conversation with her at tea; he liked her very much. Nikolai Petrovich had at that time only just moved into his new home, and not wishing to keep serfs in the house, he was on the lookout for hired servants; the woman of the inn on her side complained of the small number of visitors to the town and the hard times; he proposed to her to come into his house in the capacity of housekeeper; she consented. Her husband had long been dead, leaving her an only daughter, Fenichka. Within a fortnight Arina Savishna (that was the new housekeeper's name) arrived with her daughter at Marino and installed herself in the little lodge. Nikolai Petrovich's choice proved a successful one. Arina brought order into the household. As for Fenichka, who was at that time seventeen, no one spoke of her, and scarcely any one saw her; she lived quietly and modéstly, and only on Sundays Nikolai Petrovich noticed in the parish church, somewhere on the side, the delicate profile of her white face. More than a year passed thus.

One morning, Arina came into his study, and bowing low as usual, she asked him if he could do anything for her daughter, who had got a spark from the stove in her eye. Nikolai Petrovich, like all stay-at-homes had studied simple cures and even ordered a homœpathic medicine chest. He at once told Arina to bring the patient to him. Fenichka was much frightened when she heard the master had sent for her; however, she followed her mother. Nikolai Petrovich led her to the window and took her head in his two hands. After thoroughly examining her red and swollen eye, he prescribed a fomentation, which he made up himself at once, and tearing his handkerchief in pieces, he showed her how to apply it. Fenichka listened to all he had to say, and then was going. "Kiss the master's hand, silly girl," said Arina. Nikolai Petrovich did not give her his hand, and in confusion himself kissed her bent head on the part. Fenichka's eye was soon well again, but the impression she had made on Nikolai Petrovich did not pass quickly. He kept thinking of that pure, tender, timidly raised face; he felt that soft hair on the palms of his hands, and saw those innocent, slightly parted lips, through which pearly teeth gleamed with moist brilliance in the sunshine. He began to watch her with greater attention in church, and tried to get into conversation with her. At first she was shy of him, and one day meeting him at the approach of evening in a narrow footpath through a field of rye, she ran into the tall thick rye, overgrown with cornflowers and wormwood, so as not to meet him face to face. He caught sight of her little head through a golden network of ears of rye, from which she was peeping out like a little animal, and called affectionately to her:

"Good-evening, Fenichka! I don't bite."

"Good-evening," she whispered, not coming out of her ambush.

By degrees she began to be more at home with him, but was still shy in his presence, when suddenly her mother, Arina, died of cholera. What was to become of Fenichka? She inherited from her mother a love for order, regularity, and sedateness; but she was so young, so alone. Nikolai Petrovich was himself so good and considerate. . . . It's needless to relate the rest. . . .

"So my brother came in to see you?" Nikolai Petrovich questioned her. "He knocked and came in?"

"Yes sir."

"Well, that's a good thing. Let me give Mitya a swing."

And Nikolai Petrovich began tossing him almost up to the ceiling, to the huge delight of the baby, and to the considerable uneasiness of the mother, who every time he flew up stretched her arms up towards his little bare legs.

Pavel Petrovich went back to his elegant study, its walls covered with handsome bluish-grey wall paper, with weapons hanging upon a colorful Persian rug nailed to the wall; with walnut furniture, upholstered in dark green velveteen, with a *renaissance* bookcase of old black oak, with bronze statuettes on the magnificent desk, with a fireplace. He threw himself on the sofa, clasped his hands behind his head, and remained without moving, looking at the ceiling almost in despair. Whether he wanted to hide from the very walls that which was reflected in his face, or for some other reason, he got up, drew the heavy window curtains, and again threw himself on the sofa.

IX

On that same day Bazarov too became acquainted with Fenichka. He was walking with Arkady in the garden, and explaining to him why some of the trees, especially the young oaks had not done well.

"You ought to plant silver poplars here mostly, and firs, and perhaps lindens, adding loam. The arbor there has done well," he added, "because it's acacia and lilac; they're good fellows, they don't need much care. Why, there's some one in here."

In the arbor Fenichka was sitting with Dunyasha and Mitya. Bazarov stood still, while Arkady nodded to Fenichka like an old friend.

"Who's that?" Bazarov asked him as soon as they had passed by. "What a pretty girl!"

"Whom are you speaking of?"

"You know who; only one of them was pretty."

Arkady, not without embarrassment, explained to him briefly who Fenichka was.

"Aha!" remarked Bazarov; "your father's got good taste, one can see. I like him, your father, by George! He's a good fellow. We ought to get acquainted though," he added, and turned back towards the arbor.

"Evgeny!" Arkady cried after him in dismay; "mind what you are about, for mercy's sake."

"Don't get excited," said Bazarov; "I've been around, I'm not a country bumpkin."

Going up to Fenichka, he took off his cap.

"Allow me to introduce myself," he began, with a polite bow. "I'm a friend of Arkady Nikolaevich's and a harmless person."

Fenichka got up from the garden seat and looked at him without speaking.

"What a splendid baby!" continued Bazarov; "don't be uneasy, my praises have never brought ill-luck yet. Why are his cheeks so flushed? Is he cutting teeth?"

"Yes sir," said Fenichka; "he has cut four teeth already, and now the gums are swollen again."

"Show me, and don't be afraid, I'm a doctor."

Bazarov took the baby up in his arms, and to the great astonishment both of Fenichka and Dunyasha the child made no resistance, and was not frightened.

"I see, I see. . . . It's nothing, everything's all right, he'll have a good set of teeth. If anything goes wrong, tell me. And are you quite well yourself?"

"Quite, thank God."

"Thank God,—that's the great thing. And you?" he added, turning to Dunyasha.

Dunyasha, a very prim girl in the master's house, and a giggle-box outside the gates, only snorted in answer.

"Well, that's all right. Here's your mighty knight."

Fenichka received the baby in her arms.

"How good he was with you!" she commented in an undertone.

"Children are always good with me," answered Bazarov; "I have a way with them."

"Children know who loves them," remarked Dunyasha.

"Yes, they certainly do," Fenichka said. "Why, Mitya will not go to some people for anything."

"Will he come to me?" asked Arkady, who, after standing in the distance for some time, had gone up to the arbor.

He tried to entice Mitya to come to him, but Mitya threw his head back and started to squeal, to Fenichka's great confusion.

"Another day, when he's had time to get used to me," said Arkady indulgently, and the two friends walked away.

"What's her name?" asked Bazarov.

"Fenichka . . . Fedosya," answered Arkady.

"And her patronymic? One must know that too."

"Nikolaevna."

"*Bene.* What I like in her is that she's not too embarrassed. Some people, I suppose, would think ill of her for it. What nonsense! What is there to embarrass her? She's a mother—she's in the right."

"She is all right," observed Arkady,—"but my father. . . ."

"And he's in the right too," put in Bazarov.

"Well, no, I don't think so."

"I suppose an extra heir's not to your liking?"

"How can you not be ashamed to attribute such ideas to me!" retorted Arkady hotly; "I don't consider my father wrong from that point of view. I think he ought to marry her."

"Oho-ho!" responded Bazarov tranquilly. "What magnanimous fellows we are! You still attach significance to marriage; I did not expect that of you."

The friends walked a few paces in silence.

"I have looked at your father's entire establishment," Bazarov began again. "The cattle are inferior, the horses are broken down; the buildings also aren't much, and the workmen seem to be confirmed loafers; while the bailiff is either a fool or a knave, I haven't quite found out which yet."

"You are rather hard on everything to-day, Evgeny Vassilevich."

"And the good peasants are taking your father in for sure. You know the Russian proverb, 'The Russian peasant will cheat God Himself.' "

"I begin to agree with my uncle," remarked Arkady; "you certainly have a poor opinion of Russians."

"As though that mattered! The only good point in a Russian is his having the lowest possible opinion of himself. What does matter is that two and two make four, and the rest is all nonsense.

"And is nature nonsense?" said Arkady, looking pensively at the bright-colored fields in the distance, in the beautiful soft light of the sun, which was no longer high in the sky.

"Nature, too, is nonsense in the sense you understand it. Nature's not a temple, but a workshop, and man's the workman in it." [7]

At that instant, the long drawn notes of a violoncello floated out to them from the house. Some one was playing Schubert's *Expectation* with much feeling, though with an unpracticed hand, and the sweet melody flowed through the air like honey.

"What's that?" cried Bazarov in amazement.

"It's my father."

"Your father plays the violoncello?"

"Yes."

7. Bazarov quotes from Chernyshevsky's dissertation *The Aesthetic Relations of Art to Reality* (1855), the bible of the radicals. Chernyshevsky maintained that art is only an imitation of reality, and reality is always superior to it.

"And how old is your father?"

"Forty-four."

Bazarov suddenly burst into laughter.

"What are you laughing at?"

"Really, a man of forty-four, a *paterfamilias* in this out-of-the-way district, playing on the violoncello!"

Bazarov went on laughing; but much as he revered his mentor, this time Arkady did not even smile.

X

About a fortnight passed. Life at Marino went on its accustomed course, while Arkady played the sybarite, and Bazarov worked. Every one in the house had grown used to him, to his careless manners, and his curt and abrupt speeches. Fenichka, in particular, was so far at home with him that one night she sent to wake him up; Mitya had convulsions; and he came, and, half joking, half-yawning as usual, stayed two hours with her and relieved the child. On the other hand Pavel Petrovich had grown to detest Bazarov with all the strength of his soul; he regarded him as stuck-up, impudent, cynical, and plebeian; he suspected that Bazarov had no respect for him, that he had all but contempt for him—him, Pavel Kirsanov! Nikolai Petrovich was rather afraid of the young "nihilist," and doubted whether his influence over Arkady was for the good; but he was glad to listen to him, and was glad to be present at his scientific and chemical experiments. Bazarov had brought a microscope with him, and busied himself with it for hours on end. The servants, too, took to him, though he made fun of them; they felt that he was one of themselves just the same, not a master. Dunyasha was always ready to giggle with him, and used to cast significant and stealthy glances at him when she ran by "like a quail"; Peter, an extremely vain and stupid man, forever wearing an affected frown on his brow, a man whose whole merit consisted in the fact that he looked civil, could spell out a page of reading, and brushed his coat frequently—even he smirked and brightened up as soon as Bazarov paid him any attention; the boys on the farm simply ran after the "doctor" like puppies. Old Prokofich was the only one who did not like him; he served him at table with a surly face, called him a "mule skinner" and "a humbug"; and maintained that with his side whiskers he looked like a pig in a bush. Prokofich in his own way was quite as much of an aristocrat as Pavel Petrovich.

The best days of the year had come—the first days of June. The weather kept fine; in the distance, it is true, cholera was threatening again, but the inhabitants of that province had had time to get used to its visits. Bazarov used to get up very early and go out for two or three miles, not for a walk—he couldn't bear walking without an object—but to collect specimens of plants and insects. Sometimes he took Arkady with him. On the way home an argument usually sprang up, and Arkady was usually vanquished in it, though he said more than his companion.

One day they had somehow lingered rather late; Nikolai Petrovich went to meet them in the garden, and as he reached the arbor he suddenly heard the quick step and voices of the two young men. They were walking on the other side of the arbor, and could not see him.

"You don't know my father well enough," said Arkady.

Nikolai Petrovich concealed himself.

"Your father's a nice man," said Bazarov, "but he's behind the times; his day is done."

Nikolai Petrovich listened intently. . . . Arkady made no answer.

The man whose day was done remained motionless for a couple of minutes, and plodded slowly home.

"The day before yesterday I saw him reading Pushkin," Bazarov was continuing meanwhile. "Explain to him, please, that that's entirely useless.[8] He's not a boy, you know; it's time to throw up that rubbish. And what an idea to be a romantic these days! Give him something sensible ro read."

"What ought I to give him?" asked Arkady.

"Oh, I think Büchner's *Stoff und Kraft* [9] to begin with."

"I think so too," observed Arkady approvingly, "*Stoff und Kraft* is written in popular language. . . ."

"So it seems," Nikolai Petrovich said the same day after dinner to his brother, as he sat in his study, "you and I are behind the times, our day's over. Well, well. Perhaps Bazarov is right; but one thing hurts, I confess; I did hope, precisely now, to get on close, intimate terms with Arkady, and it turns out I'm left behind, and he has gone forward, and we can't understand one another."

"But how has he gone forward? And in what way is he so superior to us?" cried Pavel Petrovich impatiently. "It's that signor, that nihilist, who's knocked all that into his head. I hate that doctor fellow; in my opinion, he's simply a quack; I'm convinced, for all his frogs, he's not got very far even in physics."

"No, brother, you mustn't say that; Bazarov is clever, and knows his subject."

8. Bazarov again echoes Dobrolyubov, who maintained that Pushkin wrote only for the educated class and that few people were interested in him.

9. "Matter and Force." Actually, *Force and Matter* (1855), Russian translation 1860. Ludwig Büchner was the brother of Georg, the German dramatist.

"And his conceit's something revolting," Pavel Petrovich broke in again.

"Yes," observed Nikolai Petrovich, "he is conceited. But there's no doing without that, it seems; only that's what I did not take into account. I thought I was doing everything to keep up with the times; I have done well by the peasants, I have started a farm so that I am positively called a "Red" all over the province; I read, I study, I try in every way to keep abreast with the requirements of the day—and they say my day's over. And, brother, I begin to think that it is."

"Why so?"

"I'll tell you why. This morning I was sitting reading Pushkin. . . . I remember, it happened to be *The Gypsies* . . . all of a sudden Arkady came up to me, and, without speaking, with such a kindly compassion on his face, as gently as if I were a baby, took the book away from me, and laid another before me—a German book . . . smiled, and went away, carrying Pushkin off with him."

"Upon my word! What book did he give you?"

"This one here."

And Nikolai Petrovich pulled the famous treatise of Büchner, in the ninth edition, out of his coat-tail pocket.

Pavel Petrovich turned it over in his hands. "Hm!" he growled. "Arkady Nikolaevich is taking your education in hand. Well, did you try reading it?"

"Yes, I tried it."

"Well, what did you think of it?"

"Either I'm stupid, or it's all—nonsense. I must be stupid, I suppose."

"Haven't you forgotten your German?" queried Pavel Petrovich.

"I understand the German."

Pavel Petrovich again turned the book over in his hands, and glanced from under his brows at his brother. Both were silent.

"Oh, by the way," began Nikolai Petrovich, obviously wishing to change the subject, "I've got a letter from Kolyazin."

"Matvey Ilyich?"

"Yes. He has come to inspect the province. He's a bigwig now, and writes to me that, as a relation, he should like to see us, and invites you and me and Arkady to the town."

"Are you going?" asked Pavel Petrovich.

"No; are you?"

'No, I won't go either. Much object there would be in dragging oneself over thirty miles on a wild-goose chase. *Mathieu* wants to show himself in all his glory. The hell with him! he will have the whole province doing him homage; he can get on without us. A grand dignity, indeed, a privy councillor! If I had stayed in the service, if I had trudged on in that stupid harness, I should have been a general-adjutant by now. Besides, you and I are behind the times, you know."

"Yes, brother; it's time, it seems, to order a coffin and cross one's arms on one's breast," remarked Nikolai Petrovich, with a sigh.

"Well, I'm not going to give in quite so soon," muttered his brother. "I've got a tussle with that doctor fellow before me, I have a premonition."

A tussle came off that same day at evening tea. Pavel Petrovich came into the drawing-room, all ready for the fray, irritable and determined. He was only waiting for an excuse to fall upon the enemy; but for a long while an excuse did not present itself. As a rule, Bazarov said little in the presence of the "old Kirsanovs" (that was how he spoke of the brothers), and that evening he felt out of humor, and drank off cup after cup of tea without a word. Pavel Petrovich was all aflame with impatience; his wishes were fulfilled at last.

The conversation turned on one of the neighboring landowners. "Trash, a rotten little aristocrat," observed Bazarov indifferently. He had met him in Petersburg.

"Allow me to ask you," began Pavel Petrovich, and his lips were trembling, "according to your ideas, have the words 'trash' and 'aristocrat' the same meaning?"

"I said 'rotten little aristocrat,' " replied Bazarov, lazily swallowing a sip of tea.

"Precisely so, sir; but I imagine you have the same opinion of aristocrats as of rotten little aristocrats. I consider it my duty to inform you that I do not share that opinion. I venture to say that every one knows me for a man of liberal ideas and devoted to progress; but, exactly for that reason, I respect aristocrats—real aristocrats. Kindly remember, sir" (at these words Bazarov lifted his eyes and looked at Pavel Petrovich), "kindly remember, sir," he repeated, with acrimony—"the English aristocracy. They do not abate one iota of their rights, and for that reason they respect the rights of others; they demand the fulfillment of obligations in dealing with them, and for that reason they fulfill their own obligations. The aristocracy has given freedom to England, and supports it for her."

"We've heard that song a good many times," replied Bazarov; "but what are you trying to prove by that?"

"I am tryin' to prove by that, sir" (when Pavel Petrovich was angry he intentionally clipped his words in this way, though, of course, he knew very well that such forms are not strictly grammatical. In this whim could be discerned a survival of the habits of the times of Alexander I. The exquisites of those days, on the rare occasions when they spoke their own language, made use of such slipshod forms; as much as to say, "We, of course, are genuine Russians, at the same time we are grandees, who are at liberty to neglect the rules of scholars"); I am tryin' to prove by that, sir, that without the sense of personal dignity, without self-respect—and these two sentiments are well developed in the aristocrat—there is no secure foundation for the social . . . *bien public* . . . the social fabric. Character, sir—that is the chief thing; a man's character must be firm as a rock, since everything is built on it. I am very well aware, for instance, that you are pleased to consider my habits, my dress, my neatness, in short, ridiculous; but all that proceeds from a sense of self-respect, from a sense of duty—yes sir, yes sir, of duty. I live in the country, in the wilds, but I will not lower myself. I respect the dignity of man in myself."

"Let me ask you, Pavel Petrovich," said Bazarov; "you respect yourself, and sit with your arms folded; what sort of benefit does that do to the *bien public?* If you didn't respect yourself, you'd do just the same."

Pavel Petrovich turned white. "That's a different question. It's absolutely unnecessary for me to explain to you now why I sit with my arms folded, as you are pleased to express yourself. I wish only to tell you that aristocracy is a *principe,* and in our days none but immoral or silly people can live without *principes.* I said that to Arkady the day after he came home, and I repeat it now. Isn't it so, Nikolai?"

"Nikolai Petrovich nodded his head.

"Aristocracy, Liberalism, progress, principles," Bazarov was saying meanwhile; "if you think of it, what a lot of foreign . . . and useless words! No Russian needs them, even as a gift."

"What is good for something according to you? According to you we are outside humanity, outside its laws. Come—the logic of history demands . . ."

"But what's that logic to us? We can get on without it too."

"How do you mean?"

"Why, this. You don't need logic, I hope, to put a piece of bread in your mouth when you're hungry. What are these abstractions to us?"

Pavel Petrovich flung up his hands.

"I don't understand you, after that. You insult the Russian people. I don't understand how it's possible not to acknowledge *principes,* rules! By virtue of what do you act then?"

"I've told you already, uncle, that we don't recognize any authorities," put in Arkady.

"We act by virtue of what we recognize as useful," observed Bazarov. "At the present time, negation is the most useful of all—and we deny——"

"Everything?"

"Everything!"

"What, not only art and poetry . . . but even . . . horrible to say . . ."

"Everything," repeated Bazarov, with indescribable composure.

Pavel Petrovich stared at him. He had not expected this; while Arkady fairly blushed with delight.

"Allow me, though," began Nikolai Petrovich. "You deny everything; or, speaking more precisely, you destroy everything . . . But one must construct too, you know."

"That's not our business now. . . . The ground has to be cleared first."

"The present condition of the people requires it," added Arkady, with dignity; "we are bound to carry out these requirements, we have no right to yield to the satisfaction of our personal egoism."

This last phrase apparently displeased Bazarov; there was a flavor of philosophy, that is to say, romanticism about it, for Bazarov called philosophy, too, romanticism, but he did not think it necessary to correct his young disciple.

"No, no!" cried Pavel Petrovich, with sudden energy. "I'm not willing to believe that you, gentlemen, know the Russian people really, that you are the representatives of their requirements, their aspirations! No; the Russian people is not what you imagine it. It holds tradition sacred; it is a patriarchal people; it cannot live without faith . . ."

"I'm not going to dispute that," Bazarov interrupted. I'm even ready to agree that in *that* you're right."

"But if I am right. . . ."

"It still proves nothing."

"It just proves nothing," repeated Arkady, with the confidence of a practised chess-player, who has forseen an apparently dangerous move on the part of his adversary, and so is not at all taken aback by it.

"How does it prove nothing?" muttered Pavel Petrovich, astounded. "You must be going against the people then?"

"And what if we are?" cried Bazarov. "The people imagine that when it thunders the prophet Elijah's riding across the sky in his chariot. What then? Are we to agree with them? Besides, the people's Russian; but am I not Russian, too?"

"No, you are not Russian, after all you have just been saying!

I can't acknowledge you as Russian."

"My grandfather ploughed the land," answered Bazarov with haughty pride. "Ask any one of your peasants which of us—you or me—he'd readily acknowledge as a fellow-countryman. You don't even know how to talk to them."

"While you talk to him and despise him at the same time."

"Well, suppose he deserves contempt. You find fault with my attitude, but who told you that it's accidental in me, that it's not a product of that very national spirit, in the name of which you wage war?"

"To be sure! Much we need nihilists!"

"It is not for us to decide whether they're needed or not. Why, even you suppose you're not a useless person."

"Gentlemen, gentlemen, no personalities, please!" cried Nikolai Petrovich, getting up.

Pavel Petrovich smiled, and laying his hand on his brother's shoulder, forced him to sit down again.

"Don't be uneasy," he said; "I shall not forget myself, just through that sense of dignity which is made fun of so mercilessly by Mr. . . . by the doctor. Let me ask," he resumed, turning again to Bazarov; "perhaps you suppose, that your doctrine is a novelty? That is quite a mistake. The materialism you advocate has already been in vogue more than once, and has always proved insufficient . . ."

"A foreign word again!" broke in Bazarov. He was beginning to feel angry, and his face assumed a peculiar coarse coppery hue. "In the first place, we advocate nothing; that's not our way . . ."

"What do you do, then?"

"I'll tell you what we do. Formerly, not long ago, we used to say that our officials took bribes, that we had no roads, no commerce, no real justice . . ." [1]

"Well yes, yes, you are accusers;—that's what it's called, I think. I too agree with many of your denunciations, but . . ."

"Then we figured out that talk, perpetual talk, and nothing but talk about our social sores, was not worthwhile, that it all led to nothing but banality and doctrinairism. We saw that even our clever ones, so-called advanced people and accusers, were no good; that we were occupied by nonsense, talked about some sort of art, unconscious creativeness, parliamentarianism, the legal profession, and the devil knows what all, while it's a question of daily bread, while we're stifling under the grossest superstition, while all our corporations come to grief simply because there

1. Bazarov now echoes in part Dobrolyubov's article "What is Oblomovitis?" (1859), an obtuse sermon on Goncharov's tragi-comic novel *Oblomov*. Dobrolyubov found the cause for Oblomov's sloth in the institution of serfdom!

aren't enough honest men to carry them on, while the very emancipation our Government's busy upon will hardly come to any good, because peasants are glad to rob even themselves to get drunk at the pot-house."

"Yes," interposed Pavel Petrovich, "yes; you become convinced of all this, and decided not to undertake anything seriously yourselves."

"We decided not to undertake anything," repeated Bazarov grimly. He suddenly felt vexed with himself for having been so expansive before this gentleman.

"But to confine yourselves to abuse?"

"To confine ourselves to abuse."

"And that is called nihilism?"

"And that is called nihilism," Bazarov repeated again, this time with peculiar rudeness.

Pavel Petrovich puckered up his face a little. "So that's it!" he observed in a strangely composed voice. "Nihilism is to cure all our woes, and you, you are our heroes and saviors. But why do you abuse others, even those accusers? Don't you do as much talking as every one else?"

"Whatever faults we have, we do not err in that way," Bazarov muttered between his teeth.

"What, then? Do you act, or what? Are you preparing for action?"

Bazarov made no answer. Something like a tremor passed over Pavel Petrovich, but he at once regained control of himself.

"Hm! . . . Action, destruction . . ." he went on. "But how destroy without even knowing why?"

"We shall destroy, because we are a force," observed Arkady.

Pavel Petrovich looked at his nephew and smiled.

"Yes, a force is not to be called to account," said Arkady, drawing himself up.

"Unhappy boy!" groaned Pavel Petrovich; he was positively incapable of restraining himself any longer. "If you could only realise *what* you are supporting in Russia with your vile sententiousness. No; it's enough to try the patience of an angel! Force! There's forces both in the savage Kalmuck and in the Mongolian; but what is it to us? What is precious to us is civilization; yes, yes, honored sir, its fruits are precious to us. And don't tell me those fruits are worthless; the poorest scribbler, *un barbouilleur*, the man who plays dance music for five farthings an evening, is of greater use than you, because they are the representatives of civilization, and not of brute Mongolian force! You fancy yourselves advanced people, and all the while you are fit only for the Kalmuck's hovel! Force! And recollect, you forcible gentlemen, that you're only four men and a half, and the others are millions, who won't let you trample their sacred traditions under foot, who will crush you!"

"If we're crushed, serves us right," observed Bazarov. "But that's an open question. We are not so few as you suppose."

"What? You seriously suppose you can overcome a whole people?"

"All Moscow was burnt down, you know, by a penny candle," answered Bazarov.

"Yes, yes. First a pride almost Satanic, then ridicule—that, that's what it is attracts the young, that's what gains an ascendancy over the inexperienced hearts of boys! Here's one of them sitting beside you, ready to worship the ground under your feet. Look at him! (Arkady turned away and frowned.) And this plague has spread far already. I have been told that in Rome our artists never set foot in the Vatican. Raphael they almost regard as a fool, because, if you please, he's an authority; yet they themselves are disgustingly impotent and sterile, men whose imagination does not soar beyond 'Girls at a Fountain,' however they try! And even the girls are miserably drawn. They are fine fellows to your mind, are they not?"

"To my mind," retorted Bazarov, "Raphael's not worth a brass farthing; and they're no better than he."

"Bravo! bravo! Listen, Arkady . . . that's how young men of to-day ought to express themselves! And if you come to think of it, how could they fail if they followed you! In old days, young men had to study; they didn't want to be called dunces, so they had to work hard whether they liked it or not. But now, they need only say, 'Everything in the world is nonsense!' and the trick's done. Young men are delighted. And, to be sure, they were simply blockheads before, and now they have suddenly turned nihilists."

"Your vaunted sense of personal dignity has given way," remarked Bazarov phlegmatically, while Arkady flared up, and his eyes were flashing. "Our argument has gone too far; it's better to cut it short, I think. I shall be quite ready to agree with you," he added, getting up, "when you bring forward a single institution in our present mode of life, in family or in social life, which does not call for complete and unqualified repudiation."

"I will bring forward millions of such institutions," cried Pavel Petrovich—"millions! Well—the village commune, for instance."

A cold smile curved Bazarov's lips. "Well, as regards the village commune," he commented; "you had better talk to your brother. He has seen by now, I should fancy, what sort of thing the village commune is in fact—its common guarantee, its sobriety, and other features of the kind."

"The family, then, the family as it exists among our peasants!" cried Pavel Petrovich.

"And that subject, too, I imagine, it will be better for yourselves not to go into detail. You've perhaps heard of the father-in-law's rights with the bride? Take my advice, Pavel Petrovich, allow yourself two days to think about it; you're not likely to find anything on the spot. Go through all our classes, and think well over each, while Arkady and I will . . ."

"Will go on turning everything into ridicule," broke in Pavel Petrovich.

"No, will go on dissecting frogs. Come, Arkady; good-bye, gentlemen!"

The two friends walked off. The brothers were left alone, and at first they only looked at one another.

"So that," began Pavel Petrovich, "so that's what our young men of this generation are! They are like that—our successors!"

"Our successors!" repeated Nikolai Petrovich, with a dejected sigh. He had been sitting on thorns, all through the argument, and had done nothing but glance stealthily, with a sore heart, at Arkady. "Do you know what I was reminded of, brother? I once had a dispute with our late mother; she shouted, and wouldn't listen to me. At last I said to her, 'Of course, you can't understand me; we belong,' I said, 'to two different generations.' She was dreadfully offended, while I thought, 'It can't be helped. It's a bitter pill, but she has to swallow it.' You see, now, our turn has come, and our successors can say to us, 'You are not of our generation; swallow your pill.' "

"You are really too generous and modest," replied Pavel Petrovich. "I'm convinced, on the contrary, that you and I are far more in the right than these young gentlemen, though we do perhaps express ourselves in old-fashioned language, *vieilli,* and have not the same insolent conceit. . . . And the swagger of the young men nowadays! You ask one, 'Do you take red wine or white?' 'It is my custom to prefer red!' he answers, in a deep bass, with a face as solemn as if the whole universe had its eyes on him at that instant. . . ."

"Do you care for any more tea?" asked Fenichka, putting her head in at the door; she had not been able to make up her mind to come into the drawing-room while there was the sound of voices in dispute there.

"No, you can tell them to take the samovar," answered Nikolai Petrovich, and he got up to meet her. Pavel Petrovich said "*bon soir*" to him abruptly, and went away to his study.

XI

Half an hour later Nikolai Petrovich went into the garden to his favorite arbor. He was overtaken by melancholy thoughts. For the first time he realized clearly the distance between him and his son; he foresaw that every day it would grow wider and wider. In vain, then, had he spent whole days sometimes in the winters at Petersburg over the newest books; in vain had he listened to the talk of the young men; in vain had he rejoiced when he succeeded in putting in his word, too, in their heated discussions. "My brother says we are right," he thought, "and apart from all vanity, I do think myself that they are further from the truth than we are, though at the same time I feel there is something behind them we have not got, some superiority over us. . . . Is it youth? No, not only youth. Doesn't their superiority consist in there being fewer traces of the slave owner in them than in us?"

Nikolai Petrovich's head sank despondently, and he passed his hand over his face.

"But to renounce poetry?" he thought again; "to have no feeling for art, for nature . . ."

And he looked round, as though trying to understand how it was possible to have no feeling for nature. Evening was already approaching; the sun was hidden behind a small copse of aspens which lay a quarter of a mile from the garden; its shadow stretched endlessly across the still fields. A peasant on a white nag went at a trot along the dark, narrow path close beside the copse; his whole figure was clearly visible even to the patch on his shoulder, in spite of his being in the shade; the white horse's legs flashed by distinctly and pleasantly. The sun's rays for their part made their way into the copse, and piercing through its thickets, threw such a warm light on the aspen trunks that they looked like pines, and their leaves were almost a dark blue, while above them rose a pale blue sky, faintly tinged by the glow of sunset. The swallows flew high; the wind had quite died away, belated bees buzzed slowly and drowsily among the lilac blossom; a swarm of midges hung like a cloud over a solitary branch which stood out against the sky. My God, how beautiful!" thought Nikolai Petrovich, and his favorite verses came to his lips; he remembered Arkady's *Stoff und Kraft*—and was silent, but still he sat there, still he gave himself up to the sorrowful consolation of solitary thought. He was fond of reverie; his country life had developed the tendency in him. How short a time ago, he had been dreaming like this, waiting for his son at the posting station, and what changes had already occurred since that day; their relations that were then undefined, were defined now—and how defined! Again his late wife came back to his imagination, but not as he had known her for many years, not as the good domestic housewife, but as a young girl with a slim figure, innocently inquiring eyes, and a tight braid on her childish neck. He remembered how he had seen her for the first time. He was still a student then. He had met her on the staircase of his lodgings, and, jostling by accident against her, he tried to apologize, and could only mutter, "*Pardon, monsieur*," while she bowed, smiled, and suddenly seemed frightened, and ran away, though at the bend of the staircase she had glanced rapidly at him, assumed a serious air, and blushed. Afterwards, the first timid visits, the half-words, the half-smiles, and embarrassment; and melancholy, and yearnings, and at last that breathing rapture. . . . Where had it all vanished? She became his wife, he had been happy as few on earth are happy. . . . "But," he mused, "these sweet first moments, why could not one live an eternal, immortal life in them?"

He did not try to make his thought clear to himself; but he felt that he longed to keep that blissful time by something stronger than memory; he longed to feel his Marya near him again, to have the sense of her warmth and breathing, and already he could fancy that over him. . . .

"Nikolai Petrovich," came the sound of Fenichka's voice close by him; "where are you?"

He started. He felt no pang, no shame. He never even admitted the possibility of comparison between his wife and Fenichka, but he was sorry she had thought of coming to look for him. Her voice at once brought back to him his grey hairs, his age, the present. . . .

The enchanted world into which he had already stepped, which already rose out of the dim mists of the past, was shaken—and vanished.

"I'm here," he answered; "I'm coming, run along." "There it is, the traces of the slave owner," flashed through his mind. Fenichka peeped into the arbor at him without speaking, and disappeared; while he noticed with astonishment that the night had come on while he had been dreaming. Everything around was dark and hushed, and Fenichka's face had glimmered so pale and slight before him. He got up, and was about to go home; but the emotion stirred in his heart could not be soothed at once, and he began slowly walking about the garden, sometimes looking at the ground at his feet, and then raising his eyes towards the sky where swarms of stars were already twinkling. He walked a great deal, till he was almost tired out, while the restlessness within him, a kind of yearning, vague, melancholy restlessness, still was not appeased. Oh, how Bazarov would have laughed at him, if he had known what was passing within him then! Arkady himself would have condemned him. He, a man forty-four years old, an agronomist and a farmer, was shedding tears, causeless tears; this was a hundred times worse than the violoncello.

Nikolai Petrovich continued to walk, and could not make up his mind to go into the house, into that snug and peaceful nest, which looked out at him so hospitably from all its lighted windows; he had not the force to tear himself away from the darkness, the garden, the sense of the fresh air in his face, from that melancholy, that restless craving.

At a turn in the path, he was met by Pavel Petrovich. "What's the matter with you?" he asked Nikolai Petrovich; "you are as pale as a ghost; you are not well; why don't you go to bed?"

Nikolai Petrovich explained to him briefly his state of feeling and moved away. Pavel Petrovich went to the end of the garden, and he too grew thoughtful, and he too raised his eyes towards the heavens. But nothing was reflected in his beautiful dark eyes except the light of the stars. He was not born a romantic, and his fastidiously dry and sensuous soul, with its French tinge of misanthropy, was not capable of dreaming. . . .

"Do you know what?" Bazarov was saying to Arkady the same night. "I've got a splendid idea. Your father was saying to-day that he had received an invitation from your illustrious relative. Your father's not going; let us be off to X——; you know that that gentleman invited you too. See what fine weather it is; we'll take a ride about and look at the town. We'll enjoy ourselves for five or six days and that's that!"

"And you'll come back here again?"

"No; I must go to my father's. You know, he lives about twenty miles from X——. I haven't seen him for a long time nor my mother; I have to please the old folks. They're good people, especially my father; he's awfully funny. I'm their only child too."

"And will you be long with them?"

"I don't suppose so. It will be dull, I suppose."

"And you'll come to us on your way back?"

"I don't know . . . I'll see. Well, what do you say? Shall we go?"

"If you like," observed Arkady languidly.

In his heart he was highly delighted with his friend's suggestion, but he thought it a duty to conceal his feeling. He was not a nihilist for nothing!

The next day he set off with Bazarov to X——. The younger part of the household at Marino were sorry at their going; Dunyasha even cried . . . but the old folks breathed more easily.

XII

The town of X——to which our friends set off was in the jurisdiction of a governor who was still young, at once a progressive and a despot, as often happens in Russia. Before the end of the first year of his government, he had managed to quarrel not only with the marshal of nobility, a retired captain of the guards, who kept open house and a stud of horses, but even with his own subordinates. The feuds arising from this at last assumed such proportions that the ministry in Petersburg had found it necessary to send down a trusted personage with a commission to investigate it all on the spot. The choice of the authorities fell upon Matvey Ilyich Kolyazin, the son of the Kolyazin under whose protection the brothers Kirsanov had once found themselves. He, too, was a "young man"; that is to say, he had not long passed forty, but he was already on the high road to becoming a statesman, and wore a star on each side of his breast—one, to be sure, a foreign star, of the undistinguished kind. Like the governor, whom he had come to pass judgment upon, he was reckoned a progressive; and though he was already a bigwig, he was not like the majority of bigwigs. He had the highest opinion of himself; looked with approval, listened condescendingly, and laughed so good-naturedly, that at first he might even be taken for "a jolly good fellow." On important occasions, however, he knew, as the saying is, how to make the fur fly. "Energy is essential," he used to say then, "*l'énergie est la première qualité d'un homme d'état;*"[2] and for all that, he was usually taken in, and any moderately experienced official could turn him round his finger. Matvey Ilyich used to speak with great respect of Guizot, and tried to impress every one with the idea that he did not belong to the class of *routiniers* and high-and-dry bureaucrats, that not a single important phenomenon of social life passed unnoticed by him. . . . All such phrases were very familiar to him. He even followed, with dignified indifference, it is true, the development of contemporary literature; so a grown-up man who meets a procession of small boys in the street will sometimes walk after it. In reality, Matvey Ilyich had not got much beyond those political men of the days of Alexander I, who used to prepare for an evening party at Madame Svetchin's by reading a page of Con-

2. "energy is the first requisite for a statesman."

dillac;[3] only his methods were different, more modern. He was an adroit courtier, a great schemer, and nothing more; he had no special aptitude for affairs, and no intellect, but he knew how to manage his own business successfully; no one could get the better of him there, and, to be sure, that's the principal thing.

Matvey Ilyich received Arkady with the good-nature, we might even call it playfulness, characteristic of the enlightened higher official. He was astonished, however, when he heard that the cousins he had invited had remained at home in the country. "Your father was always a queer fellow," he remarked, playing with the tassels of his magnificent velvet dressing-gown, and suddenly turning to a young official in a most discreetly buttoned-up uniform, he cried, with an air of concentrated attention, "What?" The young man, whose lips were glued together from prolonged silence, rose and looked in perplexity at his chief. But, having nonplussed his subordinate, Matvey Ilyich paid no further attention to him. Our higher officials are fond of nonplussing their subordinates as a rule; the methods to which they have recourse to attain that end are rather various. The following one, among others, is in great vogue, "*is quite a favourite*," as the English say; a high official suddenly ceases to understand the simplest words, assuming total deafness. He will ask, for instance, "What's to-day?"

He is respectfully informed, "To-day's Friday, your Ex-s-s-s-lency."

"Eh? What? What's that? What do you say?" the great man repeats with intense attention.

"To-day's Friday, your Ex—s—s—lency."

"Eh? What? What's Friday? What Friday?"

"Friday, your Ex—s—s—s—lency, the day of the week."

"What, do you pretend to teach me, eh?"

Matvey Ilyich was a higher official all the same, though he was reckoned a liberal.

"I advise you, my dear boy, to go and call on the Governor," he said to Arkady; "you understand, I don't advise you to do so because I adhere to old-fashioned ideas about the necessity of paying respect to authorities, but simply because the Governor's a decent fellow; besides, you probably want to become acquainted with society here. . . . You're not a bear, I hope? And he's giving a grand ball the day after to-morrow."

"Will you be at the ball?" inquired Arkady.

3. Sofya Petrovna Svechin (1782–1859) was a leader in the religious mysticism fashionable in the later part of Alexander I's reign (died 1825). Her work, republished while the novel was being written, was much discussed. Etienne Condillac (1715–80), French philosopher, would provide arguments against her views.

"He's giving it in my honor," answered Matvey Ilyich, almost pityingly. "Do you dance?"

"I dance, but badly."

"That's a pity! There are pretty girls here, and it's a disgrace for a young man not to dance. Again, I don't say that through any old-fashioned ideas; I don't in the least imagine that a man's wit lies in his feet, but Byronism is ridiculous, *il a fait son temps*." [4]

"But, uncle, it's not through Byronism at all, I . . ."

"I will introduce you to the ladies here; I will take you under my wing," interrupted Matvey Ilyich, and he laughed complacently. "You'll find it warm, eh?"

A servant entered and announced the arrival of the president of the government administration, a mild-eyed old man, with wrinkled lips who loved nature passionately, especially on a summer day, when, in his words, "every little bee takes a little bribe from every little flower." Arkady withdrew.

He found Bazarov at the inn where they were staying and was a long while persuading him to go with him to the Governor's. "Well, it can't be helped," said Bazarov at last. "It's no good doing things by halves. We came to look at the gentry; let's look at them!" The Governor received the young men affably, but he did not ask them to sit down, nor did he sit down himself. He was in an everlasting fuss and hurry; in the morning he used to put on a tight uniform and a stiff cravat; he never finished eating or drinking, for he was constantly busy administering. He was nicknamed Bourdaloue in the province, not after the renowned French preacher, but as a hint at *burda*, swill. He invited Kirsanov and Bazarov to his ball, and within a few minutes invited them a second time, regarding them as brothers, and calling them Kaisarov.

They were on their way home from the Governor's when suddenly a short man, in a Slavophile jacket,[5] leaped out of a trap that was passing them, and with a shout, "Evgeny Vassilyich!" dashed up to Bazarov.

"Ah! it's you, Herr Sitnikov," observed Bazarov, continuing to step along on the pavement; "by what fate did you come here?"

"Fancy, absolutely by chance," he replied, and turning to the trap, he waved his hand several times, and shouted, "Follow, follow us!—My father had business here," he went on, hopping across the gutter, "and so he asked me. . . . To day I heard of your arrival, and have already been to see you. . . ." (The friends did, in fact, on returning to their room find a card with the corners

4. "has had its day."

5. The Slavophiles maintained that Russia should reject the West and go back to its own traditions and cultural roots. Among their more nonsensical acts was the attempt to dress in supposedly "native" Russian clothes.

turned down, bearing the name of Sitnikov, on one side in French, on the other in Slavonic characters.) "I hope you are not coming from the Governor's?"

"It's no use hoping; we come straight from him."

"Ah! in that case I will call on him too. . . . Evgeny Vassilvich, introduce me to your . . . to the . . ."

"Sitnikov, Kirsanov," grumbled Bazarov, not stopping.

"I am greatly flattered," began Sitnikov, walking sidewise, smirking, and hurriedly pulling off his really far too elegant gloves. "I have heard so much. . . . I am an old acquaintance of Evgeny Vassilyich and, I may say—his disciple. I am indebted to him for my regeneration. . . ."

Arkady looked at Bazarov's disciple. There was an expression of worry and tension imprinted on the small but pleasant features of his well-groomed face; his small eyes, that seemed squeezed in, had a fixed and uneasy look, and his laugh, too, was uneasy—a sort of short, wooden laugh.

"Would you believe it," he continued, "when Evgeny Vassilyich said for the first time that it was not right to recognize any authorities, I felt such enthusiasm . . . as though my eyes were opened! Here, I thought, at last I have found a man! By the way, Evgeny Vassilyich, you positively must call on a lady here who is really capable of understanding you, and for whom your visit would be a real feast; you have heard of her, I suppose?"

"Who is she?" Bazarov brought out unwillingly.

"Kukshin, *Eudoxie*, Evdoksya Kukshin. She's a remarkable nature, *émancipée* in the true sense of the word, an advanced woman. Do you know what? We'll all go together to see her now. She lives only two steps from here. We'll have lunch there. You have not lunched yet, have you?"

"No; not yet."

"Well, that's capital. She has separated, you understand, from her husband; she is not dependent on any one."

"Is she pretty?" Bazarov cut in.

"N . . . no, one couldn't say that."

"Then, what the devil are you asking us to see her for?"

"Fie; you must have your joke. . . . She will give us a bottle of champagne."

"Oh, that's it. One can see the practical man at once. By the way, is your father still in the liquor business?"

"Yes," said Sitnikov, hurriedly, and laughed shrilly. "Well? Will you come?"

"I really don't know."

"You wanted to see people, go along," said Arkady in an undertone.

"And what do you say to it, Mr. Kirsanov?" Sitnikov put in. "You must come too; we can't go without you."

"But how can we burst in upon her all at once?"

"That's no matter. Kukshin's a wonderful person!"

"There will be a bottle of champagne?" asked Bazarov.

"Three!" cried Sitnikov; "that I answer for."

"What with?"

"My own head."

"Your father's purse would be better. However, let's go."

XIII

The tiny nobleman's house in the Moscow style, in which Avdotya Nikitishna, (otherwise Evodoksya) Kukshin lived was in one of the streets of X——which had lately burnt down; it is well known that our provincial towns burn down every five years. At the door, above a visiting card nailed on askew, there was a bell-handle to be seen, and in the hall the visitors were met by some one who was not exactly a servant nor exactly a companion, in a cap—unmistakable tokens of the progressive tendencies of the mistress. Sitnikov inquired whether Avdotya Nikitishna was at home.

"Is that you, *Victor*?" sounded a shrill voice from the adjoining room. "Come in."

The woman in the cap disappeared at once.

"I'm not alone," observed Sitnikov, with a bold look at Arkady and Bazarov as he briskly pulled off his jacket, beneath which appeared something of the nature of a tunic or a sackcoat.

"No matter," answered the voice. "*Entrez.*"

The young men went in. The room into which they walked resembled a study more than a drawing-room. Papers, letters, thick issues of Russian journals, for the most part uncut, lay at random on the dusty tables; cigarette ends lay scattered everywhere. On a leather-covered sofa, a lady, still young, was reclining. Her fair hair was rather dishevelled; she wore a silk gown, not altogether tidy, heavy bracelets on her short arms, and a lace handkerchief on her head. She got up from the sofa, and carelessly drawing over her shoulders a velvet cape trimmed with yellowish ermine, she said languidly, "Good-morning, *Victor*," and shook Sitnikov's hand.

"Bazarov, Kirsanov," he announced abruptly in imitation of Bazarov.

"Delighted," answered Kukshin [6] and fixing on Bazarov a pair

6. Turgenev deliberately omits any title before the lady's name; the Russian uses here the feminine ending: *Kukshina.*

of round eyes, between which was a forlorn little turned-up red nose, "I know you," she added, and shook his hand too.

Bazarov frowned. There was nothing repulsive in the little plain person of the emancipated woman; but the expression of her face produced a disagreeable effect on the spectator. One felt impelled to ask her, "What's the matter; are you hungry? Or bored? Or shy? What are you fidgeting about?" Both she and Sitnikov always had the same uneasy air. She was extremely unconstrained, and at the same time awkward; she obviously regarded herself as a good-natured, simple creature, and all the while, whatever she did, it always struck one that it was just what she did not want to do; everything with her seemed, as children say, done on purpose, that's to say, not simply, not naturally.

"Yes, yes, I know you, Bazarov," she repeated. (She had the habit—peculiar to many provincial and Moscow ladies—of calling men by their surnames from the first day of acquaintance with them.) "Will you have a cigar?"

"A cigar's all very well," put in Sitnikov, who by now was lolling in an armchair, one leg in the air; "but give us some lunch. We're awfully hungry; and tell them to bring us up a little bottle of champagne."

"Sybarite," commented Evdoksya, and she laughed. (When she laughed the gum showed above her upper teeth.) "Isn't it true, Bazarov; he's a Sybarite?"

"I like comfort in life," Sitnikov pronounced, with dignity "That does not prevent my being a Liberal."

"No, it does; it does prevent it!" cried Evdoksya. She gave directions to her maid, however, both about lunch and champagne.

"What do you think of it?" she added, turning to Bazarov. "I'm convinced you share my opinion."

"Well, no," retorted Bazarov; "a piece of meat's better than a piece of bread even from the chemical point of view."

"Are you studying chemistry? That's my passion. I've even invented a new sort of compound myself."

"A compound? You?"

"Yes. And do you know for what purpose? To make dolls' heads that won't break. I'm practical, too, you see. But every thing's not quite ready yet. I've still to read Liebig. By the way, have you read Kislyakov's article on Female Labor, in the *Moscow Gazette?* [7] Read it, please. You're interested in the woman question, aren't you? And in the schools too? What does your friend do? What is his name?"

Madame Kukshin dropped her questions one after another with spoiled negligence, not waiting for an answer; pampered children

7. The name Kislyakov (Sourpuss) is fictitious.

talk so to their nurses.

"My name's Arkady Nikolaich Kirsanov," said Arkady, "and I'm doing nothing."

Evdoksya burst into laughter. "How charming! What, don't you smoke? Victor, do you know, I'm very angry with you."

"What for?"

"They tell me you've begun singing the praises of George Sand again. A retrograde woman, and nothing else! How can people compare her with Emerson? She hasn't any ideas on education, nor physiology, nor anything. I am sure she's never heard of embryology, and in these days—what can be done without that?" (Evdoksya even threw up her hands.) "Ah, what a wonderful article Elisevich [8] has written on that subject! He's a gentleman of genius." (Evdoksya constantly used the word "gentleman" instead of the word "man.") "Bazarov, sit next to me on the sofa. Perhaps you don't know, I'm awfully afraid of you."

"Why so? Allow me to ask."

"You're a dangerous gentleman; you're such a critic. Good God! yes! why, how absurd, I'm talking like some country lady. I really am a country lady, though. I manage my property myself; and only fancy, my bailiff Erofey's a wonderful type, quite like Cooper's Pathfinder; there is something so spontaneous in him! I've come to settle here for good; it's an intolerable town, isn't it? But what can be done?"

"The town's like any other," Bazarov remarked coolly.

"All its interests are so petty, that's what's so awful! I used to spend the winters in Moscow . . . but now my lawful spouse, Monsieur Kukshin lives there. And besides, Moscow nowadays . . . there, I don't know—it's not the same as it was. I'm thinking of going abroad; last year I was on the point of setting off."

"To Paris, of course?" queried Bazarov.

"To Paris and to Heidelberg."

"Why to Heidelberg?"

"How can you ask? Why, Bunsen's there!"

To this Bazarov could find no reply.

"*Pierre* Sapozhnikov . . . do you know him?"

"No, I don't."

"Not know *Pierre* Sapozhnikov . . . he's always at Lidia Klostatov's."

"I don't know her either."

"Well, it was he undertook to escort me. Thank God, I'm free: I have no children. . . . What was that I said: *thank God!* It's no matter though."

8. Elisevich is a slightly distorted version of a contributor to the radical periodical *The Contemporary*, where Chernyshevsky and Dobrolyubov appeared.

Evdoksya rolled a cigarette up between her fingers, which were brown with tobacco stains, passed the edge across her tongue, sucked it, and began smoking. The maid came in with a tray.

"Ah, here's lunch! Will you eat? Victor, open the bottle, that's in your line."

"Yes, it's in my line," muttered Sitnikov, and again he gave vent to the same shrill laugh.

"Are there any pretty women here?" inquired Bazarov, as he drank off a third glass.

"Yes, there are," answered Evdoksya; "but they're all such empty-headed creatures. *Mon amie,* Odintsov, for instance, is nice-looking. It's a pity her reputation's rather, well . . . That wouldn't matter, though, but she has no independent views, no breadth, nothing . . . of that sort. The whole system of education wants changing. I've thought a great deal about it; our women are very badly educated."

"There's no doing anything with them," put in Sitnikov; "one ought to despise them, and I do despise them fully and completely!" (The possibility of feeling and expressing contempt was the most agreeable sensation to Sitnikov; he used to attack women in especial, never suspecting that it was to be his fate a few months later to cringe before his wife merely because she had been born a princess Durdoleosov.) "Not a single one of them would be capable of understanding our conversation; not a single one deserves to be spoken of by serious men like us!"

"But there's not the least need for them to understand our conversation," observed Bazarov.

"Whom do you mean?" put in Evdoksya.

"Pretty women."

"What? Do you share Proudhon's ideas, then?" [9]

Bazarov drew himself up haughtily. "I don't share any one's ideas; I have my own."

"Down with all authorities!" shouted Sitnikov, delighted to have a chance of expressing himself boldly before the man he slavishly admired.

"But even Macaulay," Kukshin was beginning . . .

"Down with Macaulay," thundered Sitnikov. "Are you going to stand up for the silly females?"

"For silly females, no, but for the rights of women, which I have sworn to defend to the last drop of my blood."

"Down with . . . !" but here Sitnikov stopped. "But I don't deny them," he said.

"No, I see you're a Slavophile."

9. P. J. Proudhon (1809–65), French socialist who attacked the concept of private property.

"No, I'm not a Slavophile though, of course . . ."

"No, no, no. You are a Slavophile. You're an advocate of patriarchal despotism. You want to have the whip in your hand!"

"A whip's an excellent thing," remarked Bazarov; "but we've got to the last drop."

"Of what?" interrupted Evdoksya.

"Of champagne, most honored Avdotya Nikitishna, of champagne—not of your blood."

"I can never listen calmly when women are attacked," pursued Evdoksya. "It's awful, awful. Instead of attacking them, you'd better read Michelet's book, *De l'amour*.[1] That's marvelous! Gentlemen, let us talk of love," added Evdoksya, letting her arm fall languidly on the rumpled sofa cushion.

A sudden silence followed. "No, why should we talk of love," said Bazarov; "but just now you mentioned Odintsov . . . That was what you called her, I think? Who is that lady?"

"She's charming, charming!" piped Sitnikov. "I will introduce you. Clever, rich, a widow. It's a pity, she's not yet advanced enough; she ought to see more of our Evdoksya. I drink to your health, *Eudoxie!* Let us clink glasses! *Et toc, et toc, et tin-tin-tin! Et toc, et toc, et tin-tin-tin!!*"

"Victor, you're a rascal."

The lunch dragged on a long while. The first bottle of champagne was followed by another, a third, and even a fourth. . . . Evdoksya chattered without pause; Sitnikov seconded her. They discussed at length the question whether marriage was a prejudice or a crime, and whether men were born equal or not, and precisely what individuality consists in. Things reached the point that Evdoksya, flushed from the wine she had drunk, tapped with her blunt nails on the keys of a discordant piano, and began to sing in a hoarse voice, first gipsy songs, and then Seymour Schiff's song, "Granada lies slumbering"; while Sitnikov tied a scarf round his head, and represented the dying lover at the words—

"And thy lips to mine
In burning kiss entwine."

Finally Arkady could not stand it. "Gentlemen, this has turned into something like Bedlam," he remarked aloud. Bazarov, who had at rare intervals put in an ironical word in the conversation—he paid more attention to the champagne—yawned loudly, got up, and, without taking leave of their hostess, he walked out with Arkady. Sitnikov jumped up and followed them.

"Well, what do you think of her?" he inquired, skipping

1. *On Love,* (1859).

obsequiously from right to left of them. "I told you, you see, a remarkable personality! If we only had more women like that! She is, in her own way, a highly moral phenomenon."

"And is your pop's establishment also a highly moral phenomenon?" asked Bazarov, pointing to a pot house which they were passing at that instant.

Sitnikov again went off into a shrill laugh. He was greatly ashamed of his origin, and did not know whether to feel flattered or offended at Bazarov's unexpected familiarity.

XIV

A few days later the Governor's ball took place. Matvey Ilyich was the real "hero of the occasion." The marshal of nobility declared to one and all that he had come simply out of respect for him; while the Governor, even at the ball, even while he remained perfectly motionless, was still "administering." The affability of Matvey Ilyich's demeanor could only be equalled by its dignity. He was gracious to all, to some with a shade of aversion, to others with a shade of respect; he appeared "*en vrai chevalier français*" [2] before the ladies, and was continually giving vent to a hearty, sonorous, unshared laugh, such as befits a high official. He slapped Arkady on the back, and called him loudly "little nephew"; vouchsafed Bazarov—who was attired in a rather old evening coat—a sidelong glance in passing—absentminded but condescending—and an indistinct but affable grunt, in which nothing could be distinguished but "I . . ." and "very much"; offered Sitnikov a finger and a smile, though with his head already averted; even to Kukshin, who made her appearance at the ball with dirty gloves, no crinoline, and a bird of Paradise in her hair, even to Kukshin he said "*enchanté*." There were hordes of people, and no lack of dancing men; the civilians were for the most part standing close along the walls, but the officers danced assiduously, especially one of them who had spent six weeks in Paris, where he had mastered various daring interjections like—"*zut*," "*Ah, fichtre*," "*pst, pst, mon bibi*," and such. He pronounced them to perfection with genuine Parisian *chic*, and at the same time he said "*si j'aurais*" for "*si j'avais*," "*absolument*" in the sense of "certainly" [3] expressed himself, in fact, in the Great Russo-French jargon which the French ridicule so when they have no reason for assuring us that we speak their language like angels, "*comme des anges*."

Arkady, as we are aware, danced badly, while Bazarov did not

2. "a real French cavalier."
3. That is, incorrectly uses the present conditional instead of the indicative imperfect for "if I had," and *absolument* for emphasis.

dance at all; they both took up their position in a corner, Sitnikov joined them. With an expression of contemptuous scorn on his face, and giving vent to spiteful comments, he looked insolently about him, and really seemed to be enjoying himself. Suddenly his face changed, and turning to Arkady, he said, with some show of embarrassment it seemed, "Odintsov is here!"

Arkady looked round, and saw a tall woman in a black dress standing at the door of the room. He was struck by the dignity of her carriage. Her bare arms lay gracefully beside her slender waist; gracefully some light sprays of fuchsia drooped from her shining hair on to her sloping shoulders; her clear eyes looked out from under a somewhat protruding white brow, with a tranquil and intelligent expression—tranquil it was precisely, not pensive—and on her lips was a scarcely perceptible smile. A kind of gracious and gentle force emanated from her face.

"Do you know her?" Arkady asked Sitnikov.

"Intimately. Would you like me to introduce you?"

"Please . . . after this quadrille."

Bazarov's attention, too, was directed to Odintsov.

"That's a striking figure," he remarked. "Not like the other females."

After waiting till the end of the quadrille, Sitnikov led Arkady up to Odintsov; but he hardly seemed to be intimately acquainted with her; he was embarrassed in his sentences, while she looked at him in some surprise. But her face assumed an expression of pleasure when she heard Arkady's surname. She asked him whether he was not the son of Nikolai Petrovich.

"Exactly so."

"I have seen your father twice, and have heard a great deal about him," she went on; "I am glad to meet you."

At that instant some adjutant flew up to her and begged for a quadrille. She consented.

"Do you dance then?" asked Arkady respectfully.

"Yes, I dance. Why do you suppose I don't dance? Do you think I am too old?"

"Really, how could I possibly. . . . But in that case, let me ask you for the mazurka."

Odintsov smiled graciously. "Certainly," she said, and she looked at Arkady, not exactly with an air of superiority, but as married sisters look at very young brothers. Odintsov was a little older than Arkady—she was twenty-nine—but in her presence he felt himself a schoolboy, a little student, so that the difference in age between them seemed of more consequence. Matvey Ilyich approached her with a majestic air and ingratiating speeches. Arkady moved away, but he still watched; he could not take his eyes off her even during the quadrille. She talked with as much ease to her partner as to the grand official, quietly turned her head and eyes, and twice laughed softly. Her nose—like almost all Russian noses—was a little thick; and her complexion was not perfectly clear; Arkady made up his mind, for all that, that he had never before met such an attractive woman. He could not get the sound of her voice out of his ears; the very folds of her dress seemed to hang upon her differently from all the rest—more gracefully and amply—and her movements were particularly smooth and natural at the same time.

Arkady felt some timidity in his heart when at the first sounds of the mazurka he sat down beside his partner. He had prepared to enter into a conversation with her, but he only passed his hand through his hair, and could not find a single word to say. But his timidity and agitation did not last long; Odintsov's calm communicated itself to him too: before a quarter of an hour had passed he was telling her freely about his father, his uncle, his life in Petersburg and in the country. Odintsov listened to him with polite sympathy, slightly opening and closing her fan; his chatter was broken off when partners came for her; Sitnikov, by the way, asked her twice. She would come back, sit down again, take up her fan, and her bosom did not even heave more rapidly, while Arkady fell to chattering again, permeated by the happiness of being near her, talking to her, looking at her eyes, her lovely brow, her whole sweet, dignified, clever face. She said little herself but her words showed a knowledge of life; from some of her observations, Arkady gathered that this young woman had already felt and thought much. . . .

"Who is that you were standing with?" she asked him, "when Mr. Sitnikov brought you to me?"

"Did you notice him?" Arkady asked in his turn. He has a splendid face, hasn't he? That's a certain Bazarov, my friend."

Arkady fell to discussing "his friend." He spoke of him in such detail, and with such enthusiasm, that Odintsov turned towards him and looked attentively at him. Meanwhile, the mazurka was drawing to a close. Arkady felt sorry to part from his partner; he had spent nearly an hour so happily with her! He had, it is true, during the whole time continually felt as though she were condescending to him, as though he ought to be grateful to her . . . but young hearts are not weighed down by that feeling.

The music stopped. "*Merci,*" said Odintsov, getting up. "You promised to come and see me; bring your friend with you. I shall be very curious to see a man who has the courage to believe in nothing."

The Governor came up to Odintsov, announced that supper was

ready and, with a careworn face, offered her his arm. As she moved away, she turned to give a last smile and nod to Arkady. He bowed low, looked after her (how graceful her figure seemed to him, draped in the greyish lustre of black silk!), and thinking, "This very minute she has already forgotten my existence," was conscious of an exquisite humility in his soul.

"Well?" Bazarov questioned him, as soon as he had gone back to him in the corner. "Did you have a good time? A gentleman has just been talking to me about that lady; he said, 'She's—ooh la la!' but the gentleman seems a fool. What do you think, is she really—ooh la la?"

"I don't quite understand that definition," answered Arkady.

"Oh, come! What innocence!"

"In that case, I don't understand your gentleman. Odintsov is very sweet, no doubt, but she behaves so coldly and severely, that . . ."

"Still waters . . . you know!" put in Bazarov. "That's just what gives it piquancy. You like ices, I expect?"

"Perhaps," muttered Arkady. "I can't give an opinion on that. She wishes to make your acquaintance, and has asked me to bring you to see her."

"I can imagine how you've described me! But you did very well. Take me. Whatever she may be—whether she's simply a provincial lioness, or *émancipée after* Kukshin's fashion—anyway she's got a pair of shoulders such as I've not set eyes on for a long while."

Arkady was wounded by Bazarov's cynicism, but—as often happens—he reproached his friend not precisely for what he did not like in him . . .

"Why are you unwilling to allow freethinking in women?" he said in a low voice.

"Because, my boy, as far as my observations go, the only freethinkers among women are frights."

The conversation ended with that. Both young men went away immediately after supper. The were pursued by a nervously malicious, but somewhat fearful laugh from Kukshin; her vanity had been deeply wounded by neither of them having paid any attention to her. She stayed later than any one at the ball, and after three o'clock in the morning she was dancing a polka-mazurka with Sitnikov in the Parisian style. This edifying spectacle was the final event of the Governor's ball.

XV

"Let's see what species of mammalia this person belongs to," Bazarov said to Arkady the following day, as they mounted the staircase of the hotel in which Odintsov was staying. "I scent out something wrong here."

"I'm surprised at you!" cried Arkady. "What? You, you, Bazarov, clinging to the narrow morality, which . . ."

"What a strange fellow you are!" Bazarov cut him short, carelessly. "Don't you know that 'something wrong' means 'something right' in my dialect and for me? It means there's something to be gained. Didn't you tell me yourself this morning that she made a strange marriage, though, to my mind, to marry a rich old man is by no means a strange thing to do, but, on the contrary, very sensible. I don't believe the gossip of the town; but I should like to think, as our cultivated Governor says, that it's well-grounded."

Arkady make no answer, and knocked at the door. A young servant in livery conducted the two friends into a large room, badly furnished, like all rooms in Russian hotels, but filled with flowers. Soon Odintsov herself appeared in a simple morning dress. She seemed still younger by the light of the spring sunshine. Arkady presented Bazarov, and noticed with secret amazement that he seemed embarrassed, while Odintsov remained perfectly tranquil, as she had been the previous day. Bazarov himself was conscious of being embarrassed, and was irritated by it. "There's something—frightened of a petticoat!" he thought, and lolling in an easy-chair, quite like Sitnikov, he began talking with an exaggerated appearance of ease, while Odintsov kept her clear eyes fixed on him.

Anna Sergeyevna Odintsov was the daughter of Sergey Nikolaevich Loktev, famous for his good looks, his speculations, and his gambling, who after cutting a figure and making a sensation for fifteen years in Petersburg and Moscow, finished by ruining himself completely at cards, and was forced to retire to the country, where he died soon after, leaving a very small property to his two daughters—Anna, a girl of twenty, and Katya, a child of twelve. Their mother, who came of an impoverished line of princes — the Kh—s —had died in Petersburg when her husband was in his heyday. Anna's position after her father's death was very difficult. The brilliant education she had received in Petersburg had not fitted her for putting up with the cares of the household and estate management—for an obscure existence in the country. She knew positively no one in the whole neighborhood, and there was no one she could consult. Her father had tried to avoid all contact with the neighbors, he despised them in his way, and they despised him in theirs. She did not lose her head, however, and promptly sent for a sister of her mother's, Princess Avdotya Stepanovna Kh——, a spiteful and arrogant old lady, who, on installing herself in her niece's house, appropriated all the best rooms for her own use, scolded and grumbled from morning till night, and would not go a walk even in the garden unattended by her one serf, a surly footman in a threadbare pea-green livery with light blue trimming and a three-cornered hat. Anna put up patiently with all her aunt's whims, gradually set to work on her sister's education, and was, it seemed, already getting reconciled to the idea of wasting her life in the wilds. . . . But destiny had decreed another fate for her. She chanced to be seen by Odintsov, a very wealthy man of forty-six, an eccentric hypochondriac, stout, heavy, and sour, but not stupid, and not ill-natured; he fell in love with her, and offered her his hand. She consented to become his wife, and he lived six years with her, and on his death settled all his property upon her. Anna Sergeyevna remained in the country for nearly a year after his death; then she went abroad with her sister, but only stopped in Germany; she got tired of it and came back to live at her favorite Nikolskoe, which was nearly thirty miles from the town of X———. There she had a magnificent, splendidly furnished house and a beautiful garden, with conservatories; her late husband had spared no expense to gratify his fancies. Anna Sergeyevna very rarely went to town, generally only on business, and even then she did not stay long. She was not liked in the province; there had been a fearful outcry at her marriage with Odintsov, all sorts of improbabilities were told about her: it was asserted that she had helped her father in his cardsharping tricks, and even that she had gone abroad for excellent reasons, that it had been necessary to conceal the lamentable consequences . . . "You understand?" the indignant gossips would wind up. "She has gone through fire and water," was said of her; to which a noted provincial wit usually added: "And through brass pipes." All this talk reached her; but she turned a deaf ear to it; there was much independence and a good deal of determination in her character.

Odintsov sat leaning back in her easy-chair, and listened to Bazarov with folded hands. He, contrary to his habit, was talking a good deal, and obviously trying to interest her—again a surprise for Arkady. He could not make up his mind whether Bazarov was attaining his object. It was difficult to conjecture from Anna Sergeyevna's face what impression was being made on her; it retained the same expression, gracious and refined; her beautiful eyes shined with attention, but quiet attention. Bazarov's bad manners had impressed her unpleasantly for the first minutes of the visit like a bad smell or a discordant sound; but she saw at once that he was nervous, and that even flattered her. Nothing was repulsive to her but vulgarity, and no one could have accused

Bazarov of vulgarity. Arkady was fated to meet with surprises that day. He expected Bazarov to talk to a clever woman like Odintsov about his opinions and his views; she had herself expressed a desire to listen to the man "who dares to have no belief in anything"; but, instead of that, Bazarov talked about medicine, about homœpathy, and about botany. It turned out that Odintsov had not wasted her time in seclusion; she had read several good books, and expressed herself in excellent Russian. She turned the conversation upon music; but noticing that Bazarov did not appreciate art, she quietly brought it back to botany, even though Arkady was just launching into a discourse upon the significance of national melodies. Odintsov treated him as though he were a younger brother; she seemed to appreciate his good-nature and youthful simplicity and that was all. For over three hours a lively conversation was kept up, ranging freely over various subjects.

The friends at last got up and began to take leave. Anna Sergeyevna looked cordially at them, held out her beautiful white hand to both, and, after a moment's thought, said with a doubtful but delightful smile, "If you are not afraid of being bored gentlemen, come and see me at Nikolskoe."

"Oh, Anna Sergeyevna," cried Arkady, "I shall think it the greatest happiness . . ."

"And you, Monsieur Bazarov?"

Bazarov only bowed, and a last surprise was in store for Arkady; he noticed that his friend was blushing.

"Well?" he said to him in the street; "are you still of the same opinion—that she's ooh la la?"

"Who can tell? See how frigid she's made herself!" retorted Bazarov; and after a brief pause he added, "She's a perfect duchess, a regal personage. She only needs a train behind, and a crown on her head."

"Our duchesses don't speak Russian like that," remarked Arkady.

"She's seen ups and downs, my dear boy; she's know what it is to be hard up!"

"Anyway, she's charming," observed Arkady.

"What a magnificent body," Bazarov continued. "Perfect for the dissecting-table."

"For God's sake, stop Evgeny! that's beyond everything."

"Well, don't get angry, you baby. I meant it's first-rate. We must go to stay with her."

"When?"

"Well, why not the day after to-morrow. What is there to do here? Drink champagne with Kukshin? Listen to your cousin, the Liberal dignitary? . . . Let's be off the day after to-morrow. By the way, too—my father's little place is not far from there. This Nikolskoe's on the S—— road, isn't it?"

"Yes."

"*Optime*, why hesitate? Leave that to fools and smart alecs. I tell you, it's a splendid body!"

Three days later the two friends were driving along the road to Nikolskoe. The day was bright, and not too hot, and the sleek posting-horses trotted smartly along, switching their tied and plaited tails. Arkady looked at the road, and not knowing why, he smiled.

"Congratulate me," cried Bazarov suddenly, "to-day's the 22nd of June, my guardian angel's day. Let's see how he will watch over me. To-day they expect me home," he added, dropping his voice. . . . "Well, they can go on expecting. . . . What does it matter!"

XVI

The estate on which Anna Sergeyevna lived stood on the slope of an exposed hill, a short distance from a yellow stone church with a green roof, white columns, and a fresco over the principal entrance representing the "Resurrection of Christ" in the "Italian" style. Sprawling in the foreground of the picture was a swarthy warrior in a helmet, specially conspicuous for his rotund contours. Behind the church an extensive village stretched in two rows, with chimneys peeping out here and there above the thatched roofs. The manor-house was built in the same style as the church, the style known among us as that of Alexander I; the house, too, was painted yellow, and had a green roof, and white columns, and a pediment with an escutcheon on it. The architect had designed both buildings with the approval of the deceased Odintsov, who could not endure—as he expressed it—idle and arbitrary innovations. The house was enclosed on both sides by the dark trees of an old garden; an avenue of pruned pines led up to the entrance.

Our friends were met in the hall by two tall footmen in livery; one of them at once ran for the butler. The butler, a stout man in a black dress coat, promptly appeared and led the visitors by a staircase covered with rugs to a special room, in which two bedsteads were already prepared for them, and all the necessaries. It was clear that order reigned supreme in the house; everything was clean, everywhere there was a peculiar pleasant fragrance, just as there is in the reception rooms of ministers.

"Anna Sergeyevna requests you to join her in half an hour," the butler announced; "are there any orders meanwhile?"

"No orders," answered Bazarov; "perhaps you will be so good as to trouble yourself to bring me a glass of vodka."

"Yes, sir," said the butler, looking in some perplexity, and he withdrew, his boots creaking as he walked.

"What *grand genre!*" remarked Bazarov. "That's what it's called in your set, isn't it? She's a duchess, and that's all there is to it."

"A fine duchess," retorted Arkady, "at the very first meeting she invited such great aristocrats as you and me to stay with her."

"Especially me, a future doctor, and a doctor's son, and a village sexton's grandson. . . . You know, I suppose, I'm the grandson of a sexton? Like the great Speransky," [4] added Bazarov after a brief pause, contracting his lips. "At any rate she likes to be comfortable; oh, doesn't she, this lady! Oughtn't we to put on evening dress?"

Arkady only shrugged his shoulders . . . but he, too, was conscious of a little nervousness.

Half an hour later Bazarov and Arkady went together into the drawing-room. It was a large lofty room, furnished rather luxuriously but without particular taste. Heavy, expensive furniture stood in the ordinary stiff arrangement along the walls, which were covered with cinnamon-colored paper patterned in gold; the late Odintsov had ordered the furniture from Moscow through a friend and agent of his, a liquor dealer. Over the center sofa hung a portrait of a flabby light-haired man—and it seemed to look with displeasure at the visitors. "It must be *himself*," Bazarov whispered to Arkady, and wrinkling his nose, he added, "Hadn't we better bolt . . .?" But at that instant the lady of the house entered. She wore a light barège dress; her hair smoothly combed back behind her ears gave a girlish expression to her pure and fresh face.

"Thank you for keeping your promise," she began. "You must stay a little while with me; it's really not bad here. I will introduce you to my sister; she plays the piano well. That is a matter of indifference to you, Monsieur Bazarov; but you, I think, Monsieur Kirsanov, are fond of music. Besides my sister I have an old aunt living with me, and one of our neighbors comes in sometimes to play cards; that makes up all our circle. And now let us sit down."

Odintsov delivered all of this little speech with peculiar precision, as though she had learned it by heart; then she turned to Arkady. It appeared that her mother had known Arkady's mother, and had even been her confidante in her love for Nikolai Petrovich. Arkady began talking with great warmth of his dead mother; while Bazarov fell to turning over albums. "How tame I've be-

4. The son of a priest, educated in a seminary, M. M. Speransky (1772–1839) was an outstanding statesman, responsible for a new code of law (1832) and many other major achievements. He was the first plebeian to rise to such eminence in Russia.

come!" he thought to himself.

A beautiful wolfhound with a blue collar ran into the drawing-room, tapping on the floor with her nails, and after her entered a girl of eighteen,[5] black-haired and dark-skinned, with a rather round but pleasing face, and small dark eyes. In her hands she held a basket filled with flowers.

"This is my Katya," said Odintsov, indicating her with a motion of her head. Katya made a slight curtsey, placed herself beside her sister, and began picking out flowers. The wolfhound, whose name was Fifi, went up to both of the visitors, in turn wagging her tail, and thrusting her cold nose into their hands.

"Did you pick all that yourself?" asked Odintsov.

"Yes," answered Katya.

"Is auntie coming to tea?"

"Yes."

When Katya spoke, she had a very charming smile, sweet, timid, and candid, and looked up from under her eyebrows with a sort of humorous severity. Everything about her was still green; the voice, and the bloom on her whole face, and the rosy hands, with white palms, and the rather narrow shoulders. . . . She was constantly blushing and getting out of breath.

Odintsov turned to Bazarov. "You are looking at pictures out of politeness, Evgeny Vassilyich," she began. "That does not interest you. You had better come closer to us, and let us have a discussion about something."

Bazarov came closer. "What subject have you decided upon for discussion?" he said.

"Whatever you like. I warn you, I am dreadfully argumentative."

"You?"

"Yes. That seems to surprise you. Why?"

"Because, as far as I can judge, you have a calm, cool character, and one must be impulsive to be argumentative."

"How can you have had time to understand me so soon? In the first place, I am impatient and obstinate—you should ask Katya; and secondly, I am very easily carried away."

Bazarov looked at Anna Sergeyevna. "Perhaps; you know best. And so you are in the mood for a discussion—by all means. I was looking through the views of the Saxon mountains in your album, and you remarked that that couldn't interest me. You said so, because you suppose me to have no feeling for art, and in fact I haven't any; but these views might be interesting to me from a geological standpoint, for the formation of the mountains, for instance."

5. According to Turgenev's earlier statement, she was eight years younger than her sister, hence twenty-one.

"Excuse me; but as a geologist, you would sooner have recourse to a book, to a special work on the subject and not to a drawing."

"The drawing shows me at a glance what would be spread over ten pages in a book."

Anna Sergeyevna was silent for a little.

"And so you haven't the least artistic feeling?" she observed, putting her elbow on the table, and by that very action bringing her face nearer to Bazarov. "How can you get on without it?"

"Why, what is it needed for, may I ask?"

"Well, at least to enable one to study and understand men."

Bazarov smiled. "In the first place, experience of life does that; and in the second, I assure you, studying separate individuals is not worth the trouble. All people resemble each other, in soul as in body; each of us has brain, spleen, heart, and lungs made alike; and the so-called moral qualities are the same in all; the slight variations are of no importance. A single human specimen is sufficient to judge all the rest. People are like trees in a forest; no botanist would think of studying each individual birch tree." [6]

Katya, who was arranging the flowers, one at a time in a leisurely fashion, lifted her eyes to Bazarov with a puzzled look, and meeting his rapid and careless glance, she crimsoned up to her ears. Anna Sergeyevna shook her head.

"Like trees in a forest," she repeated. "Then according to you there is no difference between the stupid and the clever person, between the good-natured and ill-natured?"

"No, there is a difference, just as between the sick and the healthy. The lungs of a consumptive patient are not in the same condition as yours and mine, though they are made on the same plan. We know approximately what physical diseases come from; moral diseases come from bad education, from all the nonsense people's heads are stuffed with from childhood up, from the deformed state of society; in short, reform society, and there will be no diseases."

Bazarov said all this with an air as though he were all the while thinking to himself, "Believe me or not, it's all the same to me!" He slowly passed his fingers over his side whiskers, while his eyes strayed about the room.

"And you conclude," observed Anna Sergeyevna, "that when society is reformed, there will be no stupid nor wicked people?"

"At any rate, in a proper organization of society, it will be absolutely the same whether a man is stupid or clever, wicked

6. Bazarov is paraphrasing a review by Chernyshevsky of Turgenev's story "Asya." The review was entitled "The Russian at the *Rendez-Vous*" (1858). It was one of the last pieces written by this leading spokesman of the radicals before turning literary criticism over to his young colleague Dobrolyubov so that he could devote himself fully to writing on political economy.

or good."

"Yes, I understand; they will all have the same spleen."

"Precisely so, madam."

Odintsov turned to Arkady. "And what is your opinion, Arkady Nikolaevich?"

"I agree with Evgeny," he answered.

Katya looked up at him from under her eyelids.

"You amaze me, gentlemen," commented Odintsov, "but we will talk together again. But now I hear my aunt coming in to tea; we must spare her."

Anna Sergeyevna's aunt, Princess Kh——, a thin little woman with a pinched-up face, drawn together like a fist, and staring, ill-natured-looking eyes under a grey wig, came in, and, scarcely bowing to the guests, she dropped into a wide velvet covered arm-chair, upon which no one but herself was privileged to sit. Katya put a footstool under her feet; the old lady did not thank her, did not even look at her, merely moving her hands under the yellow shawl which almost covered her feeble body. The Princess liked yellow; her cap, too, had bright yellow ribbons.

"How have you slept, aunt?" inquired Odintsov, raising her voice.

"That dog in here again," the old lady muttered in reply, and noticing Fifi was making two hesitating steps in her direction, she cried, "Ss—ss!"

Katya called Fifi and opened the door for her.

Fifi dashed out delighted, in the expectation of being taken out for a walk; but when she was left alone outside the door, she began scratching on it and whining. The princess scowled. Katya was about to go out. . . .

"I expect tea is ready," said Odintsov.

"Come, gentlemen; aunt, will you go in to tea?"

The princess got up from her chair without speaking and led the way out of the drawing-room. They all followed her into the dining-room. A little page in livery drew an arm-chair covered with cushions, also devoted to the princess's use, back from the table with a scraping sound; she sank into it; Katya in pouring out the tea handed her first a cup emblazoned with a heraldic crest. The old lady put some honey in her cup (she considered it both sinful and extravagant to drink tea with sugar in it, though she never spent a farthing herself on anything), and suddenly asked in a hoarse voice, "And what does Prince Ivan write?"

No one answered her. Bazarov and Arkady soon guessed that they paid no attention to her, though they treated her respectfully.

"They put up with her for *appearances,* because she's princely breed," thought Bazarov. . . .

After tea, Anna Sergeyevna suggested that they go out for a walk; but it began to rain a little, and the whole party, with the exception of the princess, returned to the drawing-room. The neighbor, the devoted card-player, arrived; his name was Porfiry Platonich, a stoutish, greyish man with short, spindly legs, very polite and ready to entertain. Anna Sergeyevna, who talked more and more principally with Bazarov, asked him whether he'd care to play an old-fashioned game of preference with them. Bazarov assented, saying that he ought to prepare himself beforehand for the duties awaiting him as a country doctor.

"Be careful," observed Anna Sergeyevna; "Porfiry Platonich and I will beat you. And you, Katya," she added, "play something for Arkady Nikolaevich; he is fond of music, and we can listen, too."

Katya went unwillingly to the piano; and Arkady, though he certainly was fond of music, unwillingly followed her; it seemed to him that Odintsov was sending him away, and already, like every young man at his age, he felt a vague and oppressive emotion surging up in his heart, like the forebodings of love. Katya raised the lid of the piano, and without looking at Arkady, asked in a low voice:

"What am I to play you?"

"Whatever you like," answered Arkady indifferently.

"What sort of music do you like best?" repeated Katya without changing her attitude.

"Classical," Arkady answered in the same tone of voice.

"Do you like Mozart?"

"Yes, I like Mozart."

Katya pull out Mozart's *Sonata-Fantasia in C minor*. She played very well, though rather overcorrectly and drily. She sat upright and immovable, her eyes fixed on the notes and her lips tightly compressed, and only at the end of the sonata her face glowed, her hair came loose, and a little lock fell on to her dark brow.

Arkady was particularly struck by the last part of the sonata, the part in which, in the midst of the captivating gaiety of the careless melody, the pangs of such mournful, almost tragic suffering, suddenly break in. . . . But the ideas stirred in him by Mozart's music had no reference to Katya. Looking at her, he simply thought, "Well, that young lady doesn't play badly, and she's not bad-looking either."

When she had finished the sonata, Katya, without taking her hands from the keyboard, asked, "Is that enough?" Arkady declared that he could not venture to trouble her further, and began talking to her about Mozart. He asked her whether she had chosen that sonata herself, or someone had recommended it to her. But Katya answered him in monosyllables; she withdrew into herself, went back into her shell. When this happened to her, she did not very quickly come out again; her face even assumed at such times an obstinate, almost stupid expression. She was not exactly shy, but diffident, and rather overawed by her sister, who had educated her, and who, of course, did not even suspect it. Arkady was reduced at last to calling Fifi, who had returned, and with an affable smile patting her on the head to save face. Katya set to work again upon her flowers.

Bazarov meanwhile was kept revoking. Anna Sergeyevna played cards in masterly fashion; Porfiry Platonich, too, could hold his own in the game. Bazarov lost a sum which, though trifling in itself, was not altogether pleasant for him. At supper Anna Sergeyevna again turned the conversation on botany.

"Let us go for a walk to-morrow morning," she said to him. "I want you to teach me the Latin names of the wild flowers and their species."

"What use are the Latin names to you?" asked Bazarov.

"Order is needed in everything," she answered.

"What an exquisite woman Anna Sergeyevna is!" cried Arkady, when he was alone with his friend in the room assigned to them.

"Yes," answered Bazarov, "a female with brains. Yes, and she's seen life too."

"In what sense do you mean that, Evgeny Vassilich?"

"In a good sense, a good sense, my dear friend, Arkady Nikolaevich! I'm convinced she manages her estate capitally too. But what's splendid is not her, but her sister."

"What, that little dark thing?"

"Yes, that little dark thing. She now is fresh and untouched, and shy and silent, and anything you like. She's worth educating and developing. You might make something fine out of her; but the other's—a stale loaf."

Arkady made no reply to Bazarov, and each of them got into bed with his own thoughts.

Anna Sergeyevna, too, thought of her guests that evening. She liked Bazarov for the absence of gallantry in him, and even for his sharply defined views. She found in him something new, which she had not chanced to meet before, and she was curious.

Anna Sergeyevna was a rather strange creature. Having no prejudices of any kind, having no strong convictions even, she never gave way or went out of her way for anything. She had seen many things very clearly; she had been interested in many things, but nothing had completely satisfied her; indeed, she hardly desired complete satisfaction. Her intellect was at the same time inquiring and indifferent; her doubts were never soothed to forgetfulness, and they never grew strong enough to distract her. Had she not been rich and independent, she would perhaps have thrown herself into the struggle, and have known passion. But life was easy for her, though she was bored at times, and she went on passing day after day with deliberation, never in a hurry, placid, and only rarely disturbed. Dreams sometimes danced in rainbow colors before her eyes even, but she breathed more freely when they died away, and did not regret them. Her imagination indeed overstepped the limits of what is reckoned permissible by conventional morality; but even then the blood flowed as quietly as ever in her fascinatingly graceful, tranquil body. Sometimes coming out of her fragrant bath all warm and languorous, she would fall to musing on the insignificance of life, the sorrow, the labor, the malice of it. . . . Her soul would be filled with sudden daring, and would flow with generous ardor, but a draft would blow from a half-closed window, and Anna Sergeyevna would shrink into herself, and feel plaintive and almost angry, and there was only one thing she cared for at that instant—to get away from that horrid wind.

Like all women who have not succeeded in loving, she wanted something, without herself knowing what. Strictly speaking, she wanted nothing; but it seemed to her that she wanted everything. She could hardly endure the late Odintsov (she had married him out of calculation, though probably she would not have consented to become his wife if she had not considered him a good man), and had conceived a secret repugnance for all men, whom she could only figure to herself as slovenly, heavy, drowsy, and feebly importunate creatures. Once, somewhere abroad, she had met a handsome young Swede, with a chivalrous expression, with honest blue eyes under a broad brow; he had made a powerful impression on her, but it had not prevented her from going back to Russia.

"A strange man this doctor!" she thought as she lay in her luxurious bed on lace pillows under a light silk coverlet. . . .

Anna Sergeyevna had inherited from her father a little of his inclination for luxury. She had deeply loved her sinful but good-natured father, and he had idolized her, used to joke with her in a friendly way as though she were an equal, and to confide in her fully, to ask her advice. She scarcely remembered her mother.

"This doctor is a strange man!" she repeated to herself. She stretched, smiled, clasped her hands behind her head, then ran her eyes over two pages of a stupid French novel, dropped the book—and fell asleep, all clean and cool, in her clean and fragrant linen.

The following morning Anna Sergeyevna went off botanizing with Barazov directly after lunch, and returned just before dinner; Arkady did not go off anywhere, and spent an hour or so with Katya. He was not bored with her; she herself offered to repeat yesterday's sonata; but when Odintsov came back at last, when he caught sight of her, he felt an instantaneous pang at his heart. She came through the garden with a rather tired step; her cheeks were glowing and her eyes shining more brightly than usual under her round straw hat. In her fingers she was twirling the thin stalk of a wildflower, a light mantle had slipped down to her elbows, and the wide gray ribbons of her hat were clinging to her bosom. Bazarov walked behind her, self-confident and careless as usual, but the expression on his face, cheerful and even friendly as it was, did not please Arkady. Muttering "Good-morning!" between his teeth, Bazarov went away to his room, while Odintsov shook Arkady's hand abstractedly, and also walked past him.

"Good-morning!" thought Arkady. . . . "As though we had not seen each other already to-day!"

XVII

Time, it is well known, sometimes flies like a bird, sometimes crawls like a worm; but man is wont to be particularly happy when he does not even notice whether it passes quickly or slowly. It was in that way Arkady and Bazarov spent a fortnight at Odintsov's. The good order she had established in her house and in her life partly contributed to this result. She adhered strictly to this order herself, and forced others to submit to it. Everything during the course of the day was done at a fixed time. In the morning, precisely at eight o'clock, every one assembled for tea; from morning tea till lunch time every one did what he pleased; the mistress herself was engaged with her bailiff (the estate was on the quitrent system), her butler, and her head housekeeper. Before dinner everyone met again for conversation or reading; the evening was devoted to walking, cards, and music; at half-past ten Anna Sergeyevna retired to her own room, gave her orders for the following day, and went to bed. Bazarov did not like this measured, somewhat ostentatious punctuality in daily life, "like moving along rails," he pronounced it to be; the footmen in livery, the decorous butlers offended his democratic sentiments. He declared that if one went so far, one might as well dine in the English style at once—

in tail-coats and white ties. He once spoke plainly upon the subject to Anna Sergeyevna.

Her attitude was such that no one hesitated to speak his mind freely before her. She heard him out; and then her comment was, "From your point of view, you are right—and perhaps, in that respect, I am too much of a lady; but there's no living in the country without order, one would be devoured by ennui," and she continued to go her own way. Bazarov grumbled, but the very reason life was so easy for him and Arkady at Odintsov's was that everything in the house "moved on rails." For all that, a change had taken place in both young men since the first days of their stay at Nikolskoe. Bazarov, in whom Anna Sergeyevna was obviously interested, though she seldom agreed with him, began to show signs of unrest, unprecedented in him; he was easily put out of temper, and unwilling to talk, he looked irritated, and could not sit still in one place, just as though something were urging him on; while Arkady, who had definitely decided in himself that he was in love with Odintsov, began to yield to a gentle melancholy. This melancholy did not, however, prevent him from becoming friendly with Katya; it even helped him to get on friendly, affectionate terms with her. "*She* does not appreciate me? So be it . . . But here is a good creature, who does not repulse me," he thought, and his heart again knew the sweetness of magnanimous emotions. Katya vaguely realized that he was seeking a sort of consolation in her company, and did not deny him or herself the innocent pleasure of a half-shy, half-confidential friendship. They did not talk to each other in Anna Sergeyevna's presence; Katya always shrank into herself under her sister's sharp eyes; while Arkady, as befits a man in love, could pay attention to nothing else when near the object of his passion; but he was happy only with Katya. He felt that he was unable to interest Odintsov; he was shy and at a loss when he was left alone with her, and she did not know what to say to him: he was too young for her. With Katya, on the other hand, Arkady felt at home; he treated her condescendingly, did not discourage her from expressing the impressions made on her by music, reading novels, verses, and other such trifles without noticing or realizing that these *trifles* were what interested him too. Katya, on her side, did not try to drive away his melancholy. Arkady was at his ease with Katya, Odintsov with Bazarov, and thus it usually came to pass that the two couples, after being a little while together, went off on their separate ways, especially during the walks. Katya *adored* nature, and Arkady loved it, though he did not dare to acknowledge it; Odintsov was rather indifferent to the beauties of nature, like Bazarov. The almost continual separation of the two friends was not without its consequences; the relations between them began to change. Bazarov gave up talking to Arkady about Odintsov, even gave up abusing her "aristocratic ways"; true, he praised Katya as before, and only advised him to restrain her sentimental tendencies, but his praises were hurried, his advice dry, and in general he talked less to Arkady than before . . . he seemed to avoid him, seemed ill at ease with him.

Arkady observed it all, but he kept his observations to himself.

The real cause of all this "newness" was the feeling inspired in Bazarov by Odintsov, a feeling which tortured and maddened him, and which he would at once have denied, with scornful laughter and cynical abuse, if any one had ever so remotely hinted at the possibility of what was taking place in him. Bazarov had a great love for women and for feminine beauty; but love in the ideal, or, as he expressed it, romantic sense, he called gibberish, unpardonable imbecility; he regarded chivalrous sentiments as something like deformity or disease, and had more than once expressed his wonder that Toggenburg and all the minnesingers and troubadors had not been put into a lunatic asylum. "If a woman takes your fancy," he used to say, "try to gain your end; but if you can't—well, turn your back on her—there are lots of good fish in the sea." Odintsov had taken his fancy; the rumors about her, the freedom and independence of her ideas, her unmistakable liking for him, all seemed to be in his favor, but he soon saw that with her he would not "gain his ends," and he found, to his own bewilderment, that it was beyond his power to turn his back on her. His blood was on fire as soon as he thought of her; he could easily have mastered his blood, but something else was taking root in him, something he had never admitted, at which he had always jeered, at which all his pride revolted. In his conversations with Anna Sergeyevna he expressed more strongly than ever his calm contempt for everything romantic; but when he was alone, with indignation he recognized the romantic in himself. Then he would set off to the forest and walk with long strides about it, breaking the twigs that came in his way, and cursing under his breath both her and himself; or he would get into the hay-loft in the barn, and, obstinately closing his eyes, try to force himself to sleep, in which, of course, he did not always succeed. Suddenly his fancy would bring before him those chaste hands twining one day about his neck, those proud lips responding to his kisses, those intellectual eyes dwelling with tenderness—yes, with tenderness—on his, and his head went round, and he forgot himself for an instant, till indignation boiled up in him again. He caught himself in all sorts of "shameful" thoughts, as though he were driven on by a devil mocking him. Sometimes it seemed to him that there was a change taking place in Odintsov too; that there were signs in the expression of her face of something special; that, perhaps . . . but at that point he would stamp, or grind his teeth, and shake his fist in his own face.

And yet Bazarov was not altogether mistaken. He had struck Odintsov's imagination; he interested her, she thought a great deal about him. In his absence, she was not dull, she was not impatient for his coming, but she always grew more lively on his appearance; she liked to be left alone with him, and she liked talking to him, even when he irritated her or offended her taste, her refined habits. She was eager, as it were, both to put him to the test and to analyze herself.

One day walking in the garden with her, he suddenly announced, in a surly voice, that he intended going to his father's place very soon. . . . She turned pale, as though something had given her a pang, and such a pang, that she was amazed and pondered long after what it could mean. Bazarov had spoken of his departure with no idea of putting her to the test, of seeing what would come of it; he never "fabricated." On the morning of that day he had an interview with his father's bailiff, who had taken care of him when he was a child, Timofeich. This Timofeich, a little old man of much experience and astuteness, with faded yellow hair, a weather-beaten red face, and tiny tear-drops in his puckered eyes, unexpectedly appeared before Bazarov, in his shortish overcoat of stout greyish-blue cloth, girt with a strip of leather, and in tarred boots.

"Hello, oldtimer; how are you?" cried Bazarov.

"How do you do, Evgeny Vassilyich?" began the little old man, and he smiled with delight, so that his whole face was all at once covered with wrinkles.

"What have you come for? They sent for me, eh?"

"Heavens, sir, how could we?" mumbled Timofeich. (He remembered the strict injunctions he had received from his master on starting.) "I was sent to town on business, and I heard news of your honor, so here I turned off on my way, that's to say—to have a look at your honor . . . as if we could think of disturbing you!"

"Come, don't lie!" Bazarov cut him short. "Do you mean to tell me this is the road to the town?" Timofeich hesitated, and made no answer. "Is my father well?"

"Thank God, yes."

"And my mother?"

"Anna Vlasyevna too, glory be to God."

"They are waiting for me, I suppose?"

The little old man held his tiny head on one side.

"Ah, Evgeny Vassilyich, how they wait for you, it makes one's heart ache to see them; it really does."

"Oh, all right, all right, don't carry on! Tell them I'm coming soon."

"Yes, sir," answered Timofeich, with a sigh.

As he went out of the house, he pulled his cap down on his head with both hands, clambered into a wretched-looking racing droshky, and went off at a trot, but not in the direction of the town.

That same evening, Odintsov was sitting in her own room with Bazarov, while Arkady walked up and down the hall listening to Katya's playing. The princess had gone upstairs to her own room; she could not bear guests as a rule, and "especially this new riff-raff lot," as she called them. In the common rooms she only sulked; but she made up for it in her own room by breaking out into such abuse before her maid that the cap danced on her head, wig and all. Odintsov was well aware of all this.

"How is it you are proposing to leave us?" she began; "how about your promise?"

Bazarov started. "What promise, madam?"

"Have you forgotten? You meant to give me some lessons in chemistry."

"It can't be helped! My father expects me; I can't loiter any longer. However, you can read Pelouse et Frémy, *Notions générales de chimie*; it's a good book, and clearly written. You will find everything you need in it."

"But do you remember; you assured me a book cannot take the place of . . . I've forgotten how you put it, but you know what I mean . . . do you remember?"

"It can't be helped!" repeated Bazarov.

"Why go away?" said Odintsov, dropping her voice.

He glanced at her. Her head had fallen on to the back of her easy-chair, and her arms, bare to the elbows, were folded on her bosom. She seemed paler in the light of the single lamp covered with a perforated paper shade. An ample white gown hid her completely in its soft folds; even the tips of her feet, also crossed, were hardly seen.

"And why stay?" answered Bazarov.

Odintsov turned her head slightly. "You ask why? Have you not enjoyed yourself here? Or do you suppose you will not be missed here"

"I am sure I won't be."

Odintsov was silent a minute. "You are wrong in thinking that. But I don't believe you. You could not have said that seriously." Bazarov still sat immovable. "Evgeny Vassilyich, why don't you speak?"

"Why, what am I to say to you? In general it's not worth missing people, and me less than most."

"Why so?"

"I'm a practical, uninteresting person. I don't know how to talk."

"You are fishing for compliments, Evgeny Vassilyich."

"That's not a habit of mine. Don't you know yourself that I've nothing in common with the elegant side of life, the side you prize so much?"

Odintsov bit the corner of her handkerchief.

"You may think what you like, but I shall be dull when you go away."

"Arkady will remain," remarked Bazarov. Odintsov shrugged her shoulders slightly. "I shall be dull," she repeated.

"Really? In any case you will not feel dull for long."

"What makes you suppose that?"

"Because you told me yourself that you are only dull when your regular routine is interrupted. You have ordered your existence with such impeccable regularity that there can be no place in it for dullness or sadness . . . for any unpleasant emotions."

"And do you consider I am so impeccable . . . that's to say, that I have ordered my life with such regularity?"

"I should think so. Here's an example: in a few minutes it will strike ten, and I know beforehand that you will drive me away."

"No; I'm not going to drive you away, Evgeny Vassilyich. You may stay. Open that window. . . . I feel somewhat stifled."

Bazarov got up and gave the window a push. It flew open with a crash. . . . He had not expected it to open so easily; besides, his hands were shaking. The soft, dark night looked in to the room with its almost black sky, its faintly rustling trees, and the fresh fragrance of the pure open air.

"Draw the blind and sit down," said Odintsov; "I want to have a chat with you before you go away. Tell me something about yourself; you never talk about yourself."

"I try to talk to you upon useful subjects, Anna Sergeyevna."

"You are very modest . . . But I should like to know something about you, about your family, about your father, for whom you are forsaking us."

"Why is she talking like that?" thought Bazarov.

"All that's not in the least interesting," he uttered aloud, "especially for you; we are obscure people. . . ."

"And you regard me as an aristocrat?"

Bazarov lifted his eyes to Madame Odintsov.

"Yes," he said, with exaggerated sharpness.

She smiled. "I see you know me very little, though you do maintain that all people are alike, and it's not worth while to study them. I will tell you my life some time or other . . . but first you tell me yours."

"I know you very little," repeated Bazarov. "Perhaps you are right; perhaps, really, every one is a riddle. You, for instance; you avoid society, you are oppressed by it, and you have invited two students to stay with you. With your intellect, with your beauty, why do you live in the country?"

"What? What was it you said?" Odintsov interposed eagerly. "With my . . . beauty?"

Bazarov scowled. "Never mind that," he muttered; "I meant to say that I don't exactly understand why you have settled in the country."

"You don't understand it. . . . But you explain it to yourself in some way?"

"Yes . . . I assume that you remain continually in the same place because you indulge yourself, because you are very fond of comfort and ease, and very indifferent to everything else."

Odintsov smiled again. "You would absolutely refuse to believe that I am capable of being carried away by anything?"

Bazarov glanced at her from under his brows.

"By curiosity, perhaps; but not otherwise."

"Really? Well, now I understand why we are such friends; you are just like me, you see."

"We are such friends . . ." Bazarov uttered in a hollow voice.

Bazarov got up. The lamp burnt dimly in the middle of the dark, fragrant, isolated room; from time to time the blind was shaken, and there flowed in the disturbing freshness of the night; its mysterious whisperings were heard. Odintsov did not move a single limb; hidden emotion gradually possessed her. It communicated itself to Bazarov. He was suddenly conscious that he was alone with a young and lovely woman. . . .

"Where are you going?" she said slowly.

He answered nothing, and sank into a chair.

"And so you consider me a placid, pampered, spoiled creature," she went on in the same voice, never taking her eyes off the window. "While I know about myself that I am unhappy."

"You unhappy? What for? Surely you can't attach any importance to idle gossip?"

Odintsov frowned. It annoyed her that he had given *that* meaning to her words.

"Such gossip does not even amuse me, Evgeny Vassilyich, and I am too proud to allow it to disturb me. I am unhappy because . . . I have no desires, no passion for life. You look at me incredulously; you think that's said by an 'aristocrat,' who is all in lace, and sitting in a velvet armchair. I don't conceal the fact: I love what you call comfort, and at the same time I have little desire to live. Explain that contradiction as best you can. But all that's romanticism in your eyes."

Bazarov shook his head. "You are in good health, independent, rich; what more would you have? What do you want?"

"What do I want?" echoed Odintsov, and she sighed. "I am very tired, I am old, I feel as if I have lived very long. Yes, I am old," she added, softly drawing the ends of her lace over her bare arms. Her eyes met Bazarov's eyes, and she faintly blushed. "I already have so many memories behind me: my life in Petersburg, wealth, then poverty, then my father's death, marriage, then the inevitable foreign tour. . . . So many memories, and nothing to remember, and before me, before me—a long, long road, and no goal. . . . I have no wish to go on."

"Are you so disillusioned?" asked Bazarov.

"No, but I am dissatisfied," Odintsov replied, dwelling on each syllable. "I think if I could interest myself strongly in something. . . ."

"You want to fall in love," Bazarov interrupted her, "and you can't love; that's where your unhappiness lies."

Odintsov began to examine the sleeve of her lace.

"Is it true I can't love?" she said.

"I should say not! Only I was wrong in calling that an unhappiness. On the contrary, any one's more to be pitied when such a mischance befalls him."

"Mischance, what?"

"Falling in love."

"And how do you come to know that?"

"By hearsay," answered Bazarov angrily.

"You're flirting," he thought; "you're bored, and teasing me for want of something to do, while I . . ." His heart really seemed as though it were being torn to pieces.

"Besides, you are perhaps too exacting," he said, bending his whole frame forward and playing with the fringe of the chair.

"Perhaps. My idea is everything or nothing. A life for a life. Take mine, give up yours, and that without regret or turning back. Or else better have nothing."

"Well?" observed Bazarov; "those are fair terms, and I'm surprised that so far you . . . have not found what you wanted."

"And do you think it would be easy to give oneself up wholly to anything whatever?"

"Not easy, if you begin reflecting, waiting and attaching value to yourself, prizing yourself, I mean; but to give oneself up without reflection is very easy."

"How can one help prizing oneself? If I am of no value, who could need my devotion?"

"That's not my affair; that's somebody else's business to assess my value. The chief thing is to be able to yield oneself."

Odintsov bent forward from the back of her chair. "You speak," she began, "as though you had experienced all that."

"It happened to come up, Anna Sergeyevna; all that, as you know, is not in my line."

"But you could yield yourself?"

"I don't know. I shouldn't like to boast."

Odintsov said nothing, and Bazarov was mute. The sounds of the piano floated up to them from the drawing-room.

"How is it Katya is playing so late?" observed Odintsov.

Bazarov got up. "Yes, it is really late now; it's time for you to go to sleep."

"Wait a little; why are you in a hurry? . . . I want to say something to you."

"What is it?"

"Wait a little," whispered Odintsov. Her eyes rested on Bazarov; it seemed as though she were examining him attentively.

He walked across the room, then suddenly went up to her, hurriedly said, "Good-bye," squeezed her hand so that she almost screamed, and was gone. She raised her crushed fingers to her lips, breathed on them, and suddenly, impulsively getting up from her low chair, she moved with rapid steps towards the door, as though she wished to bring Bazarov back. . . . A maid came into the room with a decanter on a silver tray. Odintsov stood still, told her she could go, and sat down again, and again sank into thought. Her hair slipped loose and fell in a dark coil down her shoulders. Long after the lamp was still burning in Anna Sergeyevna's room, and for long she stayed without moving, only from time to time chafing her hands, nipped by the cold of the night.

And Bazarov came back to his bedroom two hours later with his boots wet with dew, dishevelled and glum. He found Arkady at the writing table with a book in his hands, his coat buttoned up to the throat.

"You're not in bed yet?" he said in a tone, it seemed, of annoyance.

"You stopped a long while with Anna Sergeyevna this evening," remarked Arkady, not answering him.

"Yes, I stopped with her all the while you were playing the piano with Katerina Sergeyevna."

"I did not play. . ." Arkady began, and he stopped. He felt the tears were coming into his eyes, and he did not like to cry before his sarcastic friend.

XVIII

The following morning when Odintsov came down to morning tea, Bazarov sat a long while bending over his cup, then suddenly he glanced up at her. . . . She turned to him as though he had touched her, and he thought that her face had become a little paler during the night. She soon went off to her own room, and did not appear till lunch. It rained from early morning; there was no possibility of going for a walk. The whole company assembled in the drawing-room. Arkady took up the latest issue of a journal and began reading it aloud. The princess, as was her habit, at first expressed amazement on her face, as though he were doing something improper, then glared angrily at him; but he paid no attention to her.

"Evgeny Vassilyich," said Anna Sergeyevna, "come to my room. . . . I want to ask you. . . . You mentioned a manual yesterday. . . ."

She got up and went to the door. The princess looked round with an expression that seemed to say, "Look at me, look at me: see how shocked I am!" and again glared at Arkady; but he raised his voice, and exchanging glances with Katya, near whom he was sitting, he went on reading.

Odintsov went to her study with rapid steps. Bazarov followed her quickly, not raising his eyes, and only catching with his ears the delicate swish and rustle of her silk gown gliding before him. Odintsov sank into the same easy-chair in which she had sat the previous evening, and Bazarov took up the same position as before.

"Well, what was the name of that book?" she began, after a brief silence.

"Pelouse et Frémy, *Notions générales,*" answered Bazarov. "I might however also recommend to you Ganot, *Traité élémentaire de physique expérimentale*. In that book the illustrations are clearer, and in general that text-book . . ."

Odintsov stretched out her hand.

"Evgeny Vassilyich, I beg your pardon, but I didn't invite you in here to discuss text-books. I wanted to renew last night's conversation. You went away so suddenly. . . . You won't get bored?"

"I am at your service, Anna Sergeyevna. But what were we talking about last night?"

Odintsov flung a sidelong glance at Bazarov.

"We were talking of happiness, I believe. I told you about myself. By the way, I mentioned the word 'happiness.' Tell me why it is that even when we are enjoying music, for instance, or a fine evening, or a conversation with sympathetic people, it all seems an intimation of some measureless happiness existing apart somewhere rather than actual happiness—such, I mean, as we ourselves are in possession of? Why is it? Or perhaps you have no feeling like that?"

"You know the saying, 'The grass is always greener. . . .' " replied Bazarov; "besides, you told me yesterday you are discontented. I certainly never have such ideas come into my head."

"Perhaps they seem ridiculous to you?"

"No; but they don't come into my head."

"Really? Do you know, I should very much like to know what you think about?"

"What? I don't understand."

"Listen; I have long wanted to speak openly to you. There's no need to tell you—you are conscious of it yourself—that you are not an ordinary man; you are still young—all life is before you. What are you preparing yourself for? What future awaits you? I mean to say—what object do you want to attain? What are you going forward to? What is in your heart? In short, who are you, what are you?"

"You surprise me, Anna Sergeyevna. You are aware that I am studying natural sciences, and who I . . ."

"Well, who are you?"

"I have explained to you already that I am going to be a district doctor."

Anna Sergeyevna made an impatient movement.

"What do you say that for? You don't believe it yourself. Arkady might answer me in that way, but not you."

"Why, in what is Arkady . . ."

"Stop! Is it possible you could content yourself with such a humble career, and aren't you always maintaining yourself that you don't believe in medicine? You—with your ambition—a district doctor! You answer me like that to put me off, because you have no confidence in me. But, do you know, Evgeny Vassilyich, that I could understand you; I have been poor and ambitious myself, like you; I have been perhaps through the same trials as you."

"That is all very well, Anna Sergeyevna, but you must pardon me for . . . I am not in the habit of talking freely about myself at any time as a rule, and between you and me there is such a gulf . . ."

"What sort of gulf? You mean to tell me again that I am an aristocrat? No more of that, Evgeny Vassilyich; I thought I had proved to you . . ."

"And even apart from that," broke in Bazarov, "what could induce one to talk and think about the future, which for the most part does not depend on us? If a chance turns up of doing something—so much the better; and if it doesn't turn up—at least one will be glad one didn't gossip idly about it beforehand."

"You call a friendly conversation idle gossip? . . . Or perhaps you consider me as a woman unworthy of your confidence? I know you despise us all."

"I don't despise you, Anna Sergeyevna, and you know it."

"No, I don't know anything . . . but let us suppose so. I understand your disinclination to talk of your future career; but as to what is taking place within you now . . ."

"Taking place!" repeated Bazarov, "as though I were some sort of government or society! In any case, it is utterly uninteresting; and besides, can a man always speak of everything that 'takes place' in him?"

"Why, I don't see why you can't speak freely of everything you have on your mind."

"Can you?" asked Bazarov.

"Yes," answered Anna Sergeyevna, after a brief hesitation.

Bazarov bowed his head. "You are more fortunate than I am."

Anna Sergeyevna looked at him questioningly. "As you please," she went on, "but still something tells me that we have not come together for nothing; that we shall be good friends. I am sure this—what should I say, constraint, reticence in you will vanish at last."

"So you have noticed reticence . . . as you expressed it . . . constraint?"

"Yes."

Bazarov got up and went to the window. "And would you like to know the reason of this reticence? Would you like to know what is passing within me?"

"Yes," repeated Odintsov, with a sort of dread she did not at the time understand.

"And you will not be angry?"

"No."

"No?" Bazarov was standing with his back to her. "Let me tell you then that I love you like a fool, like a madman. . . . There, you've forced it out of me."

Odintsov put both her hands out before her; but Bazarov was leaning with his forehead pressed against the window pane. He breathed hard: his whole body was visibly trembling. But it was not the tremor of youthful timidity, not the sweet alarm of the first declaration that possessed him; it was passion struggling in him, strong and painful—passion not unlike hatred, and perhaps akin to it . . . Odintsov felt both afraid and sorry for him.

"Evgeny Vassilyich!" she said, and there was the ring of unconscious tenderness in her voice.

He turned quickly, flung a devouring look on her, and snatching both her hands, he drew her suddenly to his breast.

She did not at once free herself from his embrace, but an instant later she was standing far away in a corner, and looked at Bazarov from there. He rushed at her. . . .

"You have misunderstood me," she whispered hurriedly, in alarm. It seemed that if he had made another step she would have screamed. . . . Bazarov bit his lips, and went out.

Half an hour after a maid gave Anna Sergeyevna a note from Bazarov; it consisted simply of one line: "Am I to go to-day, or can I stop till to-morrow?"

"Why should you go? I did not understand you—you did not understand me," Anna Sergeyevna answered him, but to herself she thought: "I did not understand myself either."

She did not show herself till dinner time, and kept walking to and fro in her room with her arms behind her back, stopping sometimes at the window, sometimes at the looking-glass, and slowly rubbing her handkerchief over her neck, on which she still seemed to feel a burning spot. She asked herself what had induced her to "force" his confidence, in Bazarov's words, and whether she had suspected nothing. . . . "I am to blame," she decided aloud, "but I could not have foreseen this." She fell to musing, and blushed crimson, remembering Bazarov's almost bestial face when he had rushed at her. . . .

"Or?" she uttered suddenly, and she stopped short and shook back her curls. . . . She caught sight of herself in the glass; her head thrown back, with a mysterious smile on the half-closed, half-opened eyes and lips, told her, it seemed, in a flash something at which she herself was confused. . . .

"No," she made up her mind at last. "God knows what it would lead to; you can't toy with him; peace is the best thing in the world, anyway."

Her peace of mind was not shaken; but she felt gloomy, and even shed a few tears once, though she could not have said why —certainly not for the insult done her. She did not feel insulted; she was more inclined to feel guilty. Under the influence of various vague emotions, the sense of life passing by, the desire of novelty, she had forced herself to go up to a certain point, forced herself to glance behind it, and had seen behind it not even an abyss, but a void . . . or something hideous.

XIX

Though Odintsov's self-control was great, and superior as she was to every kind of prejudice, she felt awkward when she went into the dining-room to dinner. The meal went off fairly successfully, however. Porfiry Platonovich made his appearance and told various anecdotes; he had just come back from the town. Among other things, he informed them that Governor Swill had ordered his secretaries on special commissions to wear spurs, in case he might send them off anywhere for greater speed on horseback. Arkady talked in an undertone to Katya, and diplomatically attended to the princess's wants. Bazarov maintained a grim and obstinate silence. Odintsov looked at him twice, not stealthily, but straight in the face, which was bilious and forbidding, with downcast eyes, and contemptuous determination stamped on every feature, and thought: "No . . . no . . . no." . . . After dinner she went with the whole company into the garden, and seeing that Bazarov wanted to speak to her, she took a few steps to one side and stopped. He went up to her, but even then did not raise his eyes, and said in a hollow voice:

"I must apologize to you, Anna Sergeyevna. You must be in a fury with me."

"No, I'm not angry with you, Evgeny Vassilyich," answered Odintsov; "but I am sorry."

"So much the worse. Anyway, I'm sufficiently punished. My position, you will certainly agree, is most foolish. You wrote to me, 'Why go away?' But I cannot stay, and don't wish to. Tomorrow I shall be gone."

"Evgeny Vassilyich, why are you . . ."

"Why am I going away?"

"No; I didn't mean to say that."

"You can't bring back the past, Anna Sergeyevna . . . and this was bound to come about sooner or later. Consequently I must go. I can only conceive of one condition upon which I could remain; but that condition can never be. Excuse my impertinence, but you don't love me, and you never will love me, I suppose?"

Bazarov's eyes glittered for an instant under their dark brows.

Anna Sergeyevna did not answer him. "I'm afraid of this man," flashed through her brain.

"Good-bye, then," said Bazarov, as though he guessed her thought, and he went back into the house.

Anna Sergeyevna walked slowly after him, and calling Katya to her, she took her arm. She did not leave her side till quite evening. She did not play cards, and was constantly laughing, which did not at all accord with her pale and perplexed face. Arkady was bewildered, and looked on at her as all young people look on—that is to say, he was constantly asking himself, "What is the meaning of that?" Bazarov shut himself up in his room; he came back to tea, however. Anna Sergeyevna longed to say some friendly word to him, but she did not know how to address him. . . .

An unexpected incident relieved her from her embarrassment; the butler announced the arrival of Sitnikov.

It is difficult to do justice in words to the strange figure cut by the young apostle of progress as he fluttered into the room, like a quail. With his characteristic impudence, he had made up his mind to go into the country to visit a woman whom he hardly knew, who had never invited him; but with whom, according to information he had gathered, such talented and intimate friends were staying, he was nevertheless trembling to the marrow of his bones; and instead of bringing out the apologies and compliments he had learned by heart beforehand, he muttered some absurdity about Evdoksya Kukshin having sent him to inquire after Anna Sergeyevna's health, and Arkady Nicolaevich's too, having always spoken to him in the highest terms. . . . At this point he faltered and lost his presence of mind so completely that he sat down on his own hat. However, since no one turned him out, and Anna Sergeyevna even presented him to her aunt and her sister, he soon recovered himself and began to chatter volubly. The introduction of the commonplace is often an advantage in life; it relieves overstrained strings, and sobers too self-confident or self-forgetful emotions by recalling its close kinship with them. With Sitnikov's appearance everything somehow became duller and emptier; they all even ate a more solid supper, and retired to bed half an hour earlier than usual.

"I might now repeat to you," said Arkady, lying in bed, to Bazarov, who was also undressed, "what you once said to me, 'Why are you so melancholy? One would think you had fulfilled some sacred duty.' " For some time past a sort of pretense of free-and-easy banter had sprung up between the two young men, which is always an unmistakable sign of secret displeasure or unexpressed suspicions.

"I'm going to my father's to-morrow," said Bazarov.

Arkady raised himself and leaned on his elbow. He felt both surprised, and for some reason or other pleased. "Ah!" he commented, "and is that why you're sad?"

Bazarov yawned. "You'll get old if you know too much."

"And Anna Sergeyevna?" persisted Arkady.

"What about Anna Sergeyevna?"

"I mean, will she let you go?"

"I'm not her hired hand."

Arkady grew thoughtful, while Bazarov lay down and turned with his face to the wall.

Some minutes went by in silence. "Evgeny!" cried Arkady suddenly.

"Well?"

"I will leave with you to-morrow, too."

Bazarov made no answer.

"Only I will go home," continued Arkady. "We will go together as far as Khokhlovsky, and there you can get horses at Fedot's. I should be delighted to make the acquaintance of your people, but I'm afraid of being in their way and yours. You are coming to us again later, of course?"

"I've left all my things with you," Bazarov said, without turning round.

"Why doesn't he ask me why I am going, and just as suddenly as he?" thought Arkady. "In reality, why am I going, and why is he going?" he pursued his reflections. He could find no satisfactory answer to his own question, though his heart was filled with some bitter feeling. He felt it would be hard to part from this life to which he had grown so accustomed; but for him to remain alone would be rather odd. "Something has passed between them," he reasoned to himself; "what good would it be for me to hang on after he's gone? She's utterly sick of me; I'm losing the last that remained to me." He began to imagine Anna Sergeyevna to himself, then other features gradually eclipsed the lovely image of the young widow.

"It's a pity about Katya too!" Arkady whispered to his pillow, on which a tear had already fallen. . . . All at once he shook back his hair and said aloud:

"What the devil made that fool of a Sitnikov turn up here?"

Bazarov at first stirred a little in his bed, then pronounced the following: "You're still a fool, my boy, I see. Sitnikovs are indispensable to us. I—do you understand? I need dolts like him. It's not for the gods to bake bricks, in fact!" . . .

"Oho!" Arkady thought to himself, and then in a flash all the fathomless depths of Bazarov's conceit dawned upon him. "Are you and I gods then? At least, you're a god; am not I a dolt then?"

"Yes," repeated Bazarov gloomily; "you're still a fool."

Odintsov expressed no special surprise when Arkady told her the next day that he was going with Bazarov; she seemed tired and absorbed. Katya looked at him silently and seriously; the princess went so far as to cross herself under her shawl so that he could not help noticing it. Sitnikov, on the other hand, was completely disconcerted. He had only just come in to lunch in a new and fashionable get-up, not on this occasion of a Slavophile cut; the evening before he had astonished the servant assigned to him by the amount of linen he had brought with him, and now all of a sudden his comrades were deserting him! He took a few tiny steps, doubled back like a hunted hare at the edge of a copse, and abruptly, almost with dismay, almost with a wail, announced that he intended to go too. Odintsov did not attempt to detain him.

"I have a very comfortable carriage," added the unfortunate young man, turning to Arkady; "I can take you, while Evgeny Vassilyich can take your coach, so it will be even more convenient."

"But, really, it's not at all in your way, and it's a long way to my place."

"That's nothing, nothing; I've plenty of time; besides, I have business in that direction."

"Liquor?" asked Arkady, rather too contemptuously.

But Sitnikov was reduced to such desperation that he did not even laugh as usual. "I assure you, my carriage is exceedingly comfortable," he muttered; "and there will be room for all."

"Don't wound Monsieur Sitnikov by a refusal," commented Anna Sergeyevna.

Arkady glanced at her, and bowed his head significantly.

The visitors started off after lunch. As she said good-bye to Bazarov, Odintsov held out her hand to him, and said, "We shall meet again, shall we not?"

"As you command," answered Bazarov.

"In that case, we shall."

Arkady was the first to go out to the porch; he got into Sitnikov's carriage. The butler tucked him in respectfully, but he could have hit him with pleasure, or have burst into tears. Bazarov took his seat in the coach. When they reached Khokhlovsky, Arkady waited till Fedot, the keeper of the posting-station, had put in the horses, and going up to the coach he said, with his old smile, to Bazarov, "Evgeny, take me with you; I want to come to you."

"Get in," Bazarov uttered through his teeth.

Sitnikov, who had been walking to and fro round the wheels of his carriage, whistling briskly, could only gape when he heard these words; while Arkady coolly pulled his luggage out of the carriage, took his seat beside Bazarov, and bowing politely to his former fellow-traveler, he called, "Whip up!" The coach rolled away, and was soon out of sight . . . Sitnikov, utterly nonplussed, looked at his coachman, but the latter was flicking his whip about the tail of the off horse. Then Sitnikov jumped into the carriage, and thundering at two passing peasants, "Put on your caps, idiots!" he drove to town where he arrived very late, and where, next day, at Kukshin's, he dealt very severely with two "disgusting stuck-up churls."

When he was seated in the coach by Bazarov, Arkady pressed his hand warmly, and for a long while he said nothing. It seemed as though Bazarov understood and appreciated both the pressure and the silence. He had not slept at all the previous night, and had not smoked, and had eaten scarcely anything for several days. His profile, already thinner, stood out darkly and sharply under his cap, which was pulled down to his eyebrows.

"Well, brother," he said at last, "give us a cigar. But look, tell me, is my tongue yellow?"

"Yes, it is," answered Arkady.

"Hm . . . and the cigar is tasteless. The machine's out of gear."

"You really have changed lately," observed Arkady.

"It's nothing! We shall soon be all right. One thing's a bother—my mother's so tender-hearted; if you don't grow as round as a tub, and eat ten times a day, she's quite upset. My father's all right, he's known all sorts of ups and downs himself. No, I can't smoke," he added, and he flung the cigar into the dust of the road.

"Do you think it's fifteen miles?" asked Arkady.

"Yes. But ask this sage here." He indicated the peasant sitting on the box, a laborer of Fedot's.

But the sage only answered, "Who's to know—miles hereabout aren't measured," and went on swearing in an undertone at the shaft horse for "kicking with her head-piece," that is, jerking her head.

"Yes, yes," began Bazarov; "it's a lesson to you, my young friend, an instructive example. The devil knows what nonsense it is. Every man hangs on a thread, the abyss may open under his feet any minute, and yet he must go and invent all sorts of discomforts for himself, and spoil his life."

"What are you alluding to?" asked Arkady.

"I'm not alluding to anything; I'm saying straight out that we've both behaved like fools. What's the use of talking about it! Still, I've noticed in hospital practice, the man who's furious at his illness—he's sure to get over it."

"I don't quite understand you," observed Arkady; "I should have thought you had nothing to complain of."

"And since you don't quite understand me, I'll tell you this—to my mind, it's better to break stones on the highroad than to let a woman have the mastery of even the end of one's little finger. That's all . . ." Bazarov was on the point of uttering his favorite word, "romanticism," but he checked himself, and said, "nonsense. You don't believe me now, but I tell you; you and I have been in feminine society, and very nice we found it; but to leave society like that is as pleasant as a dip in cold water on a hot day. A man hasn't time to attend to such trifles; a man must be savage, says an excellent Spanish proverb. Now, you, I suppose, my sage friend," he added, turning to the peasant sitting on the box—"you've a wife?"

The peasant showed both the friends his dull blear-eyed face.

"A wife? Yes. How else?"

"Do you beat her?"

"My wife? Anything can happen. We don't beat her without good reason!"

"That's excellent. Well, and does she beat you?"

The peasant gave a tug at the reins. "That's a strange thing to say, master. You like your joke. . . ." He was obviously offended.

"You hear, Arkady Nikolaevich! But we have taken a beating . . . that's what comes of being educated people."

Arkady gave a forced laugh, while Bazarov turned away, and did not open his mouth again the whole journey.

The fifteen miles seemed a whole thirty to Arkady. But at last, on the slope of a gently rising knoll appeared the tiny village where Bazarov's parents lived. Beside it, in a small copse of young birch, could be seen a tiny house with a thatched roof. Two peasants stood with their hats on at the first hut, abusing each other. "You're a big pig," said one; "and worse than a little sucking pig."

"And your wife's a witch," retorted the other.

"From their unconstrained behavior," Bazarov remarked to Arkady, "and the playfulness of their retorts, you can guess that my father's peasants are not too much oppressed. Why, there he is himself coming out on the porch of his house. They must have heard the bells. It's he; it's he—I know his figure. Oho ho! how grey he's grown though, poor fellow!"

XX

Bazarov leaned out of the carriage, while Arkady thrust his head out behind his companion's back, and caught sight on the small porch of the little manor-house of a tall, gaunt man with dishevelled hair, and thin aquiline nose, dressed in an old military frock coat not buttoned up. He was standing, his legs wide apart, smoking a long pipe and squinting his eyes to keep the sun out of them.

The horses stopped.

"Arrived at last," said Bazarov's father, still going on smoking though the pipe was fairly dancing up and down between his fingers. "Come, get out; get out; let me hug you."

He began embracing his son. . . . "Enyusha, Enyusha," a trembling woman's voice was heard. The door was flung open, a plump, short, little old woman in a white cap and a short, striped jacket, appeared on the threshold. She oh'd, swayed, and would certainly have fallen, had not Bazarov supported her. Her small plump hands were instantly entwined round his neck, her head was pressed to his breast, and there was a complete hush. The only sound heard was her broken sobs.

Old Bazarov breathed hard and squinted his eyes up more than ever.

"There, that's enough, that's enough, Arisha! stop," he said, exchanging a glance with Arkady, who remained motionless near the coach, while the peasant on the box even turned his head away; "that's not necessary at all, please stop."

"Ah, Vassily Ivanovich," faltered the old woman, "for what ages, my dear one, my darling, Enyusha," . . . and, not unclasping her hands, she drew her wrinkled face, wet with tears and working with tenderness, a little away from Bazarov, and gazed at him with blissful and comic-looking eyes, and again fell on his neck.

"Well, well, to be sure, that's all in the nature of things," commented Vassily Ivanovich, "only we'd better come indoors. Here's a visitor come with Evgeny. You must excuse it," he added, turning to Arkady, and made a slight bow; "you understand, a woman's weakness; and well, a mother's heart . . ."

But his lips and eyebrows, too, were twitching, and his beard was quivering . . . he was obviously trying to control himself and appear almost indifferent.

"Let's come in, mother, really," said Bazarov, and he led the enfeebled old woman into the house. Putting her into a comfortable armchair, he once more hurriedly embraced his father and introduced Arkady to him.

"Heartily glad to make your acquaintance," said Vassily Ivanovich, "but you mustn't expect great things; everything here in my house is done in a plain way, on a military footing. Arina Vlasyevna, calm yourself, pray; what weakness! The gentleman our guest will think ill of you."

"My dear sir," said the old lady through her tears, "I haven't the honor of knowing your name and patronymic . . ."

"Arkady Nikolaich," put in Vassily Ivanovich solemnly, in a low voice.

"You must excuse a silly old woman like me." The old woman blew her nose, and bending her head to right and to left, carefully wiped one eye after the other. "You must excuse me. You see, I thought I should die, that I should not live to see my da . . . arling."

"Well, here we have lived to see him, madam," put in Vassily Ivanovich. "Tanyushka," he turned to a barelegged little girl of thirteen in a bright red cotton dress, who was timidly peeping in at the door, "bring your mistress a glass of water—on a tray, do you hear?—and you, gentlemen," he added, with a kind of old-fashioned playfulness "let me ask you into the study of a retired old veteran."

"Just let me embrace you once more, Enyusha," moaned Arina Vlasyevna. Bazarov bent down to her. "Why, what a handsome fellow you have grown!"

"Well, I don't know about being handsome," remarked Vassily Ivanovich, "but he's a man, as the saying is, *ommfay*.[7] And now I hope, Arina Vlasyevna, that having satisfied your maternal heart, you will turn your thoughts to satisfying the appetites of our dear guests, because, as you're aware, even nightingales can't be fed on fairy tales."

The old lady got up from her chair. "This minute, Vassily Ivanovich, the table shall be laid. I will run myself to the kitchen and order the samovar to be brought in; there will be everything, everything. Why, I have not seen him, not given him food or drink these three years; is that nothing?"

"There, mind, good mother, bustle about; don't put us to shame; while you, gentlemen, I beg you to follow me. Here's Timofeich come to pay his respects to you, Evgeny. He, too, I daresay, is delighted, the old dog. Eh, aren't you delighted, old dog? Be so good as to follow me."

And Vassily Ivanovich went bustling forward, scraping and flapping with his slippers trodden down at heel.

His whole house consisted of six tiny rooms. One of them—the one to which he led our friends—was called the study. A thick-legged table, littered over with papers black with the accumulation of ancient dust as though they had been smoked, occupied the entire space between two windows; on the walls hung Turkish firearms, whips, swords, two maps, anatomical charts of some sort, a portrait of Hufeland,[8] a monogram woven in hair in a black frame, and a glass-framed diploma; a leather sofa, torn and worn into hollows here and there, was placed between two enormous cupboards of Karelian birchwood; books, boxes, stuffed birds, jars, and phials were huddled together in confusion on the shelves; in one corner stood a broken galvanic battery.

"I warned you, my dear guest," began Vassily Ivanovich, "that we live, so to say, bivouacking. . . ."

"There, stop that, what are you apologizing for?" Bazarov interrupted. "Kirsanov knows very well we're not Crœsuses, and that you don't have a palace. Where are we going to put him, that's

7. That is, *homme fait*—"a real man."

8. A German physician (1762–1836).

the question?"

"To be sure, Evgeny; I have a capital room there in the little lodge; he will be very comfortable there."

"Have you had a lodge put up then?"

"Of course, sir, where the bathhouse is, sir," put in Timofeich.

"That is, next to the bathhouse," Vassily Ivanovich added hurriedly. "It's summer now . . . I will run over there at once, and make arrangements; and you, Timofeich, meanwhile bring in their things. You, Evgeny, I shall of course offer my study. *Suum cuique*."[9]

"There you have him! A comical old chap, and the kindest," remarked Bazarov, as soon as Vassily Ivanovich had gone. "Just such a queer fish as yours, only in another way. He chatters too much."

"And your mother seems an awfully nice woman," observed Arkady.

"Yes, there's no humbug about her. You'll see what a dinner she'll give us."

"They didn't expect you to-day, sir; they didn't buy any beef," observed Timofeich, who was just dragging in Bazarov's box.

"We shall get on very well without beef. It's no use crying for the moon. Poverty, they say, is no vice."

"How many serfs has your father?" Arkady asked suddenly.

"The estate's not his, but mother's; there are fifteen serfs, if I remember."

"Twenty-two in all," Timofeich added, with an air of displeasure.

The flapping of slippers was heard, and Vassily Ivanovich reappeared. "In a few minutes your room will be ready to receive you," he cried triumphantly. "Arkady . . . Nikolaich? I think that is right? And here is your attendant," he added, indicating a short-cropped boy, who had come in with him in a blue coat with ragged elbows and a pair of boots which did not belong to him. "His name is Fedka. Again, I repeat, even though my son tells me not to, you mustn't expect great things. He knows how to fill a pipe, though. You smoke, of course?"

"I generally smoke cigars," answered Arkady.

"And you do very sensibly. I myself give the preference to cigars, but in these isolated parts it is exceedingly difficult to obtain them."

"There, that's enough humble pie," Bazarov interrupted again. "You'd much better sit here on the sofa and let us have a look at you."

Vassily Ivanovich laughed and sat down. His face was very

9. "To each his own."

much like his son's, only his brow was lower and narrower, and his mouth rather wider, and he was forever restless, shrugging up his shoulder as though his coat cut him under the arms, blinking, clearing his throat, and gesticulating with his fingers, while his son was distinguished by a kind of nonchalant immobility.

"Humble pie!" repeated Vassily Ivanovich. "You must not imagine, Evgeny, that I want to appeal, so to speak, to our guest's sympathies by making out we live in such a wilderness. Quite the contrary, I maintain that for a thinking man nothing is a wilderness. At least, I try as far as possible not to get rusty, so to speak, not to fall behind the age."

Vassily Ivanovich drew out of his pocket a new yellow silk handkerchief, which he had had time to snatch up on the way to Arkady's room, and flourishing it in the air, he proceeded: "I am not now alluding to the fact that, for example, at the cost of considerable sacrifice for me I have put my peasants on the quit-rent-system and given up my land to them on half profits. I regarded that as my duty; common sense itself enjoins such a proceeding, though other proprietors do not even dream of it; I am alluding to the sciences, to education."

"Yes; I see you have here *The Friend of Health*[1] for 1855," remarked Bazarov.

"It's sent me by an old comrade out of friendship," Vassily Ivanovich made haste to answer; "but we even have, some idea of phrenology, for instance," he added, addressing himself principally, however, to Arkady, and pointing to a small plaster head on the cupboard, divided into numbered squares; "we are not unacquainted even with Schönlein and Rademacher."

"Why, do people still believe in Rademacher in this province?" asked Bazarov.

Vassily Ivanovich cleared his throat. "In this province. . . . Of course, gentlemen, you know best; how could we keep pace with you? You are here to take our places. In my day, too, there was some sort of a Humoralist school, Hoffmann, and Brown too with his vitalism—they seemed very ridiculous to us, but, of course, they too had been great men at one time or other. Some one new has taken Rademacher's place with you; you bow down to him, but in another twenty years it will be his turn to be laughed at."

"For your consolation I will tell you," observed Bazarov, "that nowadays we laugh at medicine altogether, and don't bow down to any one."

"How's that? Why, you're going to be a doctor, aren't you?"

1. A medical journal. The two worthy physicians next mentioned were renowned German professors in the elder Bazarov's heyday.

"Yes, but the one fact doesn't prevent the other."

Vassily Ivanovich poked his third finger into his pipe, where a little smouldering ash was still left. "Well, it may be it may be—I am not going to argue. What am I? A retired army-doctor, *volla-too;* [2] now I've turned into an agronomist. I served in your grandfather's brigade," he addressed himself again to Arkady; "yes sir, yes sir, I have seen many sights in my day. And I was thrown into all kinds of society, brought into contact with all sorts of people! I myself, the man you see before you now, have felt the pulse of Prince Wittgenstein and of Zhukovsky! [3] They were in the southern army, on the fourteenth,[4] you understand" (and here Vassily Ivanovich pursed his lips significantly). "Well, well, but my work was on the sideline; stick to your lancet, and let everything else go hang! Your grandfather was a very honorable man, a real soldier."

"Confess, now, he was a real blockhead," remarked Bazarov, lazily.

"Ah, Evgeny, how can you use such an expression! Do consider. . . . Of course, General Kirsanov was not one of the . . ."

"Come, drop him," broke in Bazarov; "I was pleased as I was driving along here to see your birch copse; it has shot up splendidly."

Vassily Ivanovich brightened up. "And you must see what a little garden I've got now! I planted every tree myself. I've fruit, and raspberries, and all kinds of medicinal herbs. However clever you young gentlemen may be, old Paracelsus spoke the holy truth: *in herbis, verbis et lapidibus*.[5]. . . I've retired from practice, you know, of course, but two or three times a week it will happen that I'm brought back to my old work. They come for advice—I can't drive them away. Sometimes the poor have recourse to me for help. And indeed there are no doctors here at all. There's one of the neighbors here, a retired major, only fancy, he doctors the people too. I asked, 'Has he studied medicine?' And they told me, 'No, he's not studied; he does it more out of philanthropy.' . . . Ha! ha! ha! out of philanthropy! What do you think of that? Ha! ha! ha!"

"Fedka, fill me a pipe!" said Bazarov rudely.

2. That is, *et voilà tout*—"and that's all."

3. A Russian field marshal, who distinguished himself during the war of 1812 and then commanded the armies in the South of Russia (1818–28). V. A. Zhukovsky (1783–1852) was Russia's leading poet at the beginning of the nineteenth century.

4. An allusion to the Decembrist Revolt (1825), a badly organized and conducted revolt by aristocratic officers, aimed at establishing a liberal constitution and abolishing serfdom. It was put down in a matter of hours, and many of the participants, the flower of the Russian aristocracy, were banished. The militant part of the conspiracy was headed by P. I. Pestel and involved those serving in the armies in the South.

5. "Through herbs, words, and minerals."

"And there's another doctor here who just got to a patient," Vassily Ivanovich persisted in a kind of desperation, "when the patient was already *ad patres;* [6] the servant didn't let the doctor speak; 'you're no longer needed,' he told him. He hadn't expected this, got confused, and asked, 'What, did your master hiccup before his death?' 'Yes sir.' 'Did he hiccup much?' 'Yes sir.' 'Ah, well, that's all right,' and off he set back again. Ha! ha! ha!"

The old man was alone in his laughter; Arkady forced a smile on his face. Bazarov only stretched. The conversation went on in this way for about an hour; Arkady had time to go to his room, which turned out to be the anteroom attached to the bathhouse, but was very snug and clean. At last Tanyusha came in and announced that dinner was ready.

Vassily Ivanovich was the first to get up. "Come, gentlemen. You must be magnanimous and pardon me if I've bored you. I daresay my good wife will satisfy you better."

The dinner, though prepared in haste, turned out to be very good, even abundant; only the wine was not quite up to the mark; it was almost black sherry, bought by Timofeich in the town from a merchant he knew and had a faint coppery, or perhaps resinous taste, and the flies were a great nuisance. On ordinary days a serf-boy used to keep driving them away with a large green branch; but on this occasion Vassily Ivanovich had sent him away through dread of the criticism of the younger generation. Arina Vlasyevna had had time to dress; she had put on a high cap with silk ribbons and a pale blue flowered shawl. She broke down again as soon as she caught sight of her Enyusha, but her husband had no need to admonish her; she made haste to wipe away her tears herself, for fear of spotting her shawl. Only the young men ate anything; the master and mistress of the house had dined long ago. Fedka waited at table, obviously encumbered by the novelty of boots; he was assisted by a woman of a masculine cast of face and one eye, by name Anfisushka, who performed the duties of housekeeper, poultry-woman, and laundress. Vassily Ivanovich walked up and down during the whole of dinner, and with a perfectly happy, positively beatific countenance, talked about the serious anxiety he felt at Napoleon's policy, and the intricacy of the Italian question. Arina Vlasyevna took no notice of Arkady; leaning on her little closed fist, her round face, to which the full cherry-colored lips and the little moles on the cheeks and over the eyebrows gave a very simple, good-natured expression, she did not take her eyes off her son, and kept sighing;

6. "to the fathers" (that is, died).

she was dying to know for how long he had come, but she was afraid to ask him.

"What if he says for two days," she thought, and her heart sank. After the roast Vassily Ivanovich disapperared for an instant, and returned with an opened half-bottle of champagne. "Here," he cried, "though we do live in the wilds, we have something to make merry with on festive occasions!" He filled three champagne glasses and a little wineglass, proposed the health of "our inestimable guests," and at once tossed off his glass in military fashion. He made Arina Vlasyevna drink her wineglass to the last drop. When the time came in due course for preserves, Arkady, who could not bear anything sweet, thought it his duty, however, to taste four different kinds which had been freshly made, all the more as Bazarov flatly refused them and began at once smoking a cigar. Then tea arrived—with cream, butter, and biscuits; then Vassily Ivanovich took them all into the garden to admire the beauty of the evening. As they passed a garden seat he whispered to Arkady—

"This is the spot I love to philosophise as I watch the sunset; it suits a recluse like me. And there, a little farther off, I have planted some of the trees beloved of Horace."

"What trees?" asked Bazarov, overhearing.

"Why acacias, of course."

Bazarov began to yawn.

"I imagine it's time our travellers were in the arms of Morpheus," observed Vassily Ivanovich.

"That is, it's time for bed," Bazarov put in. "That's a sound idea. It is time, certainly."

As he said good-night to his mother, he kissed her on the forehead, while she embraced him, and stealthily behind his back she gave him her blessing three times. Vassily Ivanovich conducted Arkady to his room, and wished him "as refreshing repose as I enjoyed at your happy age." And Arkady did in fact sleep excellently in his bathhouse; there was a smell of mint in it, and two crickets behind the stove rivalled each other in their drowsy chirping. Vassily Ivanovich went from Arkady's room to his study, and perching on the sofa at his son's feet, he was looking forward to chatting with him; but Bazarov at once sent him away, saying he was sleepy, and did not fall asleep till morning. With wide open eyes he stared vindictively into the darkness; the memories of childhood had no power over him; and besides, he had not yet had time to get rid of his recent bitter impressions. Arina Vlasyevna first prayed to her heart's content, then she had a long, long conversation with Anfisushka, who stood stockstill before her mistress, and fixing her solitary eye upon her, communicated in a mysterious whisper all her observations and conjectures in regard to Evgeny Vassilyich. The old lady's head was giddy with happiness and wine and cigar smoke: her husband tried to talk to her, but with a wave of his hand gave it up in despair.

Arina Vlasyevna was a genuine Russian gentlewoman of the olden times; she ought to have lived two centuries before, in the days of old Muscovy. She was very devout and emotional, believed in fortune-telling, charms, dreams, and omens of every possible kind; she believed in the prophecies of holy fools, in house-spirits, in wood-spirits, in unlucky meetings, in the evil eye, in popular remedies, she ate specially prepared salt on Holy Thursday, and believed that the end of the world was near; she believed that if on Easter Sunday the candles did not go out during the all night mass, then there would be a good crop of buckwheat, and that a mushroom will not grow after a human eye has seen it; she believed that the devil likes to be where there is water, and that every Jew has a blood-stained spot on his breast; she was afraid of mice, of snakes, of frogs, of sparrows, of leeches, of thunder, of cold water, of drafts, of horses, of goats, of red-haired people, and black cats and she regarded crickets and dogs as unclean beasts; she never ate veal, doves, crayfishes, cheese, asparagus, artichokes, hares, nor water-melons, because a cut water-melon suggested the head of John the Baptist, and she could not speak of oysters without a shudder; she was fond of eating—and fasted rigidly; she slept ten hours out of the twenty four—and never went to bed at all if Vassily Ivanovich had so much as a headache; she had never read a single book except *Alexis or the Cottage in the Forest;*[7] she wrote one, or at the most two letters in a year, but knew what she was about in running the household, preserving, and jam-making, though she never touched a thing with her own hands, and was generally disinclined to move from her place. Arina Vlasyevna was very kindhearted, and in her way not at all stupid. She knew that the world is divided into masters whose duty it is to command, and simple folk whose duty it is to serve them—and so she felt no repugnance to servility and prostrations to the ground; but she treated those in subjection to her kindly and gently, never let a single beggar go away empty-handed, and never spoke ill of any one, though she was fond of gossiping now and then. In her youth she had been pretty, had played the clavichord, and spoken French a little; but in the course of many years' wanderings with her husband, whom she had married against her will, she had grown stout, and forgotten both music and French. She loved and feared

7. A sentimental novel by Ducray-Dumesnil (1761–1819), very popular in the first third of the nineteenth century in Russia.

her son unutterably; she had given up the management of the property to Vassily Ivanovich—and now did not interfere in anything; she used to groan, flutter her handkerchief, and raise her eyebrows higher and higher with horror as soon as her old husband began to discuss the impending government reforms and his own plans. She was apprehensive, constantly expecting some great misfortune, and began to weep as soon as she remembered anything sorrowful. . . . Such women are not common nowadays. God knows whether we ought to rejoice!

XXI

On getting up Arkady opened the window, and the first object that met his view was Vassily Ivanovich. In an Oriental dressing-gown girt round the waist with a pocket-handkerchief he was industriously digging in his garden. He perceived his young visitor, and leaning on his spade, he called, 'The best of health to you! How have you slept?"

"Splendidly,' answered Arkady.

"Here am I, as you see, like some Cincinnatus,[8] marking out a bed for late turnips. The time has come now—and thank God for it!—when every one ought to obtain his sustenance with his own hands; it's useless to reckon on others; one must labor oneself. And it turns out that Jean-Jacques Rousseau was right. Half an hour ago, my dear young gentleman, you might have seen me in a totally different position. One peasant woman, who complained of looseness—that's how they express it, but in our language, dysentery—I . . . how can I express it best? I administered opium; and for another I extracted a tooth. I proposed an anæsthetic to her . . . but she would not consent. All that I do *gratis—anamatyer* [9] I'm used to it, though; you see, I'm a plebeian, *homo novus*—not one of the old stock, not like my spouse. . . . Wouldn't you like to come this way into the shade, to breathe the morning freshness a little before tea?"

Arkady went out to him.

"Welcome once again," said Vassily Ivanovich, raising his hand in a military salute to the greasy skull-cap which covered his head. "You, I know, are accustomed to luxury, to amusements, but even the great ones of this world do not disdain to spend a brief space under a cottage roof."

"Good heavens," protested Arkady, "as though I were one of the great ones of this world! And I'm not accustomed to luxury."

"Pardon me, pardon me," rejoined Vassily Ivanovich with a polite

8. Cincinnatus returned to his farm after saving the Roman army and state. He cultivated the land with his own hands.

9. That is, *en amateur*—"as a hobby."

simper. "Though I am laid on the shelf now, I have knocked about the world too—I can tell a bird by its flight. I am something of a psychologist, too, in my own way, and a physiognomist. If I had not, I will venture to say, been endowed with that gift, I should have come to grief long ago; I should have stood no chance, a poor man like me. I tell you without flattery, I am sincerely delighted at the friendship I observe between you and my son. I have just seen him; he got up as he usually does—no doubt you are aware of it—very early, and went for a ramble about the neighborhood. Permit me to inquire—have you known my son long?"

"Since last winter."

"Indeed. And permit me to question you further—but hadn't we better sit down? Permit me, as a father, to ask without reserve, what do you think of my Evgeny?"

"Your son is one of the most remarkable men I have ever met," Arkady answered emphatically.

Vassily Ivanovich's eyes suddenly opened wide, and his cheeks were suffused with a faint flush. The spade fell out of his hand.

"And so you expect," he began . . .

"I'm convinced," Arkady put in, "that your son has a great future before him; that he will do honor to your name. I've been certain of that ever since I first met him."

"How . . . how was that?" Vassily Ivanovich articulated with an effort. His wide mouth was relaxed in a triumphant smile, which would not leave it.

"Would you like me to tell you how we met?"

"Yes . . . and altogether. . . ."

Arkady began to tell his tale, and to talk of Bazarov with even greater warmth, even greater enthusiasm than he had done on the evening when he danced the mazurka with Odintsov.

Vassily Ivanovich listened and listened, blew his nose, rolled his handkerchief up into a ball in both his hands, cleared his throat, ruffled up his hair, and at last could stand it no longer; he bent down to Arkady and kissed him on his shoulder. "You have made me completely happy," he said, never ceasing to smile. "I ought to tell you, I . . . idolize my son; I won't speak of my old wife—we all know what mothers are!—but I dare not show my feelings before him, because he doesn't like it. He is averse to every kind of demonstration of feeling; many people even find fault with him for such firmness of character, and regard it as a proof of pride or lack of feeling, but men like him ought not to be judged by the common standard, ought they? And here, for example, many another in his place would have been a constant drag on his parents; but he, would you believe it, has never from the day he was born taken a farthing more than he could help, that's God's truth!"

"He is a disinterested, honest man," observed Arkady.

"Exactly so; he is disinterested. And I don't only idolize him, Arkady Nikolaich, I am proud of him, and the height of my ambition is that some day there will be the following lines in his biography: 'The son of a simple army-doctor, who was, however, capable of divining his greatness betimes, and spared nothing for his education . . .' " The old man's voice broke.

Arkady pressed his hand.

"What do you think," inquired Vassily Ivanovich, after a short silence, "it won't be in medicine that he will attain the celebrity you anticipate for him?"

"Of course not in medicine, though even in that department he will be one of the leading scientific men."

"In what then, Arkady Nikolaich?"

"It would be hard to say now, but he will be famous."

"He will be famous!" repeated the old man, and he sank into a reverie.

"Arina Vasyevna sent me to call you in to tea," announced Anfisushka, coming by with an immense dish of ripe raspberries.

Vassily Ivanovich started. "And will there be cooled cream for the raspberries?"

"Yes, sir."

"Cold now, mind! Don't stand on ceremony, Arkady Nikolaich; take some more. How is it Evgeny doesn't come?"

"I'm here," Bazarov's voice was heard from Arkady's room.

Vassily Ivanovich turned round quickly. "Aha! you wanted to pay a visit to your friend; but you were too late, *amice*, and I have already had a long conversation with him. Now we must go in to tea, mother summons us. By the way, I want to have a little talk with you.

"What about?"

"There's a peasant here; he's suffering from icterus. . . ."

"You mean jaundice?"

"Yes, a chronic and very obstinate case of icterus. I prescribed centaury and St. John's wort, ordered him to eat carrots, and gave him soda; but all that's merely *palliative* measures; we need something more drastic. Though you do laugh at medicine, I am certain you can give me practical advice. But we will talk of that later. Now come in to tea."

Vassily Ivanovich jumped up briskly from the garden seat, and hummed from *Robert le Diable*—[1]

1. A popular opera (1831) by Meyer-beer (1791–1864).

"The rule, the rule we set ourselves,
To live, to live for pleasure!"

"Singular vitality!" observed Bazarov, going away from the window.

It was midday. The sun was burning hot behind a thin veil of unbroken whitish clouds. Everything was hushed; there was no sound but the cocks crowing provocatively at one another in the village, producing in every one who heard them a strange sense of drowsiness and ennui; and somewhere, high up in a tree-top, the incessant plaintive cheep of a young hawk. Arkady and Bazarov lay in the shade of a small haystack, putting under themselves a couple of armfuls of dry and rustling but still greenish and fragrant grass.

"That aspen," began Bazarov, "reminds me of my childhood; it grows at the edge of the clay-pits where the brickshed used to be, and in those days I believed firmly that that clay-pit and aspen possessed a peculiar talismanic power; I never felt bored near them. I did not understand then that I was not bored because I was a child. Well, now I'm grown up, the talisman's lost its power."

"How long did you live here altogether?" asked Arkady.

"Two years on end; then we travelled about. We led a roving life, wandering from town to town for the most part."

"And has this house been standing long?"

"Yes. My grandfather built it—my mother's father."

"Who was he—your grandfather?"

"Devil knows. Some second-major. He served with Suvorov, and was always telling stories about the the crossing of the Alps. He was probably lying."

"So that's why you have a portrait of Suvorov hanging in the drawing-room. I like these little houses like yours; they're so warm and old-fashioned; and there's always a special sort of scent about them."

"A smell of lamp-oil and clover," Bazarov remarked, yawning. "And the flies in those dear little houses. . . . Faugh!"

"Tell me," began Arkady, after a brief pause, "were they strict with you when you were a child?"

'You can see what my parents are like. They're not the strict sort."

"Do you love them, Evgeny?"

"I do, Arkady."

"How they love you!"

Bazarov was silent for a while. "Do you know what I'm thinking about?" he brought out at last, clasping his hands behind his head.

"No. What is it?"

"I'm thinking life is a happy thing for my parents. My father at sixty is fussing around, talking about 'palliative' measures, doctoring people, playing the bountiful master with the peasants—having a fine time, in short; and my mother's happy too; her day's so chockful of duties of all sorts, and sighs and groans that she's no time even to think of herself; while I . . ."

"While you?"

"I think; here I lie under a haystack. . . . The tiny space I occupy is so infinitely small in comparison with the rest of space, in which I am not, and which has nothing to do with me; and the period of time in which it is my lot to live is so petty beside the eternity in which I have not been, and shall not be. . . . And in this atom, this mathematical point, the blood circulates, the brain works and wants something. . . . Isn't it hideous? Isn't it petty?"

"Allow me to remark that what you're saying applies to men in general."

"You are right," Bazarov cut in. "I was going to say that they now—my parents, I mean—are absorbed and don't trouble themselves about their own insignificance, its stench doesn't sicken them . . . while I . . . I feel nothing but weariness and malice."

"Malice? Why malice?"

"Why? How can you ask why? Have you forgotten?"

"I remember everything, but still I don't admit that you have any right to be malicious. You're unlucky, I'll allow, but . . ."

"Pooh! then you, Arkady Nikolaevich, I can see, regard love like all modern young men; cluck, cluck, cluck you call to the hen, but if the hen comes near you, you take to your heels! I'm not like that. But that's enough of that. What can't be helped, it's shameful to talk about." He turned over on his side. "Aha! there goes a valiant ant dragging off a half-dead fly. Take her, brother, take her! Don't pay attention to her resistance; it's your privilege as an animal to be free from the sentiment of pity—make the most of it—not like us conscientious self-destructive animals!"

"You shouldn't say that, Evgeny! When have you destroyed yourself!"

Bazarov raised his head. "That's the only thing I pride myself on. I haven't crushed myself, so a skirt can't crush me. Amen! It's all over! You shall not hear another word from me about it."

Both friends lay for some time in silence.

"Yes," began Bazarov, "man's a strange animal. When one gets a view from the side, sort of, or from a distance at the dull life our 'fathers' lead here, one thinks, What could be better? You eat and drink, and know you are acting in the most reasonable, most judicious manner. But no, ennui will devour you. One wants to have to do with people if only to abuse them."

"One ought so to order one's life that every moment in it should be of significance," Arkady affirmed reflectively.

"I dare say! What's of significance is sweet, however mistaken; one could make up one's mind to what's insignificant even. But pettiness, pettiness, that's what's insufferable."

"Pettiness doesn't exist for a man so long as he refuses to recognise it."

"H'm . . . what you've just said is a 'commonplace in reverse.' "

"What? What do you mean by that term?"

"I'll tell you: to say that education is beneficial, for instance, that's a commonplace; but to say that education is injurious, that's a commonplace in reverse. There's more style about it, so to say, but in reality it's one and the same."

"And the truth is—where, which side?"

"Where? Like an echo I answer, 'Where?' "

"You're in a melancholy mood to-day, Evgeny."

"Really? The sun must have softened me, I suppose, and one shouldn't eat so many raspberries either."

"In that case, a nap's not a bad thing," observed Arkady.

"Certainly; only don't look at me; every man's face is stupid when he's asleep."

"But isn't it all the same to you what people think of you?"

"I don't know what to say to you. A real man ought not to care; a real man is one whom it's no use thinking about, whom one must either obey or hate."

"That's strange! I don't hate anybody," observed Arkady, after a moment's thought.

"And I hate so many. You are a soft-hearted, sluggish creature; how could you hate any one? . . . You're timid; you don't rely on yourself much."

"And you," interrupted Arkady, "do you rely on yourself very much? Do you have a high opinion of yourself?"

Bazarov paused. "When I meet a man who can hold his own beside me," he said, dwelling on every syllable, "then I'll change my opinion of myself. Yes, hatred! You said, for instance, to-day as we passed our bailiff Philip's cottage—it's the one that's so nice and clean—well, you said Russia will attain perfection when the poorest peasant has a hut like that, and every one of us ought to work to bring it about. . . . And I felt such a hatred for this poorest peasant, this Philip or Sidor, for whom I'm to be ready to jump out of my skin, and who won't even thank me for it . . . and what do I need his thanks for? Why, suppose he does live in a clean hut, while the nettles are growing out of me,—well what comes after that?"

"Enough, Evgeny . . . to listen to you to-day one would be driven to agree with those who reproach us for lack of principles."

"You talk like your uncle. There are no general principles—you've not made out that even yet! There are feelings. Everything depends on them."

"How so?"

"Why, just so. Take me, for instance. I maintain a negative attitude, by virtue of my sensations; I like to deny—my brain's made on that plan, and that's all! Why do I like chemistry? Why do you like apples?—also by virtue of our sensations. It's all the same thing. Men will never penetrate deeper than that. Not every one will tell you that, and, in fact, I won't tell you so another time."

"What, and is honesty a matter of the senses?"

"I should say so."

"Evgeny!" Arkady was beginning in a dejected voice . . .

"Well? What? You don't like it?" broke in Bazarov. "No, brother. If you've made up your mind to mow down everything, don't spare your own legs. But we've philosophized enough. 'Nature wafts the silence of sleep,' said Pushkin."

"He never said anything of the sort," protested Arkady.

"Well, if he didn't, as a poet he might have—and ought to have said it. By the way, he must have been a military man."

"Pushkin was never a military man!"

"Why, on every page of him there's, 'To arms! to arms! for Russia's honor!' "

"Why, what stories you invent! I declare, it's outright calumny."

"Calumny? My, what a grave matter! What a word he's found to frighten me with! Whatever charge you make against a man, you may be certain he deserves twenty times worse than that in reality."

"We had better go to sleep," said Arkady, in vexation.

"With the greatest pleasure," answered Bazarov. But neither of them slept. A feeling almost of hostility came over both young men. Five minutes later, they opened their eyes and glanced at one another in silence.

"Look," said Arkady suddenly, "a dry maple leaf has come off and is falling to earth; its movement is exactly like a butterfly's flight. Isn't it strange? Gloom and death—like brightness and life."

"Oh, my friend, Arkady Nikolaich!" cried Bazarov, "one thing

I beg of you; no fine talk."

"I talk as best I can. . . . And, I declare, it's perfect despotism. An idea came into my head; why shouldn't I utter it?"

"Yes; and why shouldn't I utter my ideas? I think that fine talk's positively indecent."

"And what is decent? Abuse?"

"Ha! ha! I see you really do intend to walk in your uncle's footsteps. How pleased that idiot would have been if he had heard you!"

"What did you call Pavel Petrovich?"

"I called him, very justly, an idiot."

"But this is intolerable!" cried Arkady.

"Aha! family feeling spoke there," Bazarov commented coolly. "I've noticed how obstinately it sticks to people. A man's ready to give up everything and break with every prejudice; but to admit, for instance, that his brother, who steals handkerchiefs, is a thief—that's too much for him. And when one comes to think of it: *my* brother, *mine*—and no genius . . . that's an idea no one can swallow."

"It was a simple sense of justice spoke in me and not family feeling at all," retorted Arkady passionately. "But since that's a sense you don't understand, since you haven't that *sensation*, you can't judge it."

"In other words, Arkady Kirsanov is too exalted for my comprehension. I bow down before him and say no more."

"Don't, please, Evgeny; we shall really quarrel at last."

"Ah, Arkady! do me a favor, let's really quarrel for once till we're both laid out dead, until we're destroyed."

"But then perhaps we should end by . . ."

"Fighting?" put in Bazarov. "So what? Here, on the hay, in these idyllic surroundings, far from the world and people's eyes, it wouldn't matter. But you'd be no match for me. I'd have you by the throat in a minute."

Bazarov spread out his long, tough fingers. . . . Arkady turned round and prepared, as though in jest, to resist. . . . But his friend's face struck him as so vindictive—there was such menace in grim earnest in the smile that distorted his lips and in his glittering eyes, that he instinctively felt afraid.

"Ah! so this is where you have got to!" the voice of Vassily Ivanovich was heard at that instant, and the old army-doctor appeared before the young men, garbed in a home-made linen pea-jacket, with a straw hat, also home-made, on his head. "I've been looking and looking for you. . . . Well, you've picked out a capital place, and you're excellently employed. Lying on the 'earth,' gazing up to 'heaven.' Do you know, there's a special significance in that?"

"I never gaze up to heaven except when I want to sneeze," growled Bazarov, and turning to Arkady he added in an undertone. "Pity he interrupted us."

"Well, that's enough," whispered Arkady and stealthily pressed his friend's hand. But no friendship can long survive such collisions.

"I look at you, my youthful friends," Vassily Ivanovich was saying meantime, shaking his head, and leaning his folded arms on some sort of cunningly bent stick of his own making, with a Turk's figure for a top,—"I look, and I cannot refrain from admiration. You have so much strength, such youth in bloom, such abilities, such talents! Positively, Castor and Pollux." [2]

"Get along with you—going off into mythology!" commented Bazarov. "You can see at once that he was a great Latinist in his day! Why, I seem to remember, you gained the silver medal for Latin prose—didn't you?"

"The Dioscuri, the Dioscuri!" repeated Vassily Ivanovich.

"Come, enough, father; don't get sentimental."

"Once in a great while it's surely permissible," murmured the old man. "However, I have not been seeking for you, gentlemen, to pay you compliments; but with the object, in the first place, of announcing to you that we shall soon be dining; and secondly, I wanted to prepare you, Evgeny. . . . You are a sensible man, you know the world, and you know what women are, and consequently you will excuse. . . . Your mother wished to have a Te Deum sung on the occasion of your arrival. You must not imagine that I am inviting you to attend this thanksgiving—it is finished now; but Father Alexey . . ."

"The parson?"

"Well, yes, the priest; he . . . is to dine with us. . . . I did not anticipate this, and did not even approve of it . . . but it somehow came about . . . he did not understand me. . . . And, well . . . Arina Vlasyevna . . . Besides, he's a worthy, reasonable man."

"He won't eat my share at dinner, I suppose?" queried Bazarov.

Vassily Ivanovich laughed. "How you talk!"

"Well, that's all I ask. I'm ready to sit down to table with any man."

Vassily Ivanovich set his hat straight. "I was certain before I spoke," he said, "that you were above any kind of prejudice. Here am I, an old man of sixty-two, and I have none." (Vassily Ivanovich did not dare to confess that he had himself desired the thanksgiving service. He was just as religious as his wife.) "And Father Alexey very much wanted to make your acquaintance. You will like

2. Mythological heroes, sons of Zeus and Leda, inseparable friends. They are the Dioscuri.

him, you'll see. He's no objection even to cards, and he sometimes—but this is between ourselves . . . positively smokes a pipe."

"All right. We'll have a round of whist after dinner, and I'll clean him out."

"He! he! he! We shall see! That remains to be seen."

"What? Are you up to your old tricks?" said Bazarov, with a peculiar emphasis.

Vassily Ivanovich's bronzed cheeks were suffused with an uneasy flush.

"For shame, Evgeny. . . . Let bygones be bygones. Well, I'm ready to acknowledge before this gentleman I had that passion in my youth; and I have paid for it too! How hot it is, though! Let me sit down with you. I won't be in your way, I hope?"

"Oh, not at all," answered Arkady.

Vassily Ivanovich lowered himself, sighing, into the hay. "Your present quarters remind me, my dear sirs," he began, "of my military bivouacking existence, the dressing stations, somewhere like this under a haystack, and we were thankful even for that." He sighed. "I have had many, many experiences in my life. For example, if you will allow me, I will tell you a curious episode of the plague in Bessarabia."

"For which you got the Vladimir cross?" put in Bazarov. "We know, we know. . . . By the way, why is it you're not wearing it?"

"Why, I told you that I have no prejudices," muttered Vassily Ivanovich (he had only the evening before had the red ribbon picked off his coat), and he proceeded to relate the episode of the plague. "Why, he's fallen asleep," he whispered all at once to Arkady, pointing to Evgeny, and winking good-naturedly. "Evgeny! get up," he went on aloud. "Let's go in to dinner."

Father Alexey, a good-looking stout man with thick, carefully combed hair, with an embroidered girdle round his lilac silk cassock, appeared to be a man of much tact and adaptability. He made haste to be the first to offer his hand to Arkady and Bazarov, as though understanding beforehand that they did not want his blessing, and he behaved himself in general without constraint. He neither derogated from his own dignity, nor gave offence to others; he vouchsafed a passing smile at the seminary Latin, and stood up for his bishop; drank two small glasses of wine, but refused a third; accepted a cigar from Arkady, but did not proceed to smoke it, saying he would take it home with him. The only thing not quite agreeable about him was a way he had of constantly raising his hand with care and deliberation to catch the flies on his face, sometimes succeeding in smashing them. He took his seat at the card table, expressing his satisfaction at doing so in measured terms, and ended by winning two and a half rubles from Bazarov in paper money;[3] they had no idea of even reckoning in silver in the house of Arina Vlasyevna. . . . She was sitting, as before, near her son (she did not play cards), her cheek, as before, propped on her little fist; she only got up to order some new dainty to be served. She was afraid to caress Bazarov, and he gave her no encouragement, he did not invite her caresses; and besides, Vassily Ivanovich had advised her not to "worry" him too much. "Young men are not fond of that sort of thing," he declared to her. (It's needless to say what the dinner was like that day; Timofeich in person had galloped off at early dawn for a special variety of Circassian beef; the bailiff had gone off in another direction for turbot, gremille, and crayfish; for mushrooms alone forty-two kopecks had been paid the peasant women in copper); but Arina Vlasyevna's eyes, bent steadfastly on Bazarov, did not express only devotion and tenderness; in them was to be seen sorrow also, mingled with awe and curiosity; there was to be seen too a sort of humble reproachfulness.

Bazarov, however, was in no mood to analyse the exact expression of his mother's eyes; he seldom turned to her, and then only with some short question. Once he asked her for her hand "for luck"; she gently laid her soft, little hand on his rough, broad palm.

"Well," she asked, after waiting a little, "has it been any use?"

"Worse luck than ever," he answered, with a careless laugh.

"He plays too rashly," pronounced Father Alexey, as it were compassionately, and he stroked his beard.

"Napoleon's rule, good Father, Napoleon's rule," put in Vassily Ivanovich, leading an ace.

"It brought him to St. Helena, though," observed Father Alexey, as he trumped the ace.

"Wouldn't you like some currant tea, Enyusha?" inquired Arina Vlasyevna.

Bazarov merely shrugged his shoulders.

"No!" he said to Arkady the next day, "I'm off from here tomorrow. I'm bored; I want to work, but I can't work here. I will come to your place again; I've left all my apparatus there, too. In your house one can at any rate shut oneself up. While here my father repeats to me, 'My study is at your disposal—nobody shall interfere with you,' and all the time he himself is never a step away. And I'm somehow ashamed to shut myself away from him.

3. A silver ruble (roughly 50 cents), the monetary standard, was worth three and a half paper rubles. There are 100 kopeks in either ruble.

It's the same thing, too, with mother. I hear her sighing the other side of the wall, and when I go in to her, there is nothing to say to her."

"She will be very much grieved," observed Arkady, "and so will he."

"I shall come back again to them."

"When?"

"Why, when on my way to Petersburg."

"I feel particularly sorry for your mother."

"Why's that? Has she won your heart with berries or what?"

Arkady dropped his eyes. "You don't understand your mother, Evgeny. She's not only a very good woman, she's very clever really. This morning she talked to me for half-an-hour, and so sensibly, interestingly."

"I suppose she was expatiating upon me all the while?"

"We didn't talk only about you."

"Perhaps; an outsider sees more clearly. If a woman can keep up half-an-hour's conversation it's always a hopeful sign. But I'm going, all the same."

"It won't be very easy for you to break it to them."

"No, it won't be easy. Some demon drove me to tease my father to-day; he had one of his rent-paying peasants flogged the other day, and quite right too—yes, yes, you needn't look at me in such horror—he did quite right, because he's a terrible thief and drunkard; only my father had no idea that I, as they say, was cognizant of the facts. He was very embarrassed, and now, I'll have to upset him more than ever. . . . . Never mind! Never say die! He'll get over it!"

Bazarov said, "Never mind"; but the whole day passed before he could make up his mind to inform Vassily Ivanovich of his intentions. At last, when he was just saying good-night to him in the study, he observed, with a feigned yawn—

"Oh . . . I was almost forgetting to tell you. . . . Send to Fedot's for our horses to-morrow."

Vassily Ivanovich was dumfounded. "Is Mr. Kirsanov leaving us, then?"

"Yes; and I'm going with him."

Vassily Ivanovich positively reeled. "You are going?"

"Yes . . . I must. Make the arrangements about the horses, please."

"Very good. . . ." faltered the old man; "to Fedot's . . . very good . . . only . . . only . . . How is it?"

"I must go to stay with him for a little time. I will come back here again later."

"Ah! For a little time . . . very good." Vassily Ivanovich drew out his handkerchief, and, blowing his nose, doubled up almost to the ground. "Well . . . everything shall be done. I had thought you were to be with us . . . a little longer. Three days. . . . After three years, it's rather little; rather little, Evgeny!"

"But, I tell you, I'm coming back directly. It's necessary for me to go."

"Necessary. . . . Well! Duty before everything. So, you want the horses sent ahead? Very good. Arina and I, of course, did not anticipate this. She has just begged some flowers from a neighbor; she meant to decorate the room for you." (Vassily Ivanovich did not even mention that every morning almost at dawn he took counsel with Timofeich, standing with his bare feet in his slippers, and pulling out one dog's-eared ruble note after another, with trembling fingers, charged him with various purchases, with special reference to good things to eat, and to red wine, which, as far as he could observe, the young men liked very much.) "Freedom is the most important thing; that's my rule. . . . I don't want to hamper you . . . not . . ."

He suddenly ceased, and made for the door.

"We shall soon see each other again, father, really."

But Vassily Ivanovich, without turning round, merely waved his hand and was gone. When he got back to his bedroom he found his wife in bed, and began to say his prayers in a whisper, so as not to wake her up. She woke, however. "Is that you, Vassily Ivanovich?" she asked.

"Yes, mother."

"Have you come from Enyusha? Do you know, I'm afraid of his not being comfortable on that sofa. I told Anfisushka to put him your travelling mattress and the new pillows; I should have given him our feather-bed, but I seem to remember he doesn't like too soft a bed. . . ."

"Never mind, mother; don't worry yourself. He's all right. Lord, have mercy on me, a sinner," he went on with his prayer in a low voice. Vassily Ivanovich was sorry for his old wife; he did not mean to tell her over night what a sorrow there was in store for her.

Bazarov and Arkady set off the next day. From early morning all was dejection in the house; Anfisushka let the tray slip out of her hands; even Fedka was bewildered, and finished by taking off his boots. Vassily Ivanovich was more fussy than ever; he was obviously trying to put on a brave front, talked loudly, and stamped with his feet, but his face looked haggard, and his eyes were continually avoiding his son. Arina Vlasyevna was crying quietly; she was utterly crushed, and could not have controlled herself at all if her husband had not spent two whole hours early in the morning exhorting her. When Bazarov, after repeated promises to come back certainly not later than in a month's time, tore himself at last from the embraces detaining him, and took his seat in the coach; when the horses had started, the bell was ringing, and the wheels were turning round, and when it was no longer any good to look after them, and the dust had settled, and Timofeich, all bent and tottering as he walked, had crept back to his little room; when the old people were left alone in their little house, which seemed suddenly to have shrunken and grown decrepit too, Vassily Ivanovich, after a few more moments of hearty waving of his handkerchief on the porch, sank into a chair, and his head dropped on to his breast. "He has cast us off; he has forsaken us," he faltered; "forsaken us; he was dull with us. All by myself, like a finger, now, all by myself!" he said several times and each time thrust his hand out with the index finger separated from the rest. Then Arina Vlasyevna went up to him, and, leaning her grey head against his grey head, said, "There's no help for it, Vasya! A son is a piece cut off. He's like the falcon that flies home and flies away at his pleasure; while you and I are like mushrooms in the hollow of a tree, we sit side by side, and don't move from our place. Only I remain unchanged for you, forever, as you for me."

Vassily Ivanovich took his hands from his face and clasped his wife, his friend, more firmly than he had clasped her even in his youth; she comforted him in his grief.

XXII

In silence, only rarely exchanging a few insignificant words, our friends travelled as far as Fedot's. Bazarov was not altogether pleased with himself. Arkady was displeased with him. He was feeling, too, that causeless melancholy which is only known to very young people. The coachman changed the horses, and getting up on to the box, inquired, "To the right or to the left?"

Arkady started. The road to the right led to the town, and from there home; the road to the left led to Odintsov's.

He looked at Bazarov.

"Evgeny," he queried; "to the left?"

Bazarov turned away. "What folly is this?" he muttered.

"I know it's folly," answered Arkady. . . . "But what does that matter? It's not the first time."

Bazarov pulled his cap down over his brows. "As you like," he said at last. "Turn to the left," shouted Arkady.

The coach rolled away in the direction of Nikolskoe. But having resolved on folly, the friends were even more obstinately silent than before, and seemed positively angry.

The friends could perceive that they had acted injudiciously in giving way so suddenly to a passing impulse merely by the way the butler met them on the steps of Odintsov's house. They were evidently not expected. They sat for a rather long while, in the drawing-room looking rather foolish. Odintsov came in to them at last. She greeted them with her customary politeness, but was surprised at their hasty return, and, so far as could be judged from the deliberation of her gestures and words, she was not over-pleased at it. They hastened to announce that they had only called on their way, and had to go farther, to the town, within four hours. She confined herself to a slight exclamation, begged Arkady to remember her to his father, and sent for her aunt. The princess appeared very sleepy, which gave her wrinkled old face an even more ill-natured expression. Katya was not well; she did not leave her room. Arkady suddenly realised that he was at least as anxious to see Katya as Anna Sergeyevna herself. The four hours were spent in insignificant discussion of one thing and another; Anna Sergeyevna both listened and spoke without a smile. It was only at the very parting that her former friendliness seemed, as it were, to revive.

"I have an attack of spleen just now," she said; "but you must not pay attention to that, and come again—I say this to both of you—some time later."

Both Bazarov and Arkady responded with a silent bow, took their seats in the coach, and without stopping again anywhere went straight home to Marino, where they arrived safely on the evening of the following day. During the whole course of the journey neither one nor the other even mentioned the name of Odintsov; Bazarov in particular scarcely opened his mouth, and kept staring to the side away from the road, with a kind of exasperated intensity.

At Marino every one was exceedingly delighted to see them. The prolonged absence of his son had begun to make Nikolai Petrovich uneasy; he uttered a cry of joy, and bounced up and down on the sofa, dangling his legs, when Fenichka ran to him with sparkling eyes, and informed him of the arrival of the "young gentlemen"; even Pavel Petrovich was conscious of some degree of agreeable excitement, and smiled condescendingly as he shook hands with the returned wanderers. Talk and questions followed; Arkady talked most, especially at supper, which was prolonged long after midnight. Nikolai Petrovich ordered up several bottles of porter which had just been sent from Moscow, and himself went on such a spree that his cheeks were crimson, and he kept laughing a half-childish, half-nervous little chuckle. Even the servants were infected by the general gaiety. Dunyasha ran up and down like one possessed, and was continually slamming doors; while Peter was still attempting to strum a Cossack waltz on the guitar after two in the morning. The strings gave forth a sweet and plaintive sound in the still air; but with the exception of a small preliminary flourish, nothing came of the cultured valet's efforts; nature had given him no more musical talent than it had anything else.

Yet things were not going overharmoniously at Marino, and poor Nikolai Petrovich was having a bad time. Difficulties on the farm multiplied every day, dreary senseless difficulties. Trouble with the hired laborers had become insupportable. Some asked for their wages to be settled or for an increase of wages, while others made off with the wages they had received in advance; the horses fell sick; the harness fell to pieces as though it were burnt, the work was done carelessly; a threshing machine that had been ordered from Moscow turned out to be useless because of its great weight, another was ruined the first time it was used; half the cattle sheds were burnt down through an old blind woman on the farm going with a burning brand in windy weather to fumigate her cow . . . the old woman, it is true, maintained that the whole mischief could be traced to the master's plan of introducing newfangled cheeses and dairy-products. The overseer suddenly turned lazy and began to grow fat, as every Russian grows fat when he gets a snug berth. When he caught sight of Nikolai Petrovich in the distance, he would fling a stick at a passing pig or threaten a half-naked urchin to show his zeal, but the rest of the time he was generally asleep. The peasants who had been put on the quitrent system did not bring their money at the time due and stole the forest-timber; almost every night the keepers caught peasants' horses in the meadows of the "farm," and sometimes forcibly bore them off. Nikolai Petrovich first set a monetary fine for damages, but the matter usually ended after the horses had been kept a day or two on the master's forage by their returning to their owners. To top it all, the peasants began quarrelling among themselves; brothers asked for a division of property, their wives could not get on together in one house; all of a sudden the squabble, as though at a given signal, came to a head, and they would come running to the counting-house steps, and crawling to the master, often drunken and with battered face, demanding justice and judgment; then arose an uproar and clamor, the shrill wailing of the women mixed with the curses of the men. Then one had to examine the contending parties, and shout oneself hoarse, knowing all the while that one could never anyway arrive at a just decision. . . . There were not hands enough for the harvest; a neighboring petty landowner with the most benevolent countenance contracted to supply him with reapers for a commission of two rubles an acre, and cheated him in the most shameless fashion; his peasant women demanded unheard-of sums, and the corn meanwhile went to waste; and here they were not getting on with the mowing, and there the Council of Guardians threatened and demanded prompt payment, in full, of interest due. . . .

"I can do nothing!" Nikolai Petrovich cried more than once in despair. "I can't flog them myself, and as for calling in the police captain, my principles don't allow it, but you can do nothing with them without the fear of punishment!"

"*Du calme, du calme,*" Pavel Petrovich would remark to this, but even he hummed to himself, frowning and tugged at his moustache.

Bazarov held aloof from these "wranglings," and indeed as a guest it was not for him to meddle in other people's business. The day after his arrival at Marino, he set to work on his frogs, his infusoria, and his chemical compositions, and was forever busy with them. Arkady, on the contrary, thought it his duty, if not to help his father, at least to make a show of being ready to help him. He listened to him patiently, and once offered him some advice, not with any idea of its being acted upon, but to show his interest. Farming did not arouse any aversion in him; he used even to dream with pleasure of agricultural work, but at this time his brain was swarming with other ideas. Arkady, to his own astonishment, thought incessantly of Nikolskoe; in former days he would simply have shrugged his shoulders if any one had told him that he could ever feel dull under the same roof as Bazarov—and that roof his father's! But he actually was dull and longed to get away. He tried to go on long walks till he was tired, but that was no use. In conversation with his father one day, he found out that Nikolai Petrovich had in his possession rather interesting letters, written by Odintsov's mother to his wife, and he gave him no rest till he got hold of the letters, for which Nikolai Petrovich had to rummage in twenty different drawers and boxes. Having gained possession of these half-crumbling papers, Arkady felt soothed, as it were, just as though he had caught a glimpse of the goal towards which he ought now to go. "I mean that for both of you," he was constantly whispering—she had added that herself! "I'll go, I'll go, hang it all!" but he recalled the last visit, the cold reception, and his former embarrassment and timidity got the better of him. The "go-ahead" feeling of youth, the secret desire to try his luck, to prove his own worth without the protection of any one whatever, finally won out. Before ten days had passed after his return to Marino, on the pretext of studying the working of the Sunday schools, he galloped off to town again, and from there to Nikolskoe. Constantly urging the driver on, he flew along, like a young officer riding to battle; and he felt both frightened and light-hearted, and was breathless with impatience. "The chief thing is—one mustn't think," he kept repeating to himself. His driver happened to be a lad of spirit; he halted before every public house, saying, "A drink or not a drink?" but, to make up for it, when he had drunk he did not spare his horses. At last the lofty roof of the familiar house came in sight. . . . "What am I doing?" flashed through Arkady's head. "Well, there's no turning back now!" The three horses galloped in unison; the driver whooped and whistled at them. And now the bridge was groaning under the hoofs and wheels, and now the avenue of pruned pines seemed running to meet them. . . . There was a glimpse of a woman's pink dress against the dark green, a young face peeped out from under the light fringe of a parasol. . . . He recognised Katya, and she recognised him. Arkady told the driver to stop the galloping horses, leaped out of the carriage, and went up to her. "It's you!" she murmured, gradually flushing all over; "let us go to my sister, she's here in the garden; she will be pleased to see you."

Katya led Arkady into the garden. His meeting with her struck him as a particularly happy omen; he was as delighted to see her, as though she were very close to him. Everything had happened so splendidly; no butler, no formal announcement. At a turn in the path he caught sight of Anna Sergeyevna. She was standing with her back to him. Hearing footsteps, she turned slowly round.

Arkady began to feel confused again, but the first words she uttered soothed him at once. "Welcome back, runaway!" she said in her even, caressing voice, and came to meet him, smiling and squinting, frowning to keep the sun and wind out of her eyes. "Where did you pick him up, Katya?"

"I have brought you something, Anna Sergeyevna," he began, "which you certainly don't expect."

"You have brought yourself; that's best of all."

XXIII

Having seen Arkady off with ironical compassion, and given him to understand that he was not in the least deceived as to the real object of his journey, Bazarov shut himself up in complete solitude; he was overtaken by a fever for work. He did not dispute now with Pavel Petrovich, especially as the latter assumed an excessively aristocratic demeanor in his presence, and expressed his opinions more in inarticulate sounds than in words. Only on one occasion Pavel Petrovich fell into a controversy with the *nihilist* on the subject of the question then much discussed of the rights of the nobles of the Baltic province; but suddenly he stopped of his own accord, remarking with chilly politeness, "However, we cannot understand one another; I, at least, have not the honor of understanding you."

"I should think not!" cried Bazarov. "A man's capable of understanding anything—how the ether vibrates, and what's going on in the sun—but how any other man can blow his nose differently from him, that he's incapable of understanding."

"What, is that supposed to be clever?" observed Pavel Petrovich inquiringly, and he went off to one side.

However, he sometimes asked permission to be present at Bazarov's experiments, and once even placed his perfumed face, washed with the very best soap, to the microscope to see how a transparent infusoria swallowed a green speck, and busily munched it with two very rapid sort of clappers which were in its throat. Nikolai Petrovich visited Bazarov much oftener than his brother; he would have come every day, as he expressed it, to "study," if his worries on the farm had not kept him too busy. He did not hinder the young scientist; he would sit down somewhere in a corner of the room and look on attentively, occasionally permitting himself a discreet question. During dinner and supper he would try to turn the conversation to physics, geology, or chemistry, seeing that all other topics, even agriculture, to say nothing of politics might lead, if not to collisions, at least to mutual unpleasantness. Nikolai Petrovich surmised that his brother's dislike for Bazarov had not diminished at all. An unimportant incident, among many others, confirmed his surmises. Cholera began to appear here and there in the neighborhood, and even "carried off" two persons from Marino itself. One night Pavel Petrovich had a rather severe attack. He was in torment till morning, but did not have recourse to Bazarov's skill. And when he met him the following day, in reply to his question, "Why he had not sent for him?" answered, still quite pale, but scrupulously brushed and shaved, "Why, I seem to recollect you said yourself you didn't believe in medicine." So the days went by. Bazarov went on working obstinately and grimly . . . and meanwhile there was in Nikolai Petrovich's house one creature to whom, if he did not open his heart he at least was glad to talk. . . . That creature was Fenichka.

He used to meet her for the most part early in the morning, in the garden, or the yard; he never went to her room to see her, and she had only once been to his door to inquire—ought she to let Mitya have his bath or not? It was not only that she confided in him, that she was not afraid of him—she was positively freer and more at her ease in her behavior with him than with Nikolai Petrovich himself. It is hard to say how it came about; perhaps it was because she unconsciously felt the absence in Bazarov of anything aristocratic, of all that superiority which at once attracts and frightens. In her eyes he was both an excellent doctor and a simple man. She looked after her baby without constraint in his presence; and once when she was suddenly attacked with giddiness and headache, she took a spoonful of medicine from his hand. Before Nikolai Petrovich she kept, as it were, at a distance from Bazarov; she acted in this way not from hypocrisy, but from a kind of feeling of propriety. She was more afraid of Pavel Petrovich than ever; for some time he had begun to watch her, and would suddenly make his appearance, as though he sprang out of the earth behind her back, in his English suit, with his immovable vigilant face, and his hands in his pockets. "It's like being doused with cold water," Fenichka complained to Dunyasha, and the latter sighed in response, and thought of another "heartless" man. Bazarov, without the least suspicion of the fact, had become the *cruel tyrant* of her heart.

Fenichka liked Bazarov; but he liked her too. His face was positively transformed when he talked to her; it assumed a bright, almost kind expression, and his habitual nonchalance was replaced by a sort of jesting attentiveness. Fenichka was growing prettier every day. There is a time in the life of young women when they suddenly begin to expand and blossom like summer roses; this time had come for Fenichka. Everything furthered it, even the prevailing July heat. Dressed in a light white dress, she herself seemed lighter and whiter; she was not tanned by the sun; while the heat, from which she could not shield herself, spread a slight flush over her cheeks and ears, and, shedding a soft indolence over her whole body, was reflected in a dreamy languor in her pretty eyes. She was almost unable to work; her hands seemed to fall naturally into her lap. She scarcely walked at all, and was constantly sighing and complaining with comic helplessness.

"You should go swimming more often," Nikolai Petrovich told her. He had made a large bathing place covered in with an awning in one of his ponds which had not yet quite dried up.

"Oh, Nikolai Petrovich! By the time one gets to the pond, one's utterly dead, and, coming back, one's dead again. You see, there's no shade in the garden."

"That's true, there's no shade," replied Nikolai Petrovich, rubbing his forehead.

One day at seven o'clock in the morning, Bazarov, returning from a walk, came upon Fenichka in the lilac arbor, which was long past flowering, but was still thick and green. She was sitting on the garden seat, and had as usual thrown a white kerchief over her head; near her lay a whole heap of red and white roses still wet with dew. He said good morning to her.

"Ah! Evgeny Vassilyich!" she said, and lifted the edge of her kerchief a little to look at him, in doing which her arm was bared to the elbow.

"What are you doing here?" said Bazarov, sitting down beside her. "Are you making a bouquet?"

"Yes, for the table at lunch. Nikolai Petrovich likes it."

"But it's a long while yet to lunch time. What a heap of flowers!"

"I gathered them now, because it will be hot then, and one can't go out. This is the only time you can breathe. I feel quite weak from the heat. I'm really afraid that I'm going to be ill."

"What an idea! Let me feel your pulse." Bazarov took her hand, felt for the evenly beating pulse, but did not even begin to count its throbs. "You'll live a hundred years!" he said, dropping her hand.

"Ah, God forbid!" she cried.

"Why? Don't you want a long life?"

"Well, but a hundred years! We had a grandmother of eighty-five—and what a martyr she was! Black, deaf, bent, and coughing all the time; nothing but a burden to herself. That's a dreadful life!"

"So it's better to be young?"

"Well, isn't it?"

"But why is it better? Tell me!"

"How can you ask why? Why, while I'm young, I can do everything—go and come and carry, and needn't ask any one for anything. . . . What can be better?"

"And to me it's all the same whether I'm young or old."

"How do you say—it's all the same? What you say is impossible."

"Well, judge for yourself, Fedosya Nikolaevna, what good is my youth to me. I live alone, a poor wretch . . ."

"That always depends on you."

"It doesn't all depend on me! At least, some one ought to take pity on me."

Fenichka glanced sidelong at Bazarov, but said nothing. "What's this book you have?" she asked after a short pause.

"That? That's a scientific book, very difficult."

"And are you still studying? And don't you find it dull? You know everything already, I should say."

"It seems not everything. You try to read a little."

"But I don't understand anything here. Is it Russian?" asked Fenichka, taking the heavily bound book in both hands. "How thick it is!"

"Yes, it's Russian."

"All the same, I won't understand anything."

"Well, I didn't give it to you for you to understand it. I wanted to look at you while you were reading. When you read, the end of your little nose moves so nicely."

Fenichka, who had set to work to spell out in a low voice the article on "Creosote" she had chanced upon, laughed and threw down the book . . . it slipped from the seat to the ground.

"I like it, too, when you laugh," observed Bazarov.

"Nonsense!"

"I like it when you talk. It's just like a little brook babbling."

Fenichka turned her head away. "What a person you are to talk!" she commented, picking the flowers over with her finger. "And how can you care to listen to me? You have talked with such clever ladies."

"Ah, Fedosya Nikolaevna, believe me; all the clever ladies in the world are not worth your little elbow."

"Come, there's another invention!" murmured Fenichka, clasping her hands.

Bazarov picked the book up from the ground.

"That's a medical book; why did you throw it away?"

"Medical?" repeated Fenichka, and she turned to him again. "Do you know, ever since you gave me those drops—do you remember?—Mitya has slept so well! I really can't think how to thank you; you are so good, really."

"But you have to pay doctors," observed Bazarov with a smile. "Doctors, you know yourself, are grasping people."

Fenichka raised her eyes, which seemed still darker from the whitish reflection cast on the upper part of her face, and looked at Bazarov. She did not know whether he was joking or not.

"If you please, we shall be delighted. . . . I must ask Nikolai Petrovich . . ."

"Why, do you think I want money?" Bazarov interrupted. "No; I don't want money from you."

"What then?" asked Fenichka.

"What?" repeated Bazarov. "Guess!"

"A likely person I am to guess!"

"Well, I'll tell you; I want . . . one of those roses."

Fenichka laughed again, and even clapped her hands, so amusing Bazarov's request seemed to her. She laughed, and at the same time felt flattered. Bazarov was looking intently at her.

"By all means," she said at last; and bending down to the seat, she began picking over the roses. "Which will you have—a red or white one?"

"Red—and not too large."

She sat up again. "Here, take it," she said, but at once drew back her outstretched hand, and, biting her lips looked towards the entrance of the arbor, then listened.

"What is it?" asked Bazarov. "Nikolai Petrovich?"

"No . . . He went to the fields . . . besides, I'm not afraid of him . . . but Pavel Petrovich . . . I fancied . . ."

"What?"

"I fancied he was coming here. No . . . it was no one. Take it." Fenichka gave Bazarov the rose.

"Why are you afraid of Pavel Petrovich?"

"He always scares me. It's not what he says but he has a way of looking knowingly. And I know you don't like him. Do you remember, you always used to quarrel with him? I don't know what your quarrel was about, but I could see you turn him about like this and like that."

Fenichka showed with her hands how in her opinion Bazarov turned Pavel Petrovich about.

Bazarov smiled. "But if he were to get the upper hand," he asked, "would you stand up for me?"

"How could I stand up for you? But no, no one will get the better of you."

"Do you think so? But I know a hand which could overcome me if it liked."

"What hand?"

"Why, don't you know, really? Smell, how delicious this rose smells you gave me."

Fenichka stretched her little neck forward, and put her face close to the flower. . . . The kerchief slipped from her head on to her shoulders; her soft mass of dark, shining, slightly ruffled hair was visible.

"Wait a minute; I want to smell it with you," said Bazarov. He bent down and kissed her vigorously on her parted lips.

She started, pushed him back with both her hands on his breast, but pushed feebly, and he was able to renew and prolong his kiss.

A dry cough was heard behind the lilac bushes. Fenichka instantly moved away to the other end of the seat. Pavel Petrovich showed himself, made a slight bow, and saying with a sort of malicious despondence, "You are here," he retreated. Fenichka at once gathered up all her roses and went out of the arbor. "It was wrong of you, Evgeny Vassilyich," she whispered as she went. There was a note of genuine reproach in her whisper.

Bazarov remembered another recent scene, and he felt both shame and contemptuous annoyance. But he at once shook his head, ironically congratulated himself "on his formal assumption of the part of the gay Lothario," and went off to his own room.

Pavel Petrovich went out of the garden, and made his way with deliberate steps to the copse. He stayed there rather a long while; and when he returned to lunch, Nikolai Petrovich inquired anxiously whether he were quite well—his face looked so gloomy.

"You know, I sometimes suffer bilious attacks," Pavel Petrovich answered tranquilly.

XXIV

Two hours later he knocked at Bazarov's door.

"I must apologize for hindering you in your scientific pursuits," he began, seating himself on a chair near the window, and leaning with both hands on a handsome walking-stick with an ivory knob (he usually walked without a stick), "But I am constrained to beg you to spare me five minutes of your time . . . no more."

"All my time is at your disposal," answered Bazarov, over whose face there passed a quick change of expression as soon as Pavel Petrovich crossed the threshold.

"Five minutes will be enough for me. I have come to put a single question to you."

"A question? What is it about?

"I will tell you, if you will kindly hear me out. At the commencement of your stay in my brother's house, before I had denied myself the pleasure of conversing with you, I heard your opinions on many subjects; but so far as my memory serves, neither between us, nor in my presence, was the subject of single combats and duelling in general broached. Allow me to hear what are your views on that subject?"

Bazarov, who had risen to meet Pavel Petrovich, sat down on the edge of the table and folded his arms.

"My view is," he said, "that from the theoretical standpoint, duelling is absurd; from the practical standpoint, now—it's quite a different matter."

"That is, you mean to say, if I understand you right, that whatever your theoretical views on duelling, you would not in practice allow yourself to be insulted without demanding satisfaction?"

"You have guessed my meaning absolutely."

"Very good sir. I am very glad to hear you say so. Your words relieve me from a state of uncertainty."

"Of indecision, you mean to say."

"That is all the same, sir; I express myself so as to be understood; I . . . am not a seminary rat. Your words save me from a rather deplorable necessity. I have made up my mind to fight you."

Bazarov opened his eyes wide. "Me?"

"Absolutely."

"But what for, pray?"

"I could explain the reason to you," began Pavel Petrovich, "but I prefer to be silent about it. To my taste, your presence here is superfluous; I cannot endure you; I despise you; and if that is not enough for you . . ."

Pavel Petrovich's eyes glittered . . . Bazarov's, too, were flashing.

"Very well, sir," he assented. "No need for further explanations. You have taken a notion to try your chivalrous spirit upon me. I might refuse you this pleasure, but—so be it!"

"I am sensible of my obligation to you," replied Pavel Petrovich; "and may reckon then on your accepting my challenge without compelling me to resort to violent measures."

"That means, speaking without allegories, to that stick?" Bazarov remarked coolly. "That is precisely correct. It's quite unnecessary for you to insult me. As a matter of fact, it would not be quite safe. You may remain a gentleman. . . . I accept your challenge, too, like a gentleman."

"Excellent," observed Pavel Petrovich, putting his stick in the corner. "We will say a few words directly about the conditions of our duel; but I should like first to know whether you think it necessary to resort to the formality of a trifling dispute, which might serve as a pretext for my challenge?"

"No; it's better without formalities."

"I think so myself. I presume it is also out of place to go into the real grounds of our difference. We cannot endure one another. What more is necessary?"

"What more, indeed?" repeated Bazarov ironically.

"As regards the conditions of the meeting itself, seeing that we shall have no seconds—for where could we get them?"

"Exactly so; where could we get them?"

"Then I have the honor to lay the following proposition before you: The combat to take place early to-morrow, at six, let us say, behind the copse, with pistols, at a distance of ten paces . . ."

"At ten paces? [4] That will do; we hate one another at that distance."

"We might have it eight," remarked Pavel Petrovich.

"We might, why not?"

"To fire twice; and, to be ready for any result, let each put a letter in his pocket, in which he accuses himself of his end."

"Now, that I don't approve of at all," observed Bazarov. "There's a slight flavor of the French novel about it, something not very plausible."

4. The distance indicates that Pavel means this duel to result in one of the combatants' death. Twelve paces would be adequate even for a very serious duel. It represents the final line to which an adversary may advance before firing, though he may fire at any time while approaching it.

"Perhaps. You will agree, however, that it would be unpleasant to incur a suspicion of murder?"

"I agree. But there is a means of avoiding that painful reproach. We shall have no seconds, but we can have a witness."

"And whom, allow me to inquire?"

"Why, Peter."

"What Peter?"

"Your brother's valet. He's a man who has attained the acme of contemporary culture, and he will perform his part with all the *comme il faut* necessary in such cases."

"I believe you are joking, sir."

"Not at all. If you think over my suggestion, you will be convinced that it's full of common sense and simplicity. You can't hide a candle under a bushel; but I'll undertake to prepare Peter in a fitting manner, and bring him on to the field of battle."

"You persist in jesting," Pavel Petrovich declared, getting up from his chair. "But after the courteous readiness you have shown me, I have no right to pretend to lie down. . . . And so, everything is arranged. . . . By the way, perhaps you have no pistols?"

"Why should I have pistols, Pavel Petrovich? I'm not a warrior."

"In that case, I offer you mine. You may rest assured that it's five years now since I shot with them."

"That's a very consoling piece of news."

Pavel Petrovich took up his stick. . . . "And now, my dear sir, it only remains for me to thank you and to leave you to your studies. I have the honor to take leave of you."

"Till we have the pleasure of meeting again, my very dear sir," said Bazarov, conducting his visitor to the door.

Pavel Petrovich went out, while Bazarov remained standing a minute before the door, and suddenly exclaimed, "Well, I'll be damned! How fine, and how foolish! A pretty farce we've been through! Like trained dogs dancing on their hind-paws. But to decline was out of the question; why, I do believe he'd have struck me, and then . . ." (Bazarov turned white at the very thought; all his pride was up in arms at once)—"then it might have come to my strangling him like a kitten." He returned to his microscope, but his heart was beating and the composure necessary for making observations had disappeared. "He caught sight of us today," he thought; "but would he really act like this on his brother's account? And as if a kiss were so important. There must be something else in it. Bah! isn't he perhaps in love with her himself? To be sure, he's in love himself; of course he's in love; it's as clear as day. What a complication! It's a nuisance!" he decided at last; "it's bad any way you look at it. In the first place, to risk a bullet through one's brains, and in any case to go away; and then Arkady . . . and that ladybug, Nikolai Petrovich. It's a bad job."

The day passed in a kind of peculiar stillness and languor. Fenichka gave no sign of her existence; she sat in her little room like a mouse in its hole. Nikolai Petrovich had a careworn air. He had just heard that blight had begun to appear in his wheat, upon which he had in particular rested his hopes. Pavel Petrovich overwhelmed every one, even Prokofich, with his icy courtesy. Bazarov began a letter to his father, but tore it up, and threw it under the table.

"If I die," he thought, "they will find it out; but I'm not going to die. No, I shall struggle along in this world a good while yet." He gave Peter orders to come to him on important business the next morning as soon as it was light. Peter imagined that he wanted to take him to Petersburg with him. Bazarov went to bed late, and all night long he was harassed by disordered dreams . . . Odintsov kept appearing in them, now she was his mother, and she was followed by a kitten with black whiskers, and this kitten seemed to be Fenichka; then Pavel Petrovich took the shape of a big forest with which he had to fight anyway. Peter woke him up at four o'clock; he dressed at once, and went out with him.

It was a lovely, fresh morning; tiny flecked clouds hovered overhead like little lambs in the pale clear blue; a fine dew lay in drops on the leaves and grass, and sparkled like silver on the spiders' webs; the damp, dark earth seemed still to keep traces of the rosy dawn; from the whole sky poured the songs of larks. Bazarov walked as far as the copse, sat down in the shade at its edge, and only then disclosed to Peter the nature of the service he expected of him. The refined valet was scared to death; but Bazarov soothed him by the assurance that he would have nothing to do but stand at a distance and look on, and that he would not incur any sort of responsibility. "And meantime," he added, "only think what an important part you have to play!" Peter threw up his hands, looked down, and leaned against a birch-tree, his face turning green.

The road from Marino skirted the copse; a light dust lay on it, untouched by wheel or foot since the previous day. Bazarov unconsciously stared along this road, picked and gnawed a blade of grass, while he kept repeating to himself, "What a piece of foolery!" The chill of the early morning made him shiver twice. . . . Peter looked at him dejectedly, but Bazarov only smiled; he was not afraid.

The tramp of horses' hoofs was heard along the road. . . . A peasant came into sight from behind the trees. He was driving before him two horses hobbled together, and as he passed Bazarov he looked at him rather strangely, without doffing his cap, which it was easy to see disturbed Peter, as an unlucky omen. "There's some one else up early too," thought Bazarov; "but he at least got up for work, while we . . ."

"I think he's coming, sir," Peter whispered suddenly.

Bazarov raised his head and saw Pavel Petrovich. Dressed in a light check jacket and snow-white trousers, he was walking rapidly along the road; under his arm he carried a box wrapped up in green cloth.

"I beg your pardon, I believe I have kept you waiting," he observed, bowing first to Bazarov, then to Peter, whom he treated respectfully at that instant, as representing something in the nature of a second. "I was unwilling to wake my man."

"It doesn't matter, sir," answered Bazarov; "we've only just arrived ourselves."

"Ah! so much the better!" Pavel Petrovich took a look round. "There's no one in sight; no one hinders us. We can proceed?"

"Let us proceed."

"You do not, I presume, desire any fresh explanations?"

"No, I don't."

"Would you like to load?" inquired Pavel Petrovich, taking the pistols out of the box.

"No; you load, and I will measure out the paces. My legs are longer," added Bazarov with a smile. "One, two, three."

"Evgeny Vassilyich," Peter babbled with an effort (he was shaking as though he were in a fever), "say what you like, I am going farther off."

"Four . . . five . . . Move away, my good fellow, move away; you may get behind a tree even, and stop up your ears, only don't shut your eyes; and if any one falls, run and pick him up. Six . . . seven . . . eight . . ." Bazarov stopped. "Is that enough?" he said, turning to Pavel Petrovich; "or shall I add two paces more?"

"As you like," replied the latter, pressing down the second bullet.

"Well, we'll add two more paces." Bazarov drew a line on the ground with the toe of his boot. "There's the barrier then. By the way, how many paces may each of us go back from the barrier? That's an important question too. That point was not discussed yesterday."

"I imagine, ten," replied Pavel Petrovich, handing Bazarov both pistols. "Will you be so good as to choose?"

"I will be so good. But, Pavel Petrovich, you must admit our combat is singular to the point of absurdity. Only look at the countenance of our second."

"You are disposed to laugh at everything," answered Pavel

Petrovich. "I acknowledge the strangeness of our duel, but I think it my duty to warn you that I intend to fight seriously. *A bon entendeur, salut!*" [5]

"Oh! I don't doubt that we've made up our minds to make away with each other; but why not laugh too and unite *utile dulci?* [6] You talk to me in French, while I talk to you in Latin."

"I am going to fight in earnest," repeated Pavel Petrovich, and he walked off to his place. Bazarov on his side counted off ten paces from the barrier, and stood still.

"Are you ready?" asked Pavel Petrovich.

"Perfectly."

"We can approach one another."

Bazarov moved slowly forward, and Pavel Petrovich, his left hand thrust in his pocket, walked towards him, gradually raising the muzzle of his pistol. . . . "He's aiming straight at my nose," thought Bazarov, "and doesn't he blink down it carefully, the ruffian! Not an agreeable sensation, though. I'm going to look at his watch chain."

Something whizzed sharply by his very ear, and at the same instant there was the sound of a shot. "I heard it, so it must be all right," had time to flash through Bazarov's brain. He took one more step, and without taking aim pressed the trigger.

Pavel Petrovich gave a slight start, and clutched at his thigh. A stream of blood began to trickle down his white trousers.

Bazarov flung aside the pistol, and went up to his antagonist. "Are you wounded?" he said.

"You had the right to call me up to the barrier," said Pavel Petrovich, "the wound is a trifle. According to our agreement, each of us has the right to one more shot."

"Well, excuse me, that'll do for another time," answered Bazarov, catching hold of Pavel Petrovich, who was beginning to turn pale. "Now I'm not a duellist but a doctor, and I must have a look at your wound before anything else. Peter, come here, Peter, where have you gone to?"

"That's all nonsense . . . I need no one's aid," Pavel Petrovich declared jerkily, "and . . . we must . . . again . . ." He tried to pull at his moustache, but his hand failed him, his eyes grew dim, and he lost consciousness.

"Here's something new! A fainting fit! What next!" Bazarov cried involuntarily, as he laid Pavel Petrovich on the grass. "Let's have a look at what's wrong." He pulled out a handkerchief, wiped away the blood, and began feeling round the wound. . . . "The bone's not touched," he muttered through his teeth; "the bullet

5. "May he who has ears listen."
6. "The pleasant to the useful" (Horace, *Ars poetica*).

went through but not too deep; one muscle, *vastus externus,* grazed. He'll be dancing about in three weeks! . . . And to faint! Oh, these nervous people, how I hate them! Look, what a delicate skin!"

"Is he killed?" the quavering voice of Peter came rustling behind his back.

Bazarov looked round. "Go for some water as quick as you can, my good fellow, and he'll outlive us yet."

But the perfected servant apparently did not understand his words, and did not stir. Pavel Petrovich slowly opened his eyes. "He is dying!" whispered Peter, and he began crossing himself.

"You are right. . . . What an imbecile countenance!" remarked the wounded gentleman with a forced smile.

"Well, go for the water, damn you!" shouted Bazarov.

"No need. . . . It was a momentary *vertige.* . . . Help me to sit up. . . . there, that's right. . . . I only need something to bind up this scratch, and I can reach home on foot, or else you can send a droshky for me. The duel, if you are willing, shall not be renewed. You have behaved honorably . . . to-day, to-day—observe."

"There's no need to recall the past," rejoined Bazarov; "and as regards the future, it's not worth while for you to trouble your head about that either, for I intend being off without delay. Let me bind up your leg now; your wound's not serious, but it's always best to stop bleeding. But first I must bring this corpse to his senses."

Bazarov shook Peter by the collar, and sent him for a droshky.

"Mind, you don't frighten my brother," Pavel Petrovich said to him; "don't dream of informing him."

Peter flew off; and while he was running for a droshky, the two antagonists sat on the ground and said nothing. Pavel Petrovich tried not to look at Bazarov; he did not want to be reconciled to him in any case; he was ashamed of his own haughtiness, of his failure; he was ashamed of the whole position he had brought about, even while he felt it could not have ended in a more favorable manner. "At any rate, he won't be hanging around," he consoled himself by reflecting, "and that's something to be thankful for." The silence continued, a distressing and awkward silence. Both of them were ill at ease. Each was conscious that the other understood him. That is pleasant to friends, and very unpleasant to those who are not friends, especially when it is impossible either to have things out or to separate.

"Have I bound up your leg too tight?" inquired Bazarov at last.

"No, not at all; it's splendid," answered Pavel Petrovich; and after a brief pause, he added, "There's no deceiving my brother; we shall have to tell him we quarrelled over politics."

"Very good," assented Bazarov. "You can say I insulted all Anglomaniacs."

"That will do splendidly. What do you imagine that man thinks of us now?" continued Pavel Petrovich, pointing to the same peasant who had driven the hobbled horses past Bazarov a few minutes before the duel, and going back again along the road, took off his cap at the sight of the "masters."

"Who knows?" answered Bazarov. "It is quite likely he thinks nothing. The Russian peasant is that mysterious stranger about whom Mrs. Radcliffe [7] used to talk so much. Who is to understand him! He doesn't understand himself!"

"Ah! so that's your idea!" Pavel Petrovich began; and suddenly he cried, "Look what your fool of a Peter has done! Here's my brother galloping up to us!"

Bazarov turned round and saw the pale face of Nikolai Petrovich, who was sitting in the droshky. He jumped out of it before it had stopped, and rushed up to his brother.

"What does this mean?" he said in an agitated voice. "Evgeny Vassilyich, please, what is this?"

"Nothing," answered Pavel Petrovich; "you have been alarmed for nothing. I had a little dispute with Mr. Bazarov, and I have had to pay for it a little."

"But what was it all about, for God's sake!"

"How can I tell you? Mr. Bazarov alluded disrespectfully to Sir Robert Peel. I must hasten to add that I am the only person to blame in all this, while Mr. Bazarov has behaved most honorably. I called him out."

"But you're covered with blood, good heavens!"

"Well, did you suppose I had water in my veins? But this bloodletting is positively beneficial to me. Isn't that so, doctor? Help me to get into the droshky, and don't give way to melancholy. I shall be quite well to-morrow. That's it; splendid. Drive on, coachman."

Nikolai Petrovich walked after the droshky; Bazarov remained where he was. . . .

"I must ask you to look after my brother," Nikolai Petrovich said to him, "till we get another doctor from the town."

Bazarov nodded his head without speaking. In an hour's time Pavel Petrovich was already lying in bed with a skillfully bandaged leg. The whole house was alarmed; Fenichka became ill. Nikolai Petrovich kept stealthily wringing his hands, while Pavel Petrovich laughed and joked, especially with Bazarov; he had put on a fine cambric night shirt, an elegant morning jacket, and a fez, did not allow the blinds to be drawn down, and humorously complained of the necessity of being kept from food.

Towards night, however, he began to be feverish; his head ached.

7. Ann Radcliffe (1764–1823), writer of extremely popular "gothic" novels.

The doctor arrived from the town. (Nikolai Petrovich would not listen to his brother, and indeed Bazarov himself did not wish him to; he sat the whole day in his room, looking yellow and vindictive, and only went in to the invalid for as brief a time as possible; twice he happened to meet Fenichka, but she shrank away from him with horror.) The new doctor advised cooling drinks; he confirmed, however, Bazarov's assertion that there was no danger. Nikolai Petrovich told him his brother had wounded himself by accident, to which the doctor responded, "Hm!" but having twenty-five silver rubles slipped into his hand on the spot, he observed, "You don't say so! Well, it's a thing that often happens, to be sure."

No one in the house went to bed or undressed. Nikolai Petrovich kept going in to his brother on tiptoe, retreating on tiptoe again; the latter dozed, moaned a little, told him in French, *Couchez-vous*,[8] and asked for drink. Nikolai Petrovich sent Fenichka twice to take him a glass of lemonade; Pavel Petrovich gazed at her intently, and drank off the glass to the last drop. Towards morning the fever had increased a little; there was slight delirium. At first Pavel Petrovich uttered incoherent words; then suddenly he opened his eyes, and seeing his brother near his bed bending anxiously over him, he said, "Don't you think, Nikolai, Fenichka has something in common with Nellie?"

"What Nellie, Pavel dear?"

"How can you ask? Princess R——. Especially in the upper part of the face. *C'est de la même famille.*"[9]

Nikolai Petrovich made no answer, while inwardly he marveled at the persistence of old passions in man. "Just see when its come to the surface," he thought.

"Ah, how I love that light-headed creature!" moaned Pavel Petrovich, clasping his hands mournfully behind his head. "I can't bear any insolent upstart to dare to touch . . ." he whispered a few minutes later.

Nikolai Petrovich only sighed; he did not even suspect to whom these words referred.

Bazarov presented himself before him at eight o'clock the next day. He had already had time to pack, and to set free all his frogs, insects, and birds.

"You have come to say good-bye to me?" said Nikolai Petrovich, getting up to meet him.

"Yes."

"I understand you, and approve of you fully. My poor brother, of course, is to blame; and that's why he was punished. He told me himself that he made it impossible for you to act otherwise. I

8. "Go to sleep."

9. "It is of the same family (sort)."

believe that you could not avoid this duel, which . . . which to some extent is explained by the almost constant antagonism of your respective views." (Nikolai Petrovich began to get a little mixed up in his words.) "My brother is a man of the old school, hot-tempered and obstinate. . . . Thank God that it has ended as it has. I have taken every precaution to avoid publicity."

"I'm leaving you my address, in case there's any fuss," Bazarov remarked casually.

"I hope there will be no fuss, Evgeny Vassilyich. . . . I am very sorry your stay in my house should have such a . . . such an end. It is the more distressing to me since Arkady . . ."

"I shall be seeing him, I expect," replied Bazarov, in whom "explanations" and "protestations" of every sort always aroused a feeling of impatience; "in case I don't, I beg you to say good-bye to him for me, and accept the expression of my regret."

"And I beg . . ." answered Nikolai Petrovich. But Bazarov went off without waiting for the end of his sentence.

When he heard of Bazarov's going, Pavel Petrovich expressed a desire to see him, and shook his hand. But even then he remained as cold as ice; he realized that Pavel Petrovich wanted to play a magnanimous role. He did not succeed in saying good-bye to Fenichka; he only exchanged glances with her at the window. Her face struck him as looking dejected. "She'll come to grief, perhaps," he said to himself. . . . "But who knows? she'll pull through somehow, I daresay!" Peter, however, was so overcome that he wept on his shoulder, till Bazarov damped him by asking if he'd a constant supply of water laid in for his eyes; while Dunyasha was obliged to run away into the wood to hide her emotion. The originator of all this woe got into a light cart, lit a cigar, and when at the third mile, at the bend in the road, the Kirsanovs' estate, with its new house, could be seen in a long line, he merely spat, and muttering "Damned aristocrats!" wrapped himself closer in his cloak.

Pavel Petrovich was soon better; but he had to remain in bed about a week. He bore his captivity, as he called it, pretty patiently, though he took great pains over his toilette, and had everything scented with eau-de-cologne. Nikolai Petrovich used to read him the journals; Fenichka waited on him as before, brought him lemonade, bouillon, boiled eggs, and tea; but she was overcome with secret dread whenever she went into his room. Pavel Petrovich's unexpected action had alarmed every one in the house, and her more than any one; Prokofich was the only person not agitated by it; he discoursed upon how gentlemen in his day used to fight, but "only with real gentlemen; low curs like that they ordered horsewhipped in the stable for their insolence."

Fenichka's conscience scarcely reproached her; but she was

tormented at times by the thought of the real cause of the quarrel; and Pavel Petrovich, too, looked at her so strangely . . . so that even when her back was turned she felt his eyes upon her. She grew thinner from constant inward agitation, and, as is usually the way, became still more charming.

One day—the incident took place in the morning—Pavel Petrovich felt better, and moved from his bed to the sofa, while Nikolai Petrovich, having satisfied himself he was better, went off to the threshing floor. Fenichka brought him a cup of tea, and setting it down on a little table, was about to withdraw. Pavel Petrovich detained her.

"Where are you going in such a hurry, Fedosya Nikolaevna?" he began; "are you busy?"

"No, sir . . . I have to pour out tea."

"Dunyasha will do that without you; sit a little while with a sick man. By the way, I must have a little talk with you."

Fenichka sat down on the edge of an easy-chair, without speaking.

"Listen," said Pavel Petrovich, tugging at his moustaches; "I have long wanted to ask you something; you seem somehow afraid of me?"

"I, sir?"

"Yes, you. You never look at me, as though your conscience were not at rest."

Fenichka crimsoned, but looked at Pavel Petrovich. He impressed her as looking strange, and her heart began throbbing slowly.

"Is your conscience at rest?" he questioned her.

"Why should it not be at rest?" she faltered.

"Goodness knows why! Besides, whom can you have wronged? Me? That is not likely. Any other people in the house here? That, too, is something incredible. Can it be my brother? But you love him, don't you?"

"I love him."

"With your whole soul, with your whole heart?"

"I love Nikolai Petrovich with my whole heart."

"Truly? Look at me, Fenichka." (It was the first time he had called her that name.) "You know, it's a great sin to lie!"

"I am not lying, Pavel Petrovich. Not love Nikolai Petrovich—I shouldn't care to live after that."

"And will you never give him up for any one?"

"For whom could I give him up?"

"For whom indeed! Well, how about that gentleman who has just gone away from here?"

Fenichka got up. "My God, Pavel Petrovich, what are you torturing me for? What have I done to you? How can such things be said!" . . .

"Fenichka," said Pavel Petrovich, in a sorrowful voice, "you know I saw . . ."

"What did you see, sir?"

"Well, there . . . in the arbor."

Fenichka crimsoned to her hair and to her ears. "How was I to blame for that?" she articulated with an effort.

Pavel Petrovich raised himself up. "You were not to blame? No? Not at all?"

"I love Nikolai Petrovich, and no one else in the world, and I shall always love him!" cried Fenichka with sudden force, while sobs rose in her throat. "As for what you saw, at the Last Judgment I will say I'm not to blame, and wasn't to blame for it, and I would rather die at once if people can suspect me of such a thing against my benefactor, Nikolai Petrovich."

But here her voice broke, and at the same time she felt that Pavel Petrovich was snatching and pressing her hand. . . . She looked at him, and was fairly petrified. He had turned even paler than before; his eyes were shining, and what was most marvelous of all, one large solitary tear was rolling down his cheek.

"Fenichka!" he was saying in a strange whisper; "love him, love my brother! He is such a kind, good man! Don't give him up for any one in the world; don't listen to any one else! Think what can be more terrible than to love and not be loved! Never leave my poor Nikolai!"

Fenichka's eyes were dry, and her terror had passed away, so great was her amazement. But what were her feelings when Pavel Petrovich, Pavel Petrovich himself, put her hand to his lips and kept it there without kissing it, only heaving convulsive sighs from time to time. . . .

"Goodness," she thought, "isn't it some attack coming on him?" . . .

At that instant his whole ruined life was stirred up within him.

The staircase creaked under rapidly approaching footsteps. . . . He pushed her away from him, and let his head drop back on the pillow. The door opened, and Nikolai Petrovich entered, cheerful, fresh, and ruddy. Mitya, as fresh and ruddy as his father, in nothing but his little shirt, was bouncing on his chest, catching the big buttons of his rough country coat with his little bare toes.

Fenichka simply flung herself upon him, and clasping him and her son together in her arms, dropped her head on his shoulder. Nikolai Petrovich was surprised; Fenichka, the reserved and staid Fenichka, had never given him a caress in the presence of a third person.

"What's the matter?" he said, and, glancing at his brother, he gave her Mitya. "You don't feel worse?" he inquired, going up to Pavel Petrovich.

He buried his face in a cambric handkerchief. "No . . . not at all . . . on the contrary, I am much better."

"You were in too great a hurry to move on to the sofa. Where are you going?" added Nikolai Petrovich, turning round to Fenichka; but she had already closed the door behind her. "I was bringing in my young hero to show you; he's been crying for his uncle. Why has she carried him off? What's wrong with you, though? Has anything passed between you, eh?"

"Brother!" said Pavel Petrovich solemnly.

Nikolai Petrovich started. He felt dismayed, he could not have said why himself.

"Brother," repeated Pavel Petrovich, "give me your word that you will carry out my one request."

"What request? Tell me."

"It is very important; the whole happiness of your life, as I see it, depends on it. I have been thinking a great deal all this time over what I want to say to you now. . . . Brother, do your duty, the duty of an honest and generous man; put an end to the scandal and bad example you are setting—you, the best of men!"

"What do you mean, Pavel?"

"Marry Fenichka. . . . She loves you; she is the mother of your son."

Nikolai Petrovich stepped back a pace, and flung up his hands. "Do you say that, Pavel? You whom I have always regarded as the most determined opponent of such marriages! You say that? Don't you know that it has simply been out of respect for you that I have not done what you so rightly call my duty?"

"You were wrong to respect me in that case," Pavel Petrovich responded, with a weary smile. "I begin to think Bazarov was right in accusing me of being an aristocrat. No, dear brother, don't let us worry ourselves about appearances and the world's opinion any more; we are old folks now and resigned; it's time we laid aside vanity of all kinds. Let us, just as you say, do our duty; and mind, we shall get happiness that way into the bargain."

Nikolai Petrovich rushed to embrace his brother.

"You have opened my eyes completely!" he cried. "I was right in always declaring you the wisest and kindest-hearted fellow in the world, and now I see you are just as reasonable as you are noble-hearted."

"Easy, easy," Pavel Petrovich interrupted him; "don't hurt the leg of your reasonable brother, who at close upon fifty has been fighting a duel like an ensign. So, then, it's a settled matter;

Fenichka is to be my . . . *belle soeur*."[1]

"My dearest Pavel! But what will Arkady say?"

"Arkady? He'll be in ecstasies, you may depend upon it! Marriage is against his principles, but then the sentiment of equality in him will be gratified. And, after all, what sense have class distinctions *au dix-neuvième siècle?*"[2]

"Ah, Pavel, Pavel, let me kiss you once more! Don't be afraid, I'll be careful."

The brothers embraced each other.

"What do you think, should you not inform her of your intention now?" queried Pavel Petrovich.

"Why be in a hurry?" responded Nikolai Petrovich. "Has there been any conversation between you?"

"Conversation between us? *Quelle idée!*"[3]

"Well, that is all right then. First of all, you must get well, and meanwhile there's plenty of time. We must think it over well, and consider . . ."

"But your mind is made up, I suppose?"

"Of course, my mind is made up, and I thank you from the bottom of my heart. I will leave you now; you must rest; any excitement is bad for you. . . . But we will talk it over again. Sleep well, dear heart, and God bless you!"

"What is he thanking me like that for?" thought Pavel Petrovich, when he was left alone. "As though it did not depend on him! I will go away as soon as he is married, somewhere a long way off—to Dresden or Florence, and will live there till I drop."

Pavel Petrovich moistened his forehead with eau de cologne, and closed his eyes. His handsome, emaciated head, the glaring daylight shining full upon it, lay on the white pillow like the head of a dead man. . . . And indeed he was a dead man.

XXV

At Nikolskoe Katya and Arkady were sitting in the garden on a turf seat in the shade of a tall ash tree; Fifi had placed herself on the ground near them, giving her slender body that graceful curve which is known among hunters as "the hare bend." Both Arkady and Katya were silent; he was holding a half-open book in his hands, while she was picking out of a basket the few crumbs of bread left in it and throwing them to a small family of sparrows, who with the frightened impudence peculiar to them were hopping and chirping at her very feet. A faint breeze stirring in the ash leaves kept slowly moving pale-gold flecks of sunlight back and forth over Fifi's tawny back and the shady path; a patch

1. "sister-in-law."
2. "in the nineteenth century."
3. "What an idea!"

of unbroken shade fell upon Arkady and Katya; only from time to time a bright streak gleamed on her hair. Both were silent, but the very way in which they were silent, in which they were sitting together, was expressive of confidential intimacy; each of them seemed not even to be thinking of his companion, while secretly rejoicing in his presence. Their faces, too, had changed since we saw them last; Arkady looked more tranquil, Katya brighter and more daring.

"Don't you think," began Arkady, "that the ash has been very well named in Russian *yasen;* no other tree is so lightly and clearly *(yasno)* transparent against the air as it is."

Katya raised her eyes to look upward, and assented "Yes", while Arkady thought, "Well, this one does not reproach me for *talking finely.*"

"I don't like Heine,[4]" said Katya, glancing towards the book which Arkady was holding in his hands, "either when he laughs or when he weeps; I like him when he's thoughtful and melancholy."

"And I like him when he laughs," remarked Arkady.

"That's the relics of your old satirical tendencies left in you." ("Relics!" thought Arkady—"if Bazarov had heard that?") "Wait a little; we shall transform you."

"Who will transform me? You?"

"Who?—my sister; Porfiry Platonovich, whom you've given up quarrelling with; auntie, whom you escorted to church the day before yesterday."

"Well, I couldn't refuse! And as for Anna Sergeyevna, she agreed with Evgeny in a great many things, you remember?"

"My sister was under his influence then, just as you were."

"As I was? Do you find that I've shaken off his influence now?"

Katya did not speak.

"I know," pursued Arkady, "you never liked him."

"I can have no opinion about him."

"Do you know what, Katerina Sergeyevna, every time I hear that answer I disbelieve it. . . . There is no man that every one of us could not have an opinion about! That's simply a way of getting out of it."

"Well, I'll say then, I don't. . . . It's not exactly that I don't like him, but I feel that he's of a different order from me, and I am different from him . . . and you, too, are different from him."

"How's that?"

"How can I tell you? . . . He's a wild animal, and you and I are tame."

4. German poet (1797–1856).

"Am I tame too?"

Katya nodded.

Arkady scratched his ear. "Let me tell you, Katerina Sergeyevna, do you know, that's really an insult?"

"Why, would you like to be wild."

"Not wild, but strong, energetic."

"It's no good wishing for that. . . . Your friend, you see, doesn't wish for it, but he has it."

"Hm! So you imagine he had a great influence on Anna Sergeyevna?"

"Yes. But no one can keep the upper hand of her for long," added Katya in a low voice.

"Why do you think that?"

"She's very proud. . . . I didn't mean that . . . she values her independence a great deal."

"Who doesn't value it?" asked Arkady, and the thought flashed through his mind, "What good is it?" "What good is it?" occurred to Katya too. When young people are often together on friendly terms, they are constantly stumbling on the same ideas.

Arkady smiled, and coming slightly closer to Katya, he said in a whisper, "Confess that you are a little afraid of her."

"Of whom?"

"Her," repeated Arkady, significantly.

"And how about you?" Katya asked in her turn.

"I am too, observe I said I am, *too*."

Katya threatened him with her finger. "I wonder at that," she began; "my sister has never felt so friendly to you as just now; much more so than when you first came."

"Really!"

"Why, haven't you noticed it? Aren't you glad of it?"

Arkady grew thoughtful.

"How have I succeeded in gaining Anna Sergeyevna's good opinion? Wasn't it because I brought her your mother's letters?"

"Both that and other causes, which I won't tell you."

"Why?"

"I won't say."

"Oh! I know; you're very obstinate."

"Yes, I am."

"And observant."

Katya gave Arkady a sidelong look. "Perhaps that irritates you? What are you thinking of?"

"I am wondering how you come to be as observant as you really are. You are so shy, so distrustful; you keep every one at a distance."

"I have lived alone a great deal; that drives one to reflection.

But do I really keep every one at a distance?"

Arkady flung a grateful glance at Katya.

"That's all very well," he pursued; "but people in your position —I mean in your circumstances—don't often have this faculty; it is as hard for them as it is for sovereigns to get at the truth."

"But, you see, I am not rich."

Arkady was taken aback, and did not at once understand Katya. "Why, of course, the property's all her sister's!" struck him suddenly; the thought was not unpleasing to him. "How nicely you said that!" he commented.

"What?"

"You said it nicely, simply, without being ashamed or posturing. By the way, I imagine there must always be something special, a kind of pride of a sort in the feeling of any man, who knows and says he is poor."

"I have never experienced anything of that sort, thanks to my sister. I only referred to my position just now because it happened to come up."

"Well; but you must admit that you have a share of that pride I spoke of just now."

"For instance?"

"For instance, you—forgive the question—you wouldn't marry a rich man, I fancy, would you?"

"If I loved him very much. . . . No, I think even then I wouldn't marry him."

"There! you see!" cried Arkady, and after a short pause he added, "And why wouldn't you marry him?"

"Because unequal matches even appear in songs."

"You want to rule, perhaps, or . . .

"Oh, no! why should I? On the contrary, I am ready to obey; only inequality is hard to bear. To respect oneself and obey, that I can understand, that's happiness; but a subordinate existence . . . No, I've had enough of that as it is."

"Enough of that as it is," Arkady repeated after Katya. "Yes, yes," he went on, "you're not Anna Sergeyevna's sister for nothing; you're just as independent as she is; but you're more reserved. I'm certain you wouldn't be the first to give expression to your feeling, however strong and holy it might be . . ."

"Well, what would you expect?" asked Katya.

"You're equally clever; and you've as much, if not more, character than she."

"Don't compare me with my sister, please," interposed Katya hurriedly; "that's too much to my disadvantage. You seem to forget my sister's beautiful and clever and . . . you in particular, Arkady Nikolaevich, ought not to say such things, and with such a serious face, too."

"What do you mean by 'you in particular'—and what makes you suppose I am joking?"

"Of course, you are joking."

"You think so? But what if I'm convinced of what I say? If I believe I have not even put it strongly enough?"

"I don't understand you."

"Really? Well, now I see; I certainly took you to be more observant than you are."

"How?"

Arkady made no answer, and turned away, while Katya looked for a few more crumbs in the basket, and began throwing them to the sparrows; but she moved her arm too vigorously, and they flew away, without stopping to pick them up.

"Katerina Sergeyevna!" began Arkady suddenly; "it's of no consequence to you, probably; but, let me tell you, I put you not only above your sister, but above every one in the world."

He got up and went quickly away, as though he were frightened at the words that had fallen from his lips.

Katya let her two hands drop together with the basket on to her lap, and with bent head she stared a long while after Arkady. Gradually a crimson flush came faintly over her cheeks; but her lips did not smile, and her dark eyes had a look of perplexity and some other, as yet undefined, feeling.

"Are you alone?" she heard the voice of Anna Sergeyevna near her; "I thought you came into the garden with Arkady."

Katya slowly raised her eyes to her sister (elegantly, even exquisitely dressed, she was standing in the path and tickling Fifi's ears with the tip of her open parasol), and slowly replied, "Yes, I'm alone."

"So I see," she answered with a smile; "I suppose he has gone to his room."

"Yes."

"Have you been reading together?"

"Yes."

Anna Sergeyevna took Katya by the chin and lifted her face up.

"You have not been quarrelling, I hope?"

"No," said Katya, and she quietly removed her sister's hand.

"How solemnly you answer! I expected to find him here, and meant to suggest his coming for a walk with me. He keeps asking me. They have sent you some shoes from the town; go and try them on; I noticed only yesterday your old ones are quite shabby. In general you don't think enough about such things, and you have such charming little feet! Your hands are nice too . . . though they're large; so you must make the most of your little feet. But you're not vain."

Anna Sergeyevna went farther along the path with a light rustle of her beautiful gown; Katya got up from the grass, and, taking Heine with her, went away too—but not to try on her shoes.

"Charming little feet!" she thought, as she slowly and lightly mounted the stone steps of the terrace, which were burning with the heat of the sun; "charming little feet you call them. . . . Well, he shall be at them."

But all at once a feeling of shame came upon her, and she ran swiftly upstairs.

Arkady was going along the corridor to his room; the butler overtook him, and announced that Mr. Bazarov was in his room.

"Evgeny!" murmured Arkady, almost with dismay; "has he been here long?"

"Mr. Bazarov arrived this minute, sir, and gave orders not to announce him to Anna Sergeyevna, but to show him straight up to you."

"Can any misfortune have happened at home?" thought Arkady, and running hurriedly up the stairs, he at once opened the door. The sight of Bazarov at once reassured him, though a more experienced eye might very probably have discerned signs of inward agitation in the sunken, though still energetic face of the unexpected visitor. With a dusty cloak over his shoulders, with a cap on his head, he was sitting at the window; he did not even get up when Arkady flung himself with noisy exclamations on his neck.

"This is unexpected! What good luck brought you?" he kept repeating, bustling about the room like one who both imagines himself and wishes to show himself delighted. "I suppose everything's all right at home; every one's well, eh?"

"Everything's all right, but not every one's well," said Bazarov. "Don't be a chatterbox, but send for some kvass for me, sit down, and listen while I tell you all about it in a few, but, I hope, pretty vigorous sentences."

Arkady quieted down, and Bazarov described his duel with Pavel Petrovich. Arkady was very much surprised, and even grieved, but he did not think it necessary to show this; he only asked whether his uncle's wound was really not serious; and on receiving the reply that it was most interesting, but not from a medical point of view, he gave a forced smile, but at heart he felt both wounded and as it were ashamed. Bazarov seemed to understand him.

"Yes, my dear fellow," he commented, "you see what comes

of living with feudal people. You turn feudal yourself, and find yourself taking part in knightly tournaments. Well, so I set off 'to the fathers,' "[5] Bazarov wound up, "and I've turned in here on the way. . . . to tell you all this, I should say, if I didn't think a useless lie stupid. No, I turned in here—the devil only knows why. You see, it's sometimes a good thing for a man to take himself by the scruff of the neck and pull himself up, like a radish out of its bed; that's what I've been doing of late. . . . But I wanted to have one more look at what I'm giving up, at the bed where I've been planted."

"I hope those words don't refer to me," responded Arkady with some emotion; "I hope you don't think of giving me up?"

Bazarov turned an intent, almost piercing look upon him.

"Would that be such a grief to you? It strikes me *you* have given me up already, you look so fresh and smart. . . . Your affair with Anna Sergeyevna must be getting on successfully."

"What do you mean by my affair with Anna Sergeyevna?"

"Why, didn't you come here from the town on her account, little bird? By the way, how are those Sunday schools getting on? Do you mean to tell me you're not in love with her? Or have you already reached the stage of discretion?"

"Evgeny, you know I have always been open with you; I can assure you, I will swear to you, you're making a mistake."

"Hm! That's a new story," remarked Bazarov in an undertone. "But there is no reason for you to get excited, it's a matter of absolute indifference to me. A romantic would say, 'I feel that our paths are beginning to part,' but I will simply say that we're tired of each other."

"Evgeny . . ."

"My dear soul, there's no great harm in that. One gets tired of much more than that in this life. And now I suppose we'd better say good-bye, hadn't we? Ever since I've been here I've had such a loathsome feeling, just as if I'd been reading Gogol's letter to the governor of Kaluga's wife.[6] By the way, I didn't tell them to unhitch the horses."

"Upon my word, this is too much!"

"Why?"

"I'll say nothing of myself; but that would be highly discourteous to Anna Sergeyevna, who will certainly wish to see you."

"Oh, you're mistaken there."

5. Bazarov mockingly (and ominously) recalls the *ad patres* of p. 95 (note 6).

6. Gogol's letter of June 6, 1846, was deleted from his *Selected Correspondence With Friends* and first appeared in 1860, that is, a year after the purported setting of the novel, under the title "What a Governor's Wife Is." Like the original volume, which had aroused Belinsky's ire, it offended both radicals and liberals with its sententiousness.

"On the contrary, I am certain I'm right," retorted Arkady. "And what are you pretending for? If it comes to that, haven't you come here on her account yourself?"

"That may be so, but you're mistaken anyway."

But Arkady was right. Anna Sergeyevna desired to see Bazarov, and sent word to him by the butler. Bazarov changed his clothes before going to her; it turned out that he had packed his new suit so as to be able to get it out easily.

Odintsov did not receive him in the room where he had so unexpectedly declared his love to her, but in the drawing-room. She held her finger tips out to him cordially, but her face betrayed an involuntary sense of tension.

"Anna Sergeyevna," Bazarov hastened to say, "before everything else I must set your mind at rest. Before you is a mortal who has come to his senses long ago, and who hopes other people, too, have forgotten his follies. I am going away for a long while; and though, as you will allow, I'm by no means a very soft creature, it would be anything but cheerful for me to carry away with me the idea that you remember me with repugnance."

Anna Sergeyevna sighed deeply, like one who has just climbed up a high mountain, and her face was lit up by a smile. She held out her hand a second time to Bazarov, and responded to his pressure.

"Let bygones be bygones," she said. "I am all the readier to do so because, speaking in all conscience, I was to blame then, too, for flirting or something like that. In a word, let us be friends as before. That was a dream, wasn't it? And who remembers dreams?"

"Who remembers them? And besides, love . . . you know, is a purely imaginary feeling."

"Really? I am very glad to hear that."

So Anna Sergeyevna spoke, and so spoke Bazarov; they both supposed they were speaking the truth. Was the truth, the whole truth, to be found in their words? They could not themselves have said, and much less could the author. But a conversation followed between them precisely as though they completely believed one another.

Anna Sergeyevna asked Bazarov, among other things, what he had been doing at the Kirsanovs'. He was on the point of telling her about his duel with Pavel Petrovich, but he checked himself with the thought that she might imagine he was trying to make himself interesting, and answered that he had been at work all the time.

"And I," observed Anna Sergeyevna, "had a fit of depression at first, goodness knows why; I even made plans for going abroad, fancy! . . . Then it passed off, your friend Arkady Nikolaich came, and I fell back into my old routine, and took up my real part again."

"What part is that, may I ask?"

"The character of aunt, guardian, mother—call it what you like. By the way, do you know I used not quite to understand your close friendship with Arkady Nikolaich; I thought him rather insignificant. But now I have come to know him better, and to see that he is clever. . . . And he's young, he's young . . . that's the great thing . . . not like you and me, Evgeny Vassilyich."

"Is he still as shy in your company?" queried Bazarov.

"Why, was he?" . . . Anna Sergeyevna began, and after a brief pause she went on: "He has grown more confiding now; he talks to me. He used to avoid me before. Though, indeed, I didn't seek his society either. He and Katya are great friends."

Bazarov felt irritated. "A woman can't help being crafty, of course!" he thought. "You say he used to avoid you," he said aloud, with a chilly smile; "but it is probably no secret to you that he was in love with you?"

"What! he too?" fell from Anna Sergeyevna's lips.

"He too," repeated Bazarov, with a submissive bow. "Can it be you didn't know it, and I've told you something new?"

Anna Sergeyevna dropped her eyes. "You are mistaken, Evgeny Vassilyich."

"I don't think so. But perhaps I ought not to have mentioned it." "And don't you try telling me lies again," he added to himself.

"Why not mention it? But I imagine that in this, too, you are attributing too much importance to a passing impression. I begin to suspect you are inclined to exaggeration."

"We had better not talk about it, Anna Sergeyevna."

"Oh, why?" she retorted; but she herself led the conversation into another channel. She was still ill at ease with Bazarov, though she had told him and assured herself that everything was forgotten. While she was exchanging the simplest remarks with him, even while she was jesting with him, she was conscious of a faint spasm of dread. So people on a steamer at sea talk and laugh carelessly, for all the world as though they were on dry land; but let only the slightest hitch occur, let the least sign be seen of anything out of the common, and at once on every face there emerges an expression of peculiar alarm, betraying the constant consciousness of constant danger.

Anna Sergeyevna's conversation with Bazarov did not last long. She began to seem absorbed in thought, answered abstractedly, and suggested at last that they should go into the hall, where they found the princess and Katya. "But where is Arkady Nikolaich?" inquired the lady of the house; and on hearing that he had not shown himself for more than an hour, she sent for him. He was not very quickly found; he had hidden himself in the very thickest part of the garden, and with his chin propped on his clasped hands, he was sitting lost in meditation. They were deep and serious meditations, but not mournful. He knew Anna Sergeyevna was sitting alone with Bazarov, but he felt no jealousy as once he had; on the contrary, his face slowly brightened; he seemed to be at once wondering and rejoicing, and resolving on something.

XXVI

The deceased Odintsov had not liked innovations, but he had tolerated "a certain play of ennobled taste," and had in consequence put up in his garden, between the hothouse and the lake, something like a greek portico, made of Russian brick. Along the dark wall at the back of this portico or gallery were six niches for statues, which Odintsov had proceeded to order from abroad. These statues were to represent Solitude, Silence, Meditation, Melancholy, Modesty, and Sensibility. One of them, the goddess of Silence, with her finger on her lip, had been sent and put up; but on the very same day some boys on the farm had broken her nose; and though a plasterer of the neighborhood undertook to make her a new nose "twice as good as the old one," Odintsov ordered her to be taken away, and she was still to be seen in the corner of the threshing barn, where she had stood many long years, a source of superstitious terror to the peasant women. The front part of the portico had long been overgrown with thick bushes; only the pediments of the columns could be seen above the dense green. In the portico itself it was cool even at midday. Anna Sergeyevna did not like to visit this place ever since she had seen a snake there; but Katya often came and sat on the wide stone seat under one of the niches. Here, in the midst of the shade and coolness, she used to read and work, or to give herself up to that sensation of perfect peace, doubtless known to each of us, the charm of which consists in the half-unconscious, silent listening to the vast current of life that flows forever both around us and within us.

The day after Bazarov's arrival Katya was sitting on her favorite stone seat, and beside her Arkady was sitting again. He had besought her to come with him to the portico.

There was still about an hour to lunch time; the dewy morning had already given place to sultry day. Arkady's face retained the expression of the preceding day; Katya had a preoccupied look. Her sister had called her into her room directly after their morning tea, and after some preliminary caresses, which always scared Katya a little, she had advised her to be more guarded in her behavior with Arkady, and especially to avoid solitary talks with him, which had supposedly attracted the notice of her aunt and the entire household. Besides this, even the previous evening Anna Sergeyevna had not been herself; and Katya herself had felt ill at ease, as though she were conscious of some fault in herself. As she yielded to Arkady's entreaties, she said to herself that it was for the last time.

"Katerina Sergeyevna," he began with a sort of bashful easiness. "since I've had the happiness of living in the same house with you, I have discussed a great many things with you; but meanwhile there is one, very important . . . for me . . . one question, which I have not touched upon up till now. You remarked yesterday that I have been changed here," he went on, at once catching and avoiding the questioning glance Katya was turning upon him. "I certainly have changed a great deal, and you know that better than any one else—you to whom I really owe this change."

"I? . . . Me? . . ." said Katya.

"I am not now the conceited boy I was when I came here," Arkady went on. "I've not reached twenty-three for nothing; as before, I want to be useful, I want to devote all my powers to the truth; but I no longer look for my ideals where I did; they present themselves to me . . . much closer to hand. Up till now I did not understand myself; I set myself tasks which were beyond my powers. . . . My eyes have been opened lately, thanks to one feeling. . . . I'm not expressing myself quite clearly, but I hope you understand me."

Katya made no reply, but she ceased looking at Arkady.

"I suppose," he began again, this time in a more agitated voice, while above his head a chaffinch sang its song unheeding among the leaves of the birch—"I suppose it's the duty of every one to be open with those . . . with those people who . . . in fact, with those who are near to him, and so I . . . I resolved . . ."

But here Arkady's eloquence deserted him; he lost the thread, stammered, and was forced to be silent for a moment. Katya still did not raise her eyes. She seemed not to understand what he was leading up to in all this, and to be waiting for something.

"I foresee I shall surprise you," began Arkady, pulling himself together again with an effort, "especially since this feeling relates in a way . . . in a way, notice . . . to you. You reproached me, if you remember, yesterday with a want of seriousness," Arkady went on, with the air of a man who has got into a bog, feels that he is sinking further and further in at every step, and yet hurries onwards in the hope of crossing it as soon as possible;

"that reproach is often aimed . . . often falls . . . on young men even when they cease to deserve it; and if I had more self-confidence . . . " ("Come, help me, do help me!" Arkady was thinking, in desperation; but, as before, Katya did not turn her head.) "If I could hope . . ."

"If I could feel sure of what you say," was heard at that instant the clear voice of Anna Sergeyevna.

Arkady was still at once, while Katya turned pale. Close by the bushes that screened the portico ran a little path. Anna Sergeyevna was walking along it escorted by Bazarov. Katya and Arkady could not see them, but they heard every word, the rustle of their clothes, their very breathing. They walked on a few steps, and, as though on purpose, stood still just opposite the portico.

"You see," pursued Anna Sergeyevna, "you and I made a mistake; we are both past our first youth, I especially so; we have seen life, we are tired; we are both—why affect not to know it?—clever; at first we interested each other, curiosity was aroused . . . and then . . ."

"And then I grew stale," put in Bazarov.

"You know that was not the cause of our misunderstanding. But however that may be, we had no need of one another, that's the chief point; there was too much . . . what shall I say? . . . that was alike in us. We did not realize it all at once. Now, Arkady . . ."

"Do you need him?" queried Bazarov.

"Hush, Evgeny Vassilyich. You tell me he is not indifferent to me, and it always seemed to me he liked me. I know that I might well be his aunt, but I don't wish to conceal from you that I have come to think more often of him. In such youthful, fresh feeling there is a special charm . . ."

"The word *fascination* is most usual in such cases," Bazarov interrupted; suppressed spleen could be heard in his choked though hollow voice. "Arkady was mysterious over something with me yesterday, and didn't talk either of you or of your sister. . . . That's a serious symptom."

"He is just like a brother with Katya," commented Anna Sergeyevna, "and I like that in him, though, perhaps, I ought not to have allowed such intimacy between them."

"That idea is prompted by . . . your feelings as a sister?" Bazarov brought out, drawling.

"Of course . . . but why are we standing still? Let us go on. What a strange talk we are having, aren't we? I would never have believed I should talk to you like this. You know, I am afraid of you . . . and at the same time I trust you, because in reality you are so good."

"In the first place, I am not in the least good; and in the second place, I have lost all significance for you, and you tell me I am good . . . It's like laying a wreath of flowers on the head of a corpse."

"Evgeny Vassilyich, we are not responsible . . ." Anna Sergeyevna began; but a gust of wind blew across, set the leaves rustling, and carried away her words. "Of course, you are free . . ." Bazarov declared after a brief pause. Nothing more could be distinguished; the steps retreated . . . everything was still.

Arkady turned to Katya. She was sitting in the same position, but her head was bent still lower. "Katerina Sergeyevna," he said with a shaking voice, and clasping his hands tightly together, "I love you forever and irrevocably, and I love no one but you. I wanted to tell you this, to find out your opinion of me, and to ask for your hand, since I am not rich, and I feel ready for any sacrifice. . . . You don't answer me? You don't believe me? Do you think I speak lightly? But remember these last days! Surely for a long time past you must have known that everything—understand me—everything else has vanished long ago and left no trace? Look at me, say one word to me . . . I love . . . I love you . . . believe me!"

Katya glanced at Arkady with a bright and serious look, and after long hesitation, with the faintest smile, she said, "Yes."

Arkady leaped up from the stone seat. "Yes! You said Yes, Katerina Sergeyevna! What does that word mean? Only that I do love you, that you believe me . . . or . . . or . . . I daren't go on . . ."

"Yes," repeated Katya, and this time he understood her. He snatched her large beautiful hands, and, breathless with rapture, pressed them to his heart. He could scarcely stand on his feet, and could only repeat, "Katya, Katya . . ." while she began weeping in a guileless way, smiling gently at her own tears. He who has not seen those tears in the eyes of the beloved, does not yet know to what a point, faint with shame and gratitude, a man may be happy on earth.

The next day, early in the morning, Anna Sergeyevna sent to ask Bazarov to her boudoir, and with a forced laugh handed him a folded sheet of notepaper. It was a letter from Arkady; in it he asked for her sister's hand.

Bazarov quickly scanned the letter, and made an effort to control himself, that he might not show the malignant feeling which was instantaneously aflame in his breast.

"So that's how it is," he commented; "and you, I fancy, only yesterday imagined he loved Katerina Sergeyevna as a brother. What do you intend to do now?"

"What do you advise me?" asked Anna Sergeyevna, still laughing.

"Well, I suppose," answered Bazarov, also with a laugh, though he felt anything but cheerful, and had no more inclination to laugh than she had; "I suppose you ought to give the young people your blessing. It's a good match in every respect; Kirsanov's position is passable, he's the only son, and his father's a good-natured fellow, he won't try to thwart him."

Odintsov walked up and down the room. By turns her face flushed and grew pale. "You think so," she said. "Well, I see no obstacles . . . I am glad for Katya . . . and for Arkady Nikolaevich too. Of course, I will wait for his father's answer. I will send him in person to him. But it turns out, you see, that I was right yesterday when I told you we were both old people. . . . How was it I saw nothing? That's what amazes me!" Anna Sergeyevna laughed again, and quickly turned her head away.

"The younger generation have grown awfully sly," remarked Bazarov, and he, too, laughed. "Good-bye," he began after a short silence. "I hope you will bring the matter to the most satisfactory conclusion; and I will rejoice from a distance."

Odintsov turned quickly to him. "You are not going away? Why should you not stay *now*? Stay . . . it's enjoyable to talk to you . . . one seems walking on the edge of a precipice. At first one feels timid, but one gains courage as one goes on. Do stay."

"Thanks for the suggestion, Anna Sergeyevna, and for your flattering opinion of my conversational talents. But I think I have already been moving too long in a sphere which is not my own. Flying fish can hold out for a time in the air, but soon they must splash back into the water; allow me, too, to paddle in my own element."

Odintsov looked at Bazarov. His pale face was twitching with a bitter smile. "This man loves me!" she thought, and she felt pity for him, and held out her hand to him with sympathy.

But he, too, understood her. "No!" he said, stepping back a pace. "I'm a poor man, but I've never taken charity so far. Good-bye, and good luck to you."

"I am certain we are not seeing each other for the last time," Anna Sergeyevna declared with an involuntary gesture.

"Anything may happen!" answered Bazarov, and he bowed and went away.

"So you are thinking of making yourself a nest?" he said the same day to Arkady, as he packed his box, crouching on the floor. "Well, it's a fine thing. But you needn't have been so foxy. I expected something from you in quite another quarter. Perhaps, though, it took you by surprise yourself?"

"I certainly didn't expect this when I parted from you," answered Arkady; "but why are you so foxy yourself, calling it 'a fine thing,' as though I didn't know your opinion of marriage."

"Ah, my dear friend," said Bazarov, "how you talk! You see what I'm doing; there seems to be an empty space in the box, and I am putting hay in; that's how it is in the box of our life; we would stuff it up with anything rather than have a void. Don't be offended, please; you remember, no doubt, the opinion I have always had of Katerina Sergeyevna. Many a young lady's called clever simply because she can sigh cleverly; but yours can hold her own, and, indeed, she'll hold it so well that she'll have you under her thumb—to be sure, though, that's quite as it ought to be." He slammed the lid to, and got up from the floor. "And now, I say again, good-bye, for it's useless to deceive ourselves—we are parting for good, and you know that yourself . . . you have acted sensibly; you're not made for our bitter, rough, lonely existence. There's no daring, no hate in you, but you've the dash of youth and the fire of youth. Your sort, you gentry, can never get beyond refined submission or refined indignation, and that's a mere trifle. You won't fight—and yet you fancy yourselves gallant chaps—but we mean to fight. But what's that! Our dust would get into your eyes, our mud would bespatter you, and you're not yet up to our level, you're admiring yourselves unconsciously, you like to upbraid yourself; but we're sick of that—we want something else! we want to smash other people! You're a good fellow; but you're a mild, liberal gentleman for all that—*ay volla-too,* as my parent is fond of saying."

"You are parting from me for ever, Evgeny," sadly responded Arkady; "and have you nothing else to say to me?"

Bazarov scratched the back of his head. "Yes, Arkady, yes, I have other things to say to you, but I'm not going to say them, because that's romanticism—that means, mawkishness. And you get married as soon as you can; and build your nest, and have lots of children. They'll be clever because they'll be born at a better time than you and me. Aha! I see the horses are ready. Time's up! I've said good-bye to every one. . . . What now? embracing, eh?"

Arkady flung himself on the neck of his former mentor and friend, and the tears fairly gushed from his eyes.

"That's what comes of being young!" Bazarov commented calmly. "But I rest my hopes on Katerina Sergeyevna. You'll see how quickly she'll console you!"

"Good-bye, friend!" he said to Arkady when he had got into the light cart, and, pointing to a pair of jackdaws sitting side by side on the stable roof, he added, "That's for you! follow that example."

"What does that mean?" asked Arkady.

"What? Are you so weak in natural history, or have you forgotten that the jackdaw is a most respectable family bird? An example to you! . . . Good-bye, signor!"

Bazarov had spoken truly. In talking that evening with Katya, Arkady completely forgot about his former teacher. He already began to follow her lead, and Katya was conscious of this, and not surprised at it. He was to set off the next day for Marino, to see Nikolai Petrovich. Anna Sergeyevna was not disposed to put any constraint on the young people, and only on account of the proprieties did not leave them by themselves for too long together. She magnanimously kept the princess out of their way; the latter had been reduced to a state of tearful frenzy by the news of the proposed marriage. At first Anna Sergeyevna was afraid the sight of their happiness might prove rather trying to herself, but it turned out quite the other way; this sight not only did not distress her, it interested her, it even softened her at last. Anna Sergeyevna felt both glad and sorry at this. "It is clear that Bazarov was right," she thought; "it has been curiosity, nothing but curiosity, and love of ease, and egoism . . ."

"Children," she said aloud, "what do you say, is love a purely imaginary feeling?"

But neither Katya nor Arkady even understood her. They were shy with her; the fragment of conversation they had involuntarily overheard haunted their minds. But Anna Sergeyevna soon set their minds at rest; and it was not difficult for her—she had set her own mind at rest.

XXVII

Bazarov's old parents were all the more overjoyed by their son's arrival, as it was quite unexpected. Arina Vlasyevna was so flustered, and kept running backwards and forwards in the house, that Vassily Ivanovich compared her to a "hen partridge"; the short tail of her abbreviated jacket did, in fact, give her something of a birdlike appearance. He himself merely growled and gnawed the amber mouth piece of his pipe, or, clutching his neck with his fingers turned his head round, as though he were trying whether it were properly screwed on, then all at once he opened his wide mouth and went off into a perfectly noiseless chuckle.

"I've come to you for six whole weeks, old thing," Bazarov said to him. "I want to work, so please don't hinder me now."

"You shall forget my face completely, that's how I'll hinder you!" answered Vassily Ivanovich.

He kept his promise. After installing his son as before in his study, he almost hid himself away from him, and kept his wife from all superfluous demonstrations of tenderness. "On Enyusha's first visit, my dear soul," he said to her, "we bothered him a little; we must be wiser this time." Arina Vlasyevna agreed with her husband, but that was small compensation since she saw her son only at meals, and was now absolutely afraid to address him. "Enyushenka," she would say sometimes—and before he had time to look round, she was nervously fingering the tassels of her reticule and faltering, "Never mind, never mind, I only——" and afterwards she would go to Vassily Ivanovich and, her cheek in her hand, would consult him: "If you could only find out, darling, which Enyusha would like for dinner to-day—borsch or *shchi?*" [7]—"But why didn't you ask him yourself?"—"Oh, he will get sick of me!" Bazarov, however, soon ceased to shut himself up; the fever of work fell away, and was replaced by dreary boredom or vague restlessness. A strange weariness began to show itself in all his movements; even his walk, firm and impetuously bold, was changed. He gave up walking in solitude, and began to seek company; he drank tea in the drawing-room, strolled about the kitchen-garden with Vassily Ivanovich, and smoked with him in silence; once even asked after Father Alexey. Vassily Ivanovich at first rejoiced at this change, but his joy was not long-lived. "Enyusha's breaking my heart," he complained in secret to his wife: "it's not that he's discontented or angry—that would be nothing; he's sad, he's sorrowful—that's what's so terrible. He's always silent. If he'd only abuse us; he's growing thin, he's lost his color."—"Mercy on us, mercy on us!" whispered the old woman; "I would put an amulet on his neck, but, of course, he won't allow it." Vassily Ivanovich several times attempted in the most circumspect manner to question Bazarov about his work, about his health, and about Arkady. . . . But Bazarov's replies were reluctant and casual; and, once noticing that his father was gradually leading up to something in conversation, he said to him in a tone of vexation: "Why do you always seem to be walking round me on tiptoe? That way's worse than the old one."—

7. The standbys of Russian cooking. Both are thick soups—borsch (literally *borshch*) is made with beets, *shchi* with cabbage. Both are served with sour cream. Borsch contains, among other things, beef, sausage, and potatoes; *shchi* is identical with the *pot-au-feu*, or boiled beef, except for the sour cream and a tablespoon of chopped dill.

"There, there, I meant nothing!" poor Vassily Ivanovich answered hurriedly. So his political hints remained fruitless. He hoped to awaken his son's sympathy one day by beginning, apropos the approaching emancipation of the peasantry, to talk about progress; but the latter responded indifferently: "Yesterday I was walking past the fence, and I heard the peasant boys here, instead of some old ballad, bawling a popular tune. That's what progress is."

Sometimes Bazarov went into the village, and in his usual bantering tone entered into conversation with some peasant: "Come," he would say to him. "expound your views on life to me, friend; you see, they say all the strength and future of Russia lies in your hands, a new epoch in history will be started by you—you give us our real language and our laws." The peasant either answered nothing or articulated a few words of this sort, "Well, we'll try . . . because, you see, that's the extent of the land . . ."

"You explain to me what your *mir* (world) [8] is," Bazarov interrupted; "and is it the same *mir* that is said to rest on three fishes?"

"It's the earth that rests on three fishes," the peasant would declare soothingly, in a kind of patriarchal, good-natured singsong; "and as against ours, that's to say, the *mir*, we know there's the master's will; because you are our fathers. And the stricter the master's rule, the better for the peasant."

After listening to such a reply one day, Bazarov shrugged his shoulders contemptuously and turned away, while the peasant sauntered slowly homewards.

"What was he talking about?" inquired another peasant of middle age and surly aspect, who at a distance from the door of his hut had been following his conversation with Bazarov.—"Arrears? eh?"

"Arrears, no indeed, mate!" answered the first peasant, and now there was no trace of patriarchal singsong in his voice; on the contrary, there was a certain scornful gruffness to be heard in it: "Oh, he clacked away about something or other; wanted to stretch his tongue a bit. Of course, he's a gentleman; what does he understand?"

"What should he understand!" answered the other peasant, and jerking back their caps and pushing down their belts, they proceeded to deliberate upon their work and their wants. Alas! Bazarov, shrugging his shoulders contemptuously, that self-confident Bazarov, who knew how to talk to peasants (as he had

8. Bazarov plays on two meanings of *mir*: the world, and the village commune. The ignorant folk believed myths that the world was supported by three fish.

boasted in his dispute with Pavel Petrovich), did not even suspect that in their eyes he was all the while something of the nature of a buffoon.

He found employment for himself at last, however. One day Vassily Ivanovich bound up a peasant's wounded leg in his presence, but the old man's hands trembled, and he could not manage the bandages; his son helped him, and from that time began to take a share in his practice, though at the same time he was constantly sneering both at the remedies he himself advised and at his father, who hastened to make use of them. But Bazarov's jeers did not in the least perturb Vassily Ivanovich; they were positively a comfort to him. Holding his greasy dressing-gown across his stomach with two fingers, and smoking his pipe, he used to listen with enjoyment to Bazarov; and the more malicious his sallies, the more good-naturedly did his delighted father chuckle, showing every one of his black teeth. He used even to repeat these sometimes flat or pointless retorts, and would, for instance, for several days without rhyme or reason, constantly reiterate, "No great shakes!" simply because his son, on hearing he was going to matins, had made use of that expression. "Thank God! he has got over his melancholy!" he whispered to his wife; "how he gave it to me to-day, it was splendid!" Moreover, the idea of having such an assistant made him ecstatic and filled him with pride. "Yes, yes," he would say to some peasant woman in a man's coat, and a cap shaped like a horn, as he handed her a bottle of Goulard's extract or a box of white ointment, "you ought to thank God every minute, my good woman, that my son is staying with me; you will be treated now by the most scientific, most modern method. Do you know what that means? The Emperor of the French, Napoleon, even, has no better doctor." And the peasant woman, who had come to complain that her "stiches were rising" (the exact meaning of these words, however, she was not able to explain herself), merely bowed low and rummaged in her bosom, where four eggs lay tied up in the corner of a towel.

Bazarov once even pulled out a tooth for a passing pedlar; and though this tooth was an average specimen, Vassily Ivanovich preserved it as a curiosity, and incessantly repeated, as he showed it to Father Alexey, "Just look, what a fang! The force Evgeny has! The pedlar seemed to leap into the air. If it had been an oak, he'd have rooted it up!"

"Most promising!" Father Alexey would comment at last, not knowing what answer to make, and how to get rid of the ecstatic old man.

One day a peasant from a neighboring village brought his brother who was ill with typhus to Vassily Ivanovich. The unhappy man, lying face down on a truss of straw, was dying; his body was covered with dark patches, he had long ago lost consciousness. Vassily Ivanovich expressed his regret that no one had taken steps to procure medical aid sooner, and declared there was no hope. And, in fact, the peasant did not get his brother home again; he died in the cart.

Three days later Bazarov came into his father's room and asked him if he had any caustic.

"Yes; what do you want it for?"

"I must have some . . . to burn a cut."

"For whom?"

"For myself."

"What, yourself? Why is that? What sort of a cut? Where is it?"

"Look here, on my finger. I went to-day to the village, you know, where they brought that peasant with typhus fever. They were just going to do an autopsy for some reason or other, and I've had no practice of that sort for a long while."

"Well?"

"Well, so I asked the district doctor about it; and so I cut myself."

Vassily Ivanovich all at once turned quite white, and, without uttering a word, rushed to his study, from which he returned at once with a bit of caustic in his hand. Bazarov was about to take it and go away.

"For mercy's sake," said Vassily Ivanovich, "let me do it myself."

Bazarov smiled. "What a devoted practitioner!"

"Don't laugh, please. Show me your finger. The cut is not a large one. Do I hurt?"

"Press harder; don't be afraid."

Vassily Ivanovich stopped. "What do you think, Evgeny; wouldn't it be better to burn it with hot iron?"

"That ought to have been done sooner; even the caustic is useless, really, now. If I've taken the infection, it's too late now."

"How . . . too late. . . ." Vassily Ivanovich could scarcely articulate the words.

"I should think so! It's more than four hours ago."

Vassily Ivanovich burnt the cut a little more. "But had the district doctor no caustic?"

"No."

"How was that, good Heavens? A doctor not have such an indispensable thing as that!"

"You should have seen his lancets," observed Bazarov as he walked away.

Up till late that evening, and all the following day, Vassily Ivanovich kept catching at every possible excuse to go into his son's room; and though far from referring to the cut—he even tried to talk about the most irrelevant subjects—he looked so persistently into his face, and watched him in such trepidation, that Bazarov lost patience and threatened to go away. Vassily Ivanovich gave him his promise, that he would not worry, the more readily as Arina Vlasyevna, from whom, of course, he kept it all secret, was beginning to worry him as to why he did not sleep, and what had come over him. For two whole days he held himself in, though he did not at all like the look of his son, whom he kept watching stealthily, . . . but on the third day, at dinner, he could bear it no longer. Bazarov sat with downcast looks, and had not touched a single dish.

"Why don't you eat, Evgeny?" he inquired, putting on an expression of the most perfect carelessness. "The food, I think, is very nicely cooked."

"I don't want anything, so I don't eat."

"Have you no appetite? And your head," he added timidly; "does it ache?"

"Yes. Of course, it aches."

Arina Vlasyevna sat up and was all alert.

"Don't be angry, please, Evgeny," continued Vassily Ivanovich; "won't you let me feel your pulse?"

Bazarov got up. "I can tell you without feeling my pulse; I'm feverish."

"Has there been any shivering?"

"Yes, there has been shivering too. I'll go and lie down, and you can send me some lime-flower tea. I must have caught cold."

"To be sure, I heard you coughing last night," observed Arina Vlasyevna.

"I've caught cold," repeated Bazarov, and he went away.

Arina Vlasyevna busied herself about the preparation of lime-flower tea, while Vassily Ivanovich went into the next room and clutched at his hair in silent desperation.

Bazarov did not get up again that day, and passed the whole night in heavy, half-unconscious torpor. After midnight, opening his eyes with an effort, he saw by the light of a lamp his father's pale face bending over him, and told him to go away. The old man begged his pardon, but he quickly came back on tiptoe, and half-hidden by the cupboard door, he gazed persistently at his son. Arina Vlasyevna did not go to bed either, and leaving the study door just open a very little, she kept coming up to it to listen "how Enyusha was breathing," and to look at Vassily Ivanovich. She could see nothing but his motionless bent back, but even that afforded her some faint consolation. In the morning Bazarov tried to get up; he was seized with giddiness, his nose began to bleed; he lay down again. Vassily Ivanovich waited on him in silence; Arina Vlasyevna went in to him and asked him how he was feeling. He answered, "Better," and turned to the wall. Vassily Ivanovich gesticulated at his wife with both hands; she bit her lips so as not to cry, and went away. The whole house seemed suddenly darkened; every one looked gloomy; there was a strange hush; a shrill cock was carried away from the yard to the village, unable to comprehend why he should be treated so. Bazarov continued to lie turned to the wall. Vassily Ivanovich tried to address him with various questions, but they fatigued Bazarov, and the old man sank back into his arm-chair, motionless, only cracking his finger-joints now and then. He went for a few minutes into the garden, stood there like a statue, as though overwhelmed with unutterable bewilderment (the expression of bewilderment never left his face all through), and went back again to his son, trying to avoid his wife's questions. She caught him by the arm at last, and passionately, almost menacingly, said, "What is wrong with him?" Then he came to himself, and forced himself to smile at her in reply; but to his own horror, instead of a smile, he found himself taken somehow by a fit of laughter. He had sent at daybreak for a doctor. He thought it necessary to inform his son of this, for fear he should be angry.

Bazarov suddenly turned over on the sofa, bent a fixed dull look on his father, and asked for drink.

Vassily Ivanovich gave him some water, and as he did so felt his forehead. It seemed on fire.

"Old thing," began Bazarov, in a slow, drowsy voice; "I'm in a bad way; I've got the infection, and in a few days you'll have to bury me."

Vassily Ivanovich staggered back, as though some one had aimed a blow at his legs.

"Evgeny!" he faltered; "what do you mean! . . . God have mercy on you! You've caught cold!"

"Enough!" Bazarov interrupted deliberately. "A doctor can't be allowed to talk like that. There's every symptom of infection; you know yourself."

"Where are the symptoms . . . of infection, Evgeny? . . . Good Heavens!"

"What's this?" said Bazarov, and, pulling up his shirt-sleeve, he showed his father the ominous red patches coming out on his arm.

Vassily Ivanovich was shaking and chill with terror.

"Supposing," he said at last, "even supposing . . . if even there's something like . . . infection . . ."

"Pyæmia," put in his son.

"Well, well . . . something of the epidemic . . ."

"*Pyæmia,*" Bazarov repeated sharply and distinctly; "have you forgotten your text-books?"

"Well, well—as you like. . . . Anyway, we will cure you!"

"Come, that's humbug. But that's not the point. I didn't expect to die so soon; it's a most unpleasant incident, to tell the truth. You and mother ought to make the most of your strong religious belief; now's the time to put it to the test." He drank off a little water. "I want to ask you about one thing . . . while my head is still under my control. To-morrow or next day my brain, you know, will send in its resignation. I'm not quite certain even now whether I'm expressing myself clearly. While I've been lying here, I've kept fancying red dogs were running round me, while you were making them point at me, as if I were a woodcock. Just as if I were drunk. Do you understand me all right?"

"I assure you, Evgeny, you are talking perfectly correctly."

"All the better. You told me you'd sent for the doctor. You did that to comfort yourself . . . comfort me too; send a messenger . . ."

"To Arkady Nikolaich?" put in the old man.

"Who's Arkady Nikolaich?" said Bazarov, as though in doubt. . . . "Oh, yes! that little bird! No, let him alone; he's turned jackdaw now. Don't be surprised; that's not delirium yet. You send a messenger to Odintsov, Anna Sergeyevna; she's a lady with an estate. . . . Do you know?" (Vassily Ivanovich nodded.) "Evgeny Bazarov, say, sends his greetings, and sends word he is dying. Will you do that?"

"Yes, I will do it. . . . But is it a possible thing for you to die, Evgeny? . . . Think only! Where would divine justice be after that?"

"I know nothing about that; only you send the messenger."

"I'll send this minute, and I'll write a letter myself."

"No, why? Say I send greetings; nothing more is necessary. And now I'll go back to my dogs. Strange! I want to fix my thoughts on death, and nothing comes of it. I see a kind of blur . . . and nothing more."

He turned heavily back to the wall again; while Vassily Ivanovich went out of the study, and struggling as far as his wife's bedroom, simply dropped down on to his knees before the holy pictures.

The doctor, the same district doctor who had had no caustic, arrived, and after looking at the patient, advised them to persevere with waiting it out, and at that point said a few words of the chance of recovery.

"Have you ever chanced to see people in my state not set off for the Elysian Fields?" asked Bazarov, and suddenly snatching the leg of a heavy table that stood near his sofa, he swung it round, and pushed it away. "There's strength, there's strength," he murmured; "it's here still, and I must die! . . . An old man at least has time to be weaned from life, but I . . . Well, go and try to disprove death. Death will disprove you, and that's all! Who's crying there?" he added, after a short pause.—"Mother? Poor thing! Whom will she feed now with her exquisite borsch? You, Vassily Ivanovich, whimpering too, I do believe! Why, if Christianity's no help to you, be a philosopher, a Stoic, or what not! Why, didn't you boast you were a philosopher?"

"Me a philosopher!" wailed Vassily Ivanovich, while the tears fairly streamed down his cheeks.

Bazarov got worse every hour; the progress of the disease was rapid, as is usually the way in cases of surgical poisoning. He still had not lost consciousness, and understood what was said to him; he was still struggling. "I don't want to lose my wits," he muttered, clenching his fists; "what rot it all is!" And at once he would say, "Come, take ten from eight, what remains?" Vassily Ivanovich wandered about like one possessed, proposed first one remedy, then another, and ended by doing nothing but cover up his son's feet. "Try cold pack . . . emetic . . . mustard plasters on the stomach . . . bleeding," he would murmur with an effort. The doctor, whom he had entreated to remain, agreed with him, ordered the patient to drink lemonade, and for himself asked for a pipe and something "warming and strengthening"—that's to say vodka. Arina Vlasyevna sat on a low stool near the door, and only went out from time to time to pray. A few days before, a looking-glass had slipped out of her hands and been broken, and this she had always considered an omen of evil; even Anfisushka could say nothing to her. Timoteich had gone off to Odintsov's.

The night passed badly for Bazarov. . . . He was in the agonies of high fever. Towards morning he was a little easier. He asked Arina Vlasyevna to comb his hair, kissed her hand, and swallowed two gulps of tea. Vassily Ivanovich revived a little.

"Thank God!" he kept declaring; "the crisis is coming, the crisis is at hand!"

"There, to think now!" murmured Bazarov; "what a word can do! He's found it; he's said 'crisis,' and is comforted. It's an astounding thing how man believes in words. If he's told he's a fool, for instance, though he's not thrashed, he'll be wretched; call him a clever fellow, and he'll be delighted if you go off without paying him."

This little speech of Bazarov's, recalling his old "retorts," moved Vassily Ivanovich greatly.

"Bravo! well said, very good!" he cried, making as though he were clapping his hands.

Bazarov smiled mournfully.

"So what do you think," he said; "is the crisis over, or coming?"

"You are better, that's what I see, that's what rejoices me," answered Vassily Ivanovich.

"Well, that's good; rejoicings never come amiss. And to her, do you remember, did you send?"

"To be sure I did."

The change for the better did not last long. The disease resumed its onslaughts. Vassily Ivanovich was sitting by Bazarov. It seemed as though the old man were tormented by some special anguish. Several times he was on the point of speaking—and could not.

"Evgeny!" he brought out at last; "my son, my beloved, dear son!"

This unfamiliar mode of address produced an effect on Bazarov. He turned his head a little, and, obviously trying to fight against the load of oblivion weighing upon him, he articulated: "What is it, father?"

"Evgeny," Vassily Ivanovich went on, and he fell on his knees before Bazarov, though the latter had closed his eyes and could not see him. "Evgeny, you are better now; please God, you will get well, but make use of this time, comfort your mother and me, perform the duty of a Christian! What it means for me to say this to you, it's awful; but still more awful . . . for ever and ever, Evgeny . . . think a little, what. . . ."

The old man's voice broke, and a strange look passed over his son's face, though he still lay with closed eyes.

"I won't refuse, if that can be any comfort to you," he brought out at last; "but it seems to me there's no need to be in a hurry. You say yourself I am better."

"Oh, yes, Evgeny, better certainly; but who knows, it is all in God's hands, and in doing the duty . . ."

"No, I will wait a bit," broke in Bazarov. "I agree with you that the crisis has come. And if we're mistaken, well! they give the sacrament to men who are unconscious, you know."

"Evgeny, I beg."

"I'll wait a little. And now I want to go to sleep. Don't disturb me." And he laid his head back in its former position.

The old man rose from his knees, sat down in the arm-chair, and clutching his beard, began biting his fingers . . .

The sound of a light carriage on springs, that sound which is peculiarly impressive in the wilds of the country, suddenly struck his ears. Nearer and nearer rolled the light wheels; now even the neighing of the horses could be heard. . . . Vassily Ivanovich jumped up and ran to the little window. There drove into the courtyard of his little house a carriage with seats for two, harnessed with four horses. Without stopping to consider what it could mean, with a rush of a sort of senseless joy, he ran out on to the steps. . . . A groom in livery was opening the carriage doors; a lady in a black veil and a black mantle was getting out of it . . .

"I am Odintsov," she said. "Evgeny Vassilyich still living? Are you his father? I have a doctor with me."

"Benefactress!" cried Vassily Ivanovich, and snatching her hand, he pressed it convulsively to his lips, while the doctor brought by Anna Sergeyevna, a little man in spectacles, of German physiognomy, stepped very deliberately out of the carriage. "Still living, my Evgeny is living, and now he will be saved! Wife! wife! . . . An angel from heaven has come to us. . . ."

"What does it mean, good Lord!" faltered the old woman, running out of the drawing-room; and, comprehending nothing, she fell on the spot in the passage at Anna Sergeyevna's feet, and began kissing her garments like a mad woman.

"What are you doing!" protested Anna Sergeyevna; but Arina Vlasyevna did not heed her, while Vassily Ivanovich could only repeat, "An angel! an angel!"

"*Wo ist der Kranke?* and where is the patient?" said the doctor at last, with some impatience.

Vassily Ivanovich recovered himself. "Here, here, follow me, *werthester Herr College*," [9] he added through old associations.

"Ah!" articulated the German, grinning sourly.

Vassily Ivanovich led him into the study. "The doctor from Anna Sergeyevna Odintsov," he said, bending down quite to his

9. "Honored colleague."

son's ear, "and she herself is here."

Bazarov suddenly opened his eyes. "What did you say?"

"I say that Anna Sergeyevna is here, and has brought this gentleman, a doctor, to you."

Bazarov moved his eyes about him. "She is here. . . . I want to see her."

"You shall see her, Evgeny; but first we must have a little talk with the doctor. I will tell him the whole history of your illness since Sidor Sidorich" (this was the name of the district doctor) "has gone, and we will have a little consultation."

Bazarov glanced at the German. "Well, talk away quickly, only not in Latin; you see, I know the meaning of *jam moritur*.[1]

"Der Herr scheint des Deutschen mächtig zu sein," [2] began this new follower of Æsculapius, turning to Vassily Ivanovich.

"*Ich*. . . . *gabe* . . . We had better speak Russian," said the old man.

"*Ach* so! so that's how it is. . . . To be sure . . ." and the consultation began.

Half-an-hour later Anna Sergeyevna, conducted by Vassily Ivanovich, came into the study. The doctor had had time to whisper to her that it was hopeless even to think of the patient's recovery.

She looked at Bazarov . . . and stood still in the doorway, so greatly was she impressed by the inflamed, and at the same time deathly face, with its dim eyes fastened upon her. She was simply dismayed, with a sort of cold and suffocating fear; the thought that she would not have felt like that if she had really loved him flashed instantaneously through her brain.

"Thanks," he said painfully, "I did not expect this. It's a good deed. So we have seen each other again, as you promised."

"Anna Sergeyvena has been so kind," began Vassily Ivanovich . . .

"Father, leave us alone. Anna Sergeyevna, you will allow it, I fancy, now?"

With a motion of his head, he indicated his prostrate helpless frame.

Vassily Ivanovich went out.

"Well, thanks," repeated Bazarov. "This is royally done. Monarchs, they say, visit the dying too."

"Evgeny Vassilyich, I hope—"

"Ah, Anna Sergeyevna, let us speak the truth. It's all over with me. I'm under the wheel. So it turns out that it was useless to think of the future. Death's an old joke, but it comes fresh to every one. So far I'm not afraid . . . but there, unconsciousness

1. "Is dying now."

2. "The gentleman seems to master the German language."

will come, and then it's all over!——" he waved his hand feebly. "Well, what do I have to say to you . . . that I loved you? There was no sense in that even before, and less than ever now. Love is a form, and my own form is already breaking up. I better say how lovely you are! And now here you stand, so beautiful . . ."

Anna Sergeyevna gave an involuntary shudder.

"Never mind, don't be uneasy. . . . Sit down there . . . Don't come close to me; you know, my illness is catching."

Anna Sergeyevna swiftly crossed the room, and sat down in the arm-chair near the sofa on which Bazarov was lying.

"Noble-hearted!" he whispered. "Oh, how near, and how young, and fresh, and pure . . . in this loathsome room! . . . Well, good-bye! live long, that's the best of all, and make the most of it while there is time. You see what a hideous spectacle; the worm half crushed, but writhing still. And, you see, I thought too: I'd break down so many things, I wouldn't die, why should I, there were problems to solve, and I was a giant! And now all the problem for the giant is how to die decently, though that makes no difference to any one either . . . Never mind; I'm not going to wag my tail."

Bazarov fell silent, and began feeling with his hand for the glass. Anna Sergeyevna gave him a drink, not taking off her glove, and drawing her breath apprehensively.

"You will forget me," he began again; "the dead's no companion for the living. My father will tell you what a man Russia is losing. . . . That's nonsense, but don't contradict the old man. Whatever toy will comfort the child . . . you know. And be kind to mother. People like them aren't to be found in your great world if you look by daylight with a candle. . . . I am needed by Russia. . . . No, it's clear, I am not needed. And who is needed? The shoemaker's needed, the tailor's needed, the butcher . . . gives us meat . . . the butcher . . . wait a little, I'm getting mixed. . . . There's a forest here . . ."

Bazarov put his hand to his brow.

Anna Sergeyevna bent down to him. "Evgeny Vassilyich, I am here . . ."

He at once took his hand away, and raised himself.

"Good-bye," he said with sudden force, and his eyes gleamed with their last light. "Good-bye. . . . Listen . . . you know I didn't kiss you then. . . . Breathe on the dying lamp, and let it go out . . ."

Anna Sergeyevna put her lips to his forehead.

"Enough!" he murmured, and dropped back on to the pillow. "Now . . . darkness . . ."

Anna Sergeyevna went softly out. "Well?" Vassily Ivanovich

asked her in a whisper.

"He has fallen asleep," she answered, hardly audibly. Bazarov was not fated to awaken. Towards evening he sank into complete unconsciousness, and the following day he died. Father Alexey performed the last rites of religion over him. When they anointed him, when the holy oil touched his breast, one eye opened, and it seemed as though at the sight of the priest in his vestments, the smoking censers, the light before the ikon, something like a shudder of horror passed over the death-stricken face. When at last he had breathed his last, and there arose a universal lamentation in the house, Vassily Ivanovich was seized by a sudden frenzy. "I said I should rebel," he shrieked hoarsely, with his face inflamed and distorted, shaking his fist in the air, as though threatening some one; "and I rebel, I rebel!" But Arina Vlasyevna, all in tears, hung upon his neck, and both prostrated themselves. "Side by side," Anfisushka related afterwards in the servants' room, "they drooped their poor heads like lambs at noonday . . ."

But the heat of noonday passes, and evening comes and night, and then, too, the return to the kindly refuge, where sleep is sweet for the weary and heavy laden. . . .

XXVIII

Six months had passed by. White winter had come with the cruel stillness of unclouded frosts, the thick-lying, crunching snow, the rosy rime on the trees, the pale emerald sky, the caps of smoke above the chimneys, the clouds of steam rushing out of the doors when they are opened for an instant, with the fresh faces, that look stung by the cold, and the hurrying trot of the chilled horses. A January day was drawing to its close; the cold of evening was more keen than ever in the motionless air, and a lurid sunset was rapidly dying away. There were lights burning in the windows of the house at Marino; Prokofich in a black frock coat and white gloves, with a special solemnity laid the table for seven. A week before in the small parish church two weddings had taken place quietly, and almost without witnesses—Arkady and Katya's, and Nikolai Petrovich and Fenichka's; and on this day Nikolai Petrovich was giving a farewell dinner to his brother, who was going away to Moscow on business. Anna Sergeyevna had gone there also directly after the ceremony was over, after making very handsome presents to the young people.

Precisely at three o'clock they all gathered about the table. Mitya was placed there too; with him appeared a nurse in a cap of glazed brocade. Pavel Petrovich took his seat between Katya and Fenichka; the husbands took their places beside their wives. Our friends had changed of late; they all seemed to have grown stronger and better looking; only Pavel Petrovich was thinner, which gave an even more elegant and *grand seigneur* air to his expressive features. . . . And Fenichka, too, was different. In a fresh silk gown, with a wide velvet head-dress on her hair, with a gold chain round her neck, she sat with respectful immobility, respectful towards herself and everything surrounding her, and smiled as though she would say, "I beg your pardon; I'm not to blame." And not she alone—all the others smiled, and also seemed apologetic; they were all a little awkward, a little sorry, and in reality very happy. They all helped one another with humorous attentiveness, as though they had all agreed to rehearse a sort of artless comedy. Katya was the most composed of all; she looked confidently about her, and it could be seen that Nikolai Petrovich was already dotingly fond of her. At the end of dinner he got up, and his glass in his hand, turned to Pavel Petrovich.

"You are leaving us . . . you are leaving us, dear brother," he began; "not for long, to be sure; but still, I cannot help expressing what I . . . what we . . . how much I . . . how much we. . . . There, the worst of it is, we don't know how to make speeches. Arkady, you speak."

"No, daddy, I've not prepared anything."

"As though I were so well prepared! Well, brother, I will simply say, let me embrace you, wish you all good luck, and come back to us as quickly as you can!"

Pavel Petrovich exchanged kisses with every one, of course not excluding Mitya; in Fenichka's case, he kissed also her hand, which she had not yet learned to offer properly, and drinking off the glass which had been filled again, he said with a deep sigh, "May you be happy my friends! *Farewell!*" This English finale passed unnoticed; but all were touched.

"To the memory of Bazarov," Katya whispered in her husband's ear, as she clinked glasses with him. Arkady pressed her hand warmly in response, but he did not venture to propose this toast aloud.

This would seem to be the end. But perhaps some of our readers would care to know what each of the characters we have introduced is doing in the present, the actual present. We are ready to satisfy him.

Anna Sergeyevna has recently married, not for love but out of good sense, with one of the future leaders of Russia, a very clever man, a lawyer, with vigorous practical sense, a strong will, and remarkable eloquence—still young, good-natured, and cold as ice. They live in the greatest harmony together, and will live perhaps to attain complete happiness . . . perhaps love. The Princess K— is dead, forgotten the day of her death. The Kirsanovs, father and son, have settled down at Marino; their fortunes are beginning to mend. Arkady has become zealous in the management of the estate, and the "farm" now yields a fairly good income. Nikolai Petrovich has been made one of the mediators appointed to carry out the emancipation reforms, and works with all his energies; he is forever driving about over his district; delivers long speeches (he maintains the opinion that the peasants ought to be "brought to comprehend things," that is to say, they ought to be reduced to a state of exhaustion by the constant repetition of one and the same words); and yet, to tell the truth, he does not give complete satisfaction either to the refined gentry, who talk with *chic* or with melancholy of the *emancipation* (pronouncing it as though it were French), nor to the uncultivated gentry, who unceremoniously curse "tha' '*muncipation*.' " He is too soft-hearted for both sets. Katerina Sergeyevna has a son, little Nikolai, while Mitya runs about merrily and talks fluently. Fenichka, Fedosya Nikolaevna, after her husband and Mitya, adores no one so much as her daughter-in-law, and when the latter is at the piano, she would gladly spend the whole day at her side. A passing word of Peter. He has grown perfectly rigid with stupidity and dignity, pronounces all his *e*'s as *u*'s but he too is married, and received a respectable dowry with his bride, the daughter of a market-gardener of the town, who had refused two excellent suitors, only because they had no watch; while Peter not only had a watch—he had a pair of patent leather shoes.

In Dresden, on the Brühl Terrace, between two and four o'clock—the most fashionable time for walking—you may meet a man about fifty, quite grey, and looking as though he suffered from gout, but still handsome, elegantly dressed, and with that special stamp which is gained only by moving in the higher strata of society. That is Pavel Petrovich. From Moscow he went abroad for the sake of his health, and has settled for good at Dresden, where he associates mostly with the English and with passing Russians. With English people he behaves simply, almost modestly, but with dignity; they find him rather a bore, but respect him for being, as they say, "*a perfect gentleman*." With Russians he is more free and easy, gives vent to his spleen, and makes fun of himself and them, but that is done by him with great amiability, negligence, and propriety. He holds Slavophile views;

it is well known that in the highest society this is regarded as *très distingué!* He reads nothing in Russian, but on his writing table there is a silver ash-tray in the shape of a peasant's plaited shoe. He is much run after by our tourists. Matvey Ilyich Kolyazin, happening to be "in temporary opposition," paid him a majestic visit on his way to take the waters in Bohemia; while the natives, with whom, however, he is very little seen, positively grovel before him. No one can so readily and quickly obtain a ticket for the court chapel, for the theatre and such things as *der Herr Baron von Kirsanoff*. He does as much good as he can; he still makes some little noise in the world; it is not for nothing that he was once a great society lion, but life is a burden to him . . . a heavier burden than he suspects himself. One need but glance at him in the Russian church, when, leaning against the wall on one side, he sinks into thought, and remains long without stirring, bitterly compressing his lips, then suddenly recollects himself, and begins almost imperceptibly to cross himself. . . .

Kushkin, too, went abroad. She is in Heidelberg, and is now studying not natural science but architecture, in which, according to her own account, she has discovered new laws. She still fraternizes with students, especially with the young Russians studying physics and chemistry, with whom Heidelberg is crowded, and who astound the naïve German professors at first by the soundness of their views of things, later astound the same professor no less by their complete inactivity and absolute idleness. In company with two or three such young chemists, who don't know oxygen from nitrogen, but are filled with scepticism and self-conceit, and with the great Elisyevich, too, Sitnikov now roams about Petersburg, also getting ready to be great, and, according to himself, continues Bazarov's "work." There is talk that some one recently gave him a beating; but he paid the fellow back: in an obscure little article, hidden in an obscure little journal, he has hinted that the man who beat him was a coward. He calls this irony. His father bullies him as before, while his wife regards him as a fool . . . and a literary man.

There is a small village graveyard in one of the remote corners of Russia. Like almost all our graveyards it presents a wretched appearance; the ditches surrounding it have long been overgrown; the grey wooden crosses lie fallen and rotting under their once painted gables; the tombstones are all displaced, as though some one were pushing them up from beneath; two or three ragged trees scarcely give scant shade; the sheep wander unchecked among the tombs . . . But among them is one untouched by man, untrampled by beast, only the birds perch upon it and sing at daybreak. An iron railing runs round it; two young fir-trees have been planted, one at each end. Evgeny Bazarov is buried in this tomb. Often from the little village not far off, two quite feeble old people come to visit it—a husband and wife. Supporting one another, they move to it with heavy steps; they go up to the railing, fall down, and remain on their knees, and long and bitterly they weep, and intently they gaze at the mute stone, under which their son is lying; they exchange some brief word, wipe away the dust from the stone, set straight a branch of a fir-tree, and pray again, and cannot tear themselves from this place, where they seem to be nearer to their son, to their memories of him. . . . Can it be that their prayers and their tears are fruitless? Can it be that love, sacred, devoted love, is not all-powerful? Oh, no! However passionate, sinning, and rebellious the heart hidden in the tomb, the flowers growing over it peep serenely at us with their innocent eyes; they tell us not of eternal peace alone, of that great peace of "indifferent" nature; they tell us, too, of eternal reconciliation and of life without end.

August, 1861.

The Author on the Novel

IVAN TURGENEV

Apropos of *Fathers and Sons* †

I was sea-bathing at Ventnor, a small town on the Isle of Wight—it was in August, 1860—when the first idea occurred to me of *Fathers and Sons,* the novel which deprived me, forever I believe, of the good opinion of the Russian younger generation. I have heard it said and read it in critical articles not once but many times that in my works I always "started with an idea" or "developed an idea." Some people praised me for it, others, on the contrary, censured me; for my part, I must confess that I never attempted to "create a character" unless I had for my departing point not an idea but a living person to whom the appropriate elements were later on gradually attached and added. Not possessing a great amount of free inventive powers, I always felt the need of some firm ground on which I could plant my feet. The same thing happened with *Fathers and Sons;* at the basis of its chief character, Bazarov, lay the personality of a young provincial doctor I had been greatly struck by. (He died shortly before 1860.) In that remarkable man I could watch the embodiment of that principle which had scarcely come to life but was just beginning to stir at the time, the principle which later received the name of nihilism. Though very powerful, the impression that man left on me was still rather vague. At first I could not quite make him out myself, and I kept observing and listening intently to everything around me, as though wishing to check the truth of my own impressions. I was worried by the following fact: not in one work of our literature did I ever find as much as a hint at what I seemed to see everywhere; I could not help wondering whether I was not chasing after a phantom. On the Isle of Wight, I remember, there lived with me at the time a Russian who was endowed with excellent taste and a remarkable "nose" for everything which the late Apollon Grigoryev called "the ideas" of an epoch. I told him what I was thinking of and what interested me so much and was astonished to hear the following remark: "Haven't you created such a character already in—Rudin?" I said nothing. Rudin and Bazarov—one and the same character!

Those words produced such an effect on me that for several weeks I tried not to think of the work I had in mind. However,

† From Ivan Turgenev, *Literary Reminiscences and Autobiographical Fragments,* translated by David Magarshack, New York, 1958, pp. 193–204. Copyright 1958 by Farrar Straus & Cudahy, Inc. Reprinted by permission of the publishers, Farrar, Straus & Giroux.

on my return to Paris I sat down to it again—the *plot* gradually matured in my head; in the course of the winter I wrote the first chapters, but I finished the novel in Russia, on my estate, in July [1861]. In the autumn I read it to a few friends, revised something, added something, and in March, 1862, *Fathers and Sons* was published in *The Russian Herald*.

I shall not enlarge on the impression this novel has created. I shall merely say that when I returned to Petersburg, on the very day of the notorious fires in the Apraksin Palace, the word "nihilist" had been caught up by thousands of people, and the first exclamation that escaped from the lips of the first acquaintance I met on Nevsky Avenue was: "Look what *your* nihilists are doing! They are setting Petersburg on fire!" My impressions at that time, though different in kind, were equally painful. I became conscious of a coldness bordering on indignation among many friends whose ideas I shared; I received congratulations, and almost kisses, from people belonging to a camp I loathed, from enemies. It embarrassed and—grieved me. But my conscience was clear; I knew very well that my attitude towards the character I had created was honest and that far from being prejudiced against him, I even sympathised with him.[1] I have too great a respect for the vocation of an artist, a writer, to act against my conscience in such a matter. The word "respect" is hardly the right one here; I simply could not, and knew not how to, work otherwise; and after all, there was no reason why I should do that. My critics described my novel as a "lampoon" and spoke of my "exasperated" and "wounded" vanity; but why should I write a lampoon on Dobrolyubov, whom I had hardly met, but whom I thought highly of as a man and as a talented writer? However little I might think of my own talent as a writer, I always have been, and still am, of the opinion that the writing of a lampoon, a "squib," is unworthy of it. As for my wounded vanity, all I can say is that Dobrolyubov's article on my last work before *Fathers and Sons*—*On the Eve* (and he was quite rightly considered as the mouthpiece of public opinion)—that that article, published in 1861, is full of the warmest and—honestly speaking—the most undeserved eulogies. But the critics had to present me as an offended lampoonist: *leur siège était fait*, [they had started their seige] and even this year I could read in Supplement No. 1 to *Cosmos* (page 96) the following lines: "At last, *everyone knows*

1. I should like to quote the following extract from my diary: "30 July, Sunday. An hour and a half ago I finished my novel at last. . . . I don't know whether it will be successful. *The Contemporary* will probably treat me with contempt for my Bazarov and . . . will not believe that while writing my novel I felt an involuntary attachment to him."

[*The Contemporary* was a leading journal, in which the ideas repeated by Bazarov appeared. *Editor.*]

that the pedestal on which Turgenev stood has been destroyed chiefly by Dobrolyubov. . . ." and further on (page 98) they speak of my "feeling of bitterness," which the critic, however, "understands and—perhaps even forgives."

The critics, generally speaking, have not got quite the right idea of what is taking place in the mind of an author or of what exactly his joys and sorrows, his aims, successes and failures are. They do not, for instance, even suspect the pleasure which Gogol mentions and which consists of castigating oneself and one's faults in the imaginary characters one depicts; they are quite sure that all an author does is to "develop his ideas"; they refuse to believe that to reproduce truth and the reality of life correctly and powerfully is the greatest happiness for an author, even if this truth does not coincide with his own sympathies. Let me illustrate my meaning by a small example. I am an inveterate and incorrigible Westerner. I have never concealed it and I am not concealing it now. And yet in spite of that it has given me great pleasure to show up in the person of Panshin (in *A House of Gentlefolk*) all the common and vulgar sides of the Westerners; I made the Slavophil Lavretsky "crush him utterly." Why did I do it, I who consider the Slavophil doctrine false and futile? Because *in the given case life, according to my ideas, happened to be like that,* and what I wanted above all was to be sincere and truthful. In depicting Bazarov's personality, I excluded everything artistic from the range of his sympathies, I made him express himself in harsh and unceremonious tones, not out of an absurd desire to insult the younger generation (! ! !),[2] but simply as a result of my observations of my acquaintance, Dr. D., and people like him. "Life happened to be *like that,*" my experience told me once more, perhaps mistakenly, but, I repeat, not dishonestly. There was no need for me to be too clever about it; I just had to depict his character *like that.* My personal predilections had nothing to do with it. But I expect many of my readers will be surprised if I tell them that with the exception of Bazarov's views on art, I share almost all his convictions. And I am assured that I am on the side of the "Fathers"—I, who in the person of Pavel Kirsanov have even "sinned" against artistic truth and gone too far, to the point of caricaturing his faults and making him look ridiculous![3]

2. Among the multitude of proofs of my "spite against our youth" one critic cited the fact that I made Bazarov lose his game of cards to Father Alexey. "He simply doesn't know," the critic observed, "how most to hurt and humiliate him! He can't even play cards!" There can be no doubt that if I had made Bazarov win his game, the same critic would have exclaimed, "Isn't it abundantly clear? The author wants to suggest that Bazarov is a cardsharper!"

3. Foreigners cannot understand the cruel accusations made against me for my Bazarov. *Fathers and Sons* has been

The cause of all the misunderstandings, the whole, so to speak "trouble," arose from the fact that the Bazarov type created by me has not yet had time to go through the gradual phases through which literary types usually go. Unlike Onegin and Pechorin,[4] he had not been through a period of idealisation and sympathetic, starry-eyed adoration. At the very moment the *new* man—Bazarov —appeared, the author took up a critical, objective attitude towards him. That confused many people and—who knows?—that was, if not a mistake, an injustice. The Bazarov type had at least as much right to be idealized as the literary types that preceded it. I have just said that the author's attitude towards the character he had created confused the reader: the reader always feels ill at ease, he is easily bewildered and even aggrieved if an author treats his imaginary character like a living person, that is to say, if he sees and displays his good as well as his bad sides, and, above all, if he does not show unmistakable signs of sympathy or antipathy for his own child. The reader feels like getting angry: he is asked not to follow a well-beaten path, but to tread his own path. "Why should I take the trouble," he can't help thinking. "Books exist for entertainment and not for racking one's brains. And, besides, would it have been too much to ask the author to tell me what to think of such and such a character or what he thinks of him himself?" But it is even worse if the author's attitude towards that character is itself rather vague and undefined, if the author himself does not know whether or not he loves the character he has created (as it happened to me in my attitude towards Bazarov, for "the involuntary attraction" I mentioned in my diary is not love). The reader is ready to ascribe to the author all sorts of non-existent sympathies or antipathies, provided he can escape from the feeling of unpleasant "vagueness."

---

translated several times into German. This is what one critic writes in analysing the last translation published in Riga (*Vossische Zeitung, Donnerstag, d. 10 Juni, zweite Beilage, Seite 3*: *"Es bleibt für den unbefangenen . . . Leser schlechthin unbegreiflich, wie sich gerade die radicale Jugend Russlands über diesen geistigen Vertreter ihrer Richtung (Bazaroff), ihrer Ueberzeugungen und Bestrebungen, wie ihn T. zeichnete, in eine Wuth hinein erhitzen konnte, die sie den Dichter gleichsam in die Acht erklären und mit jeder Schmähung überhaüfen liess. Man sollte denken, jeder moderne Radicale könne nur mit froher Genungthuung in einer so stolzen Gestalt, von solcher Wucht des Charakters, solcher gründlichen Freiheit von allem Kleinlichen, Trivialen, Faulen, Schlaffen und Lügenhalften, sein und seiner Parteigenossen typisches Portrait dargestellt sehn."*

That is: "To an unprejudiced . . . reader it is utterly incomprehensible how radical Russian youth could work itself into such a fury over the spiritual representative of their movement (Bazarov), their convictions and their aspirations, as Turgenev depicted him, and at the same time send the author to Coventry and hold him up to execration. One might have supposed that every modern radical would be only too glad to recognise himself and his comrades in such a proud personality, endowed with such a strength of character, such utter freedom from everything that is trivial, vulgar and false."

4. In Pushkin's *Evgeny Onegin* and Lermontov's *Hero of Our Time* [*Editor*].

"Neither fathers nor sons," said a witty lady to me after reading my book, "that should be the real title of your novel and—you are yourself a nihilist." A similar view was expressed with even greater force on the publication of *Smoke*. I am afraid I do not feel like raising objections: perhaps, that lady was right. In the business of fiction writing everyone (I am judging by myself) does what he can and not what he wants, and—as much as he can. I suppose that a work of fiction has to be judged *en gros* and while insisting on conscientiousness on the part of the author, the other *sides* of his activity must be regarded, I would not say, with indifference, but with calm. And, much as I should like to please my critics, I cannot plead guilty to any absence of conscientiousness on my part.

I have a very curious collection of letters and other documents in connection with *Fathers and Sons*. It is rather interesting to compare them. While some of my correspondents accuse me of insulting the younger generation, of being behind the times and a reactionary, and inform me that they "are burning my photographs with a contemptuous laugh," others, on the contrary, reproach me with pandering to the same younger generation. "You are crawling at the feet of Bazarov!" one correspondent exclaims. "You are just pretending to condemn him; in effect, you are fawning upon him and waiting as a favour for one casual smile from him!" One critic, I remember, addressing me directly in strong and eloquent words, depicted Mr. Katkov and me as two conspirators who in the peaceful atmosphere of my secluded study, are hatching our despicable plot, our libellous attack, against the young Russian forces. . . . It made an effective picture! Actually, that is how this *plot* came about. When Mr. Katkov received my manuscript of *Fathers and Sons*, of whose contents he had not even a rough idea, he was utterly bewildered.[5] The Bazarov type seemed to him "almost an apotheosis of *The Contemporary Review*," and I should not have been surprised if he had refused to publish my novel in his journal. "*Et voilà comme on ècrit l'histoire!*" [And that's how history is written!] one could have

5. I hope Mr. Katkov will not be angry with me for quoting a few passages from a letter he wrote to me at the time. "If," he wrote, "you have not actually apotheosized Bazarov, I can't help feeling that he has found himself by some sort of accident on a very high pedestal. He really does tower above all those who surround him. Compared to him, everything is either rubbish, or weak and immature. Was that the impression one ought to have got? One can feel that in his novel the author wanted to characterize a principle for which he has little sympathy, but that he seems to hesitate in the choice of his tone and has unconsciously fallen under its spell. One cannot help feeling that there is something forced in the author's attitude towards the hero of his novel, a sort of awkwardness and stiffness. The author seems to be abashed in his presence, he seems not so much to dislike him as to be afraid of him!" Mr. Katkov goes on to express his regrets that I did not let Mrs. Odintsov treat Bazarov ironically, and so on—all in the some vein! It is clear, therefore, that one of the conspirators was not altogether satisfied with the other's work.

exclaimed, but—is it permissible to give such a high-sounding name to such small matters?

On the other hand, I quite understand the reasons for the anger aroused by my book among the members of a certain party. They are not entirely groundless and I accept—without false humility—part of the reproaches levelled against me. The word "nihilist" I had used in my novel was taken advantage of by a great many people who were only waiting for an excuse, a pretext, to put a stop to the movement which had taken possession of Russian society. But I never used that word as a pejorative term or with any offensive aim, but as an exact and appropriate expression of a fact, an historic fact, that had made its appearance among us; it was transformed into a means of denunciation, unhesitating condemnation and almost a brand of infamy. Certain unfortunate events that occurred at that time increased the suspicions that were just beginning to arise and seemed to confirm the widespread misgivings and justified the worries and efforts of the "saviours of our motherland," for in Russia such "saviours of the motherland" had made their appearance just then. The tide of public opinion, which is still so indeterminate in our country, turned back. . . . But a shadow fell over my name. I do not deceive myself; I know that that shadow will not disappear. But why did not others—people before whom I feel so deeply my own insignificance—utter the great words: *Périssent nos noms, pourvu que la chose publique soit sauvée* . . . i.e. may our names perish so long as the general cause is saved! Following them, I too can console myself with the thought that my book has been of some benefit. This thought compensates me for the unpleasantness of undeserved reproaches. And, indeed, what does it matter? Who twenty or thirty years hence will remember all these storms in a teacup? Or my name—with or without a shadow over it.

But enough about myself, and besides it is time to finish these fragmentary reminiscences which, I am afraid, will hardly satisfy the reader. I just want to say a few parting words to my young contemporaries, my colleagues who enter upon the slippery career of literature. I have already said once and I am ready to repeat that that I am not blinded about my position. My twenty-five-year-old "service to the Muses" has drawn to a close amid the growing coldness of the public, and I cannot think of any reason why it should grow warmer once more. New times have come and new men are needed; literary veterans, like the military ones, are almost always invalids, and blessed are those who know how to retire at the right time! I do not intend to pronounce my farewell words in preceptorial tones, to which, incidentally, I have no right whatever, but in the tone of an old friend who is listened to with half-condescending and half-impatient attention, provided he is not too longwinded. I shall do my best not to be that.

And so, my dear colleagues, it is to you that I am addressing myself.

Grief nur hinein ins volle Menschenleben!

I would like to say to you, quoting Goethe—

Ein jeder lebt's—nicht vielen ist's bekannt
Und wo ihr's packt—da ist's interessant!

[i.e. "put your hand right in (I am afraid I can't translate it any better), into the very depth of human life! Everyone lives by it, but few know it, and wherever you grasp it, there it is interesting!"] It is only talent that gives one the power for this "grasping," this "catching hold" of life, and one cannot acquire talent; but talent alone is not enough. What one needs is the constant communion with the environment one undertakes to reproduce; what one needs is truthfulness, a truthfulness that is inexorable in relation to one's own feelings; what one needs is freedom, absolute freedom of opinions and ideas, and, finally, what one needs is education, what one needs is knowledge! "Oh, we understand! We can see what you are driving at!" many will perhaps exclaim at this point. "Potugin's ideas! Ci-vi-li-za-tion, *prenez mon ours!* [It's an old, old story!]" Such exclamations do not surprise me, but they will not make me take back anything I have said. Learning is not only light, according to the Russian proverb, it is also freedom. Nothing makes a man so free as knowledge and nowhere is freedom so needed as in art, in poetry; it is not for nothing that even in official language arts are called "free." Can a man "grasp," "catch hold of" what surrounds him if he is all tied up inside? Pushkin felt this deeply; it is not for nothing that he said in his immortal sonnet, a sonnet every young writer ought to learn by heart and remember as a commandment—

. . . . by a free *road*
Go, where your free *mind may draw you. . . .*

The absence of such freedom, incidentally, explains why not a single one of the Slavophils, in spite of their undoubted gifts,[6] has ever created anything that is alive; not one of them knew how to remove—even for a moment—his rose-coloured spectacles. But the saddest example of the absence of true freedom, arising out of

6. One cannot, of course, reproach Slavophils with ignorance or lack of education; but for the achievement of an artistic result one needs—to use a modern expression—the combined action of many *factors*. The factor the Slavophils lack is freedom; others lack education, still others talent, etc. etc.

the absence of true knowledge, is provided by the last work of Count L. N. Tolstoy (*War and Peace*), which at the same time exceeds by its creative force and poetic gifts almost anything that has appeared in our literature since 1840. No, without education and without freedom in the widest sense of the word—in relation to oneself and to one's preconceived ideas and systems, and, indeed, to one's people and one's history—a true artist is unthinkable; without that air, it is impossible to breathe.

As for the final result, the final appraisal of a so-called literary career—here, too, one has to remember the words of Goethe:

Sind's Rosen—nun sie werden blüh'n

—"if these are roses, they will bloom." There are no unacknowledged geniuses as there are no merits which survive their appointed time. "Sooner or later everyone finds his niche," the late Belinsky used to say. One has to be thankful if one has done one's bit at the right time and at the right hour. Only the few chosen ones are able to leave for posterity not only the content, but also the *form*, of their ideas and opinions, their personality, to which, generally speaking, the mob remains entirely indifferent. Ordinary individuals are condemned to total disappearance, to being swallowed up by the torrent; but they have increased its force, they have widened and deepened its bed—what more do they want?

I am laying down my pen. . . . One more last advice to young writers and one more last request. My friends, never try to justify yourselves (whatever libellous stories they may tell about you). Don't try to explain a misunderstanding, don't be anxious, yourselves, either to say or to hear "the last word." Carry on with your work—and in time everything will come right. At any rate, let a considerable period of time elapse first—and then look on all the old squabbles from an historical point of view, as I have tried to do now. Let the following example serve as a lesson to you: in the course of my literary career I have only once tried "to get the facts right." Namely, when *The Contemporary Review* began assuring its subscribers in its announcements that it had dispensed with my services because of the *unfitness* of my convictions (while, in fact, it was I who, in spite of their requests, would have nothing more to do with them—of which I have documentary proof), I could not resist announcing the real state of affairs in public and—of course, suffered a complete fiasco. The younger generation were more indignant with me than ever. "How did I dare to raise my hand against their idol! What does it matter if I was right? I should have kept silent!" I profited by this lesson; I wish you, too, should profit by it.

As for my request, it is as follows: guard our Russian tongue, our beautiful Russian tongue, that treasure, that trust handed down to you by your predecessors, headed again by Pushkin! Treat this powerful instrument with respect; it may work miracles in the hands of those who know how to use it! Even those who dislike "philosophic abstractions" and "poetic sentimentalities," even to practical people, for whom language is merely a means for expressing thoughts, a means to an end, just like an ordinary lever, even to them I will say: respect at least the laws of mechanics and extract every possible use from every thing! Or else, glancing over some dull, confused, feebly longwinded diatribe in a journal, the reader will perforce think that instead of a *lever* you are using some antedeluvian props—that you are going back to the infancy of mechanics itself. . . .

But, enough, or I shall become longwinded myself.

1868–69
Baden-Baden.

From Turgenev's Letters †

P. V. Annenkov to Turgenev [1]

September 26 (*October* 9), 1861.

* * * In Moscow I took your novel from Katkov [2] and read it carefully. In my opinion it is a masterful thing in exposition and finish, surpassing in its external form everything written by its author till now. That is the general consensus rather than my own or somebody's in particular, and therefore you may rest secure on that score. Bazarov is something else. There are different opinions about him as a result of a single cause: the author himself is somewhat constrained about him and doesn't know what to consider him—a productive force in the future or a stinking abscess of an

† From I. S. Turgenev, *Pis'ma v 13–i tomakh,* Moscow, 1961 to date, Vols. 4, 7, and 8, and I. S. Turgenev, *Sobranie sochineniy,* Moscow, 1949, Vol. XI (letters of 1874–1882). Translated by Ralph E. Matlaw.

All dates are given in both old and new style. The first is the Julian calendar used in Russia until 1917, the second the Gregorian used in the West. In the nineteenth century the Julian calendar was 12 days behind the Gregorian, and in the twentieth it was 13 days behind. The liberation of the serfs, February 19, 1861, thus took place on March 3 in our calendar, and the October Revolution is annually commemorated in the Soviet Union on November 7. Almost all Turgenev's letters bear the double date.

1. This important letter, to which Turgenev frequently alludes, was published only recently in *Russkaya Literatura,* 1958, No. 1, pp. 147–49. P. V. Annenkov (1813–87) was a critic of the mid-century and friend to many leading writers, including Turgenev. His reminiscences of that period are his most important and lasting work [*Editor*].

2. M. N. Katkov (1818–87), publisher of *The Russian Herald,* where *Fathers and Sons* appeared. Katkov became increasingly conservative and by the 1860's the journal was already considered reactionary [*Editor*].

empty culture, of which one should rid oneself quickly. Bazarov cannot be both things at the same time, yet the author's indecisiveness sways the reader's thoughts too from one pole to the other. In the form that he (that is, Bazarov) appears now, he is able at one and the same time to flatter pleasantly all negators of Tryapichkin's ilk, creating for them an honored ideal, at which they will gaze very willingly, and, on the other hand, he is capable of arousing the loathing of people who work, have faith in science and in history. He is two-faced, like Janus, and each party will see only that facet which comforts it most or which it is most capable of understanding. That's precisely what I have already seen in practice. Katkov is horrified by that force, power, superiority to the crowd, and ability to subjugate people which he noted in Bazarov; he says it is *The Contemporary* raised to an apotheosis, and despairs for thought and science when people like the author of the tale instead of fighting with the corrupting tendency, strike the colors before it, yield before it, give up, venerate in thought its empty, phosphorescent, and deceptive lustre. Another person, Katkov's direct opposite, daring to do battle with him on that score, am I. In clear conscience, that gentleman, on the contrary, sees in Bazarov the same Mongol, Genghis Khan, etc., that the real ones were; his animal brute force is not only not attractive, but increases one's repulsion toward him and is tainted with sterility. The whole type *in toto* is a condemnation of the savage society wherein he could be born, and if that type becomes known to foreigners, it will be used by them as proof of that coarse, nomadic, brutal condition in which our state finds itself, though it has a gloss of books from the Leipzig Fair. That's the kind of nonsense and disagreement Bazarov already produces now.

And you, friend, are responsible for it just the same.

Let us assume that Katkov's eyes start in fear and that I, on the contrary, am completely correct, which I do not doubt for a minute, but you really did cast a Plutarchian aura over Bazarov, because you did not even give him that "burning, diseased egotism" that distinguishes the entire generation of nihilists. An inveterate romantic may still be without "egotism" among us, but is this possible for the latest negator? That is a real trait, after all, and its absence will have the effect of making people doubt that Bazarov belongs to this world, relating him to a heroic cycle, to kinship with Ossian turned inside out, etc. In order to show the other side of the character, that splendid scene with Arkady on the haystack is not enough; occasionally or at least at some time, the Sitnikov in Bazarov must creep out too. Only through venomous egotism can Bazarov be tied to reality—that artery from the real world to his navel—and there is no reason for cutting it off. For that matter it's easy to alleviate the situation if, while maintaining all his contempt for Sitnikov, he at some time mentions to Arkady that one must preserve the Sitnikovs on the basis of the rules promulgated by Prince Vorontsov, who replied to complaints about the abominations of a certain police inspector, "I know that he is a scoundrel but he has one important merit—he is genuinely devoted to me." Finally, in one of the conversations between Bazarov and Pavel Petrovich, one of them mentions Cavour, directly citing a passage in *The Contemporary*. I think that has to be changed: one must not approach such a special phenomenon of life so directly and indiscriminately. The tale reflects the guiding idea of life but not its actual statement, expression, mannerisms. Speaking entirely in the Hegel manner, that's *schlechte Realität*.[3] But having said all that, at the same time I figuratively kiss your brow for creating that type, which discloses your usual feeling for social phenomena and which is destined to teach, to sober, to make our era pensive, though, of course, our era will undergo all these with a certain amount of stubbornness.

My second remark concerns the splendid Anna Sergeyevna. That type is drawn so delicately by you that its future judges will hardly be able to understand it completely. Only in one place does it become obscure, namely in chapter XXV, where in a conversation with Bazarov a new inclination toward Arkady on A. S.'s part is expressed The traits are so minute here that strong mental magnifying glasses are needed for understanding them, and not everyone is obliged to have them. I think one ought to hint at her new psychological state with some sort of striking turn, otherwise it'll turn out something like a Japanese snuffbox, which contains miniature trees with fruit, ponds, and boats; and that's the more annoying since the general tone of the tale is sharp, in relief, and its progress completely solid. And so far as the scene with Bazarov after receiving Arkady's request for permission to marry Katya is concerned, it is simply unbearable. It's something like Prince Kuchumov or current Russian dramatic literature in general where there is talk for talk's sake and where a kind of repellent, tepid, and fetid psychology reigns. Change that scene any way you like, let it be the mutual gaiety of the conversants, one of whom laughs out of malice and the other out of despair, but change it without fail if you value my respect.

And having said that, I congratulate you on an excellent tale, which proves that its author is still in full possession of his creative power, and that's what was most important of all for me to discover. It will create a great stir—you can expect that. It will not

3. "Bad actuality" [*Editor*].

raise the question of talent and artistic merit but rather whether its author is the historian or ringleader of the party. Serious writers have always given birth to such questions among their contemporaries and that sort of argument around a well-known name always proves the importance and significance of that name. There is no point in speaking of the many splendid details in that tale, and it is so absorbing that while reading it you think the first line stands next to the last one—the middle is swallowed up so quickly! I have heard that Countess Lambert [4] is dissatisfied with the novel: don't believe it. The world into which you led her is so terrible that she has confused its hideousness with the hideousness of the creative work—that's how I explain her judgment to myself. So, it seems, I have conscientiously fulfilled the task placed before me, and would like to know to what extent you yourself share my opinions, which, for that matter, are far from incontrovertible. * * *

To P. V. Annenkov

Paris, October 1 (13), 1861

Dear Pavel Vasil'evich:

Please accept my sincere thanks for your letter in which you express your frank opinion of my tale. It made me very glad, the more so as my confidence in my own work was badly shaken. I agree completely with all your observations (the more so since V. P. Botkin [5] also finds them just), and tomorrow I will begin work on corrections and revisions, which apparently will be of considerable scope, and I have already written Katkov to that effect. I still have a great deal of time at my disposal. Botkin, who is apparently getting better, also made several apt suggestions to me and differs with you in only one thing: he does not like Anna Sergeyevna much. But I think that I know how to bring that whole business into proper balance. When I finish my work I will send it to you, and you pass it on to Katkov. But enough about that and once again my sincere and warm thanks. * * *

To M. N. Katkov

Paris, October 1 (13), 1861

Dear Mikhail Nikiforovich:

Forgive me for bombarding you with letters, but I wanted to forewarn you that as a result of letters I received from Annenkov and the remarks of Botkin to whom I read my tale here, the

4. A close friend of Turgenev's (died 1883). He valued her literary opinions [*Editor*].

5. Literary critic, author, member of liberal sets Turgenev frequented, and a lifelong friend (1810–69) [*Editor*].

revisions of *Fathers and Sons* will be more extensive than I had anticipated, and will occupy me approximately two weeks, during which time you will receive a careful list of all omissions and additions. And therefore I repeat my request *not to publish an excerpt* and also to hold on to the manuscript, that is, not to let others read it. I hope that as a result of my corrections the figure of Bazarov will become clear to you and will not create in you the impression of an apotheosis, which was not my idea at all. Other figures will gain, too, I think. In short, I consider my piece not completely finished, and since I have expended a great deal of work on it I would like to issue it in the best possible form. * * *

To M. N. Katkov

Paris, October 27 (*November* 8), 1861

Dear Mikhail Nikoforovich:

On the advice of friends and on my own conviction, which probably coincides with yours, I think that under the current circumstances [6] the publication of *Fathers and Sons* should be put off for some time, the more so since the censorship may create difficulties now. And therefore I ask you to delay publication, which, however, does not prevent me from sending you the substantial changes and corrections I have made. In any case, rest assured that *Fathers and Sons* will appear—if at all—nowhere other than in *The Russian Herald*. Drop me a note so that I will know that you have received this letter. I also repeat my request to hold on to the manuscript and not let others read it. * * *

To M. N. Katkov

Paris, October 30 (*November* 11), 1861

Dear Mikhail Nikoforovich:

I recently wrote you, but after your letter which I received yesterday I consider it necessary to write a couple of words in reply. I agree with your comments, with almost all of them, particularly about *Pavel Petrovich* and Bazarov himself. So far as Odintsov is concerned, the unclear impression produced by that character indicates to me that here, too, I have to take more pains. (Incidentally, the *argument* between Pavel Petrovich and Bazarov has been completely revised and shortened.)

* * * I cannot agree with one thing: Odintsov ought not to be ironic with Bazarov, nor should the peasant stand higher than he,

6. Turgenev refers to student demonstrations in the fall of 1861 and the arrests that followed. The censors would be far more strict and would strike anything that mentioned or implied the disorders or radical thought among students [*Editor*].

though Bazarov himself is empty and barren. Perhaps my view of Russia is more misanthropic than you suppose: in my mind he is the real hero of our time. A fine hero and a fine time you'll say. But that's how it is.

I repeat my request to keep my product hidden. * * *

To F. M. Dostoevsky

Paris, March 18 (30), 1862

Dear Fedor Mikhailovich:

I cannot tell you to what extent your opinion of *Fathers and Sons* has made me happy. It isn't a question of satisfying one's pride but in the assurance that you haven't made a mistake and haven't missed the mark, and that labor hasn't been wasted. That was the more important for me since people whom I trust very much (I am not talking about Kolbasin) seriously advised me to throw my work into the fire—and only recently (but this is confidential) Pisemsky [7] wrote me that Bazarov is a complete failure. How can one then not doubt oneself and be led astray? It is hard for an author to feel *immediately* to what extent his idea has come to life, and whether it is true, and whether he has mastered it, etc. In his own work he is lost in the woods.

You have probably experienced this more than once yourself. And therefore thank you again. You have so completely and subtly grasped what I wanted to express through Bazarov that I simply throw my hands up in amazement—and in pleasure. It's as if you had entered my soul and felt even what I didn't consider necessary to express. God grant that this indicates not only the keen penetration of a master but also the simple comprehension of a reader—that is, God grant that everyone realize at least a part of what you have seen! Now I am at ease about the destiny of my tale: it has done its work and I have nothing to repent for.

Here is another proof of the extent to which you familiarized yourself with that character: in the meeting between Arkady and Bazarov, at that place where, according to you, something was missing, Bazarov made fun of *knights* and Arkady listened to him with secret horror, etc. I struck it out and now I regret it: [8] in general I rescribbled and revised a great deal under the influence of unfavorable comments, and the sluggishness you noticed may, per-

7. A. F. Pisemsky (1820–81), an outstanding novelist and playwright [*Editor*].

8. The passage was in chapter XXV and was later reintroduced. It reads, "he became terrified and somehow ashamed. Bazarov seemed to understand him. 'Yes, friend,' he said, 'that's what it is to live with feudal people. You become feudal yourself and start participating in jousting tournaments. Well, sir . . .' [*Editor*].

haps, have come from that.

I have received a pleasant letter from Maykov and will answer him. I shall be roundly cursed—but that has to be waited out, like a summer rain. * * *

To A. N. Maykov[9]

Paris, March 18 (30), 1862

Dear Apollon Nikolaevich:

I'll tell you straight out, like a peasant, "God grant you health for your kind and good letter!" You've comforted me greatly. I have not lacked confidence in a single one of my things as strongly as in that very one. The remarks and judgments of people whom I am accustomed to believe were extremely unfavorable. But for Katkov's persistent demands *Fathers and Sons* would never have appeared. Now I can say to myself that I couldn't have written complete nonsense if people like you and Dostoevsky stroke my head and say "Good, little man, we'll give you a 'B'." The image of a student who has solidly passed an examination is much more accurate than your image of the triumphant man, and let me tell you that your comparing yourself to a pigmy is worthless. No, you are a fellow artist, extending your hand in brotherly gesture to your friend. And I reply to your embrace with mine, to your greeting with a warm greeting and with gratitude. You have really set me at ease. Not in vain did Schiller say

> Wer für die Besten seiner Zeit gelebt—
> Der hat gelebt für alle Zeiten.[1]

* * *

To A. A. Fet[2]

Paris, March 19 (31), 1862

* * * I have not yet received a copy of my tale, but three letters have already arrived about the thing from Pisemsky, Dostoevsky, and Maykov. The first abuses the main character, the other two enthusiastically praise everything. That made me rejoice, because I was full of doubts. I think I wrote you that people whom I trust advised me to burn my work. But I tell you without flattery

9. A. N. Maykov (1821–97), a poet and friend of Turgenev's [*Editor*].

1. "He who has lived for the best men of his time/Has lived for all time." The quotation is not accurate [*Editor*].

2. A. A. Fet (1820–92), one of Russia's most sensitive and delicate lyric poets, who was also a hard-fisted, reactionary landowner [*Editor*].

that I await your opinion in order to ascertain definitely what I should think. I argue with you at every step, but I firmly believe in your esthetic sense and in your taste. * * *

To A. A. Fet

Paris, April 6 (18), 1862

First of all, dear Afanasy Afanas'evich, thank you for your letter—and my thanks would be greater if you didn't consider it necessary to put on kid gloves. Believe me, I have borne and am able to bear the harshest truth from my friends. And so, despite your euphemisms, you don't like *Fathers and Sons.* I bow my head, since there is nothing to be done about it, but I want to say a few words in my defense, though I know how unseemly and pointless it is. You ascribe the whole trouble to *tendentiousness reflection,* in short, to reason. But in reality, you had only to say that the craft was inadequate. It seems that I am more naïve than you assume. Tendentiousness! But let me ask you, what kind of tendentiousness in *Fathers and Sons?* Did I want to abuse Bazarov or or to extol him? *I do not know that myself,* since I don't know whether I love him or hate him! There you have tendentiousness! Katkov took me to task for making Bazarov into an apotheosis. You also mention *parallelism.* But where is it, permit me to ask you, and where are these *pairs,* believers and nonbelievers? Does Pavel Petrovich believe or not? I wouldn't know since I simply wanted to portray in him the type of the Stolypins, the Rossets, and other Russian ex-lions. It is a strange thing: you blame me for parallelism, but others write me "Why isn't Anna Sergeyevna a lofty person, to contrast her more fully with Bazarov? Why aren't Bazarov's old people completely patriarchical? Why is Arkady banal, and wouldn't it be better to portray him as an upright young man who is carried away for a moment? What purpose does Fenichka serve, and what conclusions can be drawn from her?" I'll tell you one thing, I drew all those characters as I would draw mushrooms, leaves, and trees. They were an eyesore to me and so I started to sketch them. But it would be strange and amusing to dismiss my own impressions simply because they resemble tendentiousness. I don't want you to draw the conclusion from that that I am a courageous fellow. On the contrary: what can be concluded from my words is even more injurious to me: it's not that I have been too shrewd, but that I was not capable enough. But truth above all. But actually—*omnia vanitas.* * * *

To K. K. Sluchevsky [3]

Paris, April 14 (26), 1862

I hasten to answer your letter, for which I am very grateful to you, dear Sluchevsky. One must value the opinion of youth. In any case I very much want there to be no misunderstandings about my intentions. I'll answer point by point.

1) The first reproach is reminiscent of the accusation made against Gogol and others, why they did not introduce *good* people among the others. Bazarov crushes all the other characters in the novel just the same (Katkov thought I presented an apotheosis of *The Contemporary* in him). The qualities given to him are not accidental. I wanted to make a tragic figure out of him—there was no place for tenderness here. He is honest, upright, and a democrat to his fingertips—and you fail to find *good* sides in him? He recommends *Stoff and Kraft* precisely as a *popular* book, that is, an empty one; the duel with Pavel Petrovich is introduced precisely as graphic proof of the emptiness of elegantly noble knighthood, presented almost in an exaggeratedly comic way. And how could he decline it? After all, Pavel Petrovich would have hit him. I think Bazarov constantly beats Pavel Petrovich and not the other way around. And if he is called a "nihilist" that word must be read as "revolutionary."

2) What you said about Arkady, the rehabilitation of the fathers, etc., only proves—alas!—that I was not understood. *My entire tale is directed against the nobility as the leading class.* Look at Nikolai Petrovich, Pavel Petrovich, and Arkady. Weakness and languor, or limitations. Esthetic feelings made me choose precisely *good* representatives of the nobility, in order to prove my theme the more surely: if the cream is bad what will the milk be like? It would be coarse, *le pont aux ânes* [4]—and untrue to take functionaries, generals, exploiters, etc. All the real *negators* I have known, without exception (Belinsky, Bakunin, Herzen, Dobrolyubov, Speshnev, etc.), came from comparatively good and honest parents. A great idea is contained therein: it removes from the *men of action*, the negators, every suspicion of *personal* dissatisfaction, personal irritation. They go their way only because they are more sensitive to the demands of national life. Countess Sal'yas [5] is wrong when she says that characters like Nikolai Petrovich and Pavel Petrovich are our grandfathers: I am Nikolai Petrovich, as are Ogarev and thousands of others; Stolypin,

3. K. K. Sluchevsky (1837–1904) was voicing the objections of Russian students studying in Heidelberg. He was already then known as a poet. [*Editor*]

4. "Trite" [*Editor*].

5. Countess Sal'yas (1810–81) wrote novels, criticism, and children's stories under the pseudonym Evgeniya Tur [*Editor*].

Esakov, Rosset, our contemporaries too—are Pavel Petrovich. They are the best of the nobility and were chosen by me for precisely that reason, in order to prove their insolvency. To present grafters on the one hand and ideal youth on the other—let others draw that picture. I wanted something larger. In one place (I struck it because of the censorship), Bazarov says to Arkady, that very Arkady in whom your Heidelberg friends see *a more successful type:* "Your father is an honest fellow. But even if he were the worst grafter you wouldn't go any farther than noble resignation or flaring up because you're a little nobleman."

3) My God! You consider Kukshin, that caricature, *most successful* of all! One should not even answer that. Odintsov *falls in love* as little with Arkady as with *Bazarov*—how can you fail to see that? She, too, is the representative of our idle, dreaming, curious and cold epicurean young ladies, our female nobility. Countess Sal'yas understood *that* character completely clearly. At first she would like to stroke the wolf's fur (Bazarov's), so long as he doesn't bite, then stroke the little boy's curls—and continue to recline, all clean, on velvet.

4) Bazarov's death (which Countess Sal'yas calls *heroic* and therefore criticizes) should, I think, have added the last stroke to his tragic figure. And our young people find it, too, accidental! I close with the following remark: if the reader does not come to love Bazarov with all his coarseness, heartlessness, pitiless dryness and sharpness—if he does not come to love him, I repeat —I am at fault and have not attained my aim. But I did not want to "sugar-coat" him, to use his own words, though through that I would have had the young on my side immediately. I did not want to purchase popularity through those kinds of concessions. Better to lose the battle (and apparently I have lost it) than to win it through a trick. I dreamt of a figure that was gloomy, wild, huge, half grown out of the ground, powerful, sardonic, honest—and doomed to destruction nevertheless—since it nevertheless still stands only at the threshold of the future—I dreamt of some sort of strange *pendant* to Pugachev,[6] etc.—and my young contemporaries tell me, shaking their heads: "You, friend, have made a mistake and have even insulted us: your Arkady has turned out better, you should have taken greater pains with him." I can only "Take off my hat and bow low" as in the gypsy song. Up to now only two people, Dostoevsky and Botkin, have understood Bazarov completely, that is, under-

6. "*Pendant*"—"counterpart, offshoot." Pugachev was the Cossack leader of a major uprising against Catherine II in 1773, finally crushed in a battle with Russia's most brilliant general, Suvorov [*Editor*].

stood my intentions. I shall try to send you a copy of my tale. But now *basta* about that. * * *

A. I. Herzen to Turgenev[7]

London, April 9 (21), 1862

* * * You grew very angry at Bazarov, out of vexation lampooned him, made him say various stupidities, wanted to finish him off "with lead"—finished him off with typhus, but nevertheless he crushed that empty man with fragrant mustache and that watery gruel of a father and that blancmange Arkady. Behind Bazarov the characters of the doctor and his wife are sketched masterfully—they are completely alive and live not in order to support your polemic but because they were born. Those are real people. It seems to me that, like an amiable rowdy, you stopped at the insolent, airy, bilious exterior, at the plebeian-bourgeois turn, and taking that as an insult, went further. But where is the explanation for his young soul's turning callous on the outside, stiff, irritable? What turned away everything tender, expansive in him? Was it Büchner's book?

In general it seems to me that you are unfair toward serious, realistic experienced opinion and confound it with some sort of coarse, bragging materialism. Yet that isn't the fault of materialism but of those "Neuvazhay-Korytos" [8] who understand it in a brutish way. Their idealism is repulsive too.

The Requiem at the end, with the further moving toward the immortality of the soul is good, but dangerous: you'll slip into mysticism that way.

There for the moment are some of the impressions I've gathered on the wing. I do not think that the great strength of your talent lies in *Tendezschriften*.[9] In addition, if you had forgotten about all the Chernyshevskys in the world while you were writing it would have been better for Bazarov. * * *

To A. I. Herzen

Paris, April 16 (28), 1862

My dear Alexander Ivanovich:

I reply to your letter immediately—not in order to defend myself, but to thank you, and at the same time to declare that

7. A. I. Herzen (1812–70), a leading Russian writer, philosopher, and journalist in revolutionary causes, spent the last twenty years of his life in exile in London, publishing the most influential Russian newspaper *(The Bell)* of the time. He was a close friend of Turgenev's [*Editor*].

8. "Disrespect-pigtrough." A comical name that figures on a list of peasants in Gogol's novel *Dead Souls* (1842). He "was run over by a careless cart as he lay sleeping in the middle of the road" [*Editor*].

9. "Tendentiousness" [*Editor*].

in creating Bazarov I was not only not angry with him, but felt "an attraction, a sort of disease" [1] toward him, so that Katkov was at first horrified and saw in him the apotheosis of *The Contemporary* and as a result convinced me to delete not a few traits that would have mellowed him, which I now regret. Of course he crushes "the man with the fragrant mustache" and others! That is the triumph of democracy over the aristocracy. With hand on heart I feel no guilt toward Bazarov and could not give him an unnecessary sweetness. If he is disliked as he is, with all his ugliness, it means that *I* am at fault and was not able to cope with the figure I chose. It wouldn't take much to present him as an ideal; but to make him a wolf and justify him just the same—that was difficult. And in that I probably did not succeed; but I only want to fend off the reproach that I was exasperated with him. It seems to me, on the contrary, that the feeling opposite to exasperation appears in everything, in his death, etc. But *basta cosí*—we'll talk more when we see each other.

I haven't become addicted to mysticism and will not be; in my relations to God I share Faust's opinion:

> Wer darf ihn nennen,
> Und wer bekennen:
> Ich glaub' ihn!
> Wer empfinden
> Und sich unterwinden
> Zu sagen: Ich glaub' ihn nicht! [2]

Moreover, that feeling in me has never been a secret to you. * * *

To Ludwig Pietsch [3]
Karlsruhe, January 22 (*February* 3), 1869
[Original in German]

Dear Friend:

Your letter evinced in my heart a mixed feeling of pity, gratefulness, and adoration! Quite seriously! A man as busy as you, to whom time is so valuable, to occupy himself with the painstaking, nerve-irritating work of revision [of the translation of *Fathers and Sons* into German]! That is a great proof of friendship!

1. A quotation from Griboedov's play *Woe from Wit* (1825), (act 4, scene 4) [*Editor*].
2. Who may name him/And who confess/"I believe in him!"/Who can feel/And dare/To say "I don't believe in him!" [*Editor*].
3. Ludwig Pietsch (1824–1911), a German journalist and writer, who helped popularize Turgenev in Germany [*Editor*].

So far as the translation is concerned you naturally have complete *carte blanche!* If you wish, you can have Bazarov marry Odintsov; I won't protest! On the contrary!

Bazarov has the habit of expressing himself contemptuously: he calls his old coat *"une loque," "ein Fetzen,"* [4]—use whatever word you like. * * *

To Ludwig Pietsch

Baden-Baden, May 22 (*June* 3), 1869

[Original in German]

* * * You write that you have to do reviews of *Fathers and Sons.* Splendid! Do one of them that is cool and strict toward it, but do express in it your incomprehension and amazement that the young generation in Russia took the portrait of Bazarov as an insulting caricature and a slanderous satire. Show instead that I portrait the fellow entirely too heroically—idealistically (which is *true*) and that Russian youth has entirely too sensitive a skin. Precisely through Bazarov I was (and still am) bespattered with mud and filth. So much abuse and invective, so many curses have been heaped on my head that was consigned to all the spirits of Hell (Vidocq, Judas bought for money, fool, ass, adder, *spitoon*—that was the *least* that I was called) that it would be a satisfaction for me to show that other nations see the matter in a different light. I dare ask you for such publicity because it corresponds completely to the truth and, of course, in no way contradicts your convictions. Otherwise I would not have troubled you. If you wish to fulfill my request, do so quickly, so that I could add a translation of the most important parts of the review to my literary reminiscences, which are to appear soon.[5] * * *

To P. V. Annenkov

Baden-Baden, December 20, 1869 (*January* 1, 1870)

* * * I have reread my article "Apropos of *Fathers and Sons*" and, just think, I feel that every word seems to have poured out of my soul. It seems that one must either not speak the truth or—what is more likely—that no author understands completely what he is doing. There is a kind of contradiction here which one cannot resolve oneself no matter how one approaches it. It is clearer for an outsider. * * *

4. "A rag, a tatter" [*Editor*].

5. The request was fulfilled. See Turgenev's "Apropos of *Fathers and Sons*" [*Editor*].

To Ya. P. Polonsky [6]

Baden-Baden, December 24, 1869 (*January* 5, 1870)

* * * It seems that everyone is dissatisfied with my little article "Apropos of *Fathers and Sons*." From this I gather that one shouldn't always speak the truth; since each word in that article is the truth itself, so far as I am concerned, of course. * * *

To I. P. Borisov

Baden-Baden, December 24, 1869 (*January* 5, 1870)

* * * It seems that my little article on *Fathers and Sons* has satisfied no one. Just think I will disown my fame, like Rostopchin did the burning of Moscow. Annenkov has even scolded me roundly. And yet every word in it is the sacred truth, at least in my judgment. It seems that an author doesn't always know himself what he is creating. My feelings toward Bazarov—my own personal feelings—were of a confused nature (God only knows whether I loved him or hated him), nevertheless the figure came out so specific that it immediately entered life and started acting by itself, in its own manner. In the final analysis what does it matter what the author himself thinks about his work. He is one thing and the work is another; but I repeat, my article was as sincere as a confession. * * *

To A. F. Onegin

Baden-Baden, December 27, 1869 (*January* 8, 1870)

* * * You don't like my little article "Apropos of *Fathers and Sons*." In Russia they abuse it terribly: they see in it something like apostacy on my part from my own service in approaching the "nihilists" and so forth. But why don't you like it? I hope you will not doubt that every word in it, every letter, is true. Consequently you, as a positive man, must look upon it as a fact—bluntly, to look down upon it: that's how a man jumps in a given instance, that's how he could grapple, that's what he expressed—what can you not like about it? * * *

To A. P. Filosofov

Bougival, August 18, (30), 1874

* * * You write that in Bazarov I wanted to present a caricature of current youth. You repeat that—forgive the blunt expression—silly reproach. Bazarov is my favorite child, for whom I quarreled

6. Ya. P. Polonsky (1819–98), an important Russian poet [*Editor*].

with Katkov, on whom I expended all the colors at my disposal, Bazarov, that bright man, that hero—a caricature? But apparently it cannot be helped. As Louis Blanc, despite all his protestations, is still constantly accused of bringing about the national workshops (*ateliers nationaux*), so I am ascribed the desire to offend youth by a caricature. For a long time now I have reacted to that accusation with contempt. I did not expect that I would have to renew that feeling in reading your letter. * * *

To A. P. Filosofov

Bougival, September 11 (23), 1874

* * * You began with Bazarov: I, too, shall start with him. You seek him in real life, but you won't find him. I shall tell you why. Times have changed. Bazarovs are not necessary now. For current social activity neither special talents nor even special intelligence is needed—nothing great, outstanding, too individualistic. Assiduity and patience are necessary. One must know how to sacrifice oneself without any hue and cry; one must know how to humble oneself and not to abhor petty and obscure, even lowly work—I choose the word "lowly" in the sense of simple, straightforward, *terra à terre*. What, for example, could be more lowly than to teach a peasant to read, to help him, to found hospitals, etc.? What does talent and even erudition have to do with that? Only the heart is necessary, the ability to sacrifice one's egoism—one cannot even speak of a calling here (not to mention Mr. V. D.'s decoration). A feeling of duty, the glorious feeling of patriotism in the true sense of that word—that's all that's necessary.

And yet Bazarov is still a figure, a prophet, a huge figure endowed with a certain charm, not devoid of a certain aureole: all that is out of place now, and it is silly to speak of *heroes* or *artists* of work. . . . Yet your search for Bazarov—"the real one" —nevertheless expresses, unconsciously perhaps, the thirst for beauty, of a special kind, of course. All these dreams must be given up. * * *

To M. E. Saltykov [7]

Paris, January 3 (15), 1876

* * * Well, now I'll say a couple of words about *Fathers and Sons* too, since you mentioned it. Do you really suppose that I have not thought of everything you have reproached me with?

7. M. E. Saltykov-Schedrin (1826–89), Russia's leading satirist of that era and a major novelist [*Editor*].

That's why I did not want to disappear from the face of the earth without having finished my large novel, [*Virgin Soil*], which, so far as I can judge, would clarify many misunderstandings and would place me in the position where I really should be put. I don't wonder, incidentally, that Bazarov has remained an enigma for many people. I can hardly figure out how I wrote him. There was a *fatum* [fate] there—please don't laugh—something stronger than the author himself, something independent of him. I know one thing: there was no preconceived idea, no tendentiousness in me then. I wrote naïvely, as if I was struck myself by what came out. You refer to the disciple's teacher.[8] But it was precisely after *Fathers and Sons* that I became estranged from that circle, where, strictly speaking, I was never a member, and would have considered it stupid and shameful to write or to work for it. Tell me honestly, can a comparison to Bazarov be insulting to anyone? Do you not yourself notice that he is the most sympathetic of my characters? "A certain delicate fragrance" is added by readers. But I am ready to confess (and already did so in print in my *Reminiscences*) that I had no right to give our reactionary rabble the chance to pick up a catchword, a name. The writer in me should have sacrificed that to the citizen, and therefore I consider fair both the alienation of youth from me and all sorts of reproaches heaped on me. The problem rising then was more important than artistic truth, and I should have known it in advance. * * *

To A. V. Toporov

Paris, November 26 (*December* 8), 1882

* * * Incidentally, I forgot one important thing: under the heading *Fathers and Sons*, you must *without fail* put in brackets:

Dedicated to the memory of Vissarion Grigor'evich Belinsky. Don't forget. * * *

8. Bazarov's "teacher" is Chernyshevsky or Dobrolyubov, and the circle is that of the journal *The Contemporary* [*Editor*].

The Contemporary Reaction

DMITRY I. PISAREV

Bazarov†

Turgenev's new novel affords us all those pleasures which we have learned to expect from his works. The artistic finish is irreproachably good: the characters and situations, the episodes and scenes are rendered so graphically and yet so unobtrusively, that the most arrant repudiator of art will feel on reading the novel a kind of incomprehensible delight which can be explained neither by the inherent interest of the narrated events, nor by the striking truth of the fundamental idea. The fact is that the events are not particularly entertaining and that the idea is not startlingly true. The novel has neither plot nor denouement, nor a particularly well-considered structure; it has types and characters, it has episodes and scenes, and above all through the fabric of the narration we see the personal, deeply felt involvement of the author with the phenomena he has portrayed. And these phenomena are very close to us, so close that our whole younger generation with its aspirations and ideas can recognize itself in the characters of this novel. By this I do not mean to say that in Turgenev's novel the ideas and aspirations of the younger generation are depicted just as the younger generation itself understands them: Turgenev regards these ideas and aspirations from his own point of view, and age and youth almost never share the same convictions and sympathies. But if you go up to a mirror which while reflecting objects also changes their color a little bit, then you recognize your own physiognomy in spite of the distortions of the mirror. We see in Turgenev's novel contemporary types and at the same time we are aware of the changes which the phenomena of reality have undergone while passing through the consciousness of the artist. It is interesting to observe the effects on a man like Turgenev of the ideas and aspirations stirring in our younger generation and manifesting themselves, as do all living things, in the most diverse forms, seldom attractive, often original, sometimes misshapen.

Such an investigation may have profound significance. Turgenev is one of the best men of the last generation; to determine how

† "Bazarov," D. I. Pisarev, in *Sochineniya*, 2 (Moscow, 1955), 7–50. Translated by Lydia Hooke. Pisarev (1840–68), the most radical critic of the 1860's, published his review of *Fathers and Sons* within a month of the novel's appearance, and was in part responsible for the controversy that arose over the work. This essay is somewhat atypical of his work, where he usually sacrificed his genuine critical insight to further "The Destruction of Aesthetics," as he entitled one of his essays.

he looks at us and why he looks at us thus and not otherwise is to find the reason for that conflict which is apparent everywhere in our private family life; this same conflict which so often leads to the destruction of young lives and which causes the continual moaning and groaning of our old men and women, who have not been able to fit the deeds and ideas of their sons and daughters to their own mold. As you can see, this is a task of vital importance, substantial and complex; I probably will not be able to cope with it but I am willing to try.

Turgenev's novel, in addition to its artistic beauty, is remarkable for the fact that it stirs the mind, leads to reflection, although, it does not solve a single problem itself and clearly illuminates not so much the phenomena depicted by the author as his own attitudes toward these phenomena. It leads to reflection precisely because everything is permeated with the most complete and most touching sincerity. Every last line in Turgenev's latest novel is deeply felt; this feeling breaks through against the will and realization of thè author himself and suffuses the objective narration, instead of merely expressing itself in lyric digressions. The author himself is not clearly aware of his feelings; he does not subject them to analysis, nor does he assume a critical attitude toward them. This circumstance gives us the opportunity to see these feelings in all their unspoiled spontaneity. We see what shines through and not just what the author wants to show us or prove. Turgenev's opinions and judgments do not change our view of the younger generation or the ideas of our time by one iota; we do not even take them into consideration, we will not even argue with them; these opinions, judgments, and feelings, expressed in inimitably lifelike images, merely afford us material for a characterization of the older generation, in the person of one of its best representatives. I shall endeavor to organize this material and, if I succeed, I shall explain why our old people will not come to terms with us, why they shake their heads and, depending on the individual and the mood, are angry, bewildered, or quietly melancholy on account of our deeds and ideas.

II

The action of the novel takes place in the summer of 1859. A young university graduate, Arkady Nikolaevich Kirsanov, comes to the country to visit his father, accompanied by his friend, Evgeny Vassilyich Bazarov, who, evidently, exerts a strong influence on his young comrade's mode of thought. This Bazarov, a man of strong mind and character, occupies the center of the novel. He is the representative of our young generation; he possesses those personality traits which are distributed among the masses in small quantities; and the image of this man clearly and distinctly stands out in the reader's imagination.

Bazarov is the son of a poor district doctor; Turgenev says nothing about his life as a student, but it must be surmised that this life was poor, laborious, and difficult; Bazarov's father says of his son that he never in his life took an extra kopeck from them; to tell the truth, it would have been impossible to take very much even if he had wanted to; consequently, if the elder Bazarov says this in praise of his son, it means that Evgeny Vassilyich supported himself at the university by his own labor, eking out a living by giving cheap lessons and at the same time finding it possible to prepare himself ably for his future occupation. Bazarov emerged from this school of labor and deprivation a strong and stern man; the course of studies in natural and medical sciences which he pursued developed his innate intelligence and taught him never to accept any idea and conviction whatsoever on faith; he became a pure empiricist; experience became for him the sole source of knowledge, his own sensations—the sole and ultimate proof. "I maintain a negative attitude," he says, "by virtue of my sensations; I like to deny—my brain's made on that plan, and that's all! Why do I like chemistry? Why do you like apples?—also by virtue of our sensations. It's all the same thing. Men will never penetrate deeper than that. Not everyone will tell you that, and, in fact, I won't tell you so another time." As an empiricist, Bazarov acknowledges only what can be felt with the hands, seen with the eyes, tasted by the tongue, in a word, only what can be examined with one of the five senses. All other human feelings he reduces to the activity of the nervous system; consequently, the enjoyment of the beauty of nature, of music, painting, poetry, the love of a woman do not seem to him to be any loftier or purer than the enjoyment of a copious dinner or a bottle of good wine. What rapturous youths call an ideal does not exist for Bazarov; he calls all this "romanticism," and sometimes instead of the word "romanticism" he uses the word "nonsense." In spite of all this, Bazarov does not steal other people's handkerchiefs, he does not extract money from his parents, he works assiduously and is even not unwilling to do something useful in life. I have a presentiment that many of my readers will ask themselves: what restrains Bazarov from foul deeds and what motivates him to do anything useful? This question leads to the following doubt: is not Bazarov pretending to himself and to others? Is he not showing off? Perhaps in the depths of his soul he acknowledges much of what he repudiates aloud, and perhaps it is precisely what he thus acknowledges which secretly saves him from moral degradation and moral worthlessness. Although Bazarov is nothing to me, although I, perhaps, feel no sympathy for him, for the sake of abstract justice, I shall endeavor to answer this question and refute this silly doubt.

You can be as indignant as you please with people like Bazarov, but you absolutely must acknowledge their sincerity. These people can be honorable or dishonorable, civic stalwarts or inveterate swindlers, depending on circumstances and their personal tastes. Nothing but personal taste prevents them from killing or stealing and nothing but personal taste motivates such people to make discoveries in the realms of science and social life. Bazarov would not steal a handkerchief for the same reason that he would not eat a piece of putrid beef. If Bazarov were starving to death, then he probably would do both. The agonizing feeling of an unsatisfied physical need would conquer his aversion to the smell of rotting meat and to the secret encroachment on other people's property. In addition to direct inclination, Bazarov has one other guiding principle in life—calculation. When he is sick, he takes medicine, although he feels no direct inclination to swallow castor oil or assafetida. He acts thus through calculation: he pays the price of a minor unpleasantness in order to secure greater comfort in the future or deliverance from a greater unpleasantness. In a word, he chooses the lesser of two evils, although he feels no attraction even to the lesser evil. This sort of calculation generally proves useless to average people; they are calculatingly cunning and mean, they steal, become entangled and wind up being made fools of anyway. Very clever people act differently; they understand that being honorable is very advantageous and that every crime, from a simple lie to murder, is dangerous and consequently inconvenient. Thus very clever people can be honorable through calculation and act openly where limited people would equivocate and lay snares. By working tirelessly, Bazarov is following his direct inclination and taste, and, furthermore, acts according to the truest calculation. If he had sought patronage, bowed and scraped, acted meanly instead of working and conducting himself proudly and independently, he would have been acting against his best interests. Careers forged through one's own work are always more secure and broader than a career built with low bows or the intercession of an important uncle. By the two latter means, it is possible to wind up as a provincial or even a metropolitan bigwig, but since the world began, no one has ever succeeded in becoming a Washington, Copernicus, Garibaldi, or Heinrich Heine through such means. Even Herostratus built his career by his own efforts and did not find his way into history through patronage. As for Bazarov, he does not aspire to become a provincial bigwig: if his imagination sometimes pictures the future, then this future is somehow indefinitely broad; he works without a goal, in order to earn his crust of bread or from love of the process of work, but, nevertheless, he vaguely feels through the quantity of his own capacities that his work will not pass without a trace and will lead to something. Bazarov is exceedingly full of self-esteem, but this self-esteem is unnoticeable as a direct consequence of his vastness. He is not interested in the trifles of which commonplace human relationships are composed; it would be impossible to insult him with obvious disdain or to make him happy with signs of respect; he is so full of himself and stands so unshakably high in his own eyes that he is almost completely indifferent to other people's opinions. Kirsanov's uncle, who closely resembles Bazarov in his cast of mind and character, calls his self-esteem "satanic pride." This expression is well-chosen and characterizes our hero perfectly. In truth, it would take nothing short of a whole eternity of constantly expanding activity and constantly increasing pleasures to satisfy Bazarov, but to his misfortune, Bazarov does not believe in the eternal existence of the human personality. "You said, for instance," he says to his friend Arkady, "to-day as we passed our bailiff Philip's cottage—it's the one that's so nice and clean—well, you said Russia will attain perfection when the poorest peasant has a hut like that, and every one of us ought to work to bring it about. . . . And I felt such a hatred for this poorest peasant, this Philip or Sidor, for whom I'm to be ready to jump out of my skin, and who won't even thank me for it . . . and what do I need his thanks for? Why, suppose he does live in a clean hut, while the nettles are growing out of me,—well, what comes after that?"

Thus Bazarov, everywhere and in everything, does only what he wishes or what seems to him to be advantageous or convenient. He is ruled only by his whims or his personal calculations. Neither over himself, nor outside himself, nor within himself does he recognize a moderator, a moral law or principle; ahead—no exalted goal; in his mind—no high design, and yet he has such great capacities.—But this is an immoral man! A villain, a monster!—I hear the exclamations of indignant readers on all sides. Well, all right, a villain and a monster; abuse him further; abuse him more, persecute him with satire and epigrams, indignant lyricism and aroused public opinion, the fires of the Inquisition and the executioners' axes—and you will neither rout him out nor kill this monster, nor preserve him in alcohol for the edification of the respectable public. If Bazarovism is a disease, then it is a disease of our time, and must be endured to the end, no matter what palliatives and amputations are employed. Treat

Bazarovism however you please—that is your business; but you will not be able to put a stop to it; it is just the same as cholera.

III

The disease of an age first infects the people who by virtue of their mental powers stand higher than the common level. Bazarov, who is possessed by this disease, is distinguished by his remarkable mind and consequently produces a strong impression on people who come into contact with him. "A real man," he says, "is one whom it's no use thinking about, whom one must either obey or hate." This definition of a real man precisely fits Bazarov himself: he continually seizes the attention of the people surrounding him at once; some he frightens and antagonizes; others he conquers, not so much with arguments as with the direct force, simplicity, and integrity of his ideas. As a remarkably intelligent man, he has never yet met his equal. " 'When I meet a man who can hold his own beside me,' he said, dwelling on every syllable, 'then I'll change my opinion of myself.' "

He looks down on people and rarely even takes the trouble to conceal his half-disdainful, half-patronizing attitude toward those who hate him and those who obey him. He loves no one; although he does not break existing ties and relationships, he does not move a muscle to renew or maintain these relationships, nor does he soften one note in his harsh voice or sacrifice one cutting joke or witty remark.

He acts thus not in the name of a principle, not in order to be completely frank at every moment, but simply because he considers it completely unnecessary to lay any restraint whatsoever on himself; for the same motive from which Americans throw their legs over the backs of chairs and spit tobacco juice on the parquet floors of elegant hotels. Bazarov needs no one, fears no one, loves no one and consequently spares no one. Like Diogenes he is almost ready to live in a barrel and because of this grants himself the right to tell people to their faces the harsh truth, simply because it pleases him to do so. We can distinguish two sides to Bazarov's cynicism—an internal and an external one; a cynicism of thought and feeling and a cynicism of manner and expression. An ironic attitude toward emotion of any sort, toward dreaminess, lyrical transports and effusions, is the essence of the internal cynicism. The rude expression of this irony, and a causeless and purposeless harshness in the treatment of others relates to external cynicism. The first depends on the cast of mind and general world view; the second is conditioned by purely external conditions of development; the traits of the society in which the subject under consideration lived. Bazarov's derisive attitude toward the softhearted Kirsanov follows from the basic characteristic of the general Bazarov type. His rude clashes with Kirsanov and his uncle arise from his individual traits. Bazarov is not only an empiricist, he is also an uncouth rowdy, who has known no life other than the homeless, laborious, sometimes wildly dissipated life of the poor student. In the ranks of Bazarov's admirers there will undoubtedly be those who will be enraptured by his coarse manners, the vestiges of student life, who will imitate these manners, which are, in any case, a shortcoming and not a virtue, who will perhaps even exaggerate his harshness, gracelessness, and abruptness. In the ranks of Bazarov's enemies there will undoubtedly be those who will pay particular attention to these ugly features of his personality and will use them to reproach the general type. Both of these groups would be mistaken and would only be displaying their profound incomprehension of the real matter. We may remind them of Pushkin's lines:

> One may be a man of sense
> Yet consider the beauty of his fingernails.

It is possible to be an extreme materialist, a complete empiricist and at the same time look after your toilet, treat your acquaintances politely, be amiable in conversation and a perfect gentleman. I say this for the benefit of those readers who attribute great significance to refined manners, who look with aversion on Bazarov, as on a man who is *mal élevé*[1] and *mauvais ton.*[2] He really is *mal élevé* and *mauvais ton*, but this really has no relevance to the essence of the type and speaks neither against it nor in its favor. Turgenev decided to choose as a representative of the Bazarov type an uncouth man; of course as he delineated his hero, he did not conceal or try to gloss over his awkwardness. Turgenev's choice can be explained by two motives: first, the character's personality, the tendency to deny ruthlessly and with complete conviction everything which others consider exalted and beautiful, is most often engendered by the drab conditions of a life of labor; from hard labor the hands coarsen, so do the manners and emotions; the man grows stronger and banishes youthful dreaminess, rids himself of lachrymose sensitivity; it is not possible to daydream at work, the attention is directed on the business at hand, and after work one must rest and really satisfy one's physical needs and one has no time for dreams. This man has become used to looking on dreams as on a whim, peculiar to idleness and aristocratic pampering; he has begun to consider moral sufferings to be products of daydreams; moral aspirations

1. "Badly brought up" [*Editor*]. 2. "Ill-bred" [*Editor*].

and actions as imagined and ridiculous. For him, the laboring man, there exists only one, eternally recurring care: today he must think about how not to starve tomorrow. This simple care, terrible in its simplicity, overshadows everything else for him, secondary anxieties, the petty troubles and cares of life; in comparison with this care the artificial products of various unsolved problems, unresolved doubts, indefinite relations which poison the lives of secure, idle people seem to him to be trivial and insignificant.

Thus the proletarian laborer, by the very process of his life, independently of the process of reflection, arrives at practical realism; from lack of leisure he forgets how to dream, to pursue an ideal, to aspire to an unattainably lofty goal. By developing the laborer's energy, labor teaches him to unite thought and deed, an act of will with an act of the mind. The man who has learned to rely on himself and on his own capacities, who has become used to accomplishing today what he conceived yesterday, begins to look with more or less obvious disdain on people who dream of love, of useful activity, of the happiness of the whole human race, and yet are not capable of lifting a finger to improve even a little whether he be doctor, artisan, pedagogue, or even a writer (it is possible to be a writer and at the same time a man of action), feels a natural, indefinable aversion to phrase making, to waste of words, to sweet thoughts, to sentimental aspirations, and in general to all pretensions not based on real tangible forces. This aversion to everything estranged from life and everything that has turned into empty phrases is the fundamental characteristic of the Bazarov type. This fundamental characteristic is engendered in precisely those various workshops where man, sharpening his mind and straining his muscles, struggles with nature for the right to live in the wide world. On these grounds, Turgenev had the right to take his hero from one of these workshops and to bring him into the society of cavaliers and ladies, in a work apron, with dirty hands, and a gloomy and preoccupied gaze. But justice forces me to put forward the proposition that the author of *Fathers and Sons* acted thus not without an insidious intention. This insidious intention is the second motive to which I referred earlier. The fact is that Turgenev, evidently, looks with no great favor on his hero. His soft, loving nature, striving for faith and sympathy, is jarred by corrosive realism; his delicate esthetic sensibility, not devoid of a large dose of aristocratism, takes offense at the faintest glimmer of cynicism; he is too weak and sensitive to bear dismal repudiations; he must become reconciled with existence, if not in the realm of life, at least in the realm of thought, or, more precisely, dreams. Like a nervous woman or the plant "touch-me not," Turgenev shrinks from the slightest contact with the bouquet of Bazarovism.

This feeling, an involuntary antipathy toward this tenor of thought, he presented to the reading public in a specimen as ungraceful as possible. He knows very well that there are very many fashionable readers in our public and, counting on the refinement of their aristocratic tastes, he did not spare the coarse details, with the evident desire of debasing and vulgarizing not only his hero but the cast of ideas which form the defining characteristic of the type. He knows very well that the majority of his readers will say of Bazarov that he is badly brought up and that it would be impossible to have him in a respectable drawing room; they will go no further or deeper; but speaking with such people, a talented artist and honorable man must be extremely careful out of respect for himself and the idea which he is upholding or refuting. Here one must hold one's personal antipathy in check since under some conditions it can turn into the involuntary slander of people who do not have the opportunity to defend themselves with the same weapons. * * *

* * * Arkady's uncle, Pavel Petrovich, might be called a small-scale Pechorin; he sowed some wild oats in his time and played the fool but finally began to tire of it all; he never succeeded in settling down, it just was not in his character; when he reached the time of life when, as Turgenev puts it, regrets resemble hopes and hopes resemble regrets, the former lion moved in with his brother in the country, surrounded himself with elegant comfort and turned his life into a peaceful vegetation. The outstanding memory of Pavel Petrovich's noisy and brilliant life was his strong feeling for a woman of high society, a feeling which had afforded him much pleasure, and afterward, as is almost always the case, much suffering. When Pavel Petrovich's relations with this woman were severed, his life became perfectly empty.

"He wandered from place to place like a man possessed;" Turgenev writes, "he still went into society; he still retained the habits of a man of the world; he could boast of two or three fresh conquests; but he no longer expected anything special of himself or of others, and he undertook nothing. He aged and his hair turned grey; to spend his evenings at the club in jaded boredom, and to argue in bachelor society became a necessity for him—a bad sign as we all know. He did not even think of marriage, of course. Ten years passed in this way. They passed by colorless and fruitless—and quickly, fearfully quickly. Nowhere does time fly past as in Russia; in prison they say it flies even faster."

An acrimonious and passionate man, endowed with a versatile mind and a strong will, Pavel Petrovich is sharply distinguished from his brother and from his nephew. He does not succumb to the influence of other people; he himself dominates the people around him and he hates those people from whom he suffers a rebuff. He has no convictions, truth to tell, but he has habits by which he sets great store. From habit he speaks of the rights and duties of the aristocracy, and from habit proves in arguments the necessity for *principles.* He is used to the ideas which are held by society and he stands up for these ideas, just as he stands up for his comfort. He cannot bear it when someone refutes his ideas, although, at bottom, he has no heartfelt attachment to them. He argues with Bazarov much more energetically than does his brother, and yet Nikolai Petrovich suffers much more from his merciless repudiations. In the depths of his soul, Pavel Petrovich is just as much of a skeptic and empiricist as Bazarov himself; in practical life he always acted and acts as he sees fit, but in the realm of thought he is not able to admit this to himself and thus he adheres in words to doctrines which his actions continually contradict. It would be well if uncle and nephew were to exchange convictions, since the first mistakenly ascribes to himself a belief in *principes* and the second just as mistakenly imagines himself to be an extreme skeptic and a daring rationalist. Pavel Petrovich begins to feel a strong antipathy toward Bazarov from their first meeting. Bazarov's plebeian manners rouse the indignation of the outdated dandy; his self-confidence and unceremoniousness irritate Pavel Petrovich as a lack of respect for his elegant person. Pavel Petrovich sees that Bazarov does not allow him to predominate over himself and this arouses in him a feeling of vexation on which he seizes as a diversion amidst the profound boredom of country life. Hating Bazarov himself, Pavel Petrovich is outraged by all his opinions, he carps at him, forces him into arguments, and argues with the zealous enthusiasm which is displayed by people who are idle and easily bored.

And what does Bazarov do amidst these three personalities? First of all, he endeavors to pay them as little attention as possible and spends the greater part of his time at work; he roams about the neighborhood, collects plants and insects, dissects frogs, and occupies himself with his microscope; he regards Arkady as a child, Nikolai Petrovich as a good-natured old man or, as he puts it, an old romantic. His feeling toward Pavel Petrovich is not exactly amicable; he is annoyed by the element of haughtiness in him, but he involuntarily tries to conceal his irritation under the guise of disdainful indifference. He does not want to admit to himself that he can be angered by a "provincial aristocrat," yet his passionate nature outs, frequently he replies vehemently to Pavel Petrovich's tirades and does not immediately succeed in gaining control over himself and once more shutting himself up in his derisive coldness. Bazarov does not like to argue or, in general, to express his opinions and only Pavel Petrovich is sometimes able to draw him into a significant discussion. These two strong characters react with hostility to each other; seeing these two men face to face it is easy to be reminded of the struggle between two successive generations. Nikolai Petrovich, of course, is not capable of being an oppressor: Arkady Nikolaevich, of course, is incapable of struggling against familial despotism; but Pavel Petrovich and Bazarov could, under certain conditions, be clear representatives: the former of the congealing, hardening forces to the past, the latter of the liberating, destructive forces of the present.

On whose side are the artist's feelings? This vitally important question may be answered definitely: Turgenev does not fully sympathize with any of his characters; his analysis does not miss one weak or ridiculous trait; we see how Bazarov senselessly repudiates everything, how Arkady revels in his enlightenment, how Nikolai Petrovich is as timid as a fifteen-year-old boy, and how Pavel Petrovich shows off and is angry that he has not won the admiration of Bazarov, the only man whom he respects, despite his hatred of him.

Bazarov talks nonsense—this is unfortunately true. He bluntly repudiates things which he does not know or understand: poetry, in his opinion is rubbish; reading Pushkin is a waste of time; to be interested in music is ludicrous; to enjoy nature is absurd. It is very possible that he, a man stifled by a life of labor, lost or never had time to develop the capacity to enjoy the pleasant stimulation of the visual and auditory nerves, but it does not follow from this that he has a rational basis for repudiating or ridiculing this capacity in others. To cut other people down to fit your own measure is to fall into narrow-minded intellectual despotism. To deny completely arbitrarily one or another natural and real human need is to break with pure empiricism.

Bazarov's tendency to get carried away is very natural; it can be explained, first by the one-sidedness of his development, and secondly by the general character of the time in which we live. Bazarov knows natural and medical sciences thoroughly: with their assistance he has rid himself of all prejudices; however, he has remained an extremely uneducated man; he has heard something or other about poetry, something or other about art, and not troubling to think, he passed abrupt sentence on these subjects which were unknown to him. This arrogance is generally by characteristic of us; it has its good sides such as intellectual courage, but on the other hand, of course, it leads at times to flagrant errors. The general character of the time is practicality: we all want to live by the rule that fine words butter no parsnips. Very energetic people often exaggerate the prevailing tendency; on these grounds, Bazarov's overly indiscriminate repudiations and the very one-sidedness of his development are tied directly to the prevailing striving for tangible benefits. We have become tired of the phrases of the Hegelians, our heads have begun to spin from soaring around in the clouds, and many of us, having sobered up and come down to earth, have gone to the other extreme and while banishing dreaminess have started to persecute simple feelings and even purely physical sensations, like the enjoyment of music. There is no great harm in this extremity, but it will not hurt to point it out; and to call it ludicrous does not mean to join the ranks of the obscurantists and old romantics. Many of our realists are up in arms against Turgenev because he does not sympathize with Bazarov and does not conceal his hero's blunders from the reader; many express the desire that Bazarov had been presented as an irreproachable man, a knight of thought without fear and reproach, and that thereby the superiority of realism to all other schools of thought would thus have been proved to the reading public. In my opinion, realism is indeed a fine thing; but let us not, in the name of this very realism, idealize either ourselves or our movement. We coldly and soberly regard all that surrounds us; let us regard ourselves just as coldly and soberly; all around us is nonsense and backwardness, but, God knows, we are far from perfect. What we repudiate is ridiculous but the repudiators have also been known, at times, to commit colossal follies; all the same, they stand higher than what they repudiate, but this is no great honor; to stand higher than flagrant absurdity does not yet mean to become a great thinker. But we, the speaking and writing realists, are now too carried away by the mental struggle of the moment, by this fiery skirmish with backward idealists, with whom it is not even worthwhile to argue; we, in my view, have gotten too carried away to maintain a skeptical attitude toward ourselves and to submit to rigorous analysis the possibility that we might have fallen into the dust of the dialectic battles which go on in journalistic pamphlets and in everyday life. Our children will regard us skeptically, or, perhaps, we ourselves will learn our real value and will begin to look *à vol d'oiseau* [3] on our present beloved ideas. Then we will regard the past from the height of the present; Turgenev is now regarding the present from the height of the past. He does not follow us, but tranquilly gazes after us and

3. "As the crow flies," that is, "straight." Pisarev seems to think it means to have a "bird's eye view" [*Editor*].

describes our gait, telling us how we quicken our pace, how we jump across ditches, how now and then we stumble over rough places in the road.

There is no irritation in the tone of his description; he has simply grown tired of moving on; the development of his own world view has come to an end, but his capacity to observe the movement of another person's thought process, to understand and reproduce all its windings, has remained in all its fullness and freshness. Turgenev himself will never be a Bazarov, but he has pondered this type and gained an understanding of it so true that not one of our young realists has yet achieved it. There is no apotheosis of the past in Turgenev's novel. The author of *Rudin* and "Asya," who laid bare the weaknesses of his generation and who revealed in *A Hunter's Sketches* a whole world of wonders which had been taking place right in front of the eyes of this very generation, has remained true to himself and has not acted against his conscience in his latest work. The representatives of the past, the "fathers," are depicted with ruthless fidelity; they are good people, but Russia will not regret these good people; there is not one element in them which would be worth saving from the grave and oblivion, but still there are moments when one can sympathize more fully with these fathers than with Bazarov himself. When Nikolai Petrovich admires the evening landscape he appears more human than Bazarov who groundlessly denies the beauty of nature to every unprejudiced reader.

> "And is nature nonsense?" said Arkady, looking pensively at the bright-colored fields in the distance, in the beautiful soft light of the sun, which was no longer high in the sky.
>
> "Nature, too, is nonsense in the sense you understand it. Nature's not a temple, but a workshop, and man's the workman in it."

In these words, Bazarov's repudiation has turned into something artificial and has even ceased to be consistent. Nature is a workshop and man is a worker in it—with this idea I am ready to agree; but when I carry this idea further, I by no means arrive at the conclusion which Bazarov draws. A worker needs rest and rest does not only mean heavy sleep after exhausting labor. A man must refresh himself with pleasant sensations, life without pleasant sensations, even if all the vital needs are satisfied, turns into unbearable suffering. The consistent materialists, like Karl Vogt, Moleschotte, and Büchner do not deny a day- laborer his glass of vodka, nor the well-to-do classes the use of narcotics. They indulgently regard even the excessive use of such substances, although they acknowledge that such excesses are harmful to the health. If a worker found pleasure in spending his free time lying on his back and gazing at the walls and ceiling of his workshop, then every sensible man would say to him: gaze on, dear friend, stare as much as you please, it won't harm your health but don't you spend your working hours staring or you will make mistakes. Why then, if we permit the use of vodka and narcotics, should we not tolerate the enjoyment of beautiful scenery, mild air, fresh verdure, the gentle play of form and color? Bazarov, in his persecution of romanticism, with incredible suspiciousness seeks it in places where it never has existed. Taking arms against idealism and destroying its castles in the air, he himself, at times, becomes an idealist, that is, he begins to prescribe to man how he should enjoy himself and how he should regulate his own sensations. Telling a man not to enjoy nature is like telling him to mortify his flesh. The more harmless sources of pleasure there are, the easier it is to live in the world, and the whole task of our generation is precisely to decrease the sum of suffering and increase the strength and amount of pleasure. Many will retort that we live in such a difficult time that it is out of the question to think about pleasure; our job, they will say, is to work, to eradicate evil, disseminate good, to clear a site for the great building where our remote descendants will feast. All right, I agree that we are compelled to work for the future, since the fruit we have sown can ripen only after several centuries; let us suppose that our goal is very lofty, still this loftiness of goal affords very little comfort in everyday unpleasantnesses. It is doubtful whether an exhausted and worn-out man will become gay and contented from the thought that his great-great-grandson will enjoy his life. Comforting oneself in the hard moments of life with a lofty goal is, if you will, just the same as drinking unsweetened tea while gazing on a piece of sugar hung from the ceiling. For people without exceedingly vivid imaginations, these wistful upward looks do not make the tea any tastier. In precisely the same way, a life consisting exclusively of work is not to the taste and beyond the powers of contemporary man. Thus, with whatever viewpoint you regard life, you will still be brought up against the fact that pleasure is absolutely indispensable. Some regard pleasure as a final goal; others are compelled to acknowledge pleasure as a very important source of the strength necessary for work. This is the sole difference between the epicureans and stoics of our day.

Thus, Turgenev does not fully sympathize with anyone or anything in his novel. If you were to say to hin: "Ivan Sergeevich, you do not like Bazarov, but what would you prefer?" he would not answer the question. He would not wish the younger generation to share their fathers' ideas and enthusiasms. Neither the fathers nor the sons satisfy him, and in this case, his repudiation is more profound and more serious than the repudiations of those people, who, having destroyed everything that existed before them, imagine that they are the salt of the earth and the purest expression of total humanity. These people are perhaps right in their destruction, but in their naïve self-adoration or in their adoration of the type which they consider that represents, lies their limitation and one-sidedness. The forms and types with which we can be contented and feel no need to look further have not yet been and perhaps never will be created by life. People who give up their intellectual independence and substitute servile worship for criticism, by giving themselves over completely to one or another prevailing theory, reveal that they are narrow, impotent, and often harmful people. Arkady is capable of acting in this way, but it would be completely impossible for Bazarov, and it is precisely this trait of mind and character which produces the captivating power of Turgenev's hero. The author understands and acknowledges this captivating power, despite the fact that neither in temperment nor in the conditions of his development does he resemble his nihilist. Furthermore, Turgenev's general attitudes toward the phenomena of life which make up his novel are so calm and disinterested, so devoid of slavish worship of one or another theory, that Bazarov himself would not have found anything timid or false in these attitudes. Turgenev does not like ruthless negations, but, nevertheless, the personality of the ruthless negator appears as a powerful one—and commands the involuntary respect of every reader. Turgenev has a propensity for idealism, but, nevertheless, not one of the idealists in his novel can be compared to Bazarov either in strength of mind or in strength of character. I am certain that many of our journalistic critics will want, at all costs, to find in Turgenev's novel a repressed urge to debase the younger generation and prove that the children are worse than their parents, but I am just as certain that the readers' spontaneous feelings, unfettered by the necessity of supporting a theory, will approve Turgenev and will find in his work not a dissertation on a particular theme, but a true, deeply felt picture of contemporary life drawn without the slightest attempt at concealment of anything. If a writer belonging to our younger generation and profoundly sympathizing with the "Bazarov school" had happened upon Turgenev's theme, then, of course, the picture would have been drawn otherwise and the colors would have been applied differently. Bazarov would not have been portrayed as an awkward student dominating the people around him through the natural strength of his healthy mind; he, perhaps, would have been turned into the embodiment of the ideas which make up the essence of this type; he, perhaps, would have manifested in his personality the clear expression of the author's tendencies, but it is doubtful whether he would have been Bazarov's equal in faithfulness to life and roundness of characterization. My young artist would have said to his contemporaries of his work: "This, my friends, is what a fully developed man must be like! This is the final goal of our efforts!" But Turgenev just says calmly and simply: "This is the sort of young people there are nowadays!" and does not even try to conceal the fact that such young people are not completely to his taste. "How can this be?" many of our contemporary journalists and publicists will cry. "This is obscurantism!" Gentlemen, we could answer, why should Turgenev's personal sensations concern you? Whether he likes such people or does not like them is a matter of taste; if, for instance, feeling no sympathy for the type, he were to slander it, then every honorable man would have the right to unmask him, but you will not find such slander in the novel: even Bazarov's awkwardnesses, to which I already alluded, are perfectly satisfactorily explained by the circumstances of his life and constitute, if not an essential requirement, at least a very frequently encountered trait of people of the Bazarov type. It would, of course, have been much more pleasant for us, the young people, if Turgenev had concealed and glossed over the graceless rough places in Bazarov, but I do not think that an artist who indulged our capricious desires could better capture the phenomena of reality. Both virtues and shortcomings are more clearly apparent when regarded from a detached point of view, and, for this reason, a detached, severely critical view of Bazarov proves, at present, to be much more fruitful than indiscriminate admiration or slavish worship. By regarding Bazarov detachedly as is possible only for a man who is "behind the times" and not involved in the contemporary movement of ideas; by examining him with the cold, probing gaze which is only engendered by long experience of life, Turgenev has justified his hero and valued him at his true worth. Bazarov has emerged from this examination as a pure and a strong man. Turgenev did not find one essential indictment against this type, and thus his voice, the voice of a man who finds himself in a camp which is inconsistent with his age and his views of life, has an especially important and decisive meaning. Turgenev did not grow fond of Bazarov, but he acknowledged his strength and his superiority and offered him a full tribute of respect.

This is more than sufficient to absolve Turgenev's novel from the powerful charge of being behind the times; it is even sufficient to compel us to acknowledge his novel as practically useful for the present age.

VI

Bazarov's relations with his comrade throw a bright streak of light on his character: Bazarov has no friends, since he has not yet met a man "who could hold his own" with him; Bazarov stands alone at the cold heights of sober thought and he is not oppressed by his isolation, he is completely engrossed in himself and in his work; observations and experiments on living nature, observations and experiments on living people fill for him the emptiness of his life and insure him against boredom. He does not feel the need to look for sympathy and understanding in another person; when some thought occurs to him, he simply expresses it, paying no attention whether his listeners agree with his opinion, or whether his ideas please them. Most frequently he does not even feel the need to express himself; he thinks to himself and, from time to time, lets drop a cursory remark, which is usually seized upon with respectful eagerness by his proselytes and pupils like Arkady. Bazarov's personality is self-contained and reserved, since it finds practically no kindred elements either outside or around itself. This reserve of Bazarov's has a dampening effect on the people who would like to see tenderness and communicativeness from him, but there is nothing artificial or premeditated in this reserve. The people who surround Bazarov are insignificant intellectually and can in no way move him, thus he is either silent or speaks in abrupt aphorisms, or breaks off an argument he has begun because he recognizes its ludicrous uselessness. If you put an adult in the same room with a dozen children, you will probably feel no surprise if the adult does not begin to converse with his roommates about his humanistic, social, and scientific convictions. Bazarov does not put on airs before other people, he does not consider himself a man of genius misunderstood by his contemporaries; he is merely obliged to regard his acquaintances from above because these acquaintances only come up to his knees; what else can he do? Is he to sit on the floor so that he will be the same height as they? He cannot pretend to be a child just so that the children will share their immature ideas with him. He involuntarily remains in isolation, and this isolation does not oppress him because he is young and strong and occupied with the seething activity of his own thoughts. The process of these thoughts remains in the shadows; I doubt whether Turgenev was in a position to render the description of this process: in order to portray it, he would have had to live through it in his own head, he would have had to himself become Bazarov, but we can be sure that this did not happen to Turgenev, because anyone who had even once, even for a few minutes, looked at things through Bazarov's eyes would have remained a nihilist for the rest of his life. In Turgenev, we see only the results at which Bazarov arrived, we see the external side of the phenomena; that is, we hear what Bazarov says and we know how he acts in life, how he treats various people. But we do not find a psychological analysis or a coherent compendium of Bazarov's thoughts; we can only guess what he thought and how he formulated his convictions to himself. By not initiating the reader into the secret of Bazarov's intellectual life, Turgenev may cause bewilderment among the segment of the public which is not used to filling in through their own mental efforts what is not stated or written in the works of a writer. The inattentive reader may come to the conclusion that Bazarov has no internal substance and that his entire nihilism consists of an interweaving of daring phrases snatched from the air and not created by independent thought. It is possible to say positively that Turgenev himself does not fully understand his hero, and does not trace the gradual development and maturation of his ideas only because he cannot and does not want to render Bazarov's thoughts as they would have arisen in his hero's mind. Bazarov's thoughts are expressed in his deeds, in his treatment of people; they shine through and it is not difficult to make them out, if only the reader carefully organizes the facts and is aware of their causes.

Two episodes fill in the details of this remarkable personality: first, his treatment of the woman who attracts him; secondly, his death.

I will consider both of these, but first I consider it not out of place to turn my attention to other, secondary details.

Bazarov's treatment of his parents will predispose some readers against the character, and others against the author. The former, becoming carried away by sentimental feelings, will reproach Bazarov for callousness; the latter, becoming carried away by their attachment to the Bazarov type, will reproach Turgenev for injustice to his hero and for a desire to show him in a disadvantageous light. Both sides, in my opinion, would be completely wrong. Bazarov really does not afford his parents the pleasures which the good old people were expecting from his visit to them, but between him and his parents there is not one thing in common. * * *

In town, at the governor's ball, Arkady becomes acquainted with a young widow, Anna Sergeyevna Odintsov; while dancing the mazurka with her, he happens to mention his friend Bazarov and excites her interest with his rapturous description of his friend's daring intellect and decisive character. She invites him to visit her and asks him to bring Bazarov. Bazarov, who had noticed her the instant she appeared at the ball, speaks to Arkady about her, involuntarily intensifying the usual cynicism of his tone, partially in order to conceal both from himself and from Arkady the impression that this woman has made on him. He willingly agrees to visit Odintsov with Arkady and explains his pleasure to himself and to Arkady by his hope of beginning a pleasant intrigue. Arkady, who has not failed to succumb to Odintsov's charms, takes offense at Bazarov's jocular tone, but, of course, Bazarov pays not the slightest attention and keeps on talking about Odintsov's beautiful shoulders, he asks Arkady whether this lady is really "ooh la la!", he says that still waters run deep and that a cold woman is just like ice cream. As he approaches Odintsov's apartments Bazarov feels a certain agitation and, wanting to overcome it, at the beginning of the visit behaves unnaturally informally and, according to Turgenev, sprawls in his chair just like Sitnikov. Odintsov notices Bazarov's agitation and, partially guessing its cause, calms our hero down with the gentle affability of her manner, and the young people's unhurried, diverse, and lively conversation continues for three hours. Bazarov treats her with special respect; it is evident that he is not indifferent to what she thinks of him, to the impression he is making; contrary to his usual habit, he speaks quite a lot, tries to interest his listener, does not make cutting remarks and even, carefully avoiding topics of general concern, discusses botany, medicine, and other subjects he is well-versed in. As the young men take their leave, Odintsov invites them to visit her in the country. Bazarov bows silently to indicate his acceptance and flushes. Arkady notices all this and is astonished by it. After this first meeting with Odintsov, Bazarov endeavors to speak of her in his former jocular tone, but the very cynicism of his expressions belies an involuntary, repressed respect. It is evident that he admires this woman and wishes to come into friendship with her; he jokes about her because he does not want to speak seriously with Arkady, either about this woman or about the new sensations which he notices in himself. Bazarov could not fall in love with Odintsov at first sight or after their first meeting; such things only happen to very shallow people in very bad novels. He was simply taken by her beautiful, or as he himself puts it, splendid body; her conversation did not destroy the general harmony of impressions, and this was enough at first to reinforce his desire to know her better. Bazarov has not yet formulated a theory about love. His student years, about which Turgenev does not say a word, probably did not pass without some affair of the heart; Bazarov, as we shall see later on, proves to be an experienced man, but, in all probability, he has had to do with women who were completely uneducated and far from refined and, consequently, incapable of strongly interesting his intellect or stirring his nerves; when he meets Odintsov he sees that it is possible to speak to her as an equal and senses that she possesses the versatile mind and firm character which he is conscious of and likes in himself. When Bazarov and Odintsov speak to each other they are able, intellectually speaking, to look each other in the eye over the fledgling Arkady's head and this instinctive mutual understanding affords them both pleasant sensations. Bazarov sees an elegant figure and involuntarily admires it; beyond this figure he discerns innate strength and unconsciously begins to respect this strength. As a pure empiricist, he enjoys the pleasant sensation and gradually becomes so accustomed to it, that when the time comes to tear himself away, it is difficult and painful for him to do so. Bazarov does not subject love to an analysis because he feels no mistrust in himself. He goes to the country to see Odintsov, with curiosity and without the slightest fear, because he wants to have a closer look at this pretty woman, wants to be with her and to spend a few days pleasantly. In the country, fifteen days pass imperceptibly; Bazarov talks with Anna Sergeyevna a lot, argues with her, expresses himself fully, and finally begins to feel for her a kind of malicious, tormenting passion. Such passion is most frequently engendered in energetic men by women who are beautiful, intelligent, and cold. The beauty of the woman stirs the blood of her admirer; her mind allows her to understand and to subject to subtle psychological analysis the feelings which she does not share or even sympathize with; her coldness insures her against getting carried away, and by increasing the obstacles, increases the man's desire to overcome them. Looking at such a woman, a man involuntarily thinks: she is so beautiful, she speaks so well about emotion, at times she becomes so animated when she expresses her subtle psychological analysis or listens to my deeply felt speeches. Why are her feelings so obstinately silent? How can I touch her to the quick? Can it be that her whole being is concentrated in her brain? Can it be that she is only amusing herself with impressions and is not capable of becoming carried away by them? Time passes in strenuous efforts to puzzle out the vital enigma; the intellect labors alongside the passions; heavy, torturous sensations appear; the whole romance of the relationship between a man and a woman takes on the strange character of a struggle. Becoming acquainted with Odintsov, Bazarov thought to amuse himself with a pleasant intrigue; knowing her better, he felt respect for her but began to see that he had little hope of success; if he had not managed to become strongly attached to Odintsov, he simply would have dismissed her with a shrug and immediately have occupied himself with the practical observation that the world is very large and there are many women in it who are easier to handle; he tried to act in such a way but he did not have the strength to shrug off Odintsov. Common sense advised him to abandon the whole affair and go away so as not to torment himself in vain, but his craving for pleasure spoke more loudly than his common sense and Bazarov remained. He was angry and he was conscious of the fact that he was committing a folly but, nevertheless, went on committing it, because his desire to live for his pleasure was stronger than his desire to be consistent. This capacity consciously to behave stupidly is an enviable virtue of strong and intelligent people. A dispassionate and dried-up person always acts according to logical calculations; a timid and weak person tries to deceive himself with sophistry and assure himself of the rightness of his desires and actions; but Bazarov has no need for such trickery; he says to himself straightforwardly: this is stupid, but nevertheless, I will do what I want, and I do not want to torment myself over it. When it becomes necessary I will have the time and strength to do what I must. A wholehearted, strong nature is manifested in this capacity to become completely carried away: a healthy, incorruptible mind is expressed in this capability to recognize as folly the passion which has consumed the whole organism.

Bazarov's relationship with Odintsov is brought to an end by a strange scene which takes place between them. She draws him into a discussion about happiness and love; with the curiosity peculiar to cold and intelligent women she questions him about what is taking place within him, she extracts a confession of love from him, with a trace of involuntary tenderness she utters his name; then, when stunned by the sudden onslaught of sensation, and new hopes, he rushes to her and clasps her to his breast, she jumps away in fear to the other end of the room and assures him that he had misunderstood her, that he was mistaken.

Bazarov leaves the room and with this their relationship comes to an end. He leaves her house the day after this incident; afterward, he sees Anna Sergeyevna twice, even visits her in the company of Arkady, but for both of them past events prove to be irrevocably past, and they regard each other calmly and speak together in the tones of reasonable and sedate people. Nevertheless, it saddens Bazarov to look on his relationship with Odintsov as on an episode from his past; he loves her and, while he does not allow himself to complain, suffer, or play the rejected lover, he becomes irregular in his way of life, now throwing himself into his work, now falling into idleness, now merely becoming bored and grumbling at the people around him. He does not want to talk about it to anyone, he does not even acknowledge to himself that he feels something resembling anguish and yearning. He becomes angry and sour because of his failure, it annoys him to think that happiness beckoned to him but then passed on and it annoys him to feel that this event has made an impression on him. All this would have worked itself out in his organism, he would again have taken up his work and cursed in the most energetic manner damnable romanticism and the inaccessible lady who had led him by the nose, and would have lived as he had before, occupied with the dissection of frogs and the courting of less unconquerable beauties. But Turgenev did not bring Bazarov out of his gloomy mood. Bazarov suddenly dies, not from grief, of course, and the novel comes to an end, or, more precisely, sharply and unexpectedly breaks off. * * *

The description of Bazarov's death is one of the best passages in Turgenev's novel; indeed, I doubt whether anything more remarkable can be found in the whole body of his work. It would be impossible for me to quote an excerpt from this magnificent episode; it would destroy the integrity of the effect; I should really quote the whole ten pages, but I do not have the space; furthermore, I hope that all my readers have read or will read Turgenev's novel. Thus, without quoting a single line, I shall endeavor to trace and explicate Bazarov's mental state from the beginning to the end of his illness. Bazarov cuts his finger while dissecting a corpse and does not have the opportunity to cauterize the cut immediately with a caustic stone or iron. Only after four hours does Bazarov come to his father's room and cauterize the sore spot, without concealing either from himself or from Vassily Ivanovich that this measure is useless if the infected matter from the corpse has entered the blood. Vassily Ivanovich knows as a doctor how great the danger is, but he cannot bring himself to look it in the face and tries to deceive himself. Two days pass, Bazarov steels himself, he does not go to bed, but he has fever and chills, loses his appetite, and suffers from a severe headache. His father's sympathy and questions irritate him because he knows that all this will not help and that the old man is pampering himself and diverting himself with empty illusions. It vexes him to see a man, and a doctor besides, not daring to view the matter in its proper light. Bazarov spares Arina Vlasyevna; he tells her that he has caught cold; on the third day he goes to bed and asks for lime tea. On the fourth day he turns to his father and straightforwardly and seriously tells him that he will die soon, shows him the red spots on his body which are a sign of infection, gives him the medical term for his illness, and coldly refutes the timid objections of the broken old man. Nevertheless, he wants to live, he is sorry to give up his self-awareness, his thoughts, his strong personality, but this pain at parting with his young life and untried power expresses itself not in a gentle melancholy but in a bitter, ironic vexation, in his scornful attitude toward himself, an impotent being, and toward the crude, meaningless accident which has trampled and crushed him. The nihilist remains true to himself to the last moment.

As a doctor, he has seen that infected people always die and he does not doubt the immutability of this law, despite the fact that it condemns him to death. In precisely the same way, he does not replace his gloomy world view by another more comforting one in a crucial moment: neither as a doctor nor as a man does he comfort himself with mirages. * * *

The author sees that Bazarov loves no one, because around him all is petty, stupid, and flabby, while he himself is fresh, intelligent, and strong; the author sees this and, in his mind, relieves his hero of the last undeserved reproach. Turgenev has studied Bazarov's character, he has pondered its elements and the conditions of its development, and he has come to see that for him there can be neither occupation nor happiness. He lives as an isolated figure and dies an isolated figure, and a useless isolated figure besides, dies as a hero who has nowhere to turn, nothing to draw breath on, nothing to do with his mighty powers, no one to love with a powerful love. As there is no reason for him to live, we must observe how he dies. The whole interest, the whole meaning of the novel is contained in the death of Bazarov. If he had turned coward, if he had been untrue to himself, it would have shed a completely different light on his whole character; he would have appeared to have been an empty braggart from whom it would be impossible to expect fortitude or decisivness in a time of need; the whole novel would have been turned into a slander on the younger generation, an undeserved reproach; with such a novel, Turgenev would have been saying: look here, young people, here is an example: even the best of you is no good. But Turgenev, as an honorable man and a true artist, could not have brought himself to tell such a grievous lie. Bazarov did not become abased, and the meaning of the novel emerged as follows: today's young people become carried away and go to extremes; but this very tendency to get carried away points to fresh strength and incorruptible intellect; this strength and this intellect, without any outside assistance or influence, will lead these young people on to the right road and will support them in life.

Whoever has found this splendid thought in Turgenev's novel could not help but express his deep and warm gratitude to this great artist and honorable citizen of Russia.

But all the same, the Bazarovs have a bad time of it in this life, although they make a point of humming and whistling. There is no occupation, no love—consequently, there is no pleasure either.

They do not know how to suffer, they will not complain, but at times they feel only that all is empty, boring, drab, and meaningless.

But what is to be done? Is it possible to infect ourselves on purpose just in order to have the satisfaction of dying beautifully and tranquilly? No! What is to be done? We must live while we are alive, eat dry bread if therc is no roast beef, know many women if it is not possible to love a woman, and, in general, we must not dream about orange trees and palms, when under foot are snowdrifts and the cold tundra.

N. N. STRAKHOV

Fathers and Sons†

* * * In order to be completely consistent to the very end, Bazarov refrains from preaching, as another form of empty chatter. And in reality, preaching would be nothing other than the admission of the rights of thought and the force of ideas. Preaching would be that justification which, as we have seen, was superfluous for Bazarov. To attach importance to preaching would mean to admit intellectual activity, to admit that men are ruled not by the senses and need, but also by thought and the words in which it is vested. To start preaching would mean to start going into abstractions, would mean calling logic and history to one's aid, would mean to concern oneself with those things already admitted to be trifles in their very essence. That is why Bazarov is not fond of arguments, disputation, and does not attach great value to them. He sees that one cannot gain much by logic; he tries instead to act through his

† From N. Strakhov, *Kriticheskiya stat'i*, 1 (Kiev, 1908), 1–39. Translated by Ralph E. Matlaw. The article first appeared in Dostoevsky's periodical *Time* in April, 1862. Strakhov (1828–96) was a philosopher and literary critic, and a close friend of Tolstoy's and Dostoevsky's.

personal example, and is sure that Bazarovs will spring up by themselves in abundance, as certain plants spring up where their seeds are. Pisarev understands that position very well. He says, for example: "Indignation at stupidity and baseness in general is understandable, though it is for that matter as fruitful as indignation at autumn dampness or winter cold." He judges Bazarov's tendency in the same way: "If Bazarovism is a disease, then it is a disease of our time, and must be endured to the end, no matter what palliatives and amputations are employed. Treat Bazarovism however you please—that is your business; but you will not be able to put a stop to it; it is just the same as Cholera."

Therefore it is clear that all the chatterer-Bazarovs, the preacher-Bazarovs, the Bazarovs occupied only with their Bazarovism rather than with deeds are on the wrong road, which will lead them to endless contradictions and stupidities, that they are far less consistent and stand much lower than Bazarov.

Such is the stern cast of mind, the solid store of thoughts Turgenev embodied in Bazarov. He clothed that mind with flesh and blood, and fulfilled that task with amazing mastery. Bazarov emerged as a simple man, free of all affectation, and at the same time firm and powerful in soul and body. Everything in him fits his strong character unusually well. It is quite noteworthy that he is *more Russian*, so to speak, than all the rest of the characters in the novel. His speech is distinguished by its simplicity, appropriateness mockery, and completely Russian cast. In the same way he approaches the common people more easily than any other character in the novel and knows better than they how to behave with them.

Nothing could correspond so well as this to the simplicity and straight forwardness of the view Bazarov professes. A man who is profoundly imbued with certain convictions, who is their complete embodiment, must without fail also turn out natural and therefore close to his native traditions and at the same time a strong man. That is why Turgenev, who up to this point had created divided characters, so to speak, for example, the Hamlet of the Shchigry District, Rudin, and Lavretsky,[1] finally attained the type of an undivided personality in Bazarov. Bazarov is the first strong character, the first whole character, to appear in Russian literature from the sphere of so called educated society. Whoever fails to value that, whoever fails to understand the importance of that phenomenon, had best not judge our literature. Even Antonovich [2]

1. Characters in the story by that name (1849), the novels *Rudin* (1856), and *Nest of Noblemen* (1859) [*Editor*].

2. Reviewer for *The Contemporary* [*Editor*].

noticed it, as one may see by the following strange sentence: "Apparently Turgenev wanted to portray in his hero what is called a *demonic or Byronic character, something on the order of Hamlet.*" Hamlet—a demonic character! That indicated a confused notion of Byron and Shakespeare. Yet actually *something of a demonic order* does emerge in Turgenev's work, that is, a figure rich in force, though that force is not pure.

In what does the action of the novel really consist?

Bazarov together with his friend Arkady Kirsanov arrives in the provinces from Petersburg. Both are students who have just completed their courses, one in the medical academy, the other at the university. Bazarov is no longer a man in his first youth; he has already acquired a certain reputation, has managed to present his mode of thought; while Arkady is still completely a youth. The entire action of the novel takes place during one vacation, perhaps for both the first vacation after completing their courses. For the most part the friends visit together, in the Kirsanov family, in the Bazarov family, in the provincial capital, in the village of the widow Odintsov. They meet many people, whom they either meet for the first time or have not seen for many years. To be precise, Bazarov had not gone home in three years. Therefore there occurs a variegated collision of their new views, brought from Petersburg, with the views of the people they meet. The entire interest of the novel is contained in these collisions. There are very few events and little action in it. Toward the end of the vacation Bazarov dies, almost by accident, becoming infected from a decomposing body, and Kirsanov marries, having fallen in love with Odintsov's sister. With that the entire novel ends.

In this Bazarov appears completely the hero, despite the fact that there is apparently nothing brilliant or striking in him. The reader's attention is focused on him from the first, and all the other characters begin to turn about him as around the main center of gravity. He is least of all interested in other characters, but the others are all the more interested in him. He does not try to attach anyone to himself and does not force himself on them, and yet wherever he appears he arouses the greatest attention and becomes the main object of feelings and thoughts, love and hatred.

In setting off to spend time with his parents and with friends Bazarov had no particular aim in mind. He does not seek anything and does not expect anything from that trip. He simply wants to rest and travel. At the most he sometimes wants to *look at people.* But with that superiority he has over those around him and as a result of their all feeling his strength, these characters themselves seek closer relations with him and involve him in a drama he did not at all want and did not even anticipate.

He had hardly appeared in the Kirsanov family when he immediately arouses irritation and hatred in Pavel Petrovich, respect mixed with fear in Nikolai Petrovich, the friendly disposition of Fenichka, Dunyasha, the servants' children, even of the baby Mitya, and the contempt of Prokofich. Later on, things reach the stage that he is himself carried away for a moment and kisses Fenichka, and Pavel Petrovich challenges him to a duel. "What a piece of foolery!" Bazarov repeats, not at all having expected such *events*.

The trip to town, its purpose to *look at people*, also is not without consequences for him. Various characters begin to mill around him. Sitnikov and Kukshin, masterfully depicted characters of the false progressive and the false emancipated woman, begin to court him. Of course they do not disconcert him; he treats them with contempt and they only serve as a contrast, from which his mind and force, his total integrity emerge still more sharply and in greater relief. But here the stumbling block, Anna Sergeyevna Odintsov, is also met. Despite his coolness Bazarov begins to waver. To the great amazement of his worshipper Arkady he is even embarrassed once, and on another occasion blushes. Without suspecting any danger, however, firmly confident of himself, Bazarov goes to visit Odintsov, at Nikolskoe. And he really does control himself splendidly. And Odintsov, like all the other characters, becomes interested in him, as she probably had not become interested in anyone else in her whole life. The matter ends badly, however. Too great a passion is aroused in Bazarov, while Odintsov's inclination does not rise to real love. Bazarov leaves almost completely rejected and again begins to be amazed at himself and to upbraid himself. "The devil knows what nonsense it is! Every man hangs on a thread, the abyss may open under his feet any minute, and yet he must go and invent all sorts of discomforts for himself, and spoil his life."

But despite these wise comments, Bazarov continues involuntarily to spoil his life just the same. Even after that lesson, even during his second visit to the Kirsanovs, he is carried away with Fenichka and is forced to fight a duel with Pavel Petrovich.

Apparently Bazarov does not at all desire and does not expect a love affair, but the love affair takes place against his iron will; life, which he had thought he would rule, catches him in its huge wave.

Near the end of the story, when Bazarov visits his father and mother, he apparently is somewhat bewildered after all the shocks he had undergone. He was not so bewildered that he could not be cured, that he would not rise again in full force after a short while. But nevertheless the shadow of sorrow which lay over that iron man even at the beginning becomes deeper toward the end. He loses the desire to work, loses weight, begins to make fun of the peasants no longer in a friendly way but rather sardonically. As a result, it turns out that this time he and the peasant fail to understand each other, while formerly mutual understanding was possible up to a point. Finally, Bazarov begins to improve and becomes interested in medical practice. The infection of which he dies nevertheless seems to testify to inadequate attention and agility, to a momentary diversion of his spiritual forces.

Death is the last test of life, the last accident that Bazarov did not expect. He dies, but to the very last moment he remains foreign to that life with which he came into conflict so strangely, which bothered him with such *trifles,* made him commit such *fooleries* and, finally killed him as result of such an *insignificant* cause.

Bazarov dies altogether the hero and his death creates a shattering impression. To the very end, to the last flash of conscience, he does not betray himself by a single word nor by a single sign of cowardice. He is broken, but not conquered.

Thus despite the short time of action in the novel and despite his quick death, Bazarov was able to express himself completely and completcly show his force. Life did not destroy him—one cannot possibly draw that conclusion from the novel—but only gave him occasions to disclose his energy. In the readers' eyes Bazarov emerges the victor from his trials. Everyone will say that people like Bazarov can do much, and that with such strength one may expect much from them.

Strictly speaking, Bazarov is shown only in a narrow frame and not with all the sweep of human life. The author says practically nothing about his hero's development, how such a character could have been formed. In precisely the same way, the novel's rapid ending leaves the question "would Bazarov have remained the same Bazarov, or in general what development awaited him in the future" as a complete puzzle. And yet silence on the first as on the second question has, it seems to me, its reason in realistic basis. If the hero's gradual development is not shown, it is unquestionably because Bazarov did not become educated through the gradual accumulation of influences but, on the contrary, by a rapid, sharp break. Bazarov had not been home for three years. During that time he studied, and now suddenly he appears before us imbued with everything he has managed to learn. The morning after his arrival he already goes forth after frogs and in general he continues his *educational* life at every convenient opportunity. He is a man of theory, and theory created him, created him imperceptibly, without events, without anything that one might have related, created him with a single intellectual turnabout.

Bazarov soon dies. That was necessary to the artist in order to make the picture simple and clear. Bazarov could not long remain in his present tense mood. Sooner or later he would have to change and stop being Bazarov. We have no right to complain to the author that he did not choose a broader task and limited himself to the narrower one. He decided to stop at a single step in his hero's development. Nonetheless the *whole man,* not fragmentary traits, appear at that step of his development, as generally happens in development. In relation to the fullness of character the author's task is splendidly fulfilled.

A living, whole man is caught by the author in each of Bazarov's actions and movements. Here is the great merit of the novel, which contains its main idea, and which our hurried moralizers did not notice. Bazarov is a theoretician; he is a strange and sharply one-sided person; he preaches unusual things; he acts eccentrically; he is a schoolboy in whom the coarsest *affectation* is united with profound sincerity; as we said before, he is a man foreign to life; that is, he himself avoids life. But a warm stream of life courses beneath all these external forms. With all his sharpness and the artificiality of his actions Bazarov is a completely live person, not a phantom, not an invention but real flesh and blood. He rejects life yet at the same time lives profoundly and strongly.

After one of the most wonderful scenes in the novel, namely, after the conversation in which Pavel Kirsanov challenges Bazarov to a duel and the latter accepts the challenge and agrees on its terms, Bazarov, amazed by the unexpected turn of events and the strangeness of the conversation, exclaims: "Well, I'll be damned! How fine, and how foolish! A pretty farce we've been through! Like trained dogs dancing on their hind paws." It would be difficult to make a more caustic remark. And yet the reader feels that the conversation Bazarov so characterizes was in reality a completely live and serious conversation; that despite all the deformity and artificiality of its form, the conflict of two energetic characters has been accurately expressed in it.

The poet shows us the same thing with unusual clarity through the whole novel. It may constantly be seen that the characters and particularly Bazarov *put on a farce* and that like trained dogs they *dance on their hind legs.* Yet beneath this appearance, as beneath a transparent veil, the reader clearly discerns that the feelings and actions underlying it are not at all canine but purely and profoundly human.

That is the point of view from which the action and events of the novel may best be evaluated. Beneath the rough, deformed, artificial, and affected forms, the profound vitality of all the phenomena and characters brought to the scene is heard. If Bazarov, for example, possesses the reader's attention and sympathy, he does so because in reality all these words and actions flow out of a living soul, not because each of his words is sacred and each action fair. Apparently Bazarov is a proud man, terribly egoistic and offending others by his egoism. But the reader makes his peace with that pride because simultaneously Bazarov lacks all smugness and self-satisfaction; pride brings him no joy. Bazarov treats his parents carelessly and curtly. But no one could suspect him, in that instance, of pleasure in the feeling of his personal superiority or the feeling of his power over them. Still less can he be reproached for abusing that superiority and that power. He simply refuses tender relationship with his parent and refuses it incompletely. Something strange emerges: he is uncommunicative with his father, laughs at him, sharply accuses him either of ignorance or tenderness. And yet the father is not only not offended but rather happy and satisfied. "Bazarov's jeers did not in the least perturb Vassily Ivanovich; they were positively a comfort to him. Holding his greasy dressing-gown across his stomach with two fingers, and smoking his pipe, he used to listen with enjoyment to Bazarov; and the more malicious his sallies, the more good-naturedly did his delighted father chuckle, showing every one of his black teeth." Such are the wonders of love. Soft and good-natured Arkady could never *delight* his father as Bazarov does his. Bazarov himself, of course, feels and understands that very well. Why should he be tender with his father and betray his inexorable consistency!

Bazarov is not at all so dry a man as his external actions and the cast of his thoughts might lead one to believe. In life, in his relations to people, Bazarov is not consistent (with himself); but in that very thing his vitality is disclosed. He likes people. "Man is a strange being," he says, noticing the presence of that liking in himself, "he wants to be with people, just to curse them, so long as he can be with them." Bazarov is not an abstract theoretician who solves all problems and is completely calmed by that solution. In such a case he would be a monstrous phenomenon, a caricature, not a man. That is why Bazarov is easily excited, why everything vexes him, everything has an effect on him, despite all his firmness and consistency in words and actions. This excitement does not betray his view and his intentions at all; for the most part it only arouses his bile and vexes him. Once he says the following to his friend Arkady: "You said, for instance, to-day as we passed our bailiff Philip's cottage—it's the one that's so nice and clean—well, you said Russia will attain perfection when the poorest peasant has a house like that, and every one of us ought to work to bring it about. And I felt such a hatred for this poorest peasant, this Philip or Sidor, for whom I'm to be ready to jump out of my skin, and * * * what do I need his thanks for? Why, suppose he does live in a clean hut, while the nettles are growing out of me,—well, what comes after that?" What a terrible, shocking speech, isn't it?

A few minutes later Bazarov does still worse: he discloses a longing to choke his tender friend Arkady, to choke him for no particular reason and in the guise of a pleasant trial already spreads wide his long and hard fingers.

Why does all this not arm the reader against Bazarov? What could be worse than that? And yet the impression created by these incidents does not serve to harm Bazarov. So much so that even Antonovich (striking proof!) who with extreme diligence explains everything in Bazarov on the bad side in order to prove Turgenev's sly intention to blacken Bazarov—completely left that incident out!

What does this mean? Apparently Bazarov, who so easily meets people, takes such lively interest in them, and so easily begins to feel rancor toward them, suffers more from that rancor than those for whom it is destined. That rancor is not the expression of destroyed egoism or insulted self-esteem, it is the expression of suffering, and oppression created by the absence of love. Despite all his views, Bazarov eagerly seeks love for people. If that desire appears as rancor, that rancor only represents the reverse of love. Bazarov cannot be a cold, abstract man. His heart demands fullness and demands feeling. And so he rages at others but feels that he should really rage at himself more than at them.

From all this it at least becomes apparent what a difficult task Turgenev undertook in his latest novel and how successfully in our view he carried it out. He depicted life under the deadening influence of theory; he gave us a living being, though that man apparently embodied himself in an abstract formula without leaving a remnant behind. Through this, if one were to judge the novel superficially, it is not very comprehensible, presents little that is appealing, and seems to consist entirely of an obscure logical construction. But in reality, it is actually marvelously clear, unusually attractive, and throbs with warm life.

There is practically no need to explain why Bazarov turned out and had to turn out a theoretician. Everyone knows that our *real* representatives, that the "carriers of thought" in our generation, have long ago renounced being *practical*, that active participation in the life around them had long ago become impossible. From that point of view Bazarov is a direct and immediate imitator of Onegin, Pechorin, Rudin, and Lavretsky. Exactly like them he lives in the mental sphere for the time being and spends his spiritual forces on it. But the thirst for activity has reached the final, extreme point in him. His entire theory consists in the direct demand for action. His mood is such that he inevitably would come to grips with that action at the first convenient possibility.

The characters surrounding Bazarov unconsciously feel the living man in him. That is why so many attachments turn upon him, far more than on any other character in the novel. Not only do his father and mother remember him and pray for him with infinite and inexpressible tenderness; in other characters too the memory of Bazarov is accompanied by love; in a moment of happiness Katya and Arkady drink "to Bazarov's memory."

Such is Bazarov's image for us, too. He is not a hateful being who repels through his shortcomings; on the contrary, his gloomy figure is grandiose and attractive.

"What then is the idea of the novel?" Lovers of bare and exact conclusions will ask. Does Bazarov present a subject for imitation according to you? Or should his failure and roughness on the contrary teach the Bazarovs not to fall into the errors and extremes of the real Bazarov? In short, is the novel written *for* the young generation or *against* it? Is it progressive or reactionary?

If the question so insistently concerns the author's intentions, what he wanted to teach and what he wanted to have unlearned, then it seems these questions would have to be answered as follows: Turgenev does in fact want to be instructive, but he chooses tasks far higher and more difficult than you suppose. It is not a difficult thing to write a novel with a progressive or reactionary tendency. But Turgenev had the pretension and daring to create a novel that had *all possible* tendencies. The worshipper of eternal truth and eternal beauty, he had the proud aim of showing the eternal in the temporary and to write a novel neither progressive nor reactionary but, so to speak, *constant*. In this instance he may be compared to a mathematician who tries to find some important theorem. Let us assume that he has finally found that theorem. Would he not be terribly amazed and disconcerted if he were suddenly approached with the question whether his theorem was progressive or reactionary? Does it conform to the *modern* spirit or does it obey the *old*?

He could only answer such questions thus: your questions make no sense and have no bearing on my findings: my theorem is an *eternal truth*.

Alas! In life's furrows
By Providence's secret will
Generations are the fleeting harvest
They rise, ripen and fall;
Others come in their wake . . .

The change of generations is the outward theme of the novel. If Turgenev did not depict all fathers and sons, or not *those* fathers and sons who would like to be different, he splendidly described fathers *in general* and children *in general* and the relationship between those two generations. Perhaps the difference between generations has never been as great as it is at the present, and therefore their relationship too appears to be particularly acute. However that may be, in order to measure the difference between objects the same measure must be used for both; in order to draw a picture all objects must be described from a point of view common to all of them.

That single measure, that general point of view for Turgenev is *human life* in its broadest and fullest meaning. The reader of his novel feels that behind the mirage of external actions and scenes there flows such a profound, such an inexhaustible current of life, that all these actions and scenes, all the characters and events are insignificant in comparison to that current.

If we understand Turgenev's novel that way, then, perhaps the moral we are seeking will also be disclosed to us more clearly. There is a moral, even a very important one, for truth and poetry are very instructive.

If we look at the picture presented by the novel more calmly and at some distance, we note easily that though Bazarov stands head and shoulders above all the other characters, though he majestically passes over the scene, triumphant, bowed down to, respected, loved, and lamented, there is nevertheless something that taken as a whole stands above Bazarov. What is that? If we examine it attentively, we will find that that higher something is not a character but that *life* which inspires them. Above Bazarov stands that fear, that love, those tears he inspires. Above Bazarov is that scene he passes through. The enchantment of nature, the charm of art, feminine love, family love, parents' love, *even* religion, all that—living, full, powerful—is the background against which Bazarov is drawn. That background is so clear and sparkling that Bazarov's huge figure stands out clearly but at the same time gloomily against it. Those who think that for sake of a supposed condemnation of Bazarov the author contrasts to him one of his characters, say Pavel Petrovich, or Arkady, or Odintsov, are terribly wrong. All these characters are insignificant in comparison to Bazarov. And yet their life, the human element in their feelings is not insignificant.

We will not discuss here the description of nature, of Russian nature, which is so difficult to describe and in describing which Turgenev is such a master. It is the same in this as in previous novels. The sky, air, fields, trees, even horses, even chicks—everything is caught graphically and exactly.

Let's simply take people. What could be weaker or more insignificant than Bazarov's young friend Arkady? He apparently submits to every passing influence; he is the most ordinary of mortals. And yet he is extremely nice. The magnanimous agitation of his young feelings, his nobility and purity are emphasized by the author with great finesse and are clearly depicted. Nikolai Petrovich, as is proper, is the real father of his son. There is not a single clear trait in him and the only good thing is that he is a man, though a very simple man. Further, what could be emptier than Fenichka? The author writes "The expression of her eyes was charming, particularly when she seemed to gaze up from beneath her brow and smiled kindly and a little stupidly." Pavel Petrovich himself calls her an *empty creature*. And yet that silly Fenichka attracts almost more adorers than the clever Odintsov. Not only does Nikolai Petrovich love her, but in part Pavel Petrovich falls in love with her as does Bazarov himself. And yet that love and falling in love are real and valuable human feelings. Finally, what is Pavel Petrovich—a dandy, a fop with gray hair, completely taken up with his concern for his toilette? But even in him, despite the apparent distortion there are living and even energetic vibrations of the heartstrings.

The farther we go in the novel, the nearer to the end of the drama, the more gloomy and tense does Bazarov's figure become, while the background becomes clearer and clearer. The creation of such figures as Bazarov's mother and father is a real triumph of talent. Apparently nothing could be less significant and useless than these people who have lived out their time and who become decrepit and disfigured in the new life with all their prejudices of old. And yet what richness of *simple* human feeling! What depth and breadth of spiritual life among the most ordinary life that does not rise a jot above the lowest level.

When Bazarov becomes ill, when he rots alive and inexorably undergoes the cruel battle with illness, life around him becomes more tense and clear in proportion to his becoming gloomier. Odintsov comes to say farewell to Bazarov! She had probably done nothing generous in her life and will not do so again all her life. So far as the father and mother are concerned, it would be difficult to find anything more touching. Their love bursts forth like some sort of lightning, for a moment striking the reader. From their simple hearts there seem to be torn infinitely sad hymns, some sort of limitlessly deep and tender outcries that irresistibly touch the soul.

Bazarov dies amidst that light and that warmth. For a moment a storm flares up in his father's soul. It is harder to imagine anything more fearful. But it soon dies down and everything again becomes bright. Bazarov's very grave is illuminated by light and peace. Birds sing over it and tears are poured on it.

So there it is, there is that secret moral which Turgenev put in his work. Bazarov turns away from nature; Turgenev does not reproach him for it; he only depicts nature in all its beauty. Bazarov does not value friendship and rejects romantic love; the author does not reproach him for it; he only describes Arkady's friendship toward Bazarov and his happy love for Katya. Bazarov denies close bonds between parents and children; the author does not reproach him for it; he only develops a picture of parental love before us. Bazarov shuns life; the author does not present him as a villain for it; he only shows us life in all its beauty. Bazarov repudiates poetry; Turgenev does not make him a fool for it; he only depicts him with all the fullness and penetration of poetry.

In short, Turgenev stands for the eternal principles of human life; for those fundamental elements which can endlessly change their forms but actually always remain unchangeable. But what have we said? It turns out that Turgenev stands for those things all poets stand for, that every real poet must stand for. And, consequently, in this case Turgenev put himself above any reproach for ulterior motives; whatever the particular circumstances he chose for his work may be, he examines them from the most general and highest point of view.

All his attention is concentrated on the general forces of life. He has shown us how these forces are embodied in Bazarov, in that same Bazarov who denies them. He has shown us if not a more powerful then a more apparent, clearer embodiment of those forces in those simple people who surround Bazarov. Bazarov is a titan, rising against mother earth; no matter how great his force it only testifies to the greatness of the forces that begot him and fed him, but it does not come up to mother earth's force.

However it may be, Bazarov is defeated all the same. He is not defeated by the characters and occurrences of life but by the very idea of that life. Such an ideal victory over him is only possible if he is done all justice, if he is exalted to his appropriate grandeur. Otherwise the victory would have no force or meaning.

In his *Government Inspector* Gogol said there was a single honorable character in the play—laughter. One might say similarly about *Fathers and Sons* that it contains one character who stands higher than the others and even higher than Bazarov—*life*. That life that rises above Bazarov would apparently be smaller and lower to the extent that the main hero of the novel, Bazarov, would be portrayed smaller and lower.

APOLLON GRIGOREV

[Nihilists]†

* * * Now the matter has become clear once and for all. It is not a question of Pushkin's "rattlings" or the "vulgarity" of certain of his poems (like "The Hero," for example)—it is not at all a question of the "kingdom of darkness," supposedly described only satirically by Ostrovsky,[1]—now the matter consists of matter, that is, in that:

1. *Art* is nonsense, useful only to arouse dormant human energy to something more substantial and important, and swept away as soon as any kind of positive results are attained.
2. *Nationality*—that is, certain national organisms—is also nonsense, which must disappear during the amalgamation the result of which will be a world where the moon is joined to the earth.
3. *History* (this had been said two years ago completely clearly) is nonsense, a senseless canvas of inept errors, shameful blindness and the most amusing enthusiasms.
4. *Science*—except for its exact and positive sides, expressed in the branches of mathematics and natural science—is the greatest nonsense, the ravings of fruitlessly stultifying human heads.
5. *Thought* is a completely senseless process, useless and quite conveniently replaced by the good teachings of the five—excuse me!—six clever little books.

But any person who is accustomed to the noxious process of thinking will involuntarily repeat Galileo's words "And yet it does turn!" Since even these results, that in the final analysis deny thought any meaning, are in themselves the results of thought—whatever it may be, it is thinking nevertheless and not the digestive process. ("And perhaps the digestive process too?" You will ask me again to note.)

Certain "generalizations" so reluctantly used by the adepts of our nihilism, which they flee and fear as the devil fears holy water, were nevertheless present at the conception of their theories. In order to say "I dissect frogs," or "I make soap" [as in Ustryalov's parody of *Fathers and Sons*], certain generalizations, albeit nega-

† From A. A. Grigorev, *Sochineniya*, edited by N. N. Strakhov, St. Petersburg, 1876, pp. 626–27. Translated by Ralph E. Matlaw. This is a section of an article, "Paradoxes of Organic Criticism," that appeared in Dostoevsky's *The Epoch* in 1864. Grigorev (1822–64) was a brilliant though eccentric critic extolling traditional Russian life, and a good poet.

1. A. N. Ostrovsky (1823–86), leading Russian dramatist. His early plays, dealing with the merchant world, were "analyzed" by Dobrolyubov in a long article entitled "The Kingdom of Darkness" (1859) [*Editor*].

tive ones, are necessary—to wit, to elevate disbelief in any other knowledge than particular knowledge into a principle. These very words are insincere in Bazarov and childishly vulgar in his parody. On Bazarov's lips they simply cover a certain intellectual despair, a despair of conscience that has been scalded several times and consequently fears cold water, conscience that had been stopped short by several insubstantial systems that tried grandiosely though not completely successfully to contain all of universal life in a single principle. Such a completely comprehensible moment of consciousness, considered ideal by Bazarov and ideal by nihilism too, has a completely legitimate place in the general process of human consciousness,—and therefore though I laugh wholeheartedly at the facts, that is, at one foolish representative or another of so-called nihilism, I do not permit myself to laugh at the general stream, at the general spirit christened with that name—whether successfully or not—and am still less capable of denying the organic-historical necessity of that eructation of materialism in new forms. But that this organic-historical eructation is no more than a passing moment—no dreams about white blackamoors will dissuade me of that.

Thought, science, art, nationality, history are not at all steps in some sort of progress, a husk swept away by the human spirit as soon as it has attained some positive results, but the eternal, organic work of eternal forces inherent in him as an organism. It seems to be a very simple and clear thing, and yet that's just what one has to explain in our day, as if it were something completely new . . . and yet it would seem, it is completely simple and clear, so simple and clear that the most organic view that emerges immediately from it is nothing other than a simple, untheoretical view of life and its manifestations or expression in science, art, and the history of nations. * * *

ALEXANDER HERZEN

Bazarov Once Again†

First Letter

Instead of a letter, dear friend, I am sending you a dissertation, and an unfinished one at that. After our conversation I reread

† From Alexander Herzen, *Sobranie sochineniy*, XX (Moscow, 1954–61), 335–40. Translated by Lydia Hooke. In this essay of 1868 Herzen undertook to show other forms of civic action than those the nihilists proclaimed. In particular he emphasized the "fathers'" activity in publishing, at home and abroad, and their salutary effect on social development in Russia.

Pisarev's article on Bazarov, which I had completely forgotten, and I am very glad of it; that is, not that I had forgotten it, but that I reread it.

This article confirms my own viewpoint. In its one-sidedness it is truer and more remarkable than its adversaries thought.

Whether Pisarev understood Turgenev's Bazarov correctly does not concern me. What is important is that he recognized *himself* and *others like him* in Bazarov and supplied what was lacking in the book. The less Pisarev kept to the mold in which the angry parent sought to fit the refractory son, the more freely does he project his own ideal on him.

"But why should Pisarev's ideal interest us? Pisarev is an incisive critic, he wrote much, he wrote about everything, sometimes on subjects he knew, but all this does not give his ideal the right to claim general consideration."

But the point is that this is not just his personal ideal, but the ideal that was cherished by the young generation *before* Turgenev's Bazarov and *after him* and which was embodied, not only by various characters in stories and novels, but also by real people who endeavored to base their actions and words on Bazarovism. I have heard and seen a dozen times what Pisarev is talking about; he has artlessly given away the heartfelt idea of a whole group; he has focused diffuse rays on one point and with them illuminated the original Bazarov.

Bazarov is more than an outsider to Turgenev, but to Pisarev he is more than a brother; for heuristic purposes, of course, we should choose the viewpoint which regards Bazarov as its *desideratum*.

Pisarev's adversaries were frightened by his imprudence; they repudiated Turgenev's Bazarov as a caricature and even more vehemently rejected his transfigured double; they were displeased that Pisarev had made a fool of himself, but this does not mean that he had misunderstood Bazarov.

Pisarev knows the heart of his Bazarov to the core. He even confesses for him: "Perhaps," he says, "in the depths of his soul Bazarov acknowledges much of what he repudiates aloud and perhaps it is precisely what he thus acknowledges which secretly saves him from moral degradation and moral worthlessness." We consider this immodesty, peering so deeply into the soul of another, to be very significant.

Pisarev further characterizes his hero as follows: "Bazarov is exceedingly full of self-esteem, but this self-esteem is unnoticeable [it is clear that this is not Turgenev's Bazarov] as a direct consequence of his vastness." Bazarov could be satisfied only by "a *whole eternity of constantly expanding activity and constantly increasing pleasures.*"[1]

Bazarov, everywhere and in everything, does what he pleases or what seems to him to be advantageous or convenient. He is ruled only by his whims or his personal calculations. Neither over himself, nor outside himself, nor within himself does he recognize a moderator . . . ahead—no exalted goal; in his mind—no high design, and yet he has such great capacities. . . . If Bazarovism is a *disease,* then it is the disease of our time, and must be endured to the end no matter what palliatives and amputations are employed.

[Bazarov] looks down on people and rarely even takes the trouble to conceal *his half disdainful, half patronizing attitude* toward those who hate him and those who obey him. He loves no one. . . . he considers it completely unnecessary to lay any restraint whatsoever on himself . . .

His cynicism has two aspects, an internal and an external one, a cynicism of thought and feeling and a cynicism of manner and expression. An ironic attitude toward emotion of any sort, toward dreaminess, lyrical transports and effusions, is the essence of the internal cynicism. The rude expression of this irony, and a cause-external cynicism. . . . Bazarov is not only an empiricist, he is less and purposeless harshness in the treatment of others relates to also an uncouth rowdy . . . In the ranks of Bazarov's admirers there will undoubtedly be those who will be enraptured by his coarse manners, . . . which are, in any case, a shortcoming and not a virtue.[2]

. . . [Such people are] most often engendered by the drab conditions of a life of labor; from hard labor the hands coarsen, so do the manners and emotions; the man grows stronger and banishes youthful dreaminess, rids himself of lachrymose sensitivity; it is not possible to daydream at work . . . This man has become used to looking on dreams as on a whim, peculiar to idleness and aristocratic pampering; . . . moral aspirations and actions as imagined and ridiculous. . . . [He feels an] aversion to phrase making.

1. Youth likes to express itself in various extravagant conceits and to strike the imagination with infinitely large images. The last sentence reminds me of Karl Moor, Ferdinand, and Don Carlos [in Schiller's plays].

2. This prediction came true. This mutual interaction of people and books is a strange thing. A book takes its whole shape from the society that spawns it, then generalizes the material, renders it clearer and sharper, and as a consequence reality is transformed. The originals become caricatures of their own sharply drawn portraits and real people take on the character of their literary shadows. At the end of the last century all German men were a little like Werther, all German women like Charlotte; at the beginning of this century, the university Werthers began to turn into "robbers," Schiller's, not real ones. Young Russians were almost all out of [Chernyshevsky's] *What's to be done?* after 1862, with the addition of a few of Bazarov's traits.

Then Pisarev introduces Bazarov's family tree: the Onegins and the Pechorins begat the Rudins and Bel'tovs.[3] The Rudins and Bel'tovs begat Bazarov. (Whether the Decembrists were omitted purposely or not, I do not know.)[4]

Weary, bored people are replaced by people yearning for action, life rejects them both as unfit and incomplete. "At times they will have to suffer, but they will never succeed in accomplishing deeds. Society is deaf and implacable toward them. They are not capable of accommodating themselves to its conditions, not one of them ever attained the rank of *head of a department*. Some console themselves by becoming professors and working for the future generation." There is no doubt of the negative service they perform. They increase the number of people *incapable* of practical action, consequently, this practical action itself or, more precisely, the forms which it usually takes at present, slowly but surely are lowered in the opinion of society.

> It seemed (after the Crimean campaign) that Rudinism was coming to an end, that the epoch of fruitless dreaming and yearning was to be followed by an epoch of tireless and useful activity. But the mirage was dispelled. The Rudins did not become practical men, from them came a new generation, which regards its predecessors with *reproach and mockery*. 'What are you complaining about, what are you seeking, what do you ask of life? No doubt, you want happiness? That's not much, is it? Happiness must be won. If you have the power, take it. If not—*be silent*, things are bad enough without you.' A gloomy, intense energy is manifested in the younger generation's *unfriendly* attitude toward its mentors. In its concepts of good and evil this generation was like the best people of the preceding generation, their sympathies and antipathies were the same, they *desired one and the same thing*, but the people of the past *fussed and bustled about*. The people of the present do not fuss, they seek nothing, they submit to no compromises and they *place their hopes on nothing*. They are just as impotent as the Rudins, but they have acknowledged their impotence.
>
> 'I cannot act now,' thinks each of these new people, 'I will not even try, *I disdain everything around me* and I will not conceal my disdain. I shall enter the battle against evil only when I feel myself to be strong.' Since they cannot act, these people begin to think and analyze . . . superstitions and authorities are shattered and their world view becomes completely devoid of various illusory notions. They are not concerned with whether society is following them; they are full of themselves, of their

3. Leading character of Herzen's novel *Whose Fault?* [*Editor*].

4. The four characters named are the protagonists of novels by Pushkin, Lermontov, Turgenev, and Herzen. They formed a historic series of the "superfluous man" in Dobrolyubov's interpretation. The Decembrists were real, the participants in the abortive revolt of December, 1825 [*Editor*].

inner life. In a word, the Pechorins have *the will but not the knowledge*, the Rudins have *the knowledge but not the will*, the Bazarovs have *both the knowledge and the will*. Thought and deed merge in one stable whole.

Everything is here, if there are no errors, both characterization and classification—all is concise and clear, the sum is tallied, the account is rendered, and from the point of view from which the author approached the problem everything is perfectly correct.

But we do not accept this account, we protest against it from our premature and unready graves. We are not Karl V and do not wish to be buried alive.[5]

The fates of the *fathers and sons* are strange! Clearly Turgenev did not introduce Bazarov to pat him on the head; it is also clear that he had wanted to do something for the benefit of the fathers. But, juxtaposed to such pitiful and insignificant fathers as the Kirsanovs, the stern Bazarov captivated Turgenev and, instead of spanking the son, he flogged the fathers.

This is why it happened that a portion of the younger generation recognized itself in Bazarov. But we do not recognize ourselves at all in the Kirsanovs; just as we do not recognize ourselves in the Manilovs and Sobakeviches,[6] although the Manilovs and Sobakeviches existed right up to the time of our youth and exist today.

There is no lack of moral abortions living at the same time in different strata of society, and in its different tendencies; without doubt, they represent more or less general types, but they do not present the sharpest and most characteristic aspects of their generation—the aspects which most express its intensiveness. Pisarev's Bazarov, in one sense, is to some degree the extreme type of what Turgenev called the sons, while the Kirsanovs are the most insignificant and vulgar representatives of the fathers.

Turgenev was more of an artist in his novel than people think and because of this he lost his way, and, in my view, this is very fortunate—he was going into one room, stumbled into another, but into a better one.

What good would it have done to send Bazarov to London? The despicable Pisemsky did not stint on travel funds for his agitated monsters.[7] We, perhaps, would have proved to him, on the banks of the Thames, that it is possible, without attaining the rank of *head of a department*, to be of just as much use as any *head of a department*, that society is not always deaf and implacable when a protest

5. Charles V, Emperor of the Holy Roman Empire, abdicated in 1555 and retired to a monastery [*Editor*].

6. Characters in Gogol's *Dead Souls* [*Editor*].

7. In Pisemsky's anti-nihilist novel *The Agitated Sea* (1863) "nihilists" come to London to confront Russian political emigrants with their ostensible failure to do something worthwhile [*Editor*].

strikes the right note, that the job sometimes does get done, that the Rudins and Bel'tovs sometimes do have the will and steadfastness and that, recognizing the impossibility of the action for which they were yearning, they gave up *much*, went to a strange land and "without fussing or bustling around" started to print Russian books and disseminate Russian propaganda.

The influence of the Russian press in London from 1856 to the end of 1863—is not only a practical fact, but a historical one as well. It is impossible to erase it, it must be accepted.

In London, Bazarov would have seen that only from a distance does it seem as if we are waving our hands in the air, and that, actually, we are working with them. Perhaps he would have replaced his anger with favor and would have ceased to regard us "with reproach and mockery."

I openly admit that this throwing of stones at one's predecessors is repugnant to me. . . . I repeat what I have said before. (*My Past and Thoughts*, volume IV): "I would like to save the younger generation from historical ingratitude and even from historical errors. It is time that father Saturn refrained from making a snack of his children, but it is also time that the children stop following the example of the Kamchadals who kill their old men."

Essays in Criticism

D. S. MIRSKY

Turgénev†

Iván Sergéyevich Turgénev was born on October 28, 1818, in Orël. His father, a handsome but impoverished squire who had served in the cavalry, was married to an heiress older than himself. She had had a very unhappy childhood and girlhood and adored her husband, who never loved her. This combined with the control of a large fortune to make of Mme Turgénev an embittered and intolerable domestic tyrant. Though she was attached to her son, she treated him with exasperating despotism, and with her serfs and servants she was plainly cruel. It was in his mother's house that the future author of *A Sportsman's Sketches* saw serfdom in its least attractive form.

In 1833 Turgénev entered the University of Moscow, but remained there only one year, for in 1834 his mother moved to Petersburg and he went over to the other university. He studied under Púshkin's friend, Professor Pletnëv, and had occasion to meet the great poet himself. His first verses were published in Pletnëv's, formerly Púshkin's, *Sovreménnik* (1838). This connection with the "literary aristocracy" is of importance: alone of all his contemporaries, Turgénev had a living link with the age of poetry. After taking his degree he went to Berlin to complete his philosophical education at the university that had been the abode and was still the temple of Hegel—the divinity of the young generation of Russian idealists. Several of them, including Stankévich and Granóvsky, Turgénev met at Berlin, and henceforward he became the friend and ally of the Westernizers. His three years at Berlin (1838–41) imbued him with a lifelong love for Western civilization and for Germany. When in 1841 he returned to Russia he at first intended to devote himself to a university career. As this did not come off, he entered the Civil Service, but there also he remained only two years, and after 1845 abandoned all pursuits except literature. His work at first was chiefly in verse, and in the midforties he was regarded, chiefly on the strength of the narrative poem *Parásha* (1843), as one of the principal hopes of the young generation in poetry.

In 1845 Turgénev fell out with his mother, who ceased to give him money, and for the following years, till her death, he had to live the life of a literary Bohemian. The reason for Mme Turgénev's

† From D. S. Mirsky, *A History of Russian Literature from Its Beginnings to 1900*, edited by Francis J. Whitfield, New York: 1958. Pp. 193-208. Copyright 1958 by Alfred A. Knopf, Inc., reprinted by permission of the publishers.

displeasure was partly that she resented her son's leaving the Civil Service and becoming a scribbler of a dangerous, revolutionary kind, but especially that she strongly disapproved of his infatuation for the famous singer Pauline García (Mme Viardot). This infatuation proved to be the love of his life. Mme Viardot tolerated it and liked Turgénev's company, and so he was able most of his life to live near her. In 1847 he went abroad, following her, and returned only in 1850, at the news of his mother's dangerous illness. On her death he found himself the possessor of a large fortune.

Meanwhile Turgénev had abandoned verse for prose. In 1847 Nekrásov's *Sovreménnik* started the publication of the short stories that were to form *A Sportsman's Sketches.* They appeared in book form in 1852, and this, together with the publication, about the same time, of other stories, gave Turgénev one of the first places, if not the first, among Russian writers. *A Sportsman's Sketches* was a great social as well as literary event. On the background of the complete silence of those years of reaction, the *Sketches,* seemingly harmless if taken one by one, produced a cumulative effect of considerable power. Their consistent presentation of the serf as a being, not only human, but superior in humanity to his masters, made the book a loud protest against the system of serfdom. It is said to have produced a strong impression on the future Emperor Alexander II and caused in him the decision to do away with the system. Meanwhile the authorities were alarmed. The censor who had passed the book was ordered to leave the service. Shortly after that an obituary notice of Gógol by Turgénev, written in what seemed to the police a too enthusiastic tone, led to his arrest and banishment to his estate, where he remained eighteen months (1852–3). When he was released he came to Petersburg already in the full glory of success. For several years he was the *de facto* head of Petersburg literature, and his judgment and decisions had the force of law.

The first years of Alexander II's reign were the summer of Turgénev's popularity. No one profited more than he from the unanimity of the progressive and reforming enthusiasm that had taken hold of Russian society. He was accepted as its spokesman. In his early sketches and stories he had denounced selfdom; in *Rúdin* (1856) he paid homage to the idealism of the elder generation while exposing its inefficiency; in *A Nest of Gentlefolk* (1859) he glorified all that was noble in the old Orthodox ideals of the old gentry; in *On the Eve* (1860) he attempted to paint the heroic figure of a young girl of the new generation. Dobrolyúbov and Chernyshévsky, the leaders of advanced opinion, chose his works for the texts of their journalistic sermons. His art answered to the demands of everyone. It was civic but not "tendentious." It painted life as it was, and chose for its subjects the most burning problems of the day. It was full of truth and, at the same time, of poetry and beauty. It satisfied Left and Right. It was the mean term, the middle style for which the forties had groped in vain. It avoided in an equal measure the pitfalls of grotesque caricature and of sentimental "philanthropy." It was perfect. Turgénev was very sensitive to his success, and particularly sensitive to the praise of the young generation and of advanced opinion, whose spokesman he appeared, and aspired, to be.

The only thing he had been censured for (or rather, as everyone believed in the photographic veracity of Turgénev's representation of Russia, it was not he, but Russian life, that was found fault with) was that while he had given such a beautiful succession of heroines, he had failed to give a Russian hero; it was noticed that when he had wanted a man of action, he had chosen a Bulgarian (Insárov in *On the Eve*). This led the critics to surmise that he believed a Russian hero an impossibility. Now Turgénev decided to make up for this shortcoming and give a real Russian man of action—a hero of the young generation. This he did in Bazárov, the nihilist hero of *Fathers and Sons* (1862). He created him with love and admiration, but the result was unexpected. The radicals were indignant. This, they said, was a caricature and no hero. This nihilist, with his militant materialism, with his negation of all religious and aesthetic values and his faith in nothing but frogs (the dissection of frogs was the mystical rite of Darwinian naturalism and anti-spiritualism), was a caricature of the young generation drawn to please the reactionaries. The radicals raised a hue and cry against Turgénev, who was proclaimed to have "written himself out." A little later, it is true, a still younger and more extreme section of radicals, in the person of the brilliant young critic Pisarev, reversed the older radicals' verdict, accepted the name of nihilist, and recognized in Bazárov the ideal to be followed. But this belated recognition from the extreme Left did not console Turgénev for the profound wound inflicted on him by the first reception given to Bazárov. He decided to abandon Russia and Russian literature. He was abroad when *Fathers and Sons* appeared and the campaign against him began. He remained abroad in the shade of Mme Viardot, at first in Baden-Baden and after 1871 in Paris, and never returned to Russia except for short periods. His decision to abandon literature found expression in the fragment of lyrical prose *Enough*, where he gave full play to his pessimism and disillusionment. He did not, however, abandon literature, and continued writing to his death. But in by far the greater part of his later work he turned away from contemporary Russia, so distasteful and unresponsive to him, towards the times of his childhood, the old Russia of before the reforms. Most of his work after 1862 is either frankly memoirs, or fiction built out of the material of early experience. He was loath, however, to resign himself to the fate of a writer who had outlived his times. Twice again he attempted to tackle the problems of the day in big works of fiction. In *Smoke* (1867) he gave full vent to his bitterness against all classes of Russian society; and in *Virgin Soil* (1877) he attempted to give a picture of the revolutionary movement of the seventies. But the two novels only emphasized his growing estrangement from living Russia, the former by its impotent bitterness, the latter by its lack of information and of all sense of reality in the treatment of the powerful movement of the seventies. Gradually, however, as party feeling, at least in literature, sank, Turgénev returned into his own (the popularity of his *early* work had never diminished). The revival of "æsthetics" in the later seventies contributed to a revival of his popularity, and his last visit to Russia in 1880 was a triumphant progress.

In the meantime, especially after he settled in Paris, Turgénev became intimate with French literary circles—with Mérimée, Flaubert, and the young naturalists. His works began to be translated into French and German, and before long his fame became international. He was the first Russian author to win a European reputation. In the literary world of Paris he became an important personality. He was one of the first to discern the talent of the young Maupassant, and Henry James (who included an essay on Turgénev in a volume on *French* novelists) and other beginning writers looked up to him as to a master. When he died, Renan, with pardonable lack of information, proclaimed that it was through Turgénev that Russia, so long mute,[1] had at last become vocal. Turgénev felt much more at home among his French confreres than among his Russian equals (with most of whom, including Tolstóy, Dostoyévsky, and Nekrásov, he sooner or later quarreled), and there is a striking difference between the impressions he produced on foreigners and on Russians. Foreigners were always impressed by the grace, charm and sincerity of his manner. With Russians he was arrogant and vain, and no amount of hero-worship could make his Russian visitors blind to these disagreeable characteristics.

Soon after his last visit to Russia Turgénev fell ill. He died on August 22, 1883, in the small commune of Bougival, on the Seine below Paris.

Turgénev's first attempt at prose fiction[2] was in the wake of

1. One will remember the words of Carlyle on "mute Russia" written in 1840, three years after the death of Púshkin.

2. For the poetic work of Turgénev see Chapter V; for his dramatic work, Chapter VII.

Lérmontov, from whom he derived the romantic halo round his first Pechórin-like heroes (*Andréy Kólosov, The Duelist, Three Portraits*) and the method of the intensified anecdote (*The Jew*). In *A Sportsman's Sketches,* began in 1847, he was to free himself from the romantic conventions of these early stories by abandoning all narrative skeleton and limiting himself to "slices of life." But even for some time after that date he remained unable in his more distinctly narrative work to hit on what was to become his true manner. Thus, for instance, *Three Meetings* (1852) is a story of pure atmosphere woven round a very slender theme, saturated in its descriptions of moonlit nights, with an excess of romantic and "poetical" poetry. *The Diary of a Superfluous Man* (1850) is reminiscent of Gógol and of the young Dostoyévsky, developing as it does the Dostoyevskian theme of humiliated human dignity and of morbid delight in humiliation, but aspiring to a Gógol-like and very un-Turgenevian verbal intensity. (The phrase "a superfluous man" had an extraordinary fortune and is still applied by literary and social historians to the type of ineffective idealist portrayed so often by Turgénev and his contemporaries.) At last *Mumú* (1854), the well-known story of the deaf serf and his favorite dog, and of how his mistress ordered it to be destroyed, is a "philanthropic" story in the tradition of *The Greatcoat* and of *Poor Folk,* where an intense sensation of pity is arrived at by methods that strike the modern reader as illegitimate, working on the nerves rather than on the imagination.

A Sportsman's Sketches, on the other hand, written in 1847–51, belongs to the highest, most lasting, and least questionable achievement of Turgénev and of Russian realism. The book describes the casual and various meetings of the narrator during his wanderings with a gun and a dog in his native district of Bólkhov and in the surrounding country. The sketches are arranged in a random order and have no narrative skeleton, containing nothing but accounts of what the narrator saw and heard. Some of them are purely descriptive, of scenery or character; others consist of conversation, addressed to the narrator or overheard. At times there is a dramatic *motive,* but the development is only hinted at by the successive glimpses the narrator gets of his personages. This absolute matter-of-factness and studious avoidance of everything artificial and made-up were the most prominent characteristics of the book when it appeared—it was a new genre. The peasants are described from the outside, as seen (or overseen) by the narrator, not in their intimate, unoverlooked life. As I have said, they are drawn with obviously greater sympathy than the upper classes. The squires are represented as either vulgar, or cruel, or ineffective. In the peasants, Turgénev emphasized their humanity, their imaginativeness, their poetical and artistic giftedness, their sense of dignity, their intelligence. It was in this quiet and unobtrusive way that the book struck the readers with the injustice and ineptitude of serfdom. Now, when the issue of serfdom is a thing of the past, the *Sketches* seem once more as harmless and as innocent as a book can be, and it requires a certain degree of historical imagination to reconstruct the atmosphere in which they had the effect of a mild bombshell.

Judged as literature, the *Sketches* are frequently, if not always, above praise. In the representation of rural scenery and peasant character, Turgénev never surpassed such masterpieces as *The Singers* and *Bézhin Meadow*.[3] *The Singers* especially, even after *First Love* and *Fathers and Sons*, may claim to be his crowning achievement and the quintessence of all the most characteristic qualities of his art. It is the description of a singing-match at a village pub between the peasant Yáshka Túrok and a tradesman from Zhízdra. The story is representative of Turgénev's manner of painting his peasants; he does not one-sidedly idealize them; the impression produced by the match, with its revelation of the singers' high sense, of artistic values, is qualified by the drunken orgy the artists lapse into after the match is over and the publican treats Yáshka to the fruit of his victory. *The Singers* may also be taken as giving Turgénev's prose at its highest and most characteristic. It is careful and in a sense artificial, but the impression of absolute ease and simplicity is exhaled from every word and turn of phrase: It is a carefully *selected* language, rich, but curiously avoiding words and phrases, crude or journalese, that might jar on the reader. The beauty of the landscape painting is due chiefly to the choice of exact and delicately suggestive and descriptive words. There is no ornamental imagery after the manner of Gógol, no rhetorical rhythm, no splendid cadences. But the sometime poet's and poets' disciple's hand is evident in the careful, varied, and unobtrusively perfect balance of the phrases.

The first thing Turgénev wrote after the *Sketches* and *Mumú* was *The Inn*. Like *Mumú* it turns on the unjust and callous treatment of serfs by their masters, but the sentimental, "philanthropic" element is replaced for the first time in his work by the characteristic Turgenevian atmosphere of tragic necessity. *The Inn* was followed in 1853–61 by a succession of masterpieces. They were divided by the author himself into two categories: novels and *nouvelles* (in Russian, *romány* and *póvesti*). The difference between the two forms in the case of Turgénev is not so much one of size or scope as that the novels aim at social significance and

3. It is interesting to note that these pieces are precisely those Henry James singles out for particular praise.

at the statement of social problems, while the *nouvelles* are pure and simple stories of emotional incident, free from civic preoccupations. Each novel includes a narrative kernel similar in subject and bulk to that of a *nouvelle,* but it is expanded into an answer to some burning problem of the day. The novels of this period are *Rúdin* (1856), *A Nest of Gentlefolk* (1859), *On the Eve* (1860), and *Fathers and Sons* (1862); the *nouvelles, Two Friends* (1854), *A Quiet Spot* (1854), *Yákov Pásynkov* (1855), *A Correspondence* (1856), *Faust* (1856), *Ásya* (1858), and *First Love* (1860). It will be noticed that the civic novels belong chiefly to the age of reform (1856–61), while the purely private *nouvelles* predominate in the reactionary years that precede it. But even "on the eve" of the Emancipation, Turgénev could be sufficiently detached from civic issues to write the perfectly uncivic *First Love.*

The novels of Turgénev are, thus, those of his stories in which he, voluntarily, submitted to the obligation of writing works of social significance. This significance is arrived at in the first place by the nature of the characters, who are made to be representative of phases successively traversed by the Russian intellectual. Rúdin is the progressive idealist of the forties; Lavrétsky, the more Slavophil idealist of the same generation; Eléna, in *On the Eve,* personifies the vaguely generous and active fermentation of the generation immediately preceding the reforms; Bazárov, the militant materialism of the generation of 1860. Secondly, the social significance is served by the insertion of numerous *conversations* between the characters on topics of current interest (Slavophilism and Westernism, the ability of educated Russian to act, the place in life of art and science, and so on). These conversations are what especially distinguished Turgénev's novels from his *nouvelles.* They have little relation to the action, and not always much more to the character of the representative hero. They were what the civic critics seized upon for comment, but they are certainly the least permanent and most dating part of the novels. There frequently occur characters who are introduced with no other motive but to do the talking, and whom one would have rather wished away. But the central, representative characters—the heroes—are in most cases not only representative, but alive. Rúdin, the first in date, is one of the masterpieces of nineteenth-century character drawing. An eminent French novelist (who is old-fashioned enough still to prefer Turgénev to Tolstóy, Dostoyévsky, and Chékhov) has pointed out to me the wonderfully delicate mastery with which the impression produced by Rúdin on the other characters and on the reader is made gradually to change from the first appearance in the glamour of superiority to the bankruptcy of his pusillanimous breach with Natália, then to the gloomy glimpse of the undone and degenerate man, and to the redeeming flash of his heroic and ineffective death on the barricades of the faubourg St. Antoine. The French writer thought this delicate change of attitude unique in fiction. Had he known more Russian, he would have realized that Turgénev had merely been a highly intelligent and creative pupil of Pushkin's. Like Pushkin in *Evgeny Onegin,* Turgénev does not analyze and dissect his heroes, as Tolstóy and Dostoyévsky would have done; he does not uncover their souls; he only conveys their atmosphere, partly by showing how they are reflected in others, partly by an exceedingly delicate and thinly woven aura of suggestive accompaniment—a method that at once betrays its origin in a *poetic* novel. Where Turgénev attempts to show us the *inner* life of his heroes by other methods, he always fails—the description of Eléna's feelings for Insárov in *On the Eve* is distinctly painful reading. Turgénev had to use all the power of selfcriticism and self-restraint to avoid the pitfall of false poetry and false beauty.

Still, the characters, constructed though they are by means of suggestion, not dissection, are the vivifying principle of Turgénev's stories. Like most Russian novelists he makes character predominate over plot (and it is the characters that we remember. The population of Turgénev's novels (apart from the peasant stories) may be classified under several heads. First comes the division into the Philistines and the elect. The Philistines are the direct descendants of Gógol's characters—heroes of *póshlost,* self-satisfied inferiority. Of course there is not a trace in them of Gógol's exuberant and grotesque caricature; the irony of Turgénev is fine, delicate, unobtrusive, hardly at all aided by any obvious comical devices. On the other side are the elect, the men and women with a sense of values, superior to those of vegetable enjoyment and social position. The men, again, are very different from the women. The fair sex comes out distinctly more advantageously from the hands of Turgénev. The strong, pure, passionate, and virtuous woman, opposed to the weak, potentially generous, but ineffective and ultimately shallow man, was introduced into literature by Púshkin, and recurs again and again in the work of the realists, but nowhere more insistently than in Turgénev's. His heroines are famous all the world over and have done much to spread a high reputation of Russian womanhood. Moral force and courage are the keynote to Turgénev's heroine—the power to sacrifice all worldly considerations to passion (Natália in *Rúdin*), or all happiness to duty (Líza in *A Nest of Gentlefolk*). But what goes home to the general reader in these women is not so much the height of their moral beauty as the extraordinary *poetical* beauty woven round them by the delicate and perfect art of their begetter.

Turgénev reaches his highest perfection in this, his own and unique art, in two of the shorter stories, *A Quiet Spot* and *First Love*. In the first, the purely Turgenevian, tragic, poetic, and rural atmosphere reaches its maximum of concentration, and the richness of suggestion that conditions the characters surpasses all he ever wrote. It transcends mere fiction and rises into poetry, not by the beauty of the single words and parts, but by sheer force of suggestion and saturated significance. *First Love* stands somewhat apart from the rest of Turgénev's work. Its atmosphere is cooler and clearer, more reminiscent of the rarefied air of Lérmontov. The heroes—Zinaída and the narrator's father (who is traditionally supposed to portray the author's own father)—are more *animal* and vital than Turgénev usually allows his heroes to be. Their passions are tense and clear-cut, free from vagueness and idealistic haze, selfish, but with a selfishness that is redeemed by self-justifying vitality. Unique in the whole of his work, *First Love* is the least relaxing of Turgénev's stories. But, characteristically, the story is told from the point of view of the boy admirer of Zinaída and of his pangs of adolescent jealousy for his rival and father.

At the height of his popularity, in 1860, Turgénev wrote a famous essay on *Hamlet and Don Quixote*. He considered these characters as the two prototypes of the elect intellectual portion of mankind, which was divided into self-conscious, introspective, and consequently ineffective, Hamlets, and enthusiastic, single minded, courageous at the risk of seeming ridiculous, Quixotes. He himself and the great majority of his heroes were Hamlets. But he had always wanted to create Quixotes, whose freedom from reflection and questioning would make them efficient, while their possession of higher values would raise them above the Philistines. In the later forties the critics, who had taken note of the consistent inefficiency of Turgénev's heroes, clamored for him to produce a more active and effective hero. This he attempted in *On the Eve*. But the attempt was a failure. He made his hero a Bulgarian patriot, Insárov. But he failed to breathe into him the spirit of life. Insárov is merely a strong, silent puppet, at times almost ludicrous. In conjunction with the stilted and vapid Eléna, Insárov makes *On the Eve* distinctly the worst of all Turgénev's mature work.

The best of the novels and ultimately the most important of Turgénev's works is *Fathers and Sons*, one of the greatest novels of the nineteenth century. Here Turgénev triumphantly solved two tasks that he had been attempting to solve: to create a living masculine character not based on introspection, and to overcome the contradiction between the imaginative and the social theme. *Fathers and Sons* is Turgénev's only novel where the social problem is distilled without residue into art, and leaves no bits of undigested journalism sticking out. Here the delicate and poetic narrative art of Turgénev reaches its perfection, and Bazárov is the only one of Turgénev's men who is worthy to stand by the side of his women. But nowhere perhaps does the essential debility and feminineness of his genius come out more clearly than in this, the best of his novels. Bazárov is a strong man, but he is painted with admiration and wonder by one to whom a strong man is something abnormal. Turgénev is incapable of making his hero triumph, and to spare him the inadequate treatment that would have been his lot in the case of success, he lets him die, not from any natural development of the nature of the subject, but by the blind decree of fate. For fate, blind chance, crass casualty, presides over Turgénev's universe as it does over Hardy's, but Turgénev's people submit to it with passive resignation. Even the heroic Bazárov dies as resigned as a flower in the field, with silent courage but without protest.

It would be wrong to affirm that after *Fathers and Sons* Turgénev's genius began to decline, but at any rate it ceased to grow. What was more important for his contemporaries, he lost touch with Russian life and thus ceased to count as a *contemporary* writer, though he remained a permanent classic. His attempts again to tackle the problems of the day in *Smoke* (1867) and in *Virgin Soil* (1877) only emphasized his loss of touch with the new age. *Smoke* is the worst-constructed of his novels: it contains a beautiful love story, which is interrupted and interlarded with conversations that have no relation to its characters and are just dialogued journalism on the thesis that all intellectual and educated Russia was nothing but smoke. *Virgin Soil* is a complete failure, and was immediately recognized as such. Though it contains much that is in the best manner of Turgénev (the characters of the bureaucratic-aristocratic Sipyágin family are among his best satirical drawings), the whole novel is disqualified by an entirely uninformed and necessarily false conception of what he was writing about. His presentation of the revolutionaries of the seventies is like an account of a foreign country by one who had never seen it.

But while Turgénev had lost the power of writing for the times, he had not lost the genius of creating those wonderful love stories which are his most personal contribution to the world's literature. Pruned of its conversations, *Smoke* is a beautiful *nouvelle,* comparable to the best he wrote in the fifties, and so is *The Torrents of Spring* (1872). Both are on the same subject: a young man loves a pure and sweet young girl but forsakes her for a mature and lascivious woman of thirty, who is loved by many and for whom he is the plaything of a fleeting passion. The characters of Irína, the older woman in *Smoke,* and of Gemma, the Italian girl in *The Torrents of Spring,* are among the most beautiful in the whole of his gallery. *The Torrents of Spring* is given a retrospective setting, and in most of the other stories of this last period the scene is set in the old times of pre-Reform Russia. Some of these stories are purely objective little tragedies (one of the best is *A Lear of the Steppes,* 1870); others are non-narrative fragments from reminiscences, partly continuing the manner and theme of *A Sportsman's Sketches.* There are also the purely biographical reminiscences, including interesting accounts of the author's acquaintance with Púshkin and Belínsky and the remarkable account of *The Execution of Troppmann* (1870), which in its fascinated objectivity is one of the most terrible descriptions ever made of an execution.

There had always been in Turgénev a poetic or romantic vein, as opposed to the prevailing realistic atmosphere of his principal work. His attitude to nature had always been lyrical, and he had always had a lurking desire to transcend the limits imposed on the Russian novelist by the dogma of realism. Not only did he begin his career as a lyrical poet and end it with his *Poems in Prose,* but even in his most realistic and civic novels the construction and atmosphere are mainly lyrical. *A Sportsman's Sketches* includes many purely lyrical pages of natural description, and to the period of his highest maturity belongs that remarkable piece *A Tour in the Forest* (1857), where for the first time Turgénev's conception of indifferent and eternal nature opposed to transient man found expression in a sober and simple prose that attains poetry by the simplest means of unaided suggestion. His last period begins with the purely lyrical prose poem *Enough* and culminates in the *Poems in Prose.* At the same time the fantastic element asserts itself. In some stories (*The Dog, Knock! Knock! Knock!* and *The Story of Father Alexis*) it appears only in the form of a suggestion of mysterious presences in an ordinary realistic setting. The most important of these stories is his last, *Clara Mílich* (1883), written under the influence of spiritualistic readings and musings. It is as good as most of his stories of purely human love, but the mysterious element is somewhat difficult to appreciate quite whole-heartedly today. It has all the inevitable flatness of Victorian spiritualism. In a few stories Turgénev freed himself from the conventions of realistic form and wrote such things as the purely visionary *Phantoms* (1864) and *The Song of Triumphant Love* (1881), written in the style of an Italian *novella* of the sixteenth century. There can be no greater contrast than between these and such stories of Dostoyévsky as *The Double* or *Mr. Prokhárchin.* Dostoyévsky, with the material of sordid reality, succeeds in building fabrics of weird fantasy. Turgénev, in spite of all the paraphernalia introduced, never succeeded in freeing himself from the second-rate atmosphere of the medium's consulting room. *The Song of Triumphant Love* shows up his limitation of another kind—the inadequacy of his language for treating subjects of insufficient reality. This limitation Turgénev shared with all his contemporaries (except Tolstóy and Leskóv). They did not have a sufficient feeling of words, of language as language (as Púshkin and Gógol had had), to make it serve them in unfamiliar fields. Words for them were only signs of familiar things and familiar feelings. Language had entered with them on a strictly limited engagement—it would serve only in so far as it had not to leave the everyday realities of the nineteenth century.

The same stylistic limitation is apparent in Turgénev's last and most purely lyrical work, *Poems in Prose* (1879–83). (Turgénev originally entitled them *Senilia;* the present title was given them with the author's silent approval by the editor of the *Messenger of Europe,* where they first appeared.) They are a series of short prose fragments, most of them gathered round some more or less narrative kernel. They are comparable in construction to the objectivated lyrics of the French Parnassians, who used visual symbols to express their subjective experience. Sometimes they verge on the fable and the apologue. In these "poems" is to be found the final and most hopeless expression of Turgénev's agnostic pessimism, of his awe of unresponsive nature and necessity, and of his pitying contempt for human futility. The best of the "poems" are those where these feelings are given an ironic garb. The more purely poetical ones have suffered from time, and date too distinctly from about 1880—a date that can hardly add beauty to anything connected with it. The one that closes the series, *The Russian Language,* has suffered particularly—not from time only, but from excessive handling. It displays in a condensed form all the weakness and ineffectiveness of Turgénev's style when it was divorced from concrete and familiar *things.* The art of eloquence had been lost.

Turgénev was the first Russian writer to charm the Western reader. There are still retarded Victorians who consider him the only Russian writer who is not disgusting. But for most lovers of Russian he has been replaced by spicier food. Turgénev was very nineteenth century, perhaps the most representative man of its latter part, whether in Russia or west of it. He was a Victorian, a man of compromise, more Victorian than any one of his Russian contemporaries. This made him so acceptable to Europe, and this has now made him lose so much of his reputation there. Turgénev struck the West at first as something new, something typically Russian. But it is hardly necessary to insist today on the fact that he is not in any sense representative of Russia as a whole. He was representative only of his class—the idealistically educated middle gentry, tending already to become a non-class intelligentsia—and of his generation, which failed to gain real touch with Russian realities,[4] which failed to find itself a place in life and which, ineffective in the sphere of action, produced one of the most beautiful literary growths of the nineteenth century. In his day Turgénev was regarded as a leader of opinion on social problems; now this seems strange and unintelligible. Long since, the issues that he fought out have ceased to be of any actual interest. Unlike Tolstóy or Dostoyévsky, unlike Griboyédov, Púshkin, Lérmontov, and Gógol, unlike Chaadáyev, Grigóriev, and Herzen—Turgénev is no longer a teacher or even a ferment. His work has become pure art—and perhaps it has won more from this transformation than it has lost. It has taken a permanent place in the Russian tradition, a place that stands above the changes of taste or the revolutions of time. We do not seek for wisdom or guidance in it, but it is impossible to imagine a time when *The Singers*, *A Quiet Spot*, *First Love*, or *Fathers and Sons* will cease to be among the most cherished of joys to Russian readers.

AVRAHM YARMOLINSKY

Fathers and Children†

Always ill at ease when it came to traffic with abstract ideas, principles, opinions, Turgenev felt sure of himself only when he was dealing with what is visible, audible, tangible. "When I don't have to do with concrete figures," he wrote, "I am entirely lost and I don't know where to turn. It always seems to me that exactly the opposite of what I say could be asserted with equal justice. But if I am speaking of a red nose and blonde hair, then the hair is blonde and the nose red; no amount of reflection will change that."

Belinsky had said at the outset of Turgenev's career that while he was extremely observant, he had no imagination. The young author had agreed with this judgment wholeheartedly. To the end he was possessed by a self-distrust which led him to lean heavily upon what the world offered to his observation. George Moore went to the root of the matter when he said that Turgenev had the illuminative rather than the creative imagination and that

4. What Turgénev was in touch with were not the raw realities of Russian life, but only their reflection in the minds of his generation of intellectuals.

† From Avrahm Yarmolinsky, ***Turgenev, The Man, His Art and His Age***, New York, 1959. Copyright 1959 by Avrahm Yarmolinsky. Published by The Orion Press. Reprinted by permission of Grossman Publishers, Inc.

he "borrowed" his stories, leaving them, as far as structure went, much as he found them.

Turgenev confessed that he envied the English their secret of making a successful plot, an ability which he found lacking in himself as in so many Russian writers. He had a prodigious memory, which served him well. He liked to insist that his characters were not invented, but discovered. He stalked them with the patience, the eagerness, and the skill with which he pursued his woodcock and his partridge. Indeed, it appears that he almost invariably drew from living models and that his fictions were fathered by experience rather than by fancy. He told a friend that it was his custom, after meeting a stranger, to set down in his notebook any peculiarities he had observed. He studied Lavater's [1] work on physiognomy from cover to cover. Drawing rooms, railway carriages, reading rooms were his favorite observatories. He did not hesitate to incorporate verbatim in his story, "The Brigadier," a private letter which he found among his mother's papers. If he had had his choice, he once remarked, he would have been a writer like Gibbon. The novelist had the historian's need for documentation.

A writer of fiction, he held, dare not be a dilettante. He must maintain close contact with life. To represent it truthfully and fairly, without philosophizing about it or trying to improve it—that was the greatest happiness for the artist. But since reality "teemed" with adventitious matter, the novelist's gift, he insisted, lay in the ability to eliminate all superfluities, so as to render only that which, in the light of his knowledge and understanding, appeared significant, characteristic, what Turgenev liked to call *typical*. He believed that the writer, while aiming at the universal, must deal with the particular, and he quoted Johann Merck enthusiastically: "With the ancients everything was local, of the moment, and thus it became eternal." Annenkov said that he represented "the personified flair of contemporaneity" in Russian literature. Looking back at his novels toward the close of his life, Turgenev wrote: "I strove, within the limits of my power and ability, conscientiously and impartially to represent and incarnate in appropriate types both what Shakespeare called 'the body and pressure of the time' and the rapidly changing countenance of the educated Russians, who have been the predominant object of my observations."

In the case of *Fathers and Children*, as in most of his writings, the germ came to Turgenev not in the form of a situation or an idea, but in that of a person. Chancing to meet in a railway train a provincial doctor who, talking shop, had

1. J. K. Lavater (1741–1801), philosopher and writer on physiognomy [*Editor*].

something to say on the subject of anthrax, the novelist was struck by the man's rough, matter-of-fact, candid manner. (He was to end his days in Siberia.) It flashed upon the novelist that here was a representative of a type, one which was to become known as the Nihilist. An individual of a similar cast, also a physician, was among the Russians he encountered on the Isle of Wight. As he looked about him, he seemed to see everywhere signs pointing to the emergence of that type. But finding no trace of it in the fiction of the day, he wondered if he were not chasing a ghost.

The notion of building a novel around this figure occurred to him during his stay at Ventnor in August, 1860. In the fall, when he was back in Paris, the idea returned with renewed force, and he found himself increasingly absorbed in it. By October the stuff for his new novel was all in his head, but, he wrote, "the spark which must kindle everything has not yet blazed up."

It was presumably about this time that he began to get up for his characters the "dossiers" without which he could not begin work on a novel. He was in the habit, as he told Henry James among others, of setting down "a sort of biography of each of his characters, and everything that they had done and that had happened to them up to the opening of the story." As in the case of *On the Eve,* he kept a diary for on of the characters, but this time it was not the journal of a minor figure, but of the protagonist, Bazarov.

When that delightful period was over during which the figures for his novel floated like nebulæ through his mind, and once he had a good grasp of his characters, Turgenev's final move, according to James, was the arduous business of devising the action which would lead them to reveal their inner natures. In *Fathers and Children* the novelist put Bazarov through his paces by taking this brusque commoner on a visit to a house of gentlefolk; by leading him into arguments with his two middle-aged, cultivated hosts; by making him fall hopelessly in love with a beautiful lady, indolent and undersexed; by involving him in a stupid, almost comical duel with one of his hosts; by engaging him in talk with his earnest, apish, pliant disciple; by sending him home to see his pathetic old parents; by bringing upon him an untimely death, the result of an infection contracted at a rural post-mortem.

The method he followed here is his habitual one—realization of the characters not by analysis of their consciousness, but by exhibition of their behavior. Like so many of his fellow craftsmen, he exalted into a dogma his way of working. When he was brooding over the plan for *Fathers and Children* he set down for a literary protégé this precept: "The writer must be a psycholgist, but a secret one: he must sense and know the roots of phenomena, but offer only the phenomena themselves,—as they blossom or wither." Ten years earlier he had said, in the course of a critique, much the same thing in other words: "The psychologist must disappear in the artist, as the skeleton is concealed within the warm and living body, for which it serves as a firm but invisible support."

From the moment when we first see Bazarov taking his time about offering his bare red hand to his host, and turning down the collar of his nondescript coat to show his long, thin face, with its sandy side-whiskers and cool green eyes, to the moment, a few months later, when the dying atheist raises one eyelid in horror as the priest administers the last sacrament, we are in the presence of a figure that dwarfs all around him and carries the whole weight of the story. It is also a figure that shows the fullest measure of Turgenev's powers of characterization. He believed that a novelist must be "objective," concerned to represent the world about him rather than his response to it, that his art required an interest in and a cumulative knowledge of other people's lives, as well as an understanding of the forces that shaped them. Bazarov, the tough-minded, hard-fisted medic, with his brutal honesty, his faith in a crudely empirical science that he uses as a cudgel wherewith to hit out at the genteel culture he abominates, this professed "Nihilist," is an example of what the objective method can achieve. In some respects, he is perhaps fashioned after an image at the back of Turgenev's mind, the image of the man he admired and could not be.

During the winter he was at work on the first chapters, and on July 19, 1861, he was writing to Countess Lambert from Spasskoye that in about two weeks he expected to taste "the only joy in a writer's life," to wit, "penning the last line." He finished the novel on July 30. In later years he asserted that he had written it seemingly without volition, almost surprised at what came from his pen.

The agony of revision followed, the most troublesome he had known, or so he claimed. At first buoyed up with confidence in his tale, he became more and more doubtful of it as he received his friends' comments. Countess Lambert had nothing good to say for it. "People in whom I have great faith," he wrote, "advised me to throw my work into the fire." As with *On the Eve,* he had the impulse, which he did not obey, to take this advice. Katkov, the editor of *The Russian Herald,* in which *Fathers and Children* was to appear, was displeased to see that the author adulated "the younger generation" (a euphemism for the radicals) and placed Bazarov on a pedestal. Turgenev wrote back to say that it was not his intention to present an apotheosis of his protagonist and that he would try to remove that impression. He added that in his opinion Bazarov, though "empty and sterile," was nevertheless "the hero of our time." He went over and over the text, cutting, adding, altering.

What increased his uncertainty was the news of student riots in Petersburg and Moscow. Under these circumstances was it proper, he wondered, to bring out a novel that had a bearing, however remote, on the political situation? He pleaded with Katkov for a postponement of publication until spring, arguing that he found it necessary to revise the work thoroughly and unhurriedly—"to replow it," as he phrased it. The author's hemmings and hawings went on until the exasperated Annenkov, who had undertaken to see the manuscript through the press, was ready to wash his hands of it. Turgenev declared that the novel was published only because "the merchant demanded delivery of the goods he had bought" and because he himself needed money.

Fathers and Children made its appearance in the issue of *The Russian Herald* for February, 1862, and shortly afterward was published separately with a dedication to the memory of Belinsky. When in the spring of the year Turgenev returned to Petersburg from Paris, he found the capital excited by a number of conflagrations which razed a section of the city and which rumor put at the door of revolutionary incendiaries. An acquaintance, meeting him on the Nevsky, exclaimed: "See what *your* Nihilists are doing! They're setting Petersburg on fire!" Turgenev had not invented the term—it was first used by St. Augustine to denote unbelievers—any more than he had invented the type, but his employment of the word and his projection of the character made for the vogue of both. Eventually he came to regret having provided what he called "our reactionary rabble" with a convenient term for their *bête noire*. The word was also used loosely by the general public. A girl wanting a new frock was likely to face her parents with the threat of turning Nihilist if they didn't come round. Where, as in Russia, literature has great prestige, the novelist is peculiarly able to become the arbiter of fashion in personality. The novel was read by everyone, from the Empress down to people who had not opened a book since their school days, and before long one discovered at least a dash of Bazarov in every young man of independent spirit.

Turgenev's conscious attitude toward his protagonist was ambiguous. He noted in his diary an hour and a half after finishing the novel that while writing it he had felt "an involuntary attraction" toward his hero. He said the same thing in a letter to Herzen a few weeks after publication. "If the reader doesn't love Bazarov, with all his coarseness, heartlessness, pitiless dryness and brusqueness," he had written a fortnight earlier to the young versifier, Sluchevsky, "it's my fault—I haven't achieved my purpose." About the same time, however, he wrote to Fet that he did not know if he loved or hated Bazarov, and defending himself against the accusation of having produced a tendentious work, he claimed that he had drawn his character as he might have sketched "mushrooms, leaves, trees," things he had seen until, in the Russian phrase, they had "calloused his eyes." In 1869 he asserted publicly that he shared Bazarov's convictions, except for his view of the arts. Privately he admitted that in saying this he had gone too far. Unquestionably the admiration the author felt for his hero went hand in hand with a desire to preserve the values that this iconoclast rejected. We have Turgenev's word for it that Nikolay Kirsanov, one of the two landed proprietors who represent the older generation, is a self-portrait.

One of Bazarov's sentiments was undoubtedly shared by his creator—dislike of the nobility. Turgenev's treatment of it in this novel afforded him the satisfaction of the flagellant. "My entire tale," reads the letter to Sluchevsky quoted above, "is directed against the gentry as a leading class." Look at these Kirsanovs, both young and old, and what do you find? "Weakness, flabbiness, inadequacy." And these are gentlefolk of the better sort. "If the cream is bad, what can the milk be like?" How well he knew these people—their good intentions, their feeble achievements, their tender sensibilities, so readily touched by a line of verse, a point of honor, enchanted memories of a dead love, the glow of a setting sun which makes the aspens look like pines! But the knowledge that made for contempt fed his sympathy, too, and Nikolay Kirsanov, at least, is a lovable fellow.

Throughout, his craftsmanship is at its best. Even the minor characters are deftly sketched in. The description of Bazarov's illness gave Chekhov, himself a physician, the sensation of having "caught the infection from him." Bathed in an atmosphere of tenderness and pathos, the passages about Bazarov's parents are among the most moving in literature. As he wrote the last lines, in which the old couple are shown visiting the grave of their only son, Turgenev had to turn away his head, so that his tears would not blot the manuscript, and even in such a dry-eyed age as ours, there must be readers who do not finish the paragraph without blinking.

True, the comings and goings crowded into the few weeks during which the action unfolds seem somewhat contrived. The structure of the novel lacks the formal beauty of *A Nest of Gentlefolk* and *On the Eve*. The touching passage at the close is flawed by the last few lines, with their suggestion of a half-hearted piety. These blemishes are negligible, however, in a work of such wide validity. *Fathers and Children* is a novel to which Turgenev gave his full powers: his intuitions, his insights, the fruit of his contacts with a variety of men and women, his reflections on experience, his sense of the pathos of the human condition. Rudin and Lavretzky can each be fully understood only in the context of his age and his country. Bazarov, while unmistakably Russian, is a universal and a profoundly attractive figure. * * *

RENÉ WELLEK

Fathers and Sons†

Turgenev was the first Russian author to gain recognition in the West. As late as 1884, Henry James, in his obituary, could write: "He seems to us impersonal, because it is from his writings almost alone that we of English, French and German speech have derived over notions—even yet, I fear, rather meagre and erroneous—of the Russian people. His genius for us is the Slav genius, his voice the voice of those vaguely imagined multitudes."

Today Turgenev is overshadowed by his younger contemporaries, Tolstoy and Dostoevsky. But he was the man who opened the doors for them. His success was due in part to the fact that he spent a great part of his life in Paris and knew and was liked by eminent French writers such as the Goncourts, Daudet, Flaubert, and Renan, and later by Henry James, who called on him in 1875. But Turgenev's success also has deeper reasons: he was a liberal, a "Westerner," who made his reputation first by *A Sportsman's Sketches* (1852), which gave a compassionate picture of the peasant serfs before the Emancipation. Turgenev's series of novels, *Rudin* (1856), *A Nest of Gentlefolk* (1859), *On the Eve* (1860), *Fathers and Sons* (1862), *Smoke* (1867), and *Virgin Soil* (1877), presented a gallery of Russian types in which a topical interest in social and political issues of the time was combined with a romantic love interest. The tone of brooding melancholy and the descriptions of the Russian forest and steppe landscape added to the impact of the well-composed and clearly told stories. Turgenev, we might say today, succeeded because he was not exotic or eccentric or passionately intense,

† From Maynard Mack (general editor), *World Masterpieces*, Volume 2, New York, 1965. Pp. 658–62.

as Tolstoy or Dostoevsky appeared to their first Western audiences, because he was in the mainstream of the European novel and nineteenth-century ideology. Turgenev could be extolled as an example of realism for the objective method of his narration, the apparent absence of the author, and the economy of his means. At the same time he was exempt from the usual charges against the French realists: he had no predilection for "low" subject matter, he was decently restrained in erotic scenes, and he refrained from cruelty and brutal violence. Henry James could rightly call him "a beautiful genius."

Fathers and Sons (1862) stands out among Turgenev's novels for many good reasons. It is free from the sentimentality and vague melancholy of several of the other books. Unobtrusively it achieves a balanced composition, while some of the later books seem to fall apart. It shows Turgenev's power of characterization at its best. He not only draws men and women vividly but he presents an ideological conflict in human terms, succeeding in that most difficult task of dramatizing ideas and social issues, while avoiding didacticism, preaching, and treatise-writing—succeeding, in short, in making a work of art.

In Russia *Fathers and Sons* stirred up an immense and acrimonious debate which centered around the figure of Bazarov, the nihilist who is the hero of the novel. Turgenev did not invent the word "nihilism": it was used in Germany early in the century in philosophical contexts and was imported into Russia by a satirical novelist, Vasily Narezhny (1780–1825). But Turgenev's novel gave it currency as a name for the young generation which did not recognize any authority. In reading the book we must dismiss from our minds the later connotation of the term, when it was affixed to the bomb-throwing revolutionaries who, in 1881, succeeded in killing the tsar. As Turgenev uses the word, however, and as Bazarov and his pupil Arkady explain it, "nihilism" means materialism, positivism, utilitarianism. It implies a rejection of religion and of the Russian class system of the time; it implies a trust in the spread of enlightenment and in science, conceived rather naïvely as purely empirical observation and investigation, symbolized by Bazarov's collecting of frogs and peering through the microscope at insects and infusoria. It implies a contempt for the conventions of society and romantic illusions, which for Bazarov include poetry and all art. But Bazarov is only potentially a revolutionary; he has no plan, no opportunity, and no time for political action. In debate he tells us that he wants to "make a clean sweep," that he wants to "change society," but he has no allies or even friends, except the doubtful Arkady. Although Bazarov comes from the people and gets along easily with them when he wants to do so, he despises their ignorance and at the end taunts the peasants for their superstition and subservience to their masters. Bazarov is entirely unattached; he is and remains an individualist, even though he tells us that all people are alike.

The figure of this rugged, uncouth, and even rude young man aroused at first the violent anger of the Russian radical intelligentsia. M. A. Antonovich, the critic of the main opposition journal, *The Contemporary*, denounced Bazarov as a "scarecrow" and "demon" and Turgenev for having written a panegyric of the fathers and a diatribe against the sons. A secret-police report ascribed to the novel "a beneficent influence on the public mind" because it "branded our underage revolutionaries with the biting name 'Nihilist' and shook the doctrine of materialism and its representatives." Turgenev was abused by the opposition, to which he himself belonged, and became so disgusted with the misinterpretation of the book that he defended and explained himself in letters and finally, in 1869, in a long article, "A propos of *Fathers and Sons*" (reprinted in *Literary Reminiscences*). Turgenev puts forth two arguments. He did not write about ideas, but he simply described an actual person whom he had met: a young doctor who had impressed him. And besides, "many of my readers will be surprised if I tell them that with the exception of Bazarov's views on art, I shared almost all his convictions." He put this even more strongly in an earlier letter (April 26, 1862, to Sluchevsky): "Bazarov dominates all the other characters of the novel. . . . I wished to make a tragic figure of him. . . . He is honest, truthful, and a democrat to the marrow of his bones. If he is called a 'nihilist,' you must read 'revolutionary.' My entire story is directed against the gentry as a leading class." Turgenev's defense was, surprisingly enough, accepted by the radicals: at least Dmitri Pisarev (1840–1868), who wrote a paper, "The Destruction of Aesthetics" (1865) and actually thought that a cobbler is more important than Pushkin (or pretended to believe it), hailed Bazarov as the true image of the "new man" and elevated, in a genuine act of self-recognition, a fictional figure to a symbol quite independently of the intentions of the author. Soviet Russian criticism accepts this interpretation and consistently hails the novel as a forecast of the Revolution.

But surely this is a gross oversimplification, to which the critics and Turgenev himself were driven in the polemical situation of the time. The book is neither an anti-nihilist novel nor a glorification of the coming revolution. Its beauty is in the detachment, the objectivity, and even the ambivalence with which Turgenev treats his hero and his opinions and presents the conflict between his crude, arrogant, youthful nihilism and the conservative romanticism of his elders. We can delight in the delicate balance which Turgenev keeps and can admire the concrete social picture he presents: the very ancient provincials, father and mother Bazarov, devout, superstitious, kindhearted, intellectually belonging to a dead world; the finicky, aristocratic Pavel Kirsanov and his weak brother Nikolay, who represent the romantic 1840's; the sloppy, name-dropping, cigarette-smoking emancipated woman, Mme. Kukshin; and the elegant, frigid, landowning widow Mme. Odintsov.

Though the eternal conflict between the old and young is one of the main themes of the book, *Fathers and Sons* is not exhaustively described by the title. Even the preoccupation with nihilism is deceptive. The book goes beyond the temporal issues and enacts a far greater drama: man's deliverance to fate and chance, the defeat of man's calculating reason by the greater powers of love, honor, and death. It seems peculiarly imperceptive of some critics to dismiss Bazarov's death by complaining that Turgenev got weary of his hero. His accidental death is the necessary and logical conclusion: Bazarov, the man of reason, the man of hope, is defeated throughout the book. His pupil Arkady becomes unfaithful and reveals his commonplace mind. Bazarov had dismissed love as a matter of mere physiology, but fell in love himself. He is furiously angry at himself when he discovers what he feels to be an inexplicable weakness; he becomes depressed, tries to forget his love by work, and almost commits suicide when he neglects his wound. Bazarov is defeated even in the duel with Pavel, though he was the victor; he had jeered at chivalry as out of date and considered hatred irrational, but he did fight the duel after all. It was ridiculous and even grotesque, but he could not suffer humiliation or stand the charge of cowardice. He did love his parents, though he was embarrassed by their old-fashioned ways. He even consented to receive extreme unction. When death came, he took it as a cruel jest which he had to bear with Stoic endurance. He died like a man, though he knew that it made no difference to anyone how he died. He was not needed, as no individual is needed. We may feel that the moving deathbed scene is slightly marred by the rhetoric of his request to Mme. Odintsov, "Breathe on the dying lamp," and surely the very last paragraph of the book contradicts or tones down its main theme. Turgenev's reference to the "flowers" on the grave (when Bazarov himself had spoken of "weeds" before) and to "eternal reconciliation and life without end" seems a concession to the public, a gesture of vague piety which is refuted by all his other writings. Turgenev puts here "indifferent nature" in quotation marks, but as early as in *Sportsman's Sketches* he had said: "From the depths of the age-old forests, from the everlasting bosom of waters the same voice is heard: 'You are no concern of mine,' says nature to man." In the remarkable scene with Arkady on the haystack—the two friends almost come to blows—Bazarov had pronounced his disgust with "man's pettiness and insignificance beside the eternity where he has not been and will not be." There is no personal immortality, no God who cares for man; nature is indifferent, fate is blind and cruel, love is an affliction, even a disease beyond reason —this seems the message Turgenev wants to convey.

But *Fathers and Sons* is not a mere lesson or fable. It is a narrative, which with very simple means allows the author to move quietly from one location to the other—from the decaying farm of the Kirsanovs, to the provincial town, to the elegant estate of Mme. Odintsov, and from there to the small estate of the old Bazarovs, and back again—firmly situating each scene in its appropriate setting, building up each character by simple gestures, actions, or dialogue so clearly and vividly that we cannot forget him. Only rarely do we feel some lapse into satire as in Mme. Kukshin's silly conversation. But on the whole, with little comment from the author, a unity of tone is achieved which links the Russian of 1859 with the eternally human and thus vindicates the universalizing power of all great art.

RALPH E. MATLAW

Turgenev's Novels and *Fathers and Sons*†

I

It may seem far-fetched, if not deliberately perverse, to state that although Turgenev was a superlative writer of fiction, he was not a successful novelist. Such a statement is not designed to characterize the achievements of his novels, but rather to comment on the insufficient integration of social background and characters appearing against this background. More simply, Turgenev was hampered by the longer literary forms, and was keenly aware of it.

When he reviewed his literary output in 1880 for a new edition of "collected works," he specified that Volumes IV, V, and VI were "to include in order, all six of my novels (*romany*) with

† An earlier version of the first section appeared as "Turgenev's Novels: Civic Responsibility and Literary Predilection" in *Harvard Slavic Studies*, IV (1957), 249–62. Reprinted by permission of the publishers from Hugh McLean, Martin Malia, George Fischer, editors, *Russian Thought and Politics* (*Harvard Slavic Studies*, Vol. IV), Cambridge, Mass.: Harvard University Press, Copyright 1957, by the President and Fellows of Harvard College.

a special foreword." In isolating *Rudin, A Nest of Noblemen, On the Eve, Fathers and Sons, Smoke,* and *Virgin Soil* from his remaining thirty-three novellas and stories (*povesti i rasskazy*), despite the fact that only *Virgin Soil* had originally appeared with the subtitle "A Novel," [1] Turgenev was not primarily motivated by literary considerations. Throughout his life he was conscious of the artist's socio-political responsibility, established as creed by Belinsky, and constantly attempted to justify his beliefs to friends, editors, and to the public. During the process, he managed to alienate in turn the radical critics and the conservatives, the old generation and the new, the Slavophiles and the Westerners. But his justifications were invariably made after the fact, and their accuracy, not to say their honesty, is frequently questionable. It is relatively easy to find, within extremely brief periods, a series of contradictory statements on the same subject in Turgenev's correspondence, since his political opinions and his aesthetic judgments remained disparate. Thus the "Hannibalic Oath" Turgenev claims he took at the beginning of his career—to direct all his creative powers toward the elimination of serfdom—hardly corresponds to his admission in a letter to Mme. Viardot that he lacked "political pathos." Nor do the many letters written during the composition of his "novels" indicate that his concern in these works was what he ascribed to it in 1880:

> I wanted to give those of my readers who take upon them the task of reading these six novels in order the possibility to convince themselves objectively how fair those critics are who accused me of changing a direction I once took, of apostacy, etc. It seems to me, on the contrary, that one might sooner reproach me of excessive steadfastness and a sort of lineal direction. The author of *Rudin,* written in 1855, and of *Virgin Soil* (1876) appears to be one and the same man. In the course of all that time, I tried, within the limits of my powers and ability, conscientiously and impartially to describe and incarnate in appropriate types both what Shakespeare calls "the body and pressure of time," and the quickly changing countenance of educated Russians, who have been the predominating subject of my observation. To what extent I was successful is not for me to judge, but I dare to believe that the reader will now no longer doubt the honesty and homogeneity of my endeavors.

Turgenev did not consider himself the chronicler of his time when

1. *A Nest of Noblemen* and *Fathers and Sons* bore no subtitle, though the manuscript of the former bears the notation *Povest'*—"*novella.*" The other three works were called *povesti. I. S. Turgenev (k 50-iletiju so dnja smerti), sbornik statej* (Leningrad, 1934), pp. 353, 355, 358, 362, 375. The edition of Turgenev's collected works issued by the Salaev brothers (Moscow, 1868–1869) contains all Turgenev's prose works in chronological order, without distinction between novels and stories.

he wrote his works. This is a task a lesser writer, someone like Prince Boborykin, might specifically set himself. Nevertheless, because Turgenev's novels do deal in greater detail than the shorter works with social questions, and would therefore interest nineteenth-century Russian publicists more, much of the critical literature on Turgenev has concentrated on his novels and their social meaning and significance. Criticism dealing with the social and political background (beginning with the famous essays by Chernyshevsky, Dobrolyubov, and Pisarev, and culminating in H. Granjard's recent voluminously documented study), despite many incidental insights into Turgenev's work, presents a rather distorted picture of his development and artistic achievement.

Comparatively little has been written from a literary, formal point of view to balance such criticism. But what has been done indicates Turgenev's predominant concern with aesthetics rather than politics. Thus Istomin treats Turgenev's early verse, narrative poems, and short stories as attempts to find a personalized means of expression by experimenting with the language, form, and methods of Pushkin, Gogol, and Lermontov. Grossman, giving the lie to Turgenev's "Hannibalic Oath," indicates that simultaneously with *A Hunter's Sketches* Turgenev worked on comedies, literary articles, translations (including *Manon Lescaut*), and studied the Spanish drama. Grossman concludes that the *Sketches* are motivated purely by literary considerations and not by problems of serfdom. Articles by D. Blagoj on Turgénev as editor of Tyutchev's and Fet's verse emphasize Turgenev's extremely conservative poetic standards and a real "art for art's-sake" attitude. Figures like Flaubert, Henry James, and participants in the famous Magny dinners, as well as Turgenev's correspondence, attest to his constant and profound concern with problems of the writer's craft. Without attempting to fix the exact percentage of Turgenev's political and aesthetic interests, an attempt can be made to examine Turgenev's creative method and to assess the effect of social responsibility on his work, particularly on his novels.

In the preface to his novels, Turgenev states that the true artist never resigns himself to convey a program, or to write on a proposed theme; that he never serves incidental, foreign aims. "Life around him gives him the matter—he creates its *concentrated reflection*." The question should then really be asked: what is the life around him? How does he view it? What in particular appeals to him? This can be answered much more easily for the man than for the writer. We know that he was keenly interested in the latest moral and political questions; that he had about him something like the temperament and zeal of a conscientious reporter; that he was always aware of the latest cultural and intellectual events. But to what degree this sense of immediacy or contemporaneousness impelled him to literary expression remains a moot question. Apart from several stories in the *Sketches*, the novels, *Punin and Baburin*, and perhaps one or two other stories, politics and social considerations do not enter the work. Indeed, it may profitably be compared to the work of Jane Austen. Although Turgenev lacked her trenchant, unsentimental mind, he resembles her in many ways, not the least of which is a disregard for historical setting. The men in *Pride and Prejudice* go off to the Napoleonic Wars, though this cannot be determined from the book, since the war is never mentioned. Most of Turgenev's work has just this self-contained, self-sufficient quality, and can be read with practically no knowledge of nineteenth-century Russia. On the other hand, it is impossible to appreciate fully the situations and characters Turgenev presents in his novels without considering the intellectual and social milieu in which they purportedly exist. But such knowledge does not materially affect appreciation of his work's merit, and in the final analysis applies only to that part of the work which has dated most quickly and is least valuable.

Turgenev faced an artistic crisis in the early 1850's, when he realized he could no longer continue "to extract distinct essences from human characters—*triples extraits*—in order to pour them later into little phials." He felt that he must either find a new form of expression or abandon literature altogether. He experimented with dramatic forms, criticism, and translations in the attempt to find that new form, and while he continued these exercises throughout his life, they always assumed secondary importance to his prose fiction. By 1855 he discovered his "new manner," but realized that at best he was uncomfortable in it. He writes to Goncharov in 1859:

> I cannot *ad infinitum* repeat *A Hunter's Sketches*. Nor do I wish to give up writing. The remaining possibility is to create tales in which I could express whatever occurred to my mind, tales with no pretension to completeness, nor forceful characters, nor profound and all-inclusive penetration into life. There will be gaps, visibly patched up, etc. How can I help it? Whoever needs a novel in the epic sense of that word, need not come to me. I would no more entertain the idea of creating a novel than that of walking on my head. No matter what I plan to write, a series of sketches is the result. *E sempre bene!* [2]

Yet Turgenev remained a storyteller throughout his career, for that was his natural mode. Even in the middle 1850's, Turgenev's

2. "And that's fine" [*Editor*].

friend Botkin felt that Turgenev was out of his depth in the story *Asya*. Boris Eykhenbaum, an outstanding modern Russian critic, maintains that all Turgenev's stories are essentially "oral narrations." Frequently they are built on the illusion of reality created artificially by a "frame:" a man sitting with friends by the fireplace tells a story; the narrator overhears someone relating a story; an event reminds the narrator of something that happened in the past; and so on. Once the frame is set, a character begins to narrate and the story immediately assumes a verbal form. The same idea is developed by Percy Lubbock:

> Turgenev was never shy of appearing in his pages as the reflective storyteller, imparting the fruits of his observation to the reader. . . . with perfect candor he will show his hand; he will draw the reader aside and pour into his ear a flow of information about the man or woman, information that openly comes straight from Turgenev himself. . . . Who and what is this communicative participator in the business, this vocal author? He does not belong to the book, and his voice has not that compelling tone and tune of its own (as Thackeray's had) which makes a reader enjoy hearing it for its own sake. . . . There is something in that constant sense of Turgenev at one's elbow, *proffering* that little picture, that may very well damage [his work].[3]

Turgenev's true mode can be further circumscribed. Grossman, for example, emphasized Turgenev's penchant for, and striking achievement with, the miniature. Such miniatures appear throughout his work, not only in the novels (Fomushka and Fimushka in *Virgin Soil*), but also in his biographical and autobiographical writings, in *Old Portraits*, and elsewhere. Indeed, another critic maintains that the miniature is the essential component of Turgenev's style: "In Turgenev the problem of depicting the mode of life (*byt*) is ordinarily handled by miniature dialogues, brief, fleeting scenes, and even symbolic pictures." This technique need not be a drawback to the novelist provided that the framework is sufficiently sturdy. But even here Turgenev has difficulties, arising out of the peculiar nature of his dialogues in the novels.

It is generally agreed that the most dated part of Turgenev's novels are the political discussions and talks, which have lost their vitality and significance, and may be excised with profit. In *Smoke*, although there may be a tenuous connection between Potugin's diatribes and the Russians depicted, these sections could be eliminated with little loss to the novel: the resulting (mutilated) product would then be *Spring Torrents* told in realistic rather than sentimental terms. Similarly, the brief argument between Lavretsky and Panshin in *Nest of Noblemen*, Insarov's

3. Percy Lubbock, *The Craft of Fiction* (London, 1929), pp. 121–22.

melodramatic revolutionary and nationalistic pronouncements in *On the Eve,* Solomin's and Paklin's speeches in *Virgin Soil,* and several scenes of pseudo prophecy or aspiration could also be eliminated without great loss to the works.

It is possible to edit the novels so drastically because there is no real integration between the character and the political position; or because the political has little function in the novel. On the other hand, in Turgenev's most successful and profound novel, *Fathers and Sons,* such excision is impossible, for Turgenev has fused the character and his social or political view. Insarov's ideals tell us next to nothing about him. Pavel Kirsanov's, or any other person's views in *Father and Sons,* are that person, and present not a statement or argument about a topical question, but rather use the statement to characterize the person uttering it. Bazarov himself, although a fully rounded literary depiction, is essentially a temperament that expresses itself in everything he says and does. In *Fathers and Sons* even political dialogue serves to dramatize personality and conflict. In most of the other works it does not. The *reductio ad absurdum* of Turgenev's inability to dramatize the political within an artistic conception is found in the prose-poems, where ex-cathedra statements on politics and life are prettified rather than artistically concentrated. In the prose-poems Turgenev merely expresses ideas rhetorically, and their triteness is necessarily striking. Similarly, political pronouncements in the novels have, by and large, little further meaning than their immediate content: they add little to the artifact.

Yet Turgenev felt compelled to insert these dialogues, since they deal with an important part of the life he was depicting. His lack of success in doing so may indicate that politics was alien to his artistic vision, that his private dichotomy between politics and aesthetics affected his ability to integrate them artistically. Moreover, such conversations are frequently anachronistic: *Rudin,* due to confused chronology, reflects philosophical concepts rampant in the early 1830's, though the novel is set in the late 1830's or early 1840's. *Fathers and Sons* and *Virgin Soil* are, to put the kindest construction in the matter, almost prophetic, for they disclose political types and movements that came into being only later. It does not much matter that Turgenev may anticipate or reconstruct eras as much as fifteen years removed from the time of writing. But it is significant that he claims political and historical accuracy. Even if *Rudin* did depict correctly life in the 1840's, what social purpose is achieved by depicting this age in 1855? Clearly it could not have been Turgenev's intention to make a political statement in *Rudin* and, in fact, the motivating impulse is not politics, but Rudin's prototype, Bakunin.

In retrospect, however, the presence of political matter must have been important to Turgenev when he separated the novels from his other works, since "apolitical" stories like *Spring Torrents* or *The Unfortunate* (*Neschastnaya*) were not called novels, though they approximate them in length. The novels, then, have a more obviously expressed political orientation. A German scholar, Trautmann, however, finds a broader distinction between the novels and novellas:

> Turgenev's novels contain detailed portraiture, with universal, typical characters, simple plot, and carefully completed action; the whole set in the midst of life, which provides the background for his portraiture.
>
> His novellas, on the other hand, present characters of greater individuality and have more singular plots: chance plays a greater part in them and the whole work is isolated from the general progress of life.

Despite dubious concepts of typicality and isolation, this view accurately describes a substantial rather than mechanical difference. There is a technical distinction to be made as well. All the novels use the third-person, omniscient narrator, unlike the stories and novellas, twenty-six of which are framed or unframed first-person narrations. It may therefore also be said that the novels are apparently the most impersonal and objective of his work. It should be stated again, however, that this distinction on Turgenev's part is arbitrary: it elevates, retrospectively, certain works to a more impressive category and bunches together, as it were, all the social message.

It does not suffice to maintain that political background does not contribute value to the novels in proportion to the space it occupies or the disruptive effect it creates. It may be shown that the use of political matter, almost compulsory in the nineteenth-century Russian novèl, is little suited to Turgenev's literary abilities; and indeed, that the longer form does not permit him to exercise his special skills. The best way to do so is to examine his process of composition.

It is abundantly clear from his manuscripts and working notes that the core for any Turgenev work of reasonably large dimension is a characterization or a biographical event. He begins with a character sketch, usually based on a live model, and tries to see the character more and more clearly. Eventually he gathers a little group of characters, and then it is only necessary to put them into movement, to find a plot that will utilize them adequately.[4] For the purpose of analysis, characterization and description will be distinguished from action and plot, although they are, of course, interdependent. "Action" names that process which reveals character or theme; "plot" (which Turgenev called *fabula*) indicates the temporal sequence of events leading to "action."

Turgenev's biggest weakness is his inability to weave a plot. He himself states, in his defense of *Fathers and Sons*, that he was not endowed with a large gift for free invention, that he constantly needed living models, and that he always used these as his starting point, and never an "idea." When he does work back from an idea, as in *Virgin Soil* or in the plan for the projected novel *Silaev*, he is out of his depth, and the artificiality present in the former work is already apparent in the working notes to it. Moreover, his manuscript notes for *Virgin Soil* have a refrain—"I am still far from perceiving the plot" (*fabula mne ešče daleko ne vidna*)—while characters and motivations are already fixed. Character, then, is at the center of Turgenev's work, and his interest in and use of plot is minimal (*Rudin, Smoke*). Plot is strikingly absent from *Fathers and Sons*, a novel illustrating that the only requirement for Turgenev's purpose is a series of scenes each of which reveals character in a different way, illuminates it from a different angle or perspective, or demonstrates still another facet of its personality. The sociological or political aspect of the novels, which must necessarily be expressed in terms of plot rather than action, may therefore be shown as even less germane to the novels than it at first appears to be.

It may further be stated as a formal principle (rather than as an impressionistic commentary) that there is only one action in the novels—love. The inception, incubation, development, declaration, withering, or evanescence of love provides a convenient touchstone for gauging and exposing character, but also creates new problems for the critic. Women frequently assume the initiative morally as well as amatorily, thereby usurping a role more properly that of the male, and then they proceed to dominate and control him. It is tempting—but not altogether necessary—to connect this with Turgenev's own personality. Whatever the personal motivation for such displacement may be, it is curious to observe that male inadequacy, expressed through hesitation, confusion, indirection, avoidance, and resignation, does not find

4. André Mazon, *Manuscrits parisiens d'Ivan Tourguénev* (Paris, 1930), pp. 1–51, provides a detailed reconstruction of Turgenev's process of composition. It may be objected that a group of characters necessarily presupposes a plot in the author's mind. However, it would be truer to say that Turgenev only had an inkling of the *action*, not of the plot (as it is defined at the end of this paragraph).

its complementary qualities satisfactorily united in the opposing female. For Turgenev divides his female characters into two groups: the "predatory" or *diabolique* (in Barbey d'Aurévilly's sense), and those whom some commentators, apparently without facetious intent, label "passionate virgins." The first group, which includes Turgenev's most successful creations (Irina in *Smoke*, Polozova in *Spring Torrents*, Varvara Petrovna in *A Nest of Noblemen*), comes in conflict with the second, which seems to represent some moral, religious, or psychological standard, albeit of a dubious artistic quality (Tanya, Gemma, and Liza in these respective works). The love relationships are usually abortive because the males are unable to live up to the high goals of the females, or destructive because the men sacrifice all—career, position, reputation, money—to meet the demands of excessive passion. This theme reappears, with appropriate variations, beginning with the narrative poem *Andrej* (1846) and ending in *Klara Milich* (1882). Love, for Turgenev, is an absolute, and its issue is destruction. This is even more evident in the novels than in the rest of the works, for the political protagonists like Bazarov attempt to relegate love to an inferior position, and thereby impair both their private and public utility. The question should also be raised whether Turgenev does not, against his better wishes, betray his own cause. The morally upright figures frequently cede first place in artistic perfection to the vacillating male, the obviously superficial but memorably portrayed secondary figure, or the woman of the world.

Despite Turgenev's handling of the action involved in love, he hardly uses it to show personality development. Indeed, Turgenev's characters are static—he deals only with the finished product, not with the mainspring of the action. Such treatment or conception is not necessarily in itself a handicap to the novelist, but it is of crucial importance in explaining his creations. It is, for example, highly significant that Natasha in *War and Peace* seemed to Turgenev not completely successful, and, conversely, that Elena of *On the Eve*, one of Turgenev's best conceived sentimental temperaments, seemed to Tolstoy "wretchedly done." Neither procedure involves a false conception of character, but the view it represents leads to a different kind of literary product. Ovsjaniko-Kulikovsky has admirably stated the difference:

> In Turgenev's work, the analytic side is minimal. But the descriptive force of art is expressed all the stronger in it. In connection with this, the genius of Turgenev was adapted to reproduce characters and personalities not so much in their development, in their past, as in their *status quo*. His genius was adapted to painting complete, finished types. His heroes and

> heroines stand before the reader, so to speak, immovably, as if they were paintings. Tolstoy's and B. Prus' characters live before the reader.

At his best, Turgenev transmits character without really indicating its formation or progress. In the attempt to portray such development, in a *Nest of Noblemen* or *Virgin Soil* (at least the first of which may be viewed as a *Bildungsroman*—a novel tracing the education and maturing of the protagonist), he is almost always unsuccessful. He accounts for his character's past in factual digressions which are frequently too perfunctory, too close to superficial "reality," too empirical. They betray a limited imagination and a limited conception of character. By restricting his portraits to observable phenomena, by ignoring that dimension which permits the exploration of the mind and its working (and by criticizing others', specifically Dostoevsky's and Tolstoy's, depictions of these alien realms), his characters emerge somewhat foreshortened and in at least one sense superficial. Turgenev's literary works offer a unique insight into the vacillating personality or the attempt to overstep personality limitations. It is disconcerting, however, in reading his manuscripts, to note that he never attempts to find the motivation behind his characters, that he is concerned exclusively with surface phenomena. And while we gratefully accept depiction of surface phenomena when it is done with as sure a touch and with such telling effect as it is by Turgenev, it is difficult to see how such a method is really effective in presenting social or political views. A reader can be perfectly sure that Pierre Bezukhov will become a Decembrist, and that Nikolai Rostov will not, for these political views are logical and necessary extensions of their respective personalities. It is less easy, if not impossible, to find a dynamic relation between Turgenev's characters and their political views, unless one accepts the view that portraiture and description of nature are the static part of his novels, while love intrigue and the social idea provide its dynamics. The dichotomy itself, however, indicates insufficient integration.

Another kind of dichotomy, indicated above in touching on Turgenev's female characters, is the fundamental tenet of his characterization. In his essay *Hamlet and Don Quixote* (1860, planned as early as 1854), which constitutes the most important body of psychological generalizations made by Turgenev, he divides all men into two categories: the Don Quixotes—idealists, self-effacing fighters for truth, unconcerned with personal risk and aggrandizement, doers, not thinkers; and Hamlets—egotists, doubters, beset by self-analysis which leads to inaction. This kind of polarization permeates Turgenev's works and particularly the novels, where "Hamlet" types are opposed to "Don Quixotes." In the essay he has greater regard for Don Quixote, though he has considerable sympathy for Hamlet; his artistic success is clearly greater with his "Hamlet" types. And again it should be noted that particularly in Turgenev's terms, Hamlets are not and cannot be political forces; they may only be political and personal failures.

Given Turgenev's theory of character and characterization, and reading his work, one is ineluctably led to a paradox, for it is in the stories and novellas, and not in the novels, that one sees a modicum of character development. It is significant that the main action in the novels always spans a brief period, usually a summer in the country, but sometimes only two weeks (*Smoke*), while the remaining works are not so restricted. Parenthetically, political novels in general, and to a lesser extent sociological novels, usually have an urban setting. But among Turgenev's novels only *Virgin Soil* gives city life any importance. Even Bazarov, as one critic has pointed out, is a fish out of water: his natural habitat is the city.[4] So that again values of greater significance to Turgenev than politics—the countryside, hunting, leisure—tend to dominate the novels and make it difficult to introduce and subordinate political issues properly. The novels catch a personality at a vital moment and expose it to us. Some of the novellas, particularly those in the first person, span the life of a character, although even they focus on a particularly important episode or related episodes in his life.

Of course, within the novels, flashbacks, digressions, and the final summation inform the reader about the characters' past and future, and here Turgenev sometimes achieves fine effects. Thus in *Rudin*, technically his most striking though not best realized novel, Turgenev divulges information about the protagonist piecemeal, from different points of view, and at an appropriate time to balance and qualify some immediate judgment of Rudin. Lezhnev takes a dim view of Rudin while others lionize him, but he later tries to raise Rudin's stature by noting his real virtues when the other characters have condemned him. Turgenev never returned to this striking form of narration. In his next novel, *A Nest of Noblemen*, he uses the single long digression of the Lavretsky family. At first this seems to have an unnecessarily disruptive effect. However, by recapitulating the history of the Lavretsky's for four generations, Turgenev indicates the patriarchic and outmoded nature of Lavretsky's family

4. V. S. Pritchett, *The Living Novel* (New York, 1947), p. 220. It may be of further interest, though perhaps only to the curious, that Turgenev dispatches the "political" heroes of his novels—Rudin, Insarov, Bazarov, and Nezhdanov—but permits the agricultural reformers or gentlemen farmers Lavretsky and Litvinov to live beyond the confines of their novels.

and life, and he is further justified in his method since he must cope with the problem of presenting and characterizing an inarticulate mediocrity. Turgenev constantly has recourse to others in order to formulate Lavretsky's thoughts (Liza, Lemm, Mikhalevich) and to make the portrait and theme clear. In subsequent novels the procedure is refined: the flashbacks are shorter, not nearly so detailed, and in the main concentrate on features necessary to the progress of the narrative. *Smoke* refines the technique of *A Nest of Noblemen* in recapitulating the early affair of Litvinov and Irina; a comparison of Elena's diary (*On the Eve*) with Nezhdanov's letters to Silin (*Virgin Soil*) marks the increased skill and impact Turgenev achieves by interspersing Nezhdanov's attempts at self-knowledge among episodes which reveal his inability to cope with reality. In *Fathers and Sons,* quite appropriately, almost no biographical information is given about Bazarov, since he lives exclusively in the present.

Because the novellas are more restricted in scope, they confront the reader less frequently with these digressions or set pieces and impinge less on the illusion of reality created by Turgenev. Even when these set pieces appear, they can be integrated much more easily into the structure as the narrator's realistic observations. In *First Love,* for example, everything is described through the eyes of the sixteen-year-old boy, or rather a sixteen-year-old boy once removed—that is, as he remembers the events twenty-five years later. The boy's observations are limited both physically and artistically: unlike an omniscient author, he sees only what is immediately before him; and because of his age and circumstance, he does not interpret his information correctly or sufficiently. The achievement of this story lies in that it is not merely a perfect rendition of "first love," but that it also simultaneously paints and characterizes the middle-aged bachelor who is the narrator. The narrator now understands many things beyond his comprehension then. But in the very process of narration he also indicates the profound and lasting effect of this experience and how it shaped him into the personality he now is.

Technically what has happened here (and in other stories like *Spring Torrents* and *Diary of a Superfluous Man*) is a rapid shift from the *nouvelle enficelée* to a Jamesian "point of view." One should not press this idea too far: Turgenev did not master the technique nor did he consistently employ it. Where Turgenev and the narrator are not identical, the mode of narration characterizes the narrator-protagonist, and what he recounts cannot be accepted at face value but must be corrected to account for the narrator's view or distortion. In any case, Turgenev's limited use of the technique occurs only in his shorter works, but significantly enough, in those which are his most successful, like *First Love*. This again suggests an incompatibility between Turgenev's natural inclinations and those things he felt should be presented in the novels. For the "point of view" is in essence inimical if not altogether inappropriate to the social or political novel. It may observe and comment on social and political situations, but its proper technical use necessarily focuses on the individual and psychological or moral personality.

Turgenev frequently uses phrases, half-sentences, incompleted speech, and punctuation indicating ellipsis. He thereby suggests many intangible thoughts and emotional movements, and permits the reader to penetrate a little more deeply into the mind of the characters. This lack of concreteness or, from the other point of view, this suggestiveness, was noted and deftly generalized by George Moore when he stated that Turgenev's "special power seems to be in his skill in instantly laying bare not the body but rather the nerve of an emotion or passion, in indicating that which is most individual and constitutional in a character." In direct contrast, political views like those of the *raisonneurs* Potugin (*Smoke*) and Paklin (*Virgin Soil*) differ even stylistically and in details of punctuation from those passages utilizing Turgenev's best talents.

And yet in the middle of the nineteenth century no Russian writer seemed to capture so well and generalize in appropriate types certain political attitudes. It was Turgenev who created (not to speak of the "nihilists") two dominant and complementary types that begat many offspring and whose very names dominate a major portion of Russian criticism: "the superfluous man," and the "Hamlet of Shchigry District." Both are personal failures, aware of their own shortcomings and keenly conscious of the impossibility of political action under the repressive regime of Nicholas I. They talk endlessly of grandiose plans, but put nothing into operation even on the minor domestic level, sinking into a kind of weakness and melancholy that is the more naggingly dissatisfying for their consciousness of personal waste. The "Hamlet" type is based on the unfortunate interpretation of Shakespeare's play developed by Goethe and dominating the first half of the nineteenth century, which finds the clue to Hamlet's failure to carry out his task in the lines "And thus the native hue of resolution/Is sicklied o'er with the pale cast of thought." It is essentially a vitriolic type, attributing its lack of success in life to the refinement and depth of its thought, which anticipates all the implications of action and therefore cripples the desire to carry it out. The "superfluous man," on the other hand, is a lachrymose and perhaps ultimately comic version of inactivity, railing at the foibles of a life and society from which the character is excluded in various ways, psychologically, socially, or intellectually. It is the feeling of not belonging, of not having anything to do in life, that leads to the tragi-comic notion of "superfluity," or perhaps better to the emphatic concern with demonstrating one's failure.

So far as the types go, they are a major contribution of Turgenev's art. They also point, however, to the failure of Turgenev's novels to challenge the modern critical temperament in the West. For such types, no matter how interesting psychologically or artfully presented in the stories that created them, seem politically dated and somehow less than engaging in the novels. It is a measure of Turgenev's failure to move into deeper analyses of character and society that the same two types could within ten years have been projected in a way that appears to readers today entirely contemporary and significant in a work like Dostoevsky's *Notes from Underground.*

The incompatibility of Turgenev's interest and method with the social and political ideas he attempted to incorporate in his novels is evident. These works clearly contain many pages that interest the cultural historian; but these are not the same pages that appeal to the literary critic, whose rewards lie in explaining Turgenev's mastery in presenting those things closest to him: not the analysis of emotion, but its impact and manifestation; nature, which is the great mirror of emotion; and art, through whose magic and skill these may be expressed.

II

Perhaps the most suggestive insight ever made into *Fathers and Sons* was V. E. Meyerhold's attempt to cast the poet Vladimir Mayakovsky in the role of Bazarov for a film version contemplated in 1929. Among those who remember the young Mayakovsky's early appearances in films, Yuri Olesha described his face as "sad, passionate, evoking infinite pity, the face of a strong and suffering man." It is a little hard to imagine Mayakovsky with side-whiskers (Bazarov, after all, presumably wears these to resemble more closely his intellectual prototype, the studious and sickly N. A. Dobrolyubov), but apart from that one could not conceive of a better reincarnation of Bazarov than Mayakovsky. For Mayakovsky, in his flamboyant and tragic life, and frequently in his verse, was or would have been if Bazarov had not already staked out a claim to that title, the arch example of the phenomenon we now call "the angry young man."

The term, with due allowance for the changes of a century and of cultures, points to two fundamental aspects of Bazarov that underlie both his attractive and repulsive traits for most readers—his immaturity and his position as an outsider in "a world he never made." And these, in turn, point to the psychological and social verities that secure so high place for *Fathers and Sons* in modern literature. The second of these has a specifical historical context and prototype, V. G. Belinsky, to whom the novel is dedicated. Bazarov's portrait, like Belinsky's career, is associated with and typifies two important notions in Russian intellectual history. The first is the rise of the "intelligentsia," a term, apparently of Rusian invention, that designates intellectuals of all persuasions dedicated in one form or another to the improvement of life in Russia, and so carries far greater ethical implications than the mere word "intellectual." The second is that of the *raznochintsy*, literally "persons of various classes," a term applied to those members of classes other than the gentry, usually the clergy or the minor and provincial professional and bureaucratic classes, who sought to pursue a career other than the one their background would normally indicate. Frequently they became members of the intelligentsia, usually after considerable privation. Unlike members of the gentry like Herzen or Turgenev, who could always turn to other sources if necessary, they were entirely dependent upon their intellectual labors, whether as tutors, journalists, writers, or in other pursuits, and from their difficult position derived no small part of their exaltation and indefatigability. While there were factions and enmities within the intelligentsia, all its members were in principle agreed on one point: opposition to the conditions of life around them. Clearly connected with these conditions is the intrusion of the *raznochintsy* into literature, until 1830 or so the exclusive purview of the gentry, who were all too eager to avoid the imputation of professionalism. In style and in tone a sharp shift may be observed, and no one better exemplifies this change in real life than Belinsky or in literature than Bazarov.

Intellectual equality, unfortunately, offered no social prerogatives. Beyond his intellectual circles and his normal habitat, the major cities, even in the rapidly changing society of the mid-nineteenth century, the *raznochinets* was an outsider, if not an upstart. Bazarov, with his enormous sensitivity and vanity, feels out of place at the Governor's Ball and at Odintsov's estate (the wording of his request for vodka amazes the butler). He frequently and deliberately emphasizes his plebeian origin, as in the ironic reference to his similarity to the great Speransky, his sharp reaction to his father's apologies, his feelings about Pavel Kirsanov, and in numerous turns of speech that the English translation cannot convey completely. As for Pavel Kirsanov, we need only think of Prince André's disdain for Speransky in *War and Peace* to judge the gulf that in Pavel's mind separates Bazarov from him. To the aristocrat who has cultivated and refined his privileged position, the democratic virtue of being a self-made man does not appear so laudable. And from this point of view Bazarov's contempt for Pavel Petrovich, "snobism in reverse," to adapt Bazarov's witticism, is another manifestation of his discomfort when out of his class. Still, as Bazarov makes clear, his prospects are very meager, and it leads to great bitterness. Outside the "establishment," which he cannot tolerate, there is no opposition party, not even a real hierarchy, and the consciousness of insuperable obstacles leads to Bazarov's great "anger." As Turgenev chose to present the matter it appears more as a social than political theme, but its motive force is just as operative. The point may profitably be compared to a similar one in *The Red and The Black* where, in Stendhal's happier imagination, Julien Sorel rises to the top, only to insist perversely at his trial on his peasant origin and to accuse his jury of seeking "to punish in me and to discourage forever that class of young men who, born in an inferior station and in a sense burdened with poverty, have the good fortune to secure a sound education, and the audacity to mingle with what the pride of rich people calls society."

The second component is more directly implied in the novel's title as the conflict between generations, apparently an inherent problem in human nature, though manifesting itself in different forms and in different degrees. *Fathers and Sons* presents it in particularly sharp form. Nikolai Kirsanov tells his brother of the remark he made to his mother, "Of course you can't understand me. We belong to different generations," and is now resigned to his turn having come to "swallow the pill." Bazarov's father similarly remembers how he scoffed at the earlier generation, accepts Bazarov's ridiculing his outdated notions, but as a matter of course indicates that in twenty years Bazarov's idols too will be replaced. The intensity of rejection, however, does differ and is a sign of the times. For Bazarov replies "For your consolation I will tell you that nowadays we laugh at medicine altogether, and don't bow down to anyone," which his father simply cannot comprehend. Normally, the problem of generations is resolved by time: the sons gradually move toward their permanent positions, give over being "angry young men," and become husbands and fathers, angry or not. It is perhaps the hardest subject of all to handle, as the reaction to the end of *War and Peace* with its assertion of domestic permanence, and, in *Fathers and Sons,* the quick taming of Arkady Kirsanov prove: the world of struggle and aspiration is more interesting to contemplate that that of fixity and acceptance. The "angry young man" cannot remain so, and is something of an anomaly if not of outright ridicule, when he maintains that view as paterfamilias.

Bazarov denies the values of normal human behavior, but when his theory is put to a single test it collapses. Bazarov falls in love and can no longer return to his former mode. Turgenev permits him to maintain his character by shifting the problem of generations to its ultimate form, that of death. This condition, at least, Bazarov must accept: "An old man at least has time to be weaned from life, but I . . . Well, go and try to disprove death. Death will disprove you, and that's all!" And in his illness Bazarov compresses into a brief period that acceptance of traditional values—family, love, life itself—that otherwise would accrue slowly and undramatically, in the process to some extent attenuating the strident expression of his former views.

But this only occurs at the end. Throughout the novel the high-mindedness, dedication, and energy that make Bazarov tower over the other characters are occasionally expressed with an immaturity bordering on adolescent revolt. The ideas themselves thus in part express the temperament of the "sons." Superficially the state may seem to apply more readily to Arkady, but it is far more ingrained in Bazarov. There are such remarks as "Bazarov drew himself up haughtily. 'I don't share anyone's ideas: I have my own,'" and "When I meet a man who can hold his own beside me, then I'll change my opinion of myself," his deliberately offensive manners, his sponging on and abuse of Kukshin and Sitnikov, his trifling with Fenichka and his jejune declaration to Odintsov. In short, the attempt to impose his own image on the world and to reshape the world accordingly. It is a point Turgenev made quite explicit in his draft for *Virgin Soil:*

> There are *Romantics of Realism* * * * They long for a reality and strive toward it, as former Romantics did toward the ideal. In reality they seek not poetry—that is ludicrous for them—but something grand and meaningful; and that's nonsense: real life is prosaic and should be so. They are unhappy, distorted, and torment themselves with this very distortion as something completely inappropriate to their work. Moreover, their appearance —possible only in Russia, always with a *sermonizing* or educational aspect—is necessary and useful: they are preachers and prophets in their own way, but complete prophets, contained and defined in themselves. Preaching is an illness, a hunger, a desire; a healthy person cannot be a prophet or even a preacher. Therefore I put something of *that* romanticism in Bazarov too, but only Pisarev noticed it.[5]

The two problems of youth and anger, or maturity and acceptance, come to a head in Bazarov's involvement with Odintsov, the

5. André Mazon, "L'élaboration d'un roman de Turgenev: *Terres vierges*." *Revue des études slaves,* V (1925), 87–88.

central episode in the novel, which also serves as a kind of structural dividing line between the political (or social) and the psychological. The discussions of nihilism and contemporary politics, that phase of the battle between the generations dominates the opening of the novel but is practically concluded when Bazarov and Arkady leave Odintsov in Chapter Nineteen. From this point on an opposite movement assumes primary importance: Bazarov's and Arkady's liberation from involvement with theories and the turn toward life itself, that is, toward those people and things in the characters' immediate existence. It entails a shift from scenes and formulations essentially intellectual to others that are more ruminative, inwardly speculative, communicating psychological states and feelings rather than ideas. With it, Bazarov's views and behavior assume a different cast, far more personal, more indicative of his real needs and dissatisfactions. His speeches about necessary reforms now turn into expressions of personal desire ("I felt such a hatred for this poorest peasant, this Philip or Sidor, for whom I'm to be ready to jump out of my skin, and who won't even thank me for it"), his rigorous materialism into the purely Pascalian speech on man's insignificance as a point in time and space. His brusqueness and former contempt for decorum now are so tempered that he accepts a challenge to a duel, has a frock coat easily accessible as he returns to Odintsov, and practices elaborate politeness as she visits him on his deathbed. The end with Bazarov's disquisition on strength, life, and necessity strike the reader as rather mawkish and hollow, for the words now have if not a false, at least a commonplace ring. Indeed, the great effect of the ending is achieved not through Bazarov's speeches but by communicating the despair of his parents.

In the final analysis Turgenev could neither condemn nor yet wholly redeem Bazarov without falsifying or diminishing the portrait. On the last page of the novel he instead implies the reconciliation of the character with a larger, permanent order of things, expressed in terms of the touchstone and overriding image of the novel—nature. The concluding words "[the flowers] tell us, too, of eternal reconciliation and of life without end" do not at all tend toward mysticism, as Herzen claimed and Turgenev denied, but affirm that "the passionate, sinning,[6] and rebellious heart" buried beneath the ground has finally come to terms with permanent reality. The passage is secular rather than religious: life is "without end" not "eternal"; it is life on earth, not in the hereafter.

6. Perhaps "erring" conveys the spirit rather than the letter of the word better than "sinning" does.

PROSPER MÉRIMÉE

Ivan Turgénev†

The name of Turgenev is popular in France today; each of his works is awaited with the same eagerness and read with the same pleasure in Paris and in St. Petersburg. He is considered one of the leaders of the realist school. This may be criticism or praise, but I do not think he belongs to any school; he follows his own inspiration. Like all good novelists, he has devoted himself to the study of the human heart, an inexhaustible mine despite its being exploited for so long a time. A delicate, exact observer, sometimes to the point of minutiae, he creates his characters as a painter and a poet at the same time. Their passions and the features of their faces are equally familiar to him. He knows their habits and their gestures; he hears them speak and gives a stenographic report of their conversation. Such is the art with which he creates a physical and moral whole from all the parts, that the reader sees a portrait rather than a imaginary tableau. Thanks to his faculty for condensing his observations in some manner and of giving them precise form, Turgenev does not shock us more than nature when he presents an abnormal and extraordinary case to us. In his novel *Fathers and Sons* he shows us a young lady who has large hands and small feet. Ordinarily there is a certain harmony among the extremities of the human frame, but exceptions are rarer in nature than in novels. Why does that nice Katya have large hands? The author saw her thus and, through his love for truth, had the indiscretion of saying so. Why is Hamlet fat and out of breath? Ought one to agree with an ingenious German professor that Hamlet, being uncertain of his resolutions, could only have a lymphatic temperament and *therefore* a disposition toward stoutness? But Shakespeare had not read Cabanis,[1] and I would prefer to think that in representing the prince of Denmark that way he had in mind the actor who was to play that role, if it did not seem still more probable to me that the poet had a figure of his imagination before him,

† From Prosper Mérimée, *Oeuvres complètes,* XII (Paris, 1932), 241–45. Translated by Ralph E. Matlaw. The article originally appeared as a preface to a collection of Turgenev in 1868. Mérimée translated a number of works from Russian, including several stories by Turgénev.

1. P. J. G. Cabanis (1757–1808), French physician and philosopher, wrote on the relation of morality to the physique [*Editor*].

who presented himself "in the mind's eye" clearly, and completely finished. Souvenirs, associations of ideas that one cannot account for to oneself, involuntarily obsess the man who has the habit of studying nature. In his fiction he gathers at a glance a host of details united by some mysterious tie that he feels but that he cannot perhaps explain. Let us note again that the resemblance, the life in a portrait, frequently depends on a detail. I remember hearing Sir Thomas Lawrence, certainly one of the great portrait painters of this century, profess this theory. He said: "Choose a trait in your sitter's face; copy it faithfully, even servilely; later you can embellish all the others. You will have made a good likeness and the sitter will be satisfied."

Painter of the most handsome aristocracy of Europe, Lawrence took great care in choosing the trait to be copied servilely. Turgenev is no more flattering than a photographer, and has none of the weaknesses toward the children of their imagination common to novelists. He gives birth to them with their faults, lets them be seen with their ridiculous aspects, leaves to his reader the task of adding up the good and the bad and consequently coming to a conclusion. Still less does he seek to offer us his characters as types of a certain passion or as the representatives of a certain idea, a practice that has been in use for a long time. With his delicate mode of analysis he does not see general types; he knows only individuals. And really, does a man who has only a single passion or who follows a single idea without deviation, does such a man exist in nature? He would surely be much more formidable than the man *of a single book* that Terence feared.

That impartiality, that love for truth which is the distinguishing trait of Turgenev, never abandons him. It is difficult today, in writing a novel whose characters are our contemporaries, not to be led to treat some of those great questions which agitate our modern societies, or at least to disclose one's views on the revolutions that operate in *mores*. However, one could not say whether Turgenev regrets the passing of society in Alexander I's day or whether he prefers that of Alexander II to it. In his novel *Fathers and Sons* he has brought on himself the anger of the young and of the old. One and the other claim to be slandered. He has only been impartial, and this the factions will hardly forgive. I will add that one must be careful not to take Bazarov for the representative of progressive youth or Pavel Kirsanov as the perfect model of the old order. These are two figures that we have seen somewhere. They no doubt exist, but they are not personifications either of the old or new of this century. One might well wish that all young men had as much verve as Bazarov and all the old men sentiments as noble as Pavel Kirsanov's.

Turgenev banishes great crimes from his novels, and one must not look for tragic scenes in them. There are few events in his novels. Nothing more simple than their plot, nothing that more resembles ordinary life, and this too is one of the consequences of his love for truth. The progress of civilization tends to make the violence of our modern society disappear, but it has not been able to change the passions that hide in the human heart. The form they assume is softened or, if you like, worn out, like a coin that has circulated a long time. In society, even in the demi-monde, one hardly ever sees Macbeths or Othellos any more. However, there are always ambitious and jealous people, and the torments that Othello undergoes before strangling Desdemona have been endured by some Parisian bourgeois before asking for a legal separation. I knew a clerk who no doubt had not seen "a dagger, the handle pointed toward him" in a diabolic hallucination, but who constantly saw before his eyes the office manager's gilt-studded armchair, and that armchair moved him to slander his superior to obtain his place. It is in "these private dramas" as it is called today that Turgenev's talent takes pleasure in and excels. * * *

HENRY JAMES

[Ivan Turgénev]†

* * * The germ of a story, with him, was never an affair of plot—that was the last thing he thought of: it was the representation of certain persons. The first form in which a tale appeared to him was as the figure of an individual, or a combination of individuals, whom he wished to see in action, being sure that such people must do something very special and interesting. They stood before him definite, vivid, and he wished to know and to show, as much as possible of their nature. The first thing was to make clear to himself what he did know, to begin with; and to this end he wrote a sort of biography of each of his characters, and everything that they had done and had happened to them up to the opening of the story. He had their *dossier*, as

†The first paragraph is from *Partial Portraits,* London and New York: Macmillan & Co., 1888. The last two paragraphs are from the Preface to *The Portrait of a Lady* in the *Novel and Tales of Henry James,* New York Edition, Volume III (copyright 1908 by Charles Scribner's Sons, 1936 by Henry James), reprinted from *The Art of The Novel,* ed. R. P. Blackmur, New York, 1934, pp. 42-44, by permission of the publishers, Charles Scribner's Sons.

the French say, and as the police have that of every conspicuous criminal. With this material in his hand he was able to proceed; the story all lay in the question, What shall I make them do? He always made them do things that showed them completely; but, as he said, the defect of his manner and the reproach that was made him was his want of "architecture"—in other words, of composition. The great thing, of course, is to have architecture as well as precious material, as Walter Scott had them, as Balzac had them. If one reads Turgénev's stories with the knowledge that they were composed—or rather that they came into being—in this way, one can trace the process in every line. Story, in the conventional sense of the word—a fable constructed, like Wordsworth's phantom, "to startle and waylay" —there *is* as little as possible. The thing consists of the motions of a group of selected creatures, which are not the result of a preconceived action, but a consequence of the qualities of the actors. Works of art are produced from every possible point of view, and stories, and very good ones, will continue to be written in which the evolution is that of a dance—a series of steps, the more complicated and lively the better, of course, determined from without and forming a figure. This figure will always, probably, find favor with many readers, because it reminds them enough, without reminding them too much, of life. * * *

* * * "I have always fondly remembered a remark that I heard fall years ago from the lips of Ivan Turgenieff in regard to his own experience of the usual origin of the fictive picture. It began for him almost always with the vision of some person or persons, who hovered before him, soliciting him, as the active or passive figures, interesting him and appealing to him just as they were and by what they were. He saw them, in that fashion, as *disponibles,*[1] saw them subject to the chances, the complications of existence, and saw them vividly, but then had to find for them the right relations, those that would most bring them out; to imagine, to invent and select and piece together the situations most useful and favorable to the sense of the creatures themselves, the complications they would be most likely to produce and to feel.

"To arrive at these things is to arrive at my 'story'," he said, "and that's the way I look for it. The result is that I'm often accused of not having 'story' enough. I seem to myself to have as much as I need—to show my people, to exhibit their relations with each other; for that is all my measure. If I watch them long enough I see them come together, I see them *placed,* I see them

1. "Disposable" [*Editor*].

engaged in this or that act and in this or that difficulty. How they look and move and speak and behave, always in the setting I have found for them, is my account of them—of which I dare say, alas, *que cela manque souvent d'architecture*.[2] But I would rather, I think, have too little architecture than too much—when there's danger of its interfering with my measure of the truth. The French of course like more of it than I give—having by their own genius such a hand for it; and indeed one must give all one can. As for the origin of one's wind-blown germs themselves, who shall say, as you ask, where they come from? We have to go too far back, too far behind, to say. Isn't it all we can say that they come from every quarter of heaven, that they are *there* at almost any turn of the road? They accumulate, and we are always picking them over, selecting among them. They are the breath of life—by which I mean that life, in its own way, breathes them upon us. They are so, in a manner prescribed and imposed—floated into our minds by the current of life. That reduces to imbecility the vain critic's quarrel, so often, with one's subject, when he hasn't the wit to accept it. Will he point out then which other it should properly have been?—his office being, essentially *to* point out. *Il en serait bien embarrassé*[3]! Ah, when he points out what I've done or failed to do I give him up my 'architecture'," my distinguished friend concluded, "as much as he will." * * *

A. P. CHEKHOV

Letter to A. S. Suvorin, February 24, 1893 †

* * * My God! What a magnificent thing *Fathers and Sons* is! It simply makes you desperate. Bazarov's illness is so powerfully done that I turned weak and had a feeling as if I had been infected by him. And Bazarov's death? And the old people? And Kukshin? God knows how he does it. It is sheer genius. I don't like *On the Eve* except Helen's father and the ending. That ending is full of tragedy. "The Dog" is very good; its language is amazing. Please read it if you've forgotten it. "Asya" is very nice, "The Quiet Spot" is crumpled and doesn't satisfy. I don't like *Smoke* at all. *A Nest of Noblemen* is weaker than *Fathers and Sons*, but the ending is almost a marvel. Besides the old woman in Bazarov, that is, Evgeny's mother and mothers in

2. "That that frequently lacks structure" [*Editor*].
3. "He'd be hard put to do it" [*Editor*].

† From A. P. Chekhov, *Sobranie sochineniy*, XII (Moscow, 1960–64), 17–18. Translated by Ralph E. Matlaw.

general, particularly the fashionable ladies, who all resemble each other, by the way (Liza's mother, Helen's mother), and Lavretsky's mother, the former serf, and in addition the simple women, all of Turgenev's women and young ladies are unbearable with their artificiality and, forgive me, falseness. Liza, Helen—these aren't Russian young ladies but some sort of Pithians, with their pronouncements, their excessive pretensions. Irina in *Smoke,* Odintsov in *Fathers and Sons,* in general the lionesses, ardent, appetizing, insatiable, seeking something—they're all nonsense. When you think of Tolstoy's Anna Karenin, all these young ladies of Turgenev's with their tempting shoulders vanish. Women of the negative sort, where Turgenev lightly caricatures them (Kukshin), or makes merry with (the description of balls), are wonderfully drawn and so successfully come off in him that, as the saying goes, you can't find a flaw in it. The descriptions of nature are good, but—I feel that we are already becoming disaccustomed to that kind of description and that something else is needed. * * *

EDWARD GARNETT

[Bazarov] †

* * * What, then, is Bazarov?

Various writers have agreed in seeing in him only "criticism, pitiless, barren, and overwhelming analysis, and the spirit of absolute negation," but this is an error. Representing the creed which has produced the militant type of Revolutionist in every capital of Europe, *he is the bare mind of Science first applied to Politics.* His own immediate origin is German Science interpreted by that spirit of logical intensity, Russian fanaticism, or devotion to the Idea, which is perhaps the distinguishing genius of the Slav. But he represents the roots of the modern Revolutionary movements in thought as well as in politics, rather than the branches springing from those roots. Inasmuch as the early work of the pure scientific spirit, knowing itself to be fettered by the superstitions, the confusions, the sentimentalities of the Past, was necessarily destructive, Bazarov's primary duty was to Destroy. In his essence, however, he stands for *the sceptical conscience of modern Science.* His watchword is *Reality,* and not Negation, as everybody in pious horror

† From Edward Garnett, *Turgenev, A Study,* London, 1917, pp. 116–26. Reprinted by permission of William Heinemann Ltd. and Mr. David Garnett.

hastened to assert. Turgenev, whose first and last advice to young writers was, "You need truth, remorseless truth, as regards your own sensations," was indeed moved to declare, "Except Bazarov's views on Art, I share almost all his convictions." The crude materialism of the 'sixties was not the basis of the scientific spirit, it was merely its passing expression; and the early Nihilists who denounced Art, the Family and Social Institutions were simply freeing themselves from traditions preparatory to a struggle that was inevitable. Again, though Bazarov is a Democrat, perhaps his kinship with the people is best proved by the contempt he feels for them. He stands forward essentially as an Individual, with the "isms" that could aid him, mere tools in his hand; Socialist, Communist or Individualist, in his necessary phases he fought this century against the tyranny of centralized Governments, and next century he will be fighting against the stupid tyranny of the Mass. Looking at Bazarov, however, as a type that has played its part and vanished with its generation, as a man he is a new departure in history. His appearance marks the dividing-line between two religions, that of the Past—Faith, and that growing religion of to-day—Science. His is the duty of breaking away from all things that men call Sacred, and his savage egoism is essential to that duty. He is subject to neither Custom nor Law. He is his own law, and is occupied simply with the fact he is studying. He has thrown aside the ties of love and duty that cripple the advance of the strongest men. He typifies Mind grappling with Nature, seeking out her inexorable laws. Mind in pure devotion to the What Is, in startling contrast to the minds that follow their self-created kingdoms of What Appears and of What Ought to Be. He is therefore a foe to the poetry and art that help to increase Nature's glamour over man by alluring him to yield to her; for Bazarov's great aim is to see Nature at work behind the countless veils of illusions and ideals, and all the special functions of belief which she develops in the minds of the masses to get them unquestioning to do her bidding. Finally, Bazarov, in whom the comfortable compromising English mind sees only a man of bad form, bad taste, bad manners and overwhelming conceit, finally, Bazarov stands for Humanity awakened from century-old superstitions and the long dragging oppressive dream of tradition. Naked he stands under a deaf, indifferent sky, but he feels and knows that he has the strong brown earth beneath his feet.

This type, though it has developed into a network of special branches to-day, it is not difficult for us to trace as it has appeared and disappeared in the stormy periods of the last thirty years. Probably the genius and energy of the type was chiefly devoted to positive Science, and not to Politics; but it is sufficient to glance at the Revolutionary History, in theory and action, of the Continent to see that every movement was inspired by the ideas of the Bazarovs, though led by a variety of leaders. Just as the popular movements for Liberty fifty years earlier found sentimental and *romantic* expression in Byronism, so the popular movements of our time have been realistic in idea, and have looked to Science for their justification. Proudhon, Bakunin, Karl Marx, the Internationals, the Russian Terrorists, the Communists, all have a certain relation to Bazarov, but his nearest kinsmen in these and other movements we believe have worked, and have remained, obscure. It was a stroke of genius on Turgenev's part to make Bazarov die on the threshold unrecognized. He is Aggression, destroyed in his destroying. And there are many reasons in life for the Bazarovs remaining obscure. For one thing, their few disciples, the Arkadys, do not understand them; for another, the whole swarm of little interested persons who make up a movement are more or less engaged in personal interests, and they rarely take for a leader a man who works for his own set of truths, scornful of all cliques, penalties and rewards. Necessarily, too, the Bazarovs work alone, and are given the most dangerous tasks to accomplish unaided. Further, they are men whose brutal and breaking force attracts ten men where it repels a thousand. The average man is too afraid of Bazarov to come into contact with him. Again, the Bazarovs, as Iconoclasts, are always unpopular in their own circles. Yesterday in political life they were suppressed or exiled, and even in Science they were the men who were supplanted before their real claim was recognized, and to-day, when order reigns for a time, the academic circles and the popular critics will demonstrate that Bazarov's existence was a mistake, and the crowd could have got on much better without him.

The Crowd, the ungrateful Crowd! though for it Bazarov has wrested much from effete or corrupt hands, and has fought and weakened despotic and bureaucratic power, what has its opinion or memory to do with his brave heroic figure? Yes, heroic, as Turgenev, in indignation with Bazarov's shallow accusers, was betrayed into defining his own creation, Bazarov, whose very atmosphere is difficulty and danger, who cannot move without hostility carrying as he does destruction to the old worn-out truths, contemptuous of censure, still more contemptuous of praise, he goes his way against wind and tide. Brave man, given up to his cause, whatever it be, it is his joy *to stand alone,* watching the crowd as it races wherever reward is and danger is not. It is Bazarov's life to despise honours, success, opinion, and to let nothing, not love itself, come between him and his inevitable course, and, when death comes, to turn his face to the wall, while in the street below he can hear the voices of men cheering the popular hero who has last arrived. The Crowd! Bazarov is the antithesis of the cowardice of the Crowd. That is the secret why we love him.

III

As a piece of art *Fathers and Children is* the most powerful of all Turgenev's works. The figure of Bazarov is not only the political centre of the book, against which the other characters show up in their respective significance, but a figure in which the eternal tragedy of man's impotence and insignificance is realized in scenes of a most ironical human drama. How admirably this figure dominates everything and everybody. Everything falls away before this man's biting sincerity. In turn the figureheads of Culture and Birth, Nicolai and Pavel representing the Past; Arkady the sentimentalist representing the Present; the father and mother representing the ties of family that hinder a man's life-work; Madame Odintsov embodying the fascination of a beautiful woman—all fall into their respective places. But the particular power of *Fathers and Children*, of epic force almost, arises from the way in which Turgenev makes us feel the individual human tragedy of Bazarov in relation to the perpetual tragedy everywhere in indifferent Nature. In *On the Eve* Turgenev cast his figures against a poetic background by creating an atmosphere of War and Patriotism. But in *Fathers and Children* this poetic background is Nature herself, Nature who sows, with the same fling of her hand, life and death springing each from each, in the same rhythmical cast of fate. And with Nature for the background, there comes the wonderful sense conveyed to the reader throughout the novel, of the generations with their fresh vigorous blood passing away quickly, a sense of the coming generations, whose works, too, will be hurried away into the background, a sense of the silence of Earth, while her children disappear into the shadows, and are whelmed in turn by the inexorable night. While everything in the novel is expressed in the realistic terms of daily commonplace life, the characters appear now close to us as companions, and now they seem like distant figures walking under an immense sky; and the effect of Turgenev's simply and subtly drawn landscapes is to give us a glimpse of men and women in their actual relation to their mother earth and the sky over their heads. This effect is rarely conveyed in the modern Western novel, which deals so much with purely indoor life; but the Russian novelist gained artistic force for his tragedies by the vague sense ever present with him of the enormous distances of the vast steppes, bearing on their bosom the peasants' lives, which serve as a sombre background to the life of the isolated individual figures with which he is dealing. Turgenev has availed himself of this hidden note of tragedy, and with the greatest art he has made Bazarov, with all his ambition opening out before him, and his triumph awaited, the eternal type of man's conquering egoism conquered by the pin-prick of death. Bazarov, who looks neither to the right hand nor to the left, who delays no longer in his life-work of throwing off the mind-forged manacles; Bazarov, who trusts not to Nature, but would track the course of her most obscure laws; Bazarov, in his keen pursuit of knowledge, is laid low by the weapon he has selected to wield. His own tool, the dissecting knife, brings death to him, and his body is stretched beside the peasant who had gone before. Of the death scene, the great culmination of this great novel, it is impossible to speak without emotion. The voice of the reader, whosoever he be, must break when he comes to those passages of infinite pathos where the father, Vassily Ivanovitch, is seen peeping from behind the door at his dying son, where he cries, "Still living, my Yevgeny is still living, and now he will be saved. Wife, wife!" And where, when death has come, he cries, "I said I should rebel. I rebel, I rebel!" What art, what genius, we can only repeat, our spirit humbled to the dust by the exquisite solemnity of that undying simple scene of the old parents at the grave, the scene where Turgenev epitomizes in one stroke the infinite aspiration, the eternal insignificance of the life of man.

Let us end here with a repetition of a simple passage that, echoing through the last pages of *Fathers and Children*, must find an echo in the hearts of Turgenev's readers: " 'To the memory of Bazarov,' Katya whispered in her husband's ear, . . . but Arkady did not venture to propose the toast aloud." We, at all events, can drink the toast to-day as a poor tribute in recompense for those days when Turgenev in life proposed it, and his comrades looked on him with distrust, with coldness and with anger.

RICHARD FREEBORN

[The Structure of *Fathers and Sons*]†

* * * Turgenev has said that he was first prompted to write about a hero of the type of Bazarov by the example of a young provincial doctor of his acquaintance who had died, presumably, about the

†From Richard Freeborn, *Turgenev: The Novelist's Novelist*, London, 1960, pp. 68-74. Copyright 1960 by Oxford University Press. Reprinted by permission of the Clarendon Press, Oxford.

year 1859. When he mentioned his intention to a friend whom he met on the Isle of Wight in August 1860, he was amazed to hear this gentleman reply: 'But surely you have already presented a similar type in—Rudin?' Turgenev adds: 'I was speechless: what was there to say? Rudin and Bazarov—one and the same type? . . . These words had such an effect on me that for several weeks I avoided all thought of the work on which I had embarked. . . . The gentleman's remark, however, is not so extraordinary as it may appear at first sight. It simply serves to underline the fact that Bazarov, like Rudin, was conceived as a hero designed to have more intellectual interest than Lavretsky, for instance, or Yelena. Like Rudin, he was intended to dominate the fiction, although—unlike the Rudin of the original version—he was conceived as a tragic figure whose tragedy would be climaxed by his death.[1]

Fathers and Children tells the story of Bazarov's return from the university in the company of his young friend, Arkady Kirsanov. They both stay for a while on the Kirsanovs' estate, where the contrast between the Fathers and the Children is initiated in the arguments between Pavel Petrovich Kirsanov and the hero, and later they visit the local town, where Bazarov meets the heroine, Odintsova. This meeting initiates the major love theme of the novel, but the action is by no means devoted exclusively to the development of it. Subsequently Bazarov visits his parents, spends a short while with them and then, to their understandable dismay, returns to the Kirsanovs' estate where the argument between Fathers and Children is concluded by the duel between him and Pavel Petrovich. Later Bazarov returns to his parents, where he decides to help his father, a retired army doctor, in his practice. Here he contracts typhus after performing an autopsy on a peasant killed by the disease and finally succumbs to it himself. As can be seen, there is more story content in *Fathers and Children* than in the previous novels, but this does not alter the fact that it is the characterization of the central figure which provides the interest of the fiction.

The objectivity of the work is remarkable on two counts. Firstly, in portraying Bazarov Turgenev has achieved a masterly portrait of a type—the type of the 'new man' of the sixties, the *raznochinets* intellectual or 'nihilist'—with whose political and social views he was manifestly out of sympathy. Secondly, the novel possesses an

1. Hjalmar Boyesen records Turgenev as saying (originally in 'A visit to Turgenev', *The Galaxy*, xvii (1874), 456–66: 'I was once out for a walk and thinking about death. . . . Immediately there rose before me the picture of a dying man. This was Bazarov. The scene produced a strong impression on me and as a consequence the other characters and the action itself began to take form in my mind.' Quoted from the Russian in 'K biografii I. S. Turgeneva', *Minuvshiye gody*, 1908, No. 8, p. 70. Turgenev writes to the same effect in his letter to Sluchevsky of April 1862.

organic unity, in which there are no narrative devices that obtrude into the fiction to distort, however slightly, the final impression of naturalness. This is not to say that *Fathers and Children* is merely a factual document or chronicle, unenlivened by the author's technique as an artist. It simply means that the technique has been perfected to the point where such devices as the use of commentator (in *Rudin* and *A Nest of the Gentry*) or devices such as diary extracts and letters (as in *On the Eve*) are no longer necessary in the delineation of character. The emphasis now falls squarely on the scenic, pictorial objectivity of the narrative and the artistic composition of the work, leaving the impression that the novel is 'telling itself', as it were, almost without the author's agency or participation.

In every respect this is more obviously 'a novel of ideas' than *On the Eve,* although the ideological independence of each minor character is linked, without being in any sense compromised or diminished, to the development of the central figure, Bazarov, in a more compelling manner than were Shubin and Bersenev to Yelena. This is due to the fact that in *Fathers and Children* the minor characters are not only spokesmen or embodiments of ideas or ideological attitudes, but they are also representatives of a particular social class with specific class attitudes; and Bazarov, opposed to them, is not only an opponent of their ideas, but a spokesman for a new, emergent social class which is to usurp the political and social authority of the older generation. In his previous novels Turgenev had not delineated class distinctions so clearly, but in *Fathers and Children* he carefully welds the social and political issues, the ideological and class attitudes, into the structure of his novel, creating a remarkable organic unity. The result is the most artistically perfect, structurally unified and ideologically compelling of Turgenev's novels.

Arkady Kirsanov and his father, Nikolay Petrovich Kirsanov, are introduced in detail to the reader at the very beginning of the novel. All the other characters—Pavel Petrovich Kirsanov, Odintsova, Bazarov's parents and such lesser characters as Fenichka (the peasant girl who has borne Nikolay Petrovich an illegitimate son), Kukshina and Sitnikov, the talkative representatives of the younger generation—are introduced into the fiction to the accompaniment of biographical and other information sufficient to explain their significance. The exception is again the unknown quantity, the hero, whose characterization is to provide the interest of the novel. Bazarov is not introduced to the reader by means of any biographical excerpt which might set his character in perspective; he is introduced, and his background lightly sketched in, by the remarks made about him by the other characters (particularly during the conversation between Arkady and Pavel Petrovich in Chapter V). While these remarks serve to provide information about Bazarov without which the reader might not be able to understand his significance for the fiction, they also serve to illustrate the contrasting nature of Bazarov, arising from his different social background. There are, of course, intimations in the fiction that Bazarov is 'different' from the other characters, but Turgenev does not rely on his omniscient position as author of the fiction to emphasize this 'difference'. On the contrary, he allows it to be made clear by the natural contrast that arises initially from the fact that Bazarov enters the fiction unexplained and by the more definite contrast which is provided through Bazarov's contact with the other characters.

Bazarov is further highlighted in the fiction by the fact that the novel is so constructed as to isolate him from the other characters. This is achieved by giving the other characters not only biographical backgrounds, or information sufficient to make their backgrounds comprehensible, but also specific 'places' in the fiction. Each character, with the exception of Bazarov, has his or her own 'place' or situation in the fiction: Nikolay, Arkady, Pavel—the poverty-stricken Mar'ino; Odintsova, Katya—the luxurious Nikol'skoye; the elderly Bazarovs—their humble estate; Sitnikov, Kukshina—the background of the town. With the exception of Bazarov and Arkady, all these characters remain in their own particular 'places' and are only comprehensible in relation to their 'places' (Odintsova and Sitnikov, admittedly, can be said to abandon their 'places' for short episodes—Odintsova to the town and to visit Bazarov on his death-bed, Sitnikov to Nikol'skoye (Chapter XIX)—but it is still true that they are only comprehensible in relation to their own 'places'). Moreover, each 'place' in the fiction and its occupants has the purpose of illuminating, by contrast, an aspect of the hero. Pavel Petrovich in Mar'ino illuminates the ideological aspect of Bazarov's significance for the fiction, the problem of the socio-political conflict between the generations; Sitnikov and Kukshina in the town illuminate the superiority of Bazarov by comparison with other members of the younger generation; Odintsova in Nikol'skoye illuminates the essential personality of the hero as a man, the duality in his nature; Bazarov's parents illuminate his egoism, the personal, as distinct from the ideological, barrier dividing the generations, and his individual insignificance as a human being, for their adoration of him is carefully offset by his own pessimistic musings on his destiny. Each 'place' in the fiction can therefore be seen as a stage in the process of the hero's characterization, and the stages are graded to elaborate and deepen the hero's portrait. Finally, Arkady ceases to play an active part in the fiction (after becoming involved in his love-story with Katya), and Bazarov is isolated as the central figure of the novel's action. In this way it can be seen that Turgenev emphasizes the tragedy of Bazarov's isolation, both as a social type and as a human being, by emphasizing his isolation within the fiction itself.

The process of characterization is also structurally integrated with the pattern of love-stories which, loosely speaking, supplies the plot of the novel and illustrates the ideological issues at stake. There are, in all, four different love-stories: (*a*) Nikolay-Fenichka; (*b*) Pavel-Fenichka, involving Bazarov; (*c*) Bazarov-Odintsova; (*d*) Arkady-Katya. All these love-stories express in one way or another an aspect of the conflict between the Fathers and the Children. The first love-story, between the land-owner and the peasant girl, implies at once the underlying social problem of the day: the relationship between land-owner and peasant on the eve of the Emancipation in 1861 (the action of the novel, it may be noted, occurs in 1859). The nature of this particular relationship between Nikolay and Fenichka also illustrates the moral failure of the older generation, of the Fathers, and it is a point at issue, in the early stage of the novel, between Nikolay and his son. The second love-story (it scarcely obtrudes as a love-story, but it must not be overlooked) is of considerably greater importance for the structure of the novel. So far as the external action of the novel is concerned, the fact that Pavel Petrovich sees Bazarov kissing Fenichka (Chapter XXIII) simply supplies him with grounds for challenging Bazarov to a duel. But the inner meaning of this episode must also be noted. The ideological conflict has already occurred (Chapters VI and X); the contrast with the members of the younger generation has been made (Chapters XII and XIII); the relationship with Odintsova has already been explored and has reached a climax (Chapters XV-XVIII), though it has not yet been abandoned; Bazarov's awareness of his own significance as a human being and his tragic destiny, despite the great future hoped for by his parents, has been made explicit in his conversation with Arkady on his parents' estate (Chapter XXI). Bazarov is now ready to reject the ideological and social precepts of the *dvoryanstvo,* the gentry; his desire to provoke a fight with Arkady in Chapter XXI foreshadows his readiness to accept the challenge that Pavel Petrovich offers him in Chapter XXIV. Yet the fact that they fight the duel ostensibly over Fenichka, the peasant girl, shows the way in which the ideological issues are welded into the structure of the novel. For Bazarov's readiness to fight the duel must be understood in the light of the fact that he is prepared not only to reject the *dvoryanstvo*, but also to devote his life to working for the peasants. His interest in Fenichka may be purely personal, but it is also given ideological significance. Similarly, Pavel Petrovich's readiness to offer the challenge must be understood in relation to the fact that for him Fenichka bears a resemblance to a certain Princess R. . . . out of passion for whom he had ruined his career and had been obliged to retire to the splendid isolation of Mar'ino (the predicament of the 'superfluous man' *par excellence*), and in relation to the fact that the crux of his earlier argument with Bazarov (Chapter X) had been the problem of the peasantry, whom he had claimed to understand better than Bazarov. His interest in Fenichka is also a mixture of the personal and the ideological. The subsequent duel represents the climax in the personal and ideological conflict between the two generations; and the defeat of Pavel Petrovich is not simply the defeat of the older generation by the younger, it is also the defeat of the gentry, the *dvoryanstvo*, by the new class of the *raznochintsy*.

The third love-story, between Odintsova and Bazarov, is clearly the most interesting, both because it concerns two people of widely differing social status and because it serves, like all the major love-stories in Turgenev's fiction, as a means of illustrating the differing personalities of the two characters. It is, however, Bazarov who emerges more successfully from this contrast. Odintsova is almost as passive a participant in the relationship as was Insarov in *On the Eve*. But, unlike the Yelena-Insarov relationship, the relationship between Odintsova and Bazarov does not absorb the whole of the fiction. There is no definite continuity to it and it is allowed to languish, in contrast to the fourth love-story, between Arkady and Katya, which is both the most conventional in the sense that it is between two young people of similar social status and the most conventional in the sense that it has a happy outcome.

It is in the different relationships involved in these love-stories that an enlargement of both structure and content in *Fathers and Children* as compared with the previous novels is to be discerned. In *Rudin*, for instance, there had been a suggestion of triangular form about the central love-story (Rudin-Natal'ya-Volyntsev), but the Rudin-Natal'ya relationship had been the most important relationship in the fiction, paralleled by the love-story between Lezhnyov and Aleksandra Lipina. In the relationship between Rudin and Natal'ya, however, there had been no explicit suggestion of social inequality, although Rudin was banished from Dar'ya Lasunskaya's house because he was not felt to be 'suitable' for her daughter; yet, despite his lack of rank, he was of the same class.

In *A Nest of the Gentry* the major love-story between Lavretsky and Liza had been connected with the Liza-Panshin, Liza-Lemm relationships, but these latter had had little bearing on the central theme of the novel. Similarly, although Lavretsky's social standing was compromised by the fact that his mother was of peasant extraction, in other points of genealogy he was Liza's social equal. In *On the Eve* Shubin and Bersenev had been united by similar feelings for Yelena, but the love-story between Yelena and Insarov had been quite independent of them. In the social sense, the inequality between Yelena and Insarov was partly camouflaged by the fact that he was given Bulgarian nationality, although Kurnatovsky was thought to be socially more fitting for Yelena, and it can be seen that her parents' reaction to her marriage was one of shock not at the fact that Insarov was a Bulgarian but because he was of more modest social origins. In general, therefore, it can be said that in these three novels there had been a single love-story which was at the centre of the fiction and only in *On the Eve* did the relationship infer a marked social inequality. But in *Fathers and Children* there is a multiplication of love-stories in the structure of the novel, and all the love-stories, with the exception of the Arkady-Katya relationship, involve social inequalities. Inevitably this means that the novel embraces an enlarged view of Russian society, for all classes in Russian society are exemplified by this means: the gentry (*dvoryanstvo*), the new men (*raznochintsy*), and the peasantry. The single love-story in the earlier novels, standing at the centre of the fiction and absorbing the greater part of its interest, had not permitted such an enlarged view.

Yet, in structural terms, the main feature of *Fathers and Children* is the figure of Bazarov. The action of the novel hinges upon him almost exclusively. He is present in practically every scene of the novel, and it is his movement within the fiction that serves to link together the different 'places' or foci of interest which comprise the setting of the novel. Simultaneously, these 'places' and their occupants contribute, stage by stage, to the process of his characterization. A natural unity of form and content is thus achieved, which is the most striking development in Turgenev's exploration of the novel-form. The portrait of Bazarov that finally emerges from the novel is one that transcends all other issues in the fiction. Beginning on May 20th 1859, the action of the novel portrays Bazarov during approximately the last three or four months of his life. His portrait acquires finally a tragic grandeur, culminating in his death which is a moment unequalled in Turgenev's fiction. * * *

RUFUS W. MATHEWSON, JR.

[The Artist and His Relation to the Truth of His Work]†

* * * The crux of the dispute [between the liberal writers and the radical critics] is in the effort to locate the center of the creative process. For the liberals it is unquestionably fixed in the sovereign moral intelligence of the artist. For the radical it is elsewhere—in life which can always be invoked to challenge a novel's formal design, in ethical obligations which arise from the needs and suffering of the masses, or in a doctrinal truth which alone directs the writer to "the significant" in experience.

In asserting their independence from the views and aspirations of other men—above all from the tactical needs of an underground political movement—the artists were merely insisting on minimal conditions for the performance of their work, which they conceived as the discovery of the whole truth about human experience. "Truth," unadorned and without qualification, became a battle cry of the group. "My hero is truth," Tolstoy shouted at Sevastopol, refusing to falsify for patriotic purposes any of the human beings he observed there. Art's truth, Turgenev felt, was a special personal vision of experience to which the artist dedicated himself as to a holy mission. The critics simply did not understand the creative process:

> They do not imagine that enjoyment . . . which consists of punishing oneself for the shortcomings . . . in the people one invents; they are fully convinced that an author unfailingly creates only that which conducts his ideas, they do not want to believe that to reproduce powerfully and accurately the truth, the realness of life, is the greatest happiness for a writer even if this truth does not coincide with his own sympathies.[1]

Formal discipline is no end in itself—art is not a game—but a means to this greater end. Political truth is not false but "one-sided," simply one aspect of the totality of man's experience. The goal is the rendering, compactly but completely, of the whole of

† From Rufus W. Mathewson, *The Positive Hero in Russian Literature,* New York, 1958, pp. 111–17, 135–36. Copyright 1958 by Columbia University Press. Reprinted by permission of the publishers, Columbia University Press. The title for this section of a chapter entitled "Rebuttal I" is provided from a preceding section.

1. From Chapter 5, "A propos de *Fathers and Sons,*" in his *Literary Reminiscences,* dated 1868–80 (*Polnoe sobranie schinenii* [St. Petersburg, 1913], X, 104).

the human condition as one's characters share it. The writer does not address himself to the "significant" truth or to the useful truth or to the probable truth, but to the whole of its gnarled and knotty substance. Chekhov, the last and often the most perceptive spokesman for the writers, makes it clear that no limitation within the writer's awareness must be allowed to infringe on the fidelity of his image. Since it is in the artist's mind that order and meaning are discovered in experience, he must clearly be independent (though not necessarily unaware) of the imperatives derived from other disciplines, if he is to meet this challenging and exhausting standard of "absolute and honest truth."

In a sense the writers' claim to autonomy is based on the notion that the act of creation is in itself an act of discovery. Art maintains its own outposts on the frontiers of experience, conducts its own explorations according to its own rules, and presents its findings to the public without referral to any authority outside the writer's conscience. Art bears comparison in this connection with a scientific experiment. Lionel Trilling has compared the fabricated world of the work of art—Marianne Moore's "imaginary garden" —with the artificial situation of the experiment, "which is devised to force or foster a fact into being." [2] Both wings of Russian realism accepted some such view of the creative process. But there is a significant difference between them on this point. It is not that either group really rigged the experiment or allowed the unrestricted play of the experimenter's subjectivity. The distinction is rather to be found in differing stands of selectivity regulating the amount and kinds of data to be taken under consideration. The liberal in spite of his prejudices and pedispositions seemed always inclined to permit more data—in terms of variety of character and situation—as raw material to be tested in his experiment. The radical favored smaller amounts with a larger share pretested by other disciplines. To the extent that this was so, the outcome always tended to be predetermined in this kind of fiction, as Chernyshevsky's novel clearly indicated.

The writer's effort to remain true to the logic of the data, and to organize them without damage or distortion, gave rise more than once to the peculiar situation in which the writer struggled desperately, and sometimes unsuccessfully, to control the outcome of his story, and asked in bewilderment what had gone wrong when he failed. Gogol's Chichikov (*Dead Souls*), Tolstoy's Levin (*Anna Karenina*), Dostoevsky's Myshkin (*The Idiot*)—all represent intentions unfulfilled. It may be argued that Raskolnikov's questionable conversion violates the logic of the data, and the writer's

2. Lionel Trilling, "Introduction," in James, *The Princess Casamassima,* I, xiv.

better judgment, too, as it is revealed in his working notes for the novel's conclusions: "Raskolnikov goes to shoot himself." [3] Ivan Karamazov's state of suspension, far from fulfillment but as far from defeat, does not express the author's explicit beliefs as we know them to be. In all these cases the writer has created someone as strong and assertive as himself, with an independent identity and destiny. Turgenev is painfully honest and frankly at sea about his relation to Bazarov. True to his precept: to present "the whole of the living human face," he found himself unable to say, after he had done so, that Bazarov was the creature of his hopes, or even whether "I love him or hate him." [4] Working out of this ambivalence, Turgenev endowed Bazarov with a striking combination of good and bad qualities: he has in his make-up "coarseness," "heartlessness," "ruthless dryness and sharpness," yet he is "strong," "honorable, just, and a democrat to the tip of his toes." These, at least, are some of the qualities Turgenev discovered in him after the fact. But they were not the result of a calculated balancing of vices and virtues during the act of creation itself. At that moment his governing intention was to exclude arbitrary manipulation and to submit to the logic of his invention. He has described his curious feeling of helplessness before his creation:

> It seems that an author himself does not know what he is creating; my feelings for Bazarov—my personal feelings—were of a confused nature (whether I loved him or hated him, the Lord knows!), nevertheless the image came out so defined that he immediately stepped into life and started to act in his own particular way. In the end what does it matter what a writer thinks of his work. It is a thing in itself and he is a thing in himself.[5]

Turgenev would have been a happier man if he had really believed in the separate existences of author and hero. He was never able to disclaim responsibility for Bazarov entirely, but he achieved a degree of detachment that enabled him to penetrate to the real reasons for the clamorous and discordant reception of "his favorite child." The danger lay in his own ambiguity:

> If the writer's attitude toward his characters is not defined . . . if the author himself doesn't know whether he loves the character he has set forth . . . then it is thoroughly bad. The reader is prepared to attach to the author imaginary sympathies or imaginary antipathies, if only to escape from the unpleasant "uncertainty." [6]

3. F. M. Dostoevsky, *Iz arkhiva F. M. Dostoevskogo. Prestuplenie i nakazanie: neizdannye materialy,* ed. I. I. Glivenko (Moscow-Leningrad, 1931), p. 216.
4. Letter to A. A. Fet, dated April 6/18, 1862.
5. Letter to I. P. Borisov, January 5, 1870.
6. From the *Literary Reminiscences* in *Polnoe sobranie sochinenii,* X, 106.

Fathers and Sons fell, as Turgenev put it, "like oil on the fire." [7] In this superheated time readers "read through" the novel and groped for direct, immediate identification with the life around them. There was neither the leisure nor the tolerance to honor his real purpose as he explained it to Dostoevsky: "Nobody, it seems, suspects that I tried to present . . . a tragic figure—and everybody comments: why is he so sinister? or why is he so good?" [8]

Turgenev was a victim of the partisan view of truth held by the political extremists on both sides, a view impatient of paradox or ambiguity, hence unwilling to accept the complexity or the contradictions of tragedy. In the radicals' universe allowance was made for obstacles and setbacks but not for doubt or bewilderment. They felt that much larger sectors of the available truth were known than the liberal writers believed. And, in any case, important new discoveries would not, in all likelihood, be made by freely ranging writer-explorers. The writer, in the radical prescription, was expected to deal far more with the given—to illustrate the known, not to seek the unknown. Behind the words "typical," "healthy," "progressive," and "necessary" lay the certainty that such words had fixed and exclusive definitions, and, still further in the background, the implication that these definitions, constituting the essential truth, must be accepted by—or even imposed on—writers.

In deciding what truth is for the writer, certain judgments must be made about what aspects of the truth of human life or what moments in man's life cycle are of greatest fictional interest. For the great Russian novelists ideas and doctrine were not excluded, but were contained in character, and made a function of the whole man. The truth of fiction for them embraced all varieties of love, friendship, and hatred, had as its permanent backdrop the perspective of growth, decay, and death, and, because of the artist's elevation above, and independence from, his characters, included the human facts of fallibility, error, and failure. The radicals, on the other hand, were interested in ideological man. In their view of literary truth—and undoubtedly in their own private moral code—character was a function of doctrine, and men generally were most "interesting" when seen in active response to their social situation. Against the liberal creed of knowledge of life for its own sake whatever the consequences, the radicals opposed an ideology, a body of organized knowledge designed to affect men's future social behavior in a specific way. Since the doctrine was known to be valid, its spokesmen in art could not be permitted to fail, or if they did, for personal reasons, they became simply uninteresting or untypical in the radicals' special use of those words. For the

7. Letter to P. V. Annenkov, June 8, 1862.

8. Letter to F. M. Dostoevsky, April 22, 1862.

liberal with his eye focused on the individual in all his observable relations with life, this doctrinal view of man was, as Tolstoy put it, "one-sided." Turgenev was undoubtedly reacting against this view when he enjoined young writers to steer clear of any and all "dogma." Also, since an ideological view of the world involved a calculation about the future, literary truth for the radicals must contain that diagram of what is to come, as they discerned it in present events. According to the canons of realism, the future, seen either as the inevitable or as the desirable, must remain an unknown. Possibilities might be stated, but any effort to force character into one of these possibilities had unhappy results, as we have seen in the case of Chichikov, Raskolnikov, Levin, and others. * * *

* * * Turgenev, whose indictment of the radical is far gentler than his friend Herzen's, had, nevertheless, to acknowledge the presence of a towering arrogance in the radical type.[9] In Bazarov this quality provides the outlet for his admirable courage and energy and is, at the same time, a crippling malformation of his character. When his doctrinal supports have been worn away and shown to be inadequate, Bazarov lapses fleetingly into Nietzschean image of himself as a kind of superman, before he collapses under the weight of his swollen ego.[1] When charged with falsification and slander on this point, Turgenev looked beyond Herzen's concrete explanations and sought to explain it in general, psychological terms:

> What kind of artist would I be (I don't say man) if I did not understand that self confidence, exaggeration of expression . . . and posing, even a certain cynicism, constitute inevitable attributes of youth.[2]

IRVING HOWE

Turgenev: The Politics of Hesitation†

* * * If Rudin has partly been created in Turgenev's own image, Bazarov, the hero of *Fathers and Sons,* is a figure in opposition to

9. Even Chernyshevsky acknowledges this. But with Rakhmetov, his self-assurance and his abruptness in personal relations are seen as a refreshingly direct and time-saving manner which all his friends understand and appreciate. [Rakhmetov is the hero of Chernyshevsky's novel *What Is To Be Done?* Editor].

1. Turgenev makes it clear in a letter to K. K. Sluchevski that the slip of a knife that kills Bazarov is not an accident but part of a coherent tragic design (Letter of April 14/26, 1862).

2. Letter to A. P. Filosofov, August 18/30, 1874.

† From Irving Howe, *Politics and the Novel,* New York, 1957, pp. 129–33.

that image. The one rambles idealistic poetry, the other grumbles his faith in the dissection of frogs; the one is all too obviously weak, the other seems spectacularly strong. Yet between the two there is a parallel of social position. Both stand outside the manor-house that is Russia, peering in through a window; Rudin makes speeches and Bazarov would like to throw stones but no one pays attention, no one is disturbed. They together might, like Dostoevsky's Shatov and Kirillov, [in *The Possessed*] come to a whole man; but they are not together, they alternate in Russian life, as in Russian literature, each testifying to the social impotence that has made the other possible.

Like all of Turgenev's superfluous men, Bazarov is essentially good. Among our more cultivated critics, those who insist that the heroes of novels be as high-minded as themselves, it has been fashionable to look with contempt upon Bazarov's nihilism, to see him as a specimen of Russian boorishness. Such a reading is not merely imperceptive, it is humorless. Would it really be better if Bazarov, instead of devoting himself to frogs and viscera, were to proclaim about Poetry and the Soul? Would it be better if he were a metaphysician juggling the shells of Matter and Mind instead of a coarse materialist talking nonsense about the irrelevance of Pushkin?

For all that Bazarov's nihilism accurately reflects a phase of Russian and European history, it must be taken more as a symptom of political desperation than as a formal intellectual system. Bazarov is a man ready for life, and cannot find it. Bazarov is a man of the most intense emotions, but without confidence in his capacity to realize them. Bazarov is a revolutionary personality, but without revolutionary ideas or commitments. He is all potentiality and no possibility. The more his ideas seem outmoded, the more does he himself seem our contemporary.

No wonder Bazarov feels so desperate a need to be rude. There are times when society is so impervious to the kicks of criticism, when intellectual life softens so completely into the blur of gentility, that the rebellious man, who can tolerate everything but not being taken seriously, has no alternative to rudeness. How else is Bazarov to pierce the elegant composure of Pavel Petrovich, a typically "enlightened" member of the previous generation who combines the manners of a Parisian litterateur with an income derived from the labor of serfs. Bazarov does not really succeed, for Pavel Petrovich forces him to a duel, a romantic ceremony that is the very opposite of everything in which Bazarov believes. During the course of the duel, it is true, Pavel Petrovich must yield to Bazarov, but the mere fact that it takes place is a triumph for the old, not the new. Bazarov may regard Pavel

Petrovich as an "archaic phenomenon," but the "archaic phenomenon" retains social power.

The formal components of Bazarov's nihilism are neither unfamiliar nor remarkable: 19th century scientism, utilitarianism, a crude materialism, a rejection of the esthetic, a belief in the powers of the free individual, a straining for tough-mindedness and a deliberate provocative rudeness. These ideas and attitudes can gain point only if Bazarov brings them to political coherence, and the book charts Bazarov's journey, as an uprooted plebeian, in search of a means of expression, a task, an obligation. On the face of it, Bazarov's ideas have little to do with politics, yet he is acute enough to think of them in political terms; he recognizes that they are functions of his frustrated political passion. "Your sort," he says to his mild young friend Arkady, "can never get beyond refined submission or refined indignation, and that's no good. You won't fight—and yet you fancy yourselves gallant chaps—but we mean to fight . . . We want to smash other people! You're a capital fellow; but you're a sugary liberal snob for all that . . ." This is the language of politics, it might almost be Lenin talking to a liberal parliamentarian. But even as Bazarov wants to "smash other people" he senses his own helplessness: he has no weapons for smashing anything. "A harmless person," he calls himself, and a little later, "A tame cat."

In the society of his day, as Turgenev fills it in with a few quick strokes, Bazarov is as superfluous as Rudin. His young disciple Arkady cannot keep pace with him; Arkady will marry, have a houseful of children and remember to be decent to his peasants. The older generation does not understand Bazarov and for that very reason fears him: Arkady's father, a soft slothful landowner, is acute enough, however, to remark that Bazarov is different: he has "fewer traces of the slaveowner." Bazarov's brief meeting with the radicals is a fine bit of horseplay, their emptyheaded chatter being matched only by his declaration, as preposterous as it is pathetic: "I don't adopt anyone's ideas; I have my own." At which one of them, in a transport of defiance, shouts: "Down with all authorities!" and Bazarov realizes that among a pack of fools it is hard not to play the fool. He is tempted, finally, by Madame Odintzov, the country-house Delilah; suddenly he finds his awkward callow tongue, admitting to her his inability to speak freely of everything in his heart. But again he is rejected, and humiliated too, almost like a servant who has been used by his mistress and then sent packing. Nothing remains but to go home, to his good sweet uncomprehending mother and father, those remnants of old Russia; and to die.

Turgenev himself saw Bazarov in his political aspect:

> If he [Bazarov] calls himself a nihilist, one ought to read—a revolutionary . . . I dreamed of a figure that should be gloomy, wild, great, growing one half of him out of the soil, strong, angry, honorable, and yet doomed to destruction—because as yet he still stands on the threshold of the future. I dreamed of a strange parallel to Pugatchev. And my young contemporaries shake their heads and tell me, "You have insulted us . . . It's a pity you haven't worked him out a little more.' There is nothing left for me but, in the words of the gipsy song, "to take off my hat with a very low bow."

Seldom has a writer given a better cue to the meaning of his work, and most of all in the comparison between Bazarov and Pugatchev, the leader of an 18th century peasant rebellion who was hanged by a Tzar. Pugatchev, however, had his peasant followers, while Bazarov . . . what is Bazarov but a Pugatchev without the peasants?

It is at the end of *Fathers and Sons* that Turgenev reaches his highest point as an artist. The last twenty-five pages are of an incomparable elevation and intensity, worthy of Tolstoy and Dostoevsky, and in some respects, particularly in their blend of tragic power and a mute underlying sweetness, superior to them. When Bazarov, writhing in delirium, cries out, "Take ten from eight, what's left over?" we are close to the lucidity of Lear in the night. It is the lucidity of final self-confrontation, Bazarov's lament over his lost, his unused powers: "I was needed by Russia . . . No, it's clear, I wasn't needed . . ." Nothing so thoroughly undercuts his earlier protestations of self-sufficiency as this last outcry.

This ending too has failed to satisfy many critics, even one so perceptive as Prince Mirsky, who complains that there is something arbitrary in Bazarov's death. But given Russia, given Bazarov, how else *could* the novel end? Too strong to survive in Russia, what else is possible to Bazarov but death? The accident of fate that kills him comes only after he has been defeated in every possible social and personal encounter; it is the summation of those encounters. The "arbitrariness" of Bazarov's death comes as a bitterly ironic turning of his own expectations. Lying lonely and ignored in a corner of Russia, this man who was to change and destroy everything ends in pitiful helplessness. Political and not political, the ending is the only one that was available to Turgenev at the time he wrote.

MILTON HINDUS

The Duels in Mann and Turgenev †

Admiration is too mild a word to describe Mann's attitude toward the Russian novel of the nineteenth century. Reverence comes closer to the the mark. His essays on Tolstoy and Dostoevsky show with what care he studied the Slavic masters. In this note, I shall consider the practical use to which he puts one of Turgenev's inventions in his own fiction.

Faced with a problem in the resolution of the plot of *The Magic Mountain* similar to one found in *Fathers and Sons,* Mann solved it in a manner containing so many detailed resemblances to Turgenev's solution as to suggest clearly that he used the Russian author as his mode.

The fact that there are duels with pistols at climactic moments in both books is not the point. There is a duel, for example, in Tolstoy's *War and Peace* between Pierre Bezuhov and his first wife's lover Dolohov which bears not the least resemblance to either Turgenev's or Mann's duel. The duel in Tolstoy originates in passion, but the clashes in *Fathers and Sons* and *The Magic Mountain* are caused primarily by differences in ideas and temperament. It is true that the abstract reasons for the duel are somewhat disguised by Turgenev in deference to nineteenth-century notions of realism, while in Mann they stand forth bare and unadorned. The thin disguise which the fundamental conflict between the nihilist Bazarov and the romantic Uncle Pavel takes in *Fathers and Sons* is the feeling of jealousy which the latter experiences when he accidentally spies Bazarov kissing Fenichka in the orchard. But this is no more the cause of their duel than Sarajevo was the cause of the First World War or Danzig of the Second.

From the first time that Bazarov and Pavel met, they had found themselves at complete loggerheads with each other concerning values and manners. To Bazarov as to Stephen Dedalus, history is "a nightmare from which he is trying to awaken." The best thing that could happen to the relics of the past that weighed so heavily on the minds of the present generation, he felt, was that they should be completely obliterated from memory. Bazarov rejects humanistic tradition with an absolute finality which

† From *Comparative Literature,* XI (1959), 308–12. Reprinted by permission of Milton Hindus and the editors.

borders upon violence. He declares at one point that a single chemist contributes more to humanity than the best of poets. He has been called with good reason a precursor of the Bolsheviks. Uncle Pavel, on the other hand, is in love with the past for its own sake and delights in all the seemingly useless forms which it has bequeathed to us. Not quite like Miniver Cheevy in his desire for "iron clothing," he yet looks nostalgically backward in time rather than forward. It follows naturally that, while the empirical Bazarov is completely practical-minded, Uncle Pavel is no less completely ineffectual. In this connection, it is significant that, though he is considerably more experienced in the use of firearms than Bazarov, Pavel faints from the merest scratch in the struggle which he has himself provoked. The ruthless efficiency with which the Russian nihilist polishes off the pretensions of his opponent, incidentally, is to me a shade more logical and satisfactory than the suicide of Leo Naphta (which, however, is defended by Professor Weigand on the ground that since "his only positive principle is that of negation . . . it is altogether in keeping with his part that he should end by blowing out his brains").[1]

Earlier in the story, Bazarov and Pavel had found themselves in so hopeless a conflict that social relations between them had finally broken down altogether. "They renounced the pleasure of conversing with each other." The incident with Fenichka supplied the needed excuse. Pavel issued the challenge and Bazarov was constrained to accept it. The real grounds of their quarrel, says Pavel, is that "they cannot endure one another." The ideological conflict between the humanitarian Settembrini and the obscurantist Naphta is, like that of Bazarov and Pavel, inadjudicable except by force.[2] Naphta recognizes this when he says to Settembrini: "I am in your way, you are in mine—good. We will transfer the settlement of our differences to a suitable place."

In both Turgenev and Mann the fight is forced upon a reluctant antagonist, an intellectual who does not believe in dueling as a method of settling disputes. Bazarov says: "From the theoretical standpoint, duelling is absurd; from the practical standpoint, now—it's quite a different matter." In almost the same words, Settembrini says: "Theoretically, I disapprove of the duel . . . In practice, however, it is another matter." In both novels, the aggressors, Naphta and Pavel, bring the issue to a head in the

1. *Thomas Mann's Novel Der Zauberberg* by Herman J. Weigand (1933). From the portion reprinted in *The Stature of Thomas Mann,* ed. Charles Neider (New York, 1947), p. 163.

2. The thesis here expounded is anticipated by Harry Levin in his essay on *Joseph The Provider* in Neider's anthology, p. 211: "The Naphta-Settembrini debate could only be settled by force; taking a leaf from Turgenev's *Fathers and Sons,* Mann staged a duel between between them . . . "

same manner—by the implied threat of the application of raw physical violence, should the more ceremonious and ritualistic bloodletting of the duel be resisted by the intellectual's pacific principles. Pavel comes to call on Bazarov armed with a walking stick which he plainly means to use should Bazarov refuse him satisfaction, Bazarov, reflecting upon the challenge, says to himself afterwards: "Why I do believe he'd have struck me, and then . . . it might have come to my strangling him like a cat." Bazarov blanches at the very thought, for underneath his demeanor of scientific calm and objectivity he too is very much the man of touchy feelings and pride. Naphta provokes Settembrini with a similar threat of immediate violent measures: " 'I hope your civilian principles will not prevent you from knowing what you owe me—else I shall be forced to put these principles to a test that—' Settembrini drew himself up; the movement was so expressive that Naphta went on: 'Ah, I see, that will not be necessary . . .' "

Later on, Settembrini talks with Hans Castorp about the significance of Naphta's challenge, and in the conversation makes explicit what is allowed to remain implicit in the scene of Turgenev: "The duel, my friend, is not an 'arrangement' like another. It is the ultimate, the return to a state of nature, slightly mitigated by regulations that are chivalrous in character, but extremely superficial. The essential nature of the thing remains the primitive, the physical struggle; and however civilized a man is, it is his duty to be ready for such a contingency, which may any day arise." Castorp, after some thought, accepts the validity of Settembrini's analysis: "With horror he understood that at the end of everything only the physical remained, only the teeth and nails. Yes, they must fight; only thus could be assured even that small mitigation of the primitive by the rules of chivalry." That is to say, "speaking without metaphor" (as Bazarov says to Pavel), the sword or the pistol are more aesthetic ways of settling differences than the caveman's club or its equivalent, Uncle Pavel's walking stick. In Mann's novel, the outbreak of violence between Naphta and Settembrini foreshadows the beginning of the general European war; for what is true of the relations of individuals, as Proust remarks, is also true of the relations between national states. The court of last resort, physical combat, breaks man down from being a rational animal to being merely an animal that has for his protection "only the teeth and nails." Castorp's bitter acceptance of the human condition in this instance prefigures his participation in the great duel which convulsed the civilization of Europe. Between Bazarov and Pavel, too, that is to say between the future of Russia which Turgenev prophesied "with horror" and its past which he had known from living experience, no solution that was thinkable remained save violence.

There is another resemblance between the treatments of these scenes—the ironic contrast underscored by both Mann and Turgenev between the behavior of those who engage in the odd sport of dueling and those who carry on the world's necessary work. In Turgenev, as Bazarov repairs to the field of battle with Pavel he suddenly looks up to see "a peasant [who] came into sight from behind the trees. He was driving before him two horses hobbled together . . . 'There's some one else up early too,' thought Bazarov; 'but he at least has got up for work, while we . . .' " Similarly in *The Magic Mountain*: "Hans Castorp, after a restless night, left the Berghof to go to the rendezvous. The maidservants cleaning the hall looked after him in wonder." The contrast here implies perhaps the same social commentary as is to be found in Breughel's picture of the fall of Icarus, where the foreground is occupied by a team ploughing and the middle distance by a ship sailing peacefully on its voyage, while the splash made by the principal subject of the picture is an almost invisible dot somewhere off to one side. The heroism of the world is a remote and quixotic form of foolishness to its peasants, valets, and chambermaids.

T. S. Eliot has said somewhere that the difference between inferior artists and good ones is that the former borrow while the latter steal. Less pointed than this witty formulation is the observation that the good writer transforms or introduces variations upon a theme supplied by his predecessor. There are not only similarities between Turgenev's duel and Mann's but differences as well. Turgenev covers up the fundamental cause of the conflict he describes by his concession to realism in making jealousy the immediate reason. Mann, on the other hand, dispenses with any naturalistic device and delights in showing us that he is aware of his own daring. Castorp objects to Settembrini that the ground of his duel with Naphta is unreal: "If even there were a real injury,' he cried . . . 'If one of them had dragged the other's good name in the dirt, *if it was a question of a woman*, or anything else really momentous, that you could take hold of, so that you felt there was no possibility of reconciliation! For such cases the duel is the last resort . . .'" (italics mine). This objection is disposed of summarily by Settembrini, who takes the opportunity to teach his "pupil" Castorp an important lesson.

> You err, my friend, first of all in the assumption that the intellectual cannot assume a personal character . . . The point at which you go wrong is in your estimation of the things of the mind, in general. You obviously think they are too feeble to engender conflicts and passions comparable for sternness with

> those real life brings forth, the only issue of which can be the appeal to force. *All' incontro!* The abstract, the refined-upon, the ideal, is at the same time the Absolute—it is sternness itself; it contains within it more possibilities of deep and radical hatred, of unconditioned and irreconcilable hostility, than any relation of social life can. It astonishes you to hear that it leads, far more directly and inexorably than these, to radical intimacy, to grips, to the duel and actual physical struggle?

I am certain that Turgenev also believed this, and that it constitutes the central meaning of the duel in *Fathers and Sons*. But his concession to realism has somewhat weakened his idea. Mann has rescued the idea from its accidents and by his process of abstraction has succeeded in producing an effect quite as original in its own way as that of Turgenev.

JAMES H. JUSTUS

Fathers and Sons: The Novel as Idyll†

One of the most striking successes of *Fathers and Sons* is not its rather reluctant political statement, which at best reveals the division of Turgenev's mind, but the unambiguous theme of the "goodness" of nature. In a day when the concept has become philosophically banal, this achievement is all the more remarkable. However positively Bazarov preaches his nihilism, however influentially he sways disciples, however rabidly he hints of the Advent, he remains a powerless, unused talent. Arguing that he remains so because "the time is not yet at hand" is to beg the question. Moreover, Turgenev drops sufficient clues to suggest that Bazarov's fault is not in the "when" of Russia's destiny but in the "how" of his own nature.

By the time he seeks out Anna Sergyevna, observing what a "tame cat" he is becoming, the threat (or promise) of any significant influence he may have on society at large is passed; and with that passing goes the political interest Bazarov may have whipped up earlier in the reader. Yet structurally the novel gains, not loses, interest after this climax at Nikolskoe. Obviously, Turgenev's story of a young revolutionary is concerned with a more comprehensive and at the same time more personal rebellion than that which a single-demensioned political reading can give. What we face is nothing less than the very life, the focus, of the

† From *Western Humanities Review,* XV (1961), 259–65. Reprinted by permission of James H. Justus and the editors.

novel: the search for self-definition.

That which sets in relief the world view of the Fathers and records, both explicitly and implicitly, the progress of the world view of the Sons is external nature, a symbolic system observable in the varying degrees to which the two opposing world views conflict and reconcile. To see nature serving a more artistic purpose than mere scene-painting is not to deny the politics in the novel; rather, the methods by which Turgenev uses nature (particularly the suggestion of the mystic "Mother Russia" or "native soil" idea) enhance the tragedy which he foresees—the loss of communication between the generations and the ultimate rupture in revolution.

Throughout *Fathers and Sons* there is greater emphasis on the conflict between generations than between bourgeoisie and proletariat. Conflict of the latter type, inevitable though it is, is less explicit, that is, it has less ideological affection, sorrow, or even concern for the peasant who will be caught up in it than, say, Conrad's *Under Western Eyes* or even James's *Princess Casamassima.* In Turgenev's novel the hurt is both something less and something more—families dissolved by ideological postulates. Intellectually powerful as the political issues are, they are vapid compared with the moral-emotional episodes in the homes of the Fathers. These scenes are memorable not because of their vigor—as Dostoyevsky's memorable scenes are apt to be—but because of quiet, undertoned pathos. And much of this pathos is created by the repetitive use of nature symbols.

Superficially the great world of nature is associated with the Fathers, the guardians and lovers of the land, which includes the recognizable objects of an agrarian society: aspens, swallows, bees, lilac blossoms, gardens of roses, sunsets. This is the natural milieu of both Arkady and Bazarov, an environment from which they have wrenched themselves but to which they return. Though it is a harsh land with its satisfactions dearly earned, it is also a gentle land, which supports a society of individuals who show mutual respect and love and abide by the canons of traditional manners and faith.

Almost mournfully Turgenev seems to permit the naturalistic, scientific Sons to better their Fathers in argument and in their vision of a new Russia—mournfully because his heart-felt sympathy is attached to the dying class in spite of its "vanity, dandy habits, fatuity . . . perpetual talk . . . about art, unconscious creativeness, parliamentarism, trial by jury" and its sometimes hollow adherence to the principle of man's dignity.

Perhaps the single most affecting scene occurs immediately after the explosive dinner argument between Bazarov and Pavel Petrovitch. After the arrogant young nihilist challenges Pavel to take two days to think of an institution that "does not call for complete and unqualified destruction," Nikolai, overtaken by melancholy, retires in the dying day to his favorite arbor to reflect on the chasm that separates him from his son. Not even the violence of Bazarov's gibes when they are pertinent nor the shallow discipleship of Arkady when it is most excusable can overshadow the dramatic force of this scene in which Nikolai comprehends the nature of the tension. He wants to agree with his son and up to a point applauds his world view:

> . . . I feel there is something behind them we have not got, some superiority over us. . . . It is youth? No; not only youth. Doesn't their superiority consist in there being fewer traces of the slave-owner in them than in us?

But how far must he go to bridge the widening chasm? He is already known as a "Red Radical" over the province for his soft policies toward the peasants; he reads and studies, trying to keep abreast of developments. But all this is not enough. His methods smack of reform, when the young men have little patience with anything short of revolution.

But even the image of revolution, of sheer energy unleashed, is not so hateful to Nikolai as the Sons' underlying assumption that a chemist is "twenty times as useful as any poet," a materialism that ignores and even denounces the values of poetry, art, and nature:

> And he looked round, as though trying to understand how it was possible to have no feeling for nature. . . . The sun's rays from the farther side fell full on the copse, and piercing through its thickets, threw such a warm light on the aspen trunks that they looked like pines, and their leaves were almost a dark blue, while above them rose a pale blue sky, faintly tinged by the glow of sunset. . . . "How beautiful, my God!" thought Nikolai Petrovitch, and his favorite verses were almost on his lips . . . but still he sat there, still he gave himself up to the sorrowful consolation of solitary thought. He was fond of dreaming; his country life had developed the tendency in him.

Here is more than scene-painting. Couched in even more religious terms than the references to religion itself, this episode is Turgenev's most explicit use of nature as a symbolic system embodying the deepest values of the Fathers. Despite the depressing presence of streams with hollow banks, hovels with tumble-down roofs, barns with gaping doorways and neglected threshing-floors, and tattered peasants, these values are stubbornly insisted on and equated with the Fathers' native soil. At such times the scenes take on an almost sacramental cast.

Vassily Ivanovitch, even though a provincial doctor, is also identified with the Russian soil and landscape. He reads authorities in order to keep up with advances in healing, and though he understands the fad of discarding idols for more advanced ones, he cannot understand his son's concept of laughing at medicine altogether. With obvious relief he turns to Bazarov's comment on the growth of his birch trees.

> "And you must see what a little garden I've got now! I planted every tree myself. I've fruit, and raspberries, and all kinds of medicinal herbs."

After tea Vassily takes them to his garden "to admire the beauty of the evening" and whispers to Arkady,

> "At this spot I love to meditate, as I watch the sunset; it suits a recluse like me. And there, a little farther off, I have planted some of the trees beloved of Horace."

This initial impression of Bazarov's father is reinforced time and time again; Arkady sees him garbed in an Oriental dressing gown industriously digging in the garden, regaling his visitor with his plans for late turnips, and citing Rousseau's philosophy of the necessity for man's obtaining "his sustenance with his own hands." And later, when he unknowingly interrupts a hostile fight between Arkady and Bazarov in the shade of a haystack, he can see only a Castor-and-Pollux pair "excellently employed," with a special "significance" in their lying on the earth and gazing up to heaven.

II

But the Fathers' orientation to the natural world, a source of both their strength and inefficacy, does not constitute a simple opposition to the crude scientism and anti-esthetic pragmatism of the Sons. Ultimately the Sons' ideology is fuzzy and narrow, separated as it is from the deceptively simple agrarian world view. Paradoxically, it is this simple orientation that proves multidimensional, capable of absorbing both Bazarov's aggressive and Arkady's passive revolutionary airs. Both Sons consistently underrate their Fathers' world. Bazarov cannot channel his arrogance, rudeness, and frustration into political coherence (Arkady hardly tries) and so cannot overcome the settled, all-encompassing, and pervading social coherence of the Fathers. With considerable skill Turgenev traces the Sons' progress from the stages of rebellion against this social coherence to at least a partial reconciliation with it, and his methods are enhanced by the framework of nature which gives authority to this agrarian world view. Significant or not, the Sons' references to objects of nature outnumber those of the Fathers. Some are, of course, openly negative: a flourishing denial of the symbols means a denial of the entire system, which must be destroyed and built anew, presumably in an image yet to be found. On the night before the duel Bazarov has a dream in which Pavel Petrovitch takes "the shape of a great wood, with which he had yet to fight." And the same dark image recurs on his deathbed, where after his fitful siege of self-confronting, he sees the final struggle: "There's a forest here. . . ."

But the negative responses to nature—or those which take the form of "disordered dreams"—are surely no less indicative of the massive strength of the Fathers' world (and indeed of the Sons' unconscious involvement in it) than the more obvious garden scenes with the Fathers. The battle lines are not simply Sons versus Fathers but, more importantly, Sons versus Themselves. They possess too much of their Fathers' world to dismiss it successfully, even though it is a dying world, for to dismiss it outright is to deny themselves the self-definition they both crave. It is this tension that ideologically tilts the outcome to the Fathers and dramatically signifies Turgenev's theme. Without this inner tension, the story would be simply another tale of young ideals clashing against old ones. As it is, this novel is essentially a modification of the traditional story of the young hero who sets out in search of his fortune, which (according to Lionel Trilling in his essay on *The Princess Casamassima*) is "What the folktale says when it means that the hero is seeking himself." In *Fathers and Sons* it is a painful progress, and the opposing forces are not a series of physical obstacles but the ponderous irrationality of an entire social system. The irony in such a modern modification is that this society into which Arkady and Bazarov are plunged is not new to their experience. They have not only been there before; it is part of themselves. In one sense of their return, they do battle with themselves to attain a fully satisfactory self-definition.

Arkady, prone as he is to accept all premises and conclusions of Bazarov, still permits himself to recognize the symbols of the land; and in spite of that land's "endless, comfortless winter, with its storms, and frosts, and snows," he feels swayed by a familiar spring:

> All around was golden green, all—trees, bushes, grass—shone and stirred gently in wide waves under the soft breath of the warm wind; from all sides flooded the endless trilling music of the larks; . . . the rooks strutted among the half-grown short spring-corn . . . only from time to time their heads peeped out amid its grey waves.

This is the natural attraction of the land—dramatically juxtaposed against Arkady's own denial that it is his birthplace which creates this special feeling. (In the same connection he can exclaim: "What air . . . ! How delicious it smells! Really I fancy there's nowhere such fragrance . . . !") Later, countering Bazarov's declaration that "two and two make four, and the rest is all foolery," Arkady asks, "And is nature foolery?" and notes the "bright-colored fields in the distance, in the beautiful soft light of the sun. . . ."

III

Once back under the family roof, influence of the old order increases as Bazarov's declines. Finally, as a gesture, he offers to help his father with the difficult problems of the farm; doubtless the involvement would have been deeper immediately but for his preoccupation with Katya. At Nikolskoe the major scenes occur out-of-doors, primarily in various parts of the garden. Here under ash trees he and Katya feed sparrows and relax into a "confidential intimacy" where they admit that Bazarov's influence on them and Anna has passed. In the same garden but hidden "in the very thickest part," he loses himself in meditation and "at once wondering and rejoicing" he resolves to marry Katya. It is a significant scene, for it constitutes his final break with what is essentially an alien spirit; his alliance with Katya ushers in a domestic period of acceptance. It discards revolution, but not reform.

Bazarov, on the other hand, is the strong character but simultaneously the most decisively divided. His pastime is natural history, psychologically a more acceptable deference to the old order than the more esthetic, wasteful nature-observing of the others. His frog-cutting contributes to his scientific-medical knowledge. Only occasionally he permits himself observations, and then often from a pragmatic impulse. He explains to Arkady that poplars and spruce firs do better than oaks. To assure Anna that studying a single human specimen is enough to judge the entire race he makes an analogy quite in character: "People are like trees in a forest; no botanist would think of studying each individual birch-tree." His walks more often take him to the forest, and he naps regularly in the barn's hayloft. And in a rare self-revealing speech to Arkady he says:

> "That aspen-tree . . . reminds me of my childhood; it grows at the edge of the clay-pits where the bricks were dug, and in those days I believed firmly that that clay-pit and aspen-tree possessed a peculiar talismanic power; I never felt dull near them. I did not understand then that I was not dull, because I

> was a child. Well, now I'm grown up, the talisman's lost its power."

Unusually loquacious, Bazarov broods on his "loathsome pettiness." Contrasting himself to his parents, who "don't trouble themselves about their own nothingness; it doesn't sicken them," he mutters: "I feel nothing but weariness and anger." Part of his frustration derives from his unfortunate, unrealized love for Anna, and in self-pity he advises an ant dragging off a half-dead fly,

> "Take her, brother, take her! Don't pay attention to her resistance; it's your privilege as an animal to be free from the sentiment of pity—make the most of it—not like us conscientious self-destructive animals!"

His conversation with Fenichka, which culminates in their kissing, takes place in the lilac arbor; and the duel which Pavel instigates as a result of it occurs at dawn on a fresh morning, when the most salient part of the picture is the singing of the larks. Hearing of Arkady's coming marriage, he calls his friend a jackdaw, "a most respectable family bird," and later advises him with more gravity:

> "And you get married as soon as you can; and build your nest, and get children to your heart's content. They'll have the wit to be born in a better time than you and me."

Despite Bazarov's death-bed pledge to himself and to Anna ("Never mind; I'm not going to turn tail"), he realizes that any number of men are more important to Russia than he. He solves his last problem of "how to die decently," but Turgenev makes it clear that the giant succumbs in the end to the same natural processes as the pygmy Fathers and in fact on the Fathers' own terms. However wretched the graveyard with its rotting wooden crosses and scrubby shade trees, birds perch on Bazarov's tomb and sing while his parents pray. And conventional as Turgenev's personal conclusion to the tale may be, it underscores the rebellious principle quite apart from political considerations. Here is one whose self was not only divided but at war and whose reconciliation and submission to the basic pattern, the natural life, come inexorably:

> However passionate, sinning, and rebellious the heart hidden in the tomb, the flowers growing over it peep serenely at us with their innocent eyes; they tell us not of eternal peace alone, of that great peace of "indifferent" nature; they tell us, too, of eternal reconciliation and of life without end.

It is not correct to say that Bazarov's reconciliation is entirely unsought, a matter of physical necessity. Long before his death he deliberately returns, giving up dissection of frogs for the healing of humans, pleasing his parents in his perverse manner, and indulging them in their "toys," which are part of the old order.

That Turgenev as a conscious craftsman intends his novel to bear its theme partly through external nature as a referent can be deduced from his many pertinent allusions to Rousseau, Emerson, Pushkin, and even Fenimore Cooper's Natty Bumpo. But, more important, he communicates the stature of Nikolai and Vassily through identification with the land that can produce stability, affection, and even growth, as well as tradition-bound inadequacies in social and political matters. For Arkady and Bazarov, their radical notions at first dispossess them from such a heritage; but despite this open rejection, the reader can follow consistently their alliance to it through a patterned thematic thread of nature references, an alliance that the two characters recognize and admit only sporadically. The movement is reunion with and reconciliation to the mainstream of humanity, and with all its faults, that mainstream is the world of the Fathers.

P. G. PUSTOVOYT

Some Features of Composition in *Fathers and Sons*†

Dialogue plays so large a role in Turgenev's novels that it would be incorrect to consider it simply as a technical device of the writer's. The increasing role of dialogue is determined by the themes and the intellectual content of his works. In general, dialogue is the most appropriate form in the sociological novel to raise philosophical arguments on the large questions preoccupying the author's contemporary society. It makes it possible to develop actual political problems, and to cast light on them from various points of view. Finally, in dialogue characters are disclosed and discovered and appear as active agents and participants in ideological conflict.

In the novel *Fathers and Sons* dialogues are above all passionate political and philosophical arguments. Unlike his opponents, Bazarov is brief and lapidary in arguments. He does not conquer

† From P. G. Pustovoyt, ***Roman I. S. Turgeneva "Ottsy i deti" i ideynaya bor'ba 60–x godov XIX veka,*** Moscow, 1960, pp. 224–39. Translated by Ralph E. Matlaw. Much of the enormous literature on Turgenev in the Soviet Union rehashes the political and intellectual background. A smaller body of work deals with Turgenev's style and methods. This essay has been chosen as representative of the quality and tenor of Soviet criticism of ***Fathers and Sons.***

and overwhelm his opponents through long arguments and philosophical tirades as Rudin did but in laconic, pregnant replies, apt, full of meaning, appropriately expressed in aphorisms. Bazarov does not attempt to speak beautifully, he does not try "to pin down words like butterflies." And yet Bazarov emerges the victor in almost all the arguments, since his replies, thrown off almost as if in passing, are jammed full of profound thoughts and testify to the hero's colossal erudition, his knowledge of life, his resourcefulness and cleverness. Bazarov's replies may be turned into a complete system of opinions. A definite democratic scheme underlies every reply. For example, the replies "peasants are glad to rob even themselves to get dead drunk at the pot-house" or "when it thunders the common folk think Elijah the Prophet is riding through the heavens in a chariot" clearly express the educational plans formulated in Chernyshevsky's and Dobrolyubov's articles in *The Contemporary* at the end of the 1850's, and embodied in many of N. Uspensky's stories about common folk, which usually appeared in the opening pages of that periodical. Bazarov's reply "The art of making money or 'Shrink Hemorrhoids' " has been explained by N. K. Brodsky as a reference by Bazarov for polemical purposes to two works by a writer of the 1860's, I. T. Kokorev, reviewed by Chernyshevsky and Dobrolyubov. It is easy to prove that the main hero's other replies ("Raphael isn't worth a plugged nickel," "a good chemist is twenty times more useful than any poet") are based on the rich real material of the epoch.

In order to make Bazarov's speech in the dialogues broad and to make it express the hero's ideas in concentrated form, Turgenev makes Bazarov use proverbs and sayings, idiomatic expressions, and other forms of phraseology more frequently than other characters ("a scalded cat fears cold water," "that's not the whole story," "as the ale is drawn it must be drunk"). And yet it would be incorrect to consider the aphoristic and idiomatic quality of Bazarov's speech in argumentation as its only characteristic feature. Turgenev endowed his main hero with the capacity for oratorical speech in addition to these very real and characteristic marks of Bazarov's speech, which reveal in him the genuine democrat who tries to make himself understood by common folk. Thus, in Chapter Ten of the novel, in the argument with Pavel Petrovich, Bazarov does not limit himself to the brief and devastatingly apt replies ("We've heard that song a good many times," that is, he criticizes Pavel Petrovich's discussion of the English aristocracy; or "The ground has to be cleared first"), but he also delivers a fairly long critical tirade against liberal phrasemongering:

> Then we figured out that talk, perpetual talk, and nothing but talk about our social sores was not worthwhile, that it all led to

> nothing but banality and doctrinairism. We saw that even our clever ones, so-called advanced people and accusers, were no good; that we were occupied by nonsense, talked about some sort of art, unconscious creativeness, parliamentarism, the legal profession, and the devil knows what all, while it's a question of daily bread, while we're stifling under the grossest superstition, while all our corporations come to grief simply because there aren't enough honest men to carry them on . . .[1]

The syntactical construction of that sentence is itself enough to prove that before us is not an ordinary district doctor but an orator, a tribune, a leader of a certain party (that is, the presence of parallel constructions: "We figured out," "we saw," and before that "we said"; repeated conjunctions "that" and "while"). If we examine the content of Bazarov's angry tirade it becomes clear that Turgenev did not shut his hero's lips, did not limit his participation in arguments to witticisms, but permitted him to express himself "at the top of his voice," that is, as he might have expressed himself before a large mass of his partisans.

Bazarov knows how to ridicule and parry Pavel Petrovich's country squire's drawing-room manner of speech with its countless formulas of servile-courtier politeness and ingratiation like "I haven't the honor of knowing," "permit me to be so curious as to ask," "will you be so kind as." Thus, for example, when Pavel Petrovich in his usual elegant manner, which he considered a mark of special chic, offers Bazarov with solemn grandioseness to "be so good as to choose (pistols)" Bazarov answers him calmly but with deadly irony "I will be so good." Such are some of the characteristics of dialogue in Turgenev's *Fathers and Sons.*

The portraits of characters play a vital, though not the most important, role in Turgenev's novels in general and in *Fathers and Sons* in particular. Turgenev very carefully studies a character's bearing, his exterior, and his gestures before engraving it on the artistic work. Turgenev wrote "I define characters as for a play: so and so, aged such and such, dresses this way, bears himself this way. Sometimes a certain gesture occurs to me and I immediately put down: passes his hand over his hair or pulls at his moustache. And I do not start to write until he becomes an old acquaintance for me, until I see him and hear his voice. And so with all the characters." In Turgenev's works, the characters are portrayed in many different ways. Upon close examination at least three types of portraits emerge from the variety offered.

The first is a detailed portrait with a description of the height,

1. The reader will note that Pustovoyt has omitted the last part of the sentence: "while the very emancipation our Government's busy upon will hardly come to any good, because peasants are glad to rob even themselves to get drunk at the pot-house" [*Editor*].

hair, face, and eyes of the hero and also several characteristic individual traits designed for the reader's visual impression. As a rule this sort of portrait is accompanied in Turgenev by little commentaries by the author, which distinguishes Turgenev's manner from, say, Goncharov's. This type of portrait appears as early as *The Hunter's Sketches,* for example the portrait of Yashka the Turk in "The Singers":

> a lean and well-built man of twenty-three, dressed in a long-skirted blue nankeen coat. He looked like a dashing factory worker and, it seems, could hardly boast of good health. His sunken cheeks, large, restless gray eyes, straight nose with fine moving nostrils, a white, sloping brow, with flaxen curls pushed back from it, large but handsome and expressive lips—*his entire face revealed an impressionable and passionate man.*[2]

Natalia Lasunsky in *Rudin,* Lavretsky in *A Nest of Noblemen,* Shubin in *On the Eve* are other examples. * * * In *Fathers and Sons* the portraits of Bazarov and Odintsov are executed in a similar way. Here, for example, is the portrait of Bazarov in the second chapter:

> "Nikolai Petrovich turned around quickly and going up to a *tall* man in a *long,* loose, rough coat with tassels, who had only just got out of the carriage, he warmly pressed the *bare red* hand, which the latter did not at once hold out to him. . . . answered Bazarov, in a *lazy* but *manly* voice; and turning back the collar of his rough coat, he showed Nikolai Petrovich his whole face. It was *long* and *lean,* with a *broad* forehead, a nose flat at the base and *sharp* at the tip, *large greenish* eyes, and *drooping* side whiskers of a *sandy* color."

Then the author's explanations occur: "It was animated by a tranquil smile, and showed self-confidence and intelligence."

It is easy to note that dominant psychological trait of the hero is in the present case already defined through the portrait. With the aid of numerous precise details and commentary on the general impression given, Turgenev really creates that "physical and moral union" noted by Prosper Mérimée. The further description of the hero's exterior may continue even after the definition of the dominant psychological traits: the following details are added to the basic portrait of Bazarov: "his *long, thick, dark-blond* hair did not hide the prominent bumps of his *large skull.*"

The portrait of Odintsov in the fourteenth chapter is presented in the same kind of relief and in the same clear images:

2. Italics in the quoted text are Pustovoyt's throughout, except *Victor* on p. 319, Turgenev's indication that Kukshin pronounced his name in French rather than in Russian [*Editor*].

> Arkady looked round, and saw a tall woman in a *black* dress standing at the door of the room. He was struck by the dignity of her carriage. Her *bare* arms lay gracefully beside her *slender* waist; gracefully some *light* sprays of fuchsia drooped from her *shining* hair on to her *sloping* shoulders; her *clear* eyes looked out from under a somewhat *protruding white* brow, with a tranquil and intelligent expression—tranquil it was precisely, not pensive —and on her lips was a *scarcely perceptible* smile. A kind of *gracious* and *gentle* force emanated from her face.

Here too, after explaining what sort of impression the figure of Odintsov should produce on the reader, Turgenev does not stop describing the exterior of his heroine; he goes on to remark that

> her nose—like almost all Russian noses—was a little thick; and her complexion was not perfectly clear; Arkady made up his mind, for all that, that he had never before met such an attractive woman.

Second. In Turgenev's novels we encounter satirical portraits in some respects similar to Gogol's manner. These consist of portraits with extensive use of the background, characterizing the figure by oblique means. The author's commentary on the satirical portrait sometimes does not limit itself to a simple indication of one quality or another in the figure, but develops into a whole picture. * * *

In *Fathers and Sons,* the clearest satiric portraits approximating Gogol's manner, gradually disclosing the essence of character by oblique means, are those of Kukshin and Sitnikov. The portrait of Kukshin is created against a broad background, consisting of several concentric circles that increasingly strengthen the satiric element. Turgenev begins Chapter Thirteen, devoted to Kukshin, by describing the city, then discusses the city's streets, then the little house "in the Moscow style" where Madame Kukshin lives, then adduces details like the "visiting card nailed on askew," the "bell-handle," the "some one who was not exactly a servant nor exactly a companion, in a cap—unmistakable tokens of the progressive tendencies of the mistress." It is perfectly clear that the background heralds to the reader nothing great and grandiose but testifies to some sort of unfounded pretense on the part of the inhabitant of this place; while the author's comment on "the progressive tendencies of the mistress" clearly has an ironic ring.

Continuing to develop the device of oblique characterization, Turgenev moves to a narrower concentric circle of observation and presents a detailed description of Kukshin's room: "Papers, letters, thick issues of Russian journals, for the most part uncut [a very characteristic detail!], lay at random on the dusty tables; cigarette ends lay scattered everywhere." It suffices to remember how in *Dead Souls* Gogol gradually discloses the image of Manilov by means of the furnishings (the exposed house, the abandoned pond, the room, the book with a bookmark on page 14), to become convinced that Turgenev successfully uses Gogol's device of oblique characterization.

The figure Turgenev chooses as the object of his satire usually appears in the novel, as in Gogol, after a distinctive descriptive overture, after the corresponding background has been drawn and when the reader has already formed a definite impression about him or her on the basis of the preceding description of setting an environment aroung the figure. Turgenev draws Kukshin's portrait only after discussing the city, its streets, the house, and the room in which she lives:

> "On a leather-covered sofa a lady, still young, was reclining. Her fair hair was rather dishevelled; she wore a silk gown, not altogether tidy, heavy bracelets on her short arms, and a lace handkerchief on her head. She got up from the sofa, and carelessly drawing over her shoulders a velvet cape trimmed with yellowish ermine, she said languidly, "good-morning, *Victor*."

Underlining a series of incongruities in Kukshin's external appearance (young—rather dishevelled; in a silk gown—not altogether tidy; bracelets—on short arms), a series of deprecatory details ("round eyes, between which was a forlorn little turned-up red nose," "when she laughed, the gum showed above her upper teeth," "fingers brown with tobacco stains," etc.), Turgenev adds force to the author's comments to the portrait. In this case it is no longer a casual author's remark or a reply as, for example, the one about Bazarov's face "It was animated by a tranquil smile and expressed self-confidence and intelligence."

In describing Kukshin the commentaries grow into an extensive satirical characterization which is presented as it were not only through the author but also through another character, in this instance Bazarov. The author and Bazarov seem to fuse into a single character to convey the satiric judgment on Kukshin: "Bazarov frowned. There was nothing repulsive in the little plain person of the emancipated woman; but the expression of her face produced a disagreeable effect on the spectator. One felt impelled [it is hard to say who was impelled: the author or Bazarov, or everyone, including the reader] to ask her, 'What's the matter; are you hungry? Or bored? Or shy? What are you fidgeting about?' Both she and Sitnikov always had the same uneasy air. She was extremely unconstrained and at the same time awkward; she obviously regarded herself a good-natured, simple creature, and all the while, whatever she did, it always struck one that it was just what she did not want to do; everything with her seemed, as children say, done on purpose, that's to say, not simply, not naturally." We note that the satiric portrait of the imitative nihilist is presented before the dialogue in which her negative essence is disclosed.

Sitnikov's portrait is created through separate satirical brush strokes and subtle details that characterize him accurately. He is a man of small stature, he doesn't get out of the carriage but *leaps* out, *dashes* toward Bazarov like a shot although there is no reason either for shouting or for hurrying, immediately starts to *fidget* around Bazarov, *hops* over the ditch, runs now at the right of Bazarov, now at the left, advances somehow sideways, laughs *shrilly,* smiles *subserviently,* etc. "An expression of *worry* and *tension,*" Turgenev writes in Chapter Twelve, was "imprinted on the *small* but *pleasant* features of his *well-groomed* face; his small eyes, that seemed *squeezed in,* had a fixed and uneasy look, and his laugh, too, was uneasy—a sort of short, wooden laugh." The words "but pleasant" are neutralized to such an extent by the preceding "worry and tension" and subsequent "well-groomed face" that they must be taken as the author's malicious irony toward his character. Sitnikov's portrait is concluded with the following stroke: in Kukshin's room Sitnikov "by now was lolling in an armchair, one leg in the air."

When a definite impression of these caricature-like nihilists has been created through their portraits, an impression Shchedrin later so aptly called one of "flap-ears playing the fool," Turgenev discloses their foolishness in detail through dialogue and action.

In the *third place,* a portrait that contradicts the inner content of the person is very characteristic for Turgenev. The variations of that kind of portrait are determined by the nature of the contrast between that which the author emphasizes in the exterior of the person and what he later discloses his essence to be. * * * The exterior [of Pavel Petrovich] emphasizes his aristocracy and European polish, satirical traits creep into the description of the character's external anglomania, while the essence of Pavel Petrovich is not disclosed by satiric means. * * *

Several critics of Turgenev's work are inclined to consider the figure of Pavel Petrovich satirical in general, relying upon Turgenev's own words "I raised his faults to the point of making them a caricature, I made him laughable." Actually, of course, the matter is not quite so. Turgenev criticises very sharply but not by satirical means Pavel Petrovich's principles and convictions with the exception of his views on dueling and the duel itself. The bankruptcy of Pavel Petrovich's pompous speeches about reforms, government steps, committees, and deputies is exposed with "the thunder of indignation." Turgenev notes his character's complete inactivity without satire. But Turgenev permits obvious satirical strokes to appear in depicting Pavel Pavlovich's anglomania and external aristocracy. This was clearly expressed in his portrait and gave various satirical journals an opportunity to parody precisely that part of the character.

Pretensions to something special and original are seen in the figure's dress and in his manners: the English *suit,* the stylish cravate, various fezes, his custom of speaking while gently rocking, moving his shoulders, his European "shake-hands," etc.

Actually Pavel Petrovich did not create and could not create anything new and original, since the social force he represented was disappearing from the historical arena in the 1860's, yielding its place to the progressively developing democratic forces that were gathering strength. Turgenev understood that both Pavel Petrovich and Nikolay Petrovich became outmoded people, and even had his Bazarov say that their song had been sung. However, this could not please Turgenev who was a moderate liberal and therefore in dismissing the principles of liberals of the 1860's the author avoided satire. * * *

Bazarov's parents may serve as clear examples of transitional or mixed portraits. The portrait of Bazarov's father appears in Chapter Twenty as follows:

> Bazarov leaned out of the carriage, while Arkady thrust his head out behind his companion's back, and caught sight on the small porch of the little manor-house of a *tall, gaunt* man with *dishevelled* hair, and a *thin aquiline* nose, dressed in an *old military* frock coat not buttoned up. He was standing, his legs wide apart, smoking a *long* pipe and squinting his eyes to keep the sun out of them.

Here everything reminds one of the manner in which the first type of portrait is drawn (that of Bazarov, for example), but there are no author's comments in the portrait of the father. On the other hand, Turgenev later pays considerable attention to the device of oblique characterization—he presents a detailed description of Vassily Ivanovich's study:

> A thick-legged table, littered over with papers black with the accumulation of ancient dust as though they had been smoked, occupied the entire space between two windows; on the walls hung Turkish firearms, whips, swords, two maps, anatomical charts of some sort, a portrait of Hufeland, a monogram woven in hair in a black frame, and a glass-framed diploma; a leather sofa, torn and worn into hollows here and there was placed between two enormous cupboards of Karelian birchwood; books,

> boxes, stuffed birds, jars, and phials were huddled together in confusion on the shelves; in one corner stood a broken galvanic battery.

Speaking more accurately, the reader sees a museum of an ancient Aesculapius, whose archaic exhibits testify to former enthusiam in equal degree for medicine and hunting, rather than the study of a contemporary scholar and practitioner, keeping up with recent discoveries in science. Even more, it testifies to the desolation and backwardness reigning in Vassily Ivanovich's house. After such a description of Bazarov's father's study, it is clear that such details as "dishevelled hair," "old military frock coat not buttoned up," "legs wide apart" are not amassed accidentally in the portrait.

Before turning to the portrait of Arina Valasyevna, Bazarov's mother, Turgenev traces a distinctive background in Gogol's style: "at last, on the slope of a gently rising knoll, appeared the *tiny village* where Bazarov's parents lived. Beside it, in a *small copse* of young birch, could be seen a *tiny* house with a thatched roof."

One should draw attention to the use of diminutives, through which the author creates in the reader an impression of something pitiful and insignificant. In the same way and with the help of similar diminutives, the author paints a portrait "of a real Russian little gentlewoman of the former, ancient days"; "the door was flung open, *plump, short, little old woman in white cap and a short little striped jacket* appeared on the threshold. She oh'd, swayed, and would certainly have fallen had not Bazarov supported her. Her *small plump hands* were instantly entwined around his neck."

Later on, details in the external appearance of the sentimental old woman that lower the portrait are increased ("crumpled and adoring face," "blissful and comic-looking eyes") and the author seems, as it were, to create a second portrait (but now no longer in full), at which he himself looks with good-natured, kindly irony: "leaning, on her little closed fist, her *round* face, to which the *full, cherry-colored lips and the little moles* on the cheeks and over the eyebrows gave a very simple, good-natured expression, she did not take her eyes off her son, and kept sighing."

Other forms of characterization do not play a primary role in Turgenev's novels and are not distinguished from the specific traits that strike one. Thus, characterization of a figure in action is almost identical in Turgenev with Goncharov's procedure. A. Mazon correctly writes that Turgenev "conceived a novel as a succession of scenes, connected one to the other by means of a simple plot." Therefore there are no extravagances and unexpected situations in Turgenev's novels. Thereby Turgenev distinguishes himself, among others, from Dostoevsky, in whose novels the actions and behavior of characters is given before they are characterized, and therefore at times seem strange and unexpected (for instance in *The Possessed* and *The Idiot*).

The conflict of "fathers" and "sons," the characters of each of the groups, to a certain extent of course are disclosed in their actions: Bazarov's duel with Pavel Petrovich, his behavior toward Odintsov, his clash and break with Arkady, Arkady's marriage to Katya. Finally Bazarov's infection and death is presented by the author as the result of selfless, noble, but unconsidered action by the hero.

As a rule the action of Turgenev's characters is not accompanied by such long and at times tormenting reflections as frequently occurs in Dostoevsky (it suffices to mention Raskol'nikov). Nor do Turgenev's novels contain extensive "interior monologues" characteristic of Tolstoy's heroes. This fact is explained by Turgenev's special view of the role and place of psychology in the artist's creative process. As early as 1852 Turgenev published in *The Contemporary* a review, "A few Words on Ostrovsky's New Play *The Poor Bride*." Firmly protesting against the dramatist's excessive fragmentation of characters, Turgenev wrote: "In our view Mr. Ostrovsky creeps, so to speak, into the soul of every character he creates; but we permit ourselves to remark to him that this unquestionably useful operation should be completed by the author as a preliminary step. His characters must be in his complete power when he presents them to us. We will be told that that is psychology; very well, but the psychologist must disappear in the artist, as the skeleton disappears beneath the living body, which it serves as a solid but invisible support." This Turgenev affirmed before he wrote his novels. But even later, in a letter to A. A. Fet apropos of Tolstoy's *War and Peace* Turgenev didn't change his view of psychological analysis in an artistic work. He wrote,

> The second part of *The Year 1805* is also weak: how petty and sly that all is, and is Tolstoy really not fed up with those eternal reflections, 'Am I coward, or not' . . . And the historical additions . . . is a puppet show and charlatanism while the psychology—all those sharply pointed boots of Alexander, Speransky's laugh—are nonsense. . . . these delicate reflections, meditations and observations on one's own feeling are boring. * * *

From what has been said several conclusions may be made concerning Turgenev's principles of psychological analysis of characters.

In the first place, in order not to destroy the unity of the created figures, not to fragment characters and not to harm the artistry of the work, the writer must not carry on the analysis of the character psychology before the reader's eyes. All that is accomplished earlier by the writer, who offers the reader only the psychological results. We note that the psychological picture of Bazarov is presented precisely that way in *Fathers and Sons*. Odintsov evaluates Arkady's qualities in accordance with the same psychological principles after the falling out with Bazarov.

In the second place, the device of presenting the psychological process itself ("the dialectic of the soul") a characteristic feature of Tolstoy's art, is completely unacceptable and foreign to Turgenev's heart.

In the third place, opposing the fragmentation of psychological characterization into particularities, Turgenev fights for the wholeness and clarity of the general psychological portrait of the hero, for the careful choice and artistic filtering of the fundamental, primary psychological traits of the character.

All these conclusions find support in the writer's artistic practice. In the psychological tales and socio-psychological novels, where the psychological characterization plays a corresponding role, Turgenev made use of internal monologues, as well as diaries and letters and reminiscences and dreams and indirect speech—that is, all the existing components of psychological characterization, as an artistic device. He artfully alternated that artistic device with others—characterization by portrait, speech, and dialogue.

In those novels, like *Fathers and Sons*, that clearly express the dominating importance of the political, there was no great need for psychological characterization. Therefore it does not occupy so large a place in the novel *Fathers and Sons* as it does, for example, in *A Nest of Noblemen* or *First Love*. This permits us to limit ourselves to general observations on this artistic device.

ZBIGNIEW FOLEJEWSKI

The Recent Storm around Turgenev as a Point in Soviet Aesthetics†

Few works of literature have had such a mixed reception by their contemporary societies as Turgenev's novels, especially *Fathers and Sons*. Nor does interest in Turgenev in Russia seem to diminish with time. Ever since *Fathers and Sons* was first published (1862),

† From *Slavic and East European Journal,* Vol. VI, No. 1 (1962), pp. 21-27. Published by The University of Wisconsin Press. Reprinted with permission of The Regents of the University of Wisconsin.

the views and actions of its hero, Bazarov, have been constantly analyzed and praised or condemned as a social and political program in the light of the author's real or alleged views, and the author himself, in turn, has been persistently identified with this or that political group or movement. In spite of the advanced age of this novel, which is just about to celebrate its hundredth anniversary, a new literary and ideological debate has recently again flared up about it. Its reverberations seem of more than passing interest.

When in my comparative study, "Turgenev and Prus," written ten years ago,[1] I briefly referred to the background of Turgenev's conflict with his contemporaries, I thought it sufficient to note that Turgenev's artistic credo on the rights and duties of a realistic writer had been stated convincingly enough by the author himself in his essay, "Concerning *Fathers and Sons.*"[2] I limited myself to emphasizing social and intellectual situations in Turgenev's Russia which caused the writer, in defense of his artistic integrity, to voice what must have sounded like truisms to Western readers. It may be well, however, again to reassert here some of Turgenev's arguments, especially his insistence on the elementary right of a writer to "recreate reality as he sees it"—a task which he regarded as "the greatest happiness of a writer, *even if it does not coincide with his personal sympathies.*"

At the time of writing my earlier study, it looked as if the matter were settled once and for all. Turgenev's case seemed definitely closed. The novelist seemed to have been granted not only a definite "pardon" but also general posthumous recognition as a great artist, a writer of first importance in the development of Russian realism.

We all know that no real work of art can claim complete objectivity in relationship to the reality it depicts. But we also know that there must exist something called objective artistic truth to make a work of art conceived in the spirit of realism. The existence of this artistic truth in Turgenev's work had been generally recognized by nineteenth-century literary criticism, both in Russia and abroad, and the Soviet period, on the whole, did not bring any radical revaluation of Turgenev on this point. In Soviet critical literature Turgenev is usually presented as a great master whose keen interest in the fate of human beings included such grave social issues as the lot of suppressed Russian peasants, thus stamping his work as "progressive."

Naturally, because of the general social emphasis in Soviet criticism, this last item was easily overstressed, thus counter-balanc-

1. *Slavonic and East European Review,* XLX (1950), pp. 132–38.

2. "Po povodu *Otcov i detej.*" Quoted here from I. S. Turgenev, *Sobranie sočinenij,* X (Moskva, 1949), pp. 260–68.

ing Turgenev's later skepticism toward revolutionary ideas.[3] However, the most recent and quite heated discussion of Turgenev's art in Soviet literary criticism has revived the larger issue of the entire ideological content of Turgenev's work, and specifically the ideological significance of his novel, *Fathers and Sons.* Although most of the arguments in this discussion are not new, there are some that appear to me to merit serious attention by students of Russian literature and literary criticism as they bear on some wider and vital issues in Soviet aesthetics.

II

The discussion was initiated and at once brought to a boiling point by V. Arxipov's article in the first issue of the literary periodical *Russkaja literatura,* "On the Creative History of I. S. Turgenev's Novel *Fathers and Sons.*" [4]

There are several points in the article and in the ensuing polemics that seem of more than ordinary interest. The first point is the revival of the old question of whether Turgenev's novel, *Fathers and Sons,* is a true and "objective" artistic creation or a polemic pamphlet born in the atmosphere of the author's involvement in the political discussion, and serving a non-literary purpose. The second point, partly related to the first, raises the problem of distinguishing those elements in Russian culture to be treated as class products from those to be regarded as national supra-class products of the historical development of the entire people. The third and perhaps the most important point is the problem—a crucial and controversial one in Soviet criticism—of whether creations have their own autonomous life and, if so, whether methods of aesthetic analysis and especially of structural analysis should not take it into account.

In the discussion of the first point Arxipov seems to follow in part the old line of reasoning initiated by M. Antonvič in his famous article in *Russkij vestnik* (1862), "An Asmodeus of Our Time." [5] However, he makes no direct reference to Antonovič, and his own approach—especially as regards the concept of a literary hero—is in general accord with the canons of socialist realism.

Turgenev's contemporaries blamed him mainly for his literary

3. For these standard views see for example such representative works as: P. N. Sakulina, *I. S. Turgenev* (Moskva, 1918); V. Lvov-Rogačevskij, *I. S. Turgenev* (Moska, Leningrad, 1926); M. K. Kleman, *I. S. Turgenev* (Leningrad, 1936); N. L. Brodskij, *I. S. Turgenev* (Moskva, 1950); S. M. Petrov, *I. S. Turgenev* (Moskva, 1950); P. G. Pustovojt, *I. S. Turgenev* (Moskva, 1957); E. M. Efimova, *I. S. Turgenev, Seminarij* (Leningrad, 1958). This last work contains a special account (Chapter XI, parts 2 and 3, pp. 33–92) on Turgenev in Soviet literary criticism.

4. "K tvorčeskoj istorii romana I. S. Turgeneva *Otcy i deti,*" *Russkaja literatura,* 1958, No. 1 pp. 132–162.

5. "Asmodej našego vremeni." Included in M. Antonovic, *Izbrannye stat'i* (Leningrad, 1938), pp. 141–202.

choices, i. e., the distribution of light and shade in his panorama of the Russian reality of the time. They did not object on principle to a *roman à thèse;*[6] what they were not satisfied with was rather the lack of a clear social engagement on Turgenev's part. Arxipov follows the same line, only in the opposite direction; his main thesis is that the entire matrix of this novel is *strictly political history,* and that political considerations deform the artistic concept. He does not accept the notion of any specific autonomous life led by literary figures, and he challenges all attempts to divorce certain social and political aspects of Russian life at Turgenev's time from their later development. Quite logically he insists on the truth that certain issues discussed in Turgenev's novel were political issues important in Turgenev's time, and that they do have direct bearing on later ideological developments in Russia. He turns very sharply against the notion that realism is a classless phenomenon above and beyond political considerations. As for the concept of the hero of *Fathers and Sons,* to Arxipov as to other critics who consistently follow the principles of socialist realism it is a sign of artistic failure that Bazarov can be at one and the same time victorious in his skirmishes with Pavel Kirsanov and defeated in his struggle with himself. In the fact that Turgenev conceived Bazarov as a *tragic* figure such critics see political tendentiousness and artistic inconsistency; and in the fact that in Bazarov's polemics there are echoes of the views of Dobroljubov and Černyshevskij in a somewhat edited form, they see an artistically illegitimate device. Incidentally, this happens to coincide with the old accusation that in the figure of Bazarov Turgenev gave a "caricature" rather than a hero—a charge so painful to Turgenev that he could hardly find words too strong to discredit it.

Arxipov's polemic fervor leads him to statements which make literary argument with him rather easy. He asserts, for example, that Turgenev in *Fathers and Sons* "forged a weapon for fighting the democratic movement," which served both contemporary and subsequent reactionary circles well. The weakness here is that while such a statement is partly true, the conclusions Arxipov draws from it do not necessarily follow. He overlooks the fact that Turgenev was attacked with equal fervor by the "reactionary circles" and—by the same token—he admits what various Russian and foreign literary critics have pointed out, namely, that a work of "real" realism cannot be evaluated on the basis of the political context. Arxipov completely ignores the elementary truth that Turgenev's work was a contemporary novel based on his concept of literary realism, and that consequently it must be regarded

6. A novel designed to illustrate or prove an idea [*Editor*].

as a literary transformation of reality as perceived by the artist. Turgenev belongs to the school of writers who neither avoided debating contemporary issues nor denied their own sympathies, but at the same time, Turgenev's artistic integrity on these points has been quite successfully argued by people belonging to different social and political groups. Arxipov, consequently, finds himself rather isolated in his position that *Fathers and Sons* is above all a political pamphlet. After all, the "tragic" figure of Bazarov, quite apart from Turgenev's panoramic distribution of light and shade, is an epitome of the Russian intelligentsia. From the point of view of literary continuity, Bazarov is a logical development, and one could almost say that he had to appear as a literary hero whether Turgenev anticipated his function in the political struggle or not.

III

As was pointed out in one of the first polemical articles after the publication of Arxipov's arguments (G. Bjalyj, "V. Arxipov Against I. Turgenev"),[7] there is very little new evidence in support of this otherwise old argument. The only new source material introduced by Arxipov is a letter to Turgenev from P. Annenkov, in which its writer suggested that Turgenev should make certain changes in his novel. Bjalyj argues that these changes are inconsequential so far as the general character of Bazarov is concerned and that, if anything, they actually tend to free the novel of direct political implications. It might be added that some of Annenkov's suggestions may have been aimed at making Bazarov's figure less militant, less offensive for the liberals, but that Turgenev's willingness to follow them can be justified in most cases by the fact that they make the character *artistically* more convincing.

One of the key elements in Arxipov's discussion is the matter of Bazarov's "prototype." For Arxipov this is something in which the notion of class-struggle and political determination is self-evident. "In the choice of a prototype is the evaluation of this prototype," postulates Arxipov, as if the idea itself were something no one could deny. Actually, a lengthy discussion with Arxipov on this point was undertaken in an article by P. Pustovojt under a somewhat malicious title: "In Pursuit of Sensation." [8]

Arxipov is, of course, right in his statement that Bazarov's weight as a spokesman critical of the program of the liberal circles in Russia is questionable—for the simple reason that Turgenev's entire critique of liberalism is consistently developed from the positions of liberalism. But the very premise that Bazarov as a literary hero is primarily a tool in the class struggle, political

7. "V. Arxipov protiv I. Turgeneva," *Novyi mir,* 1958, No. 8, pp. 255–259.

8. "V pogone za sensaciej," *Voprosy literatury,* 1958, No. 8, pp. 241–242.

struggle, etc., would still have to be proved. In any case, Arxipov's line of reasoning, even if we accept his thesis about the strictly political character of the novel, can be easily attacked (as was done by L. Krutkova in *Neva*, 1958, No. 9, p. 242) by pointing out that Turgenev's own relationship to his hero is dual in nature.

Most of the Soviet critics participating in the debate do not agree with Arxipov's main thesis, namely, with his assertions that: (1) the entire history of the novel *Fathers and Sons* is political history; and (2) the hero concept in this novel is primarily a reflection of class struggle.

Particularly outspoken have been articles by E. Osetrov, "New Variations On the Old Theme" [9] and G. Kunicyn, "A Scholarly Essay, or a . . . Pasquil." [1] Arxipov, finding himself challenged, wrote a lengthy reply, "Against the Theory of the Single Stream," [2] sharp in tone and, on the whole, unyielding in argument.

Although he was slightly more generous this time in granting Turgenev some of the privileges due an artist, Arxipov repeated most of his main statements and even added a few new arguments in their defense. Especially in his exegesis of Marx and Lenin was he on officially firm ground. From the position of Marxist aesthetics, it was relatively easy for him to beat down arguments by his opponents which were based on the presumed internal autonomy of art and on the right of literary critics to treat literary development as an immanent "single stream" process.

IV

For an outside reader, it might have appeared at first sight that Arxipov's argumentation was absolutely authoritative. Indeed, in the context of the official theory of Socialist Realism many of his statements are quite tenable. Nevertheless, even in this context, his main thesis about the exclusively political character of *Fathers and Sons* turned out to be too extremist, especially in the light of Turgenev's entire artistic production, which after all cannot be assessed adequately today by simply applying contemporary formulae of "Critical Realism," "Socialist Realism," etc. Arxipov himself was not able to ignore the long established nineteenth-century formula (later convincingly argued, for example, by George Lukacs, and brought out in the course of the polemics by some of Arxipov's Soviet opponents) about autonomous sets of values in art which may amount to a "progressive" total effect in works of realism not necessarily pre-determined by the author's ideological platform. In any case, Arxipov's reply was not the last word in the dispute.

9. "Novye variacii na staruju temu," *Literatura i žizn'*, 1958, No. 33.
1. "Naučnaja stat'ja ili . . . paskvil'," *Pod'em*, 1958, No. 4, pp. 189–195.
2. "Protiv teorii edinogo potoka," *Russkaja literatura*, 1959, No. 2, pp. 95–130.

Especially significant from this point of view are editorial remarks in "Literary Scholarship and the Present Day" in *Voprosy literatury*.[3] What this article suggests is that the ideological premises of Arxipov's theses are not impeccable. A scrutiny of Arxipov's interpretation of statements by Marx, Lenin, and other authorities leads his opponents to repeat the argument that Arxipov's approach contains "remnants of vulgar sociologism" as well as remnants of the concepts of the so-called "voprekists," i.e., sworn opponents of the sociological school.

This article is symptomatic of the entire problem of the literary and aesthetic situation in the Soviet Union. It seems that some kind of a compromise between formal aesthetic analysis of literary art and its strictly ideological interpretation is being sought by some Soviet scholars and critics.[4] The recent renaissance of interest in structural stylistic research manifested in a number of publications and especially re-emphasized in such authoritative works as Viktor Vinogradov's *The Language of Belles-Lettres*,[5] poses interesting questions about what new direction, if any, literary research will eventually take. Given the doctrine of socialist realism, the answers are not easily foreseeable.

It is interesting to note that in the same issue of *Russkaja literatura* in which Arxipov's second article was printed, there appeared an article by G. Fridlender, "Concerning the Debate on *Fathers and Sons*," [6] which is also an attempt at some kind of compromise between the line represented by Arxipov and that taken by some of his opponents. Although Fridlender agrees with several of Arxipov's theoretical statements, he is inclined to admit that Arxipov went too far in his interpretations of purely literary facts. He sees the chief value of the debate in the fact that it reveals certain important areas in Soviet literary criticism where some clarification should be sought. One of these areas needing investigation, according to Fridlender, is the relationship between national and class elements in the literary heritage.

Thus, the controversy over Turgenev, not very fruitful, perhaps, so far as a better understanding of Turgenev is concerned, reveals some interesting divergencies in Soviet aesthetics by opening up debate of more general literary and aesthetic issues with a vigor unknown since the introduction of socialist realism.

3. "Literaturovedenie i sovremennost'," *Voprosy literatury*, 1959, No. 10. pp. 8–16. See also rebuttals to Arxipov's second article by G. Bjalyj and A. Dement'ev, under the common title "Arxipov polemiziruet," in *Novyj mir*, 1959, No. 10, pp. 261–265.

4. As an interesting attempt at such compromise, one may regard the book on Turgenev's novel by P. G. Pustovojt, *Roman I. S. Turgeneva "Otcy i deti" i idejnaja bor'ba 60-x godov XIX veka* (Moskva, 1960).

5. *O jazyke xudožestvennoj literatury* (Moskva, 1959).

6. "K sporam ob *Otcax i detjax*," *Voprosy literatury*, 1959, No. 10, pp. 130–140.

A Chronology of Turgenev's Life

(The first date represents the Russian Calendar, the second the Western. See note to Turgenev's Letters).

1818 October 28 (November 9). Born in Orel.
1819–27 Raised on the estate Spasskoe.
1827–34 Moves to Moscow, matriculates at Moscow University, 1833.
1834 Transfers to St. Petersburg University. Father dies.
1837 Graduates from university.
1838–41 European jaunt, attends University of Berlin. Returns to Russia in May (June), 1841.
1842 Passes examination for M.A. at St. Petersburg University, but does not finish required dissertation.
1843 Publishes his first narrative poem. Meets Belinsky. Meets Pauline Viardot, French singer, to whom he remained devoted till his death.
1847–50 Publication of *A Hunter's Sketches* and stay in Paris with the Viardots. Returns to Russia in June, 1850. Mother dies November 16 (28), 1850.
1852 Under arrest April 16 (28)–May 15 (27) for laudatory obituary on Gogol. Lionized (in jail and elsewhere) by society and intellectuals.
1852–53 "Exiled" to Spasskoe under police surveillance.
1856 Publishes *Rudin*. Goes abroad July 21 (August 2).
1858 Returns to Russia.
1859 Publishes *Nest of Noblemen*. Goes abroad.
1860 Publishes *On the Eve, First Love*. Goes abroad.
1861 Returns to Russia. Finishes *Fathers and Sons*. Goes abroad.
1862 Publishes *Fathers and Sons* (February). Visits Russia.
1863 Settles in Baden-Baden with the Viardots. Will make six visits to Russia in the next eight years.
1867 Publishes *Smoke*.
1869 Publishes *Reminiscences* and *Collected Works*.
1870 Publishes *A King Lear of the Steppes*.
1872 Publishes *Spring Freshets*. *A Month in the Country* (1850, published 1855), first performed in Moscow.
1875 Jointly with the Viardots buys estate in Bougival near Paris.
1877 Publishes *Virgin Soil*.
1879 Honorary degree from Oxford University.

1880 In Russia, participates in Pushkin festival. More or less makes peace with Tolstoy and Dostoevsky.

1882 Publishes "Poems in Prose," prepares new collected edition. Becomes ill.

1883 Dies in Bougival September 3 after terrible agonies (cancer), during which he for a while kept a detailed diary of the course of the disease. At one point near the end he hurled an inkwell at Pauline Viardot, an act of plagiarism (from Luther) and of ingratitude to the source of his inspiration for thirty-five years.

Selected Bibliography

A complete English bibliography may be found in *Turgenev in English. A checklist of works by and about him* compiled by Riss Yachnin and David H. Stam. New York, The New York Public Library, 1962.

Blotner, Joseph L. *The Political Novel.* New York, 1951

Bourget, Paul. *Nouveaux essais de psychologie contemporaine.* Paris, 1888.

Cecil, David Lord. *Poets and Story-tellers.* London, 1949.

Freeborn, Richard. *Turgenev. The Novelist's Novelist.* London, 1960.

Gettman, Royal A. *Turgenev in England and America.* Urbana, Illinois, 1941.

Gifford, Henry. *The Hero of His Time. A Theme in Russian Literature.* London, 1950.

Granjard, Henri. *Ivan Tourguénev et les courants politiques et sociaux de son temps.* Paris, 1954.

Hare, Richard. *Portrait of Russian Personalities Between Reform and Revolution.* New York, 1958.

Herschkowitz, Harry. *Democratic Ideas in Turgenev's Novels.* New York, 1932.

Lloyd, J. A. T., *Ivan Turgenev.* London, 1942.

Margarshack, David. *Turgenev, A Life.* New York, 1954.

Matlaw, Ralph E., editor. *Belinsky, Chernyshevsky, and Dobrolyubov. Selected Criticism,* New York, 1962.

Mirsky, Dmitry S., *A History of Russian Literature.* New York, 1949.

Maurois, Andre. *Tourguéniev.* Paris, 1952.

Moore, George. *Impressions and Opinions.* London, 1891.

Phelps, Gilbert. *The Russian Novel in English Fiction.* London, 1956.

Trautman, Reinhold. *Turgenev als Novelist.* Leipzig, 1948.

Wilson, Edmund. "Turgenev and the Life-Giving Drop." In *Turgenev's Literary Reminiscences.* New York, 1958.

Yarmolinsky, Avrahm. *Turgenev. The Man, His Art and His Age.* New York, 1959.

Zhitova, Vera. *The Turgenev Family.* London, 1947.

NORTON CRITICAL EDITIONS

AUSTEN *Emma* edited by Stephen M. Parrish
AUSTEN *Pride and Prejudice* edited by Donald J. Gray
Beowulf (the Donaldson translation) edited by Joseph M. Tuso
BOCCACCIO *The Decameron* selected, translated, and edited by Mark Musa and Peter E. Bondanella
BRONTË, CHARLOTTE *Jane Eyre* edited by Richard J. Dunn
BRONTË, EMILY *Wuthering Heights* edited by William M. Sale, Jr. *Revised Edition*
CARROLL *Alice in Wonderland* edited by Donald J. Gray
CHOPIN *The Awakening* edited by Margaret Culley
CLEMENS *Adventures of Huckleberry Finn* edited by Sculley Bradley, Richmond Croom Beatty, E. Hudson Long, and Thomas Cooley *Second Edition*
CONRAD *Heart of Darkness* edited by Robert Kimbrough *Revised Edition*
CONRAD *Lord Jim* edited by Thomas Moser
CRANE *The Red Badge of Courage* edited by Sculley Bradley, Richmond Croom Beatty, E. Hudson Long, and Donald Pizer *Second Edition*
Darwin edited by Philip Appleman
DEFOE *Moll Flanders* edited by Edward Kelly
DEFOE *Robinson Crusoe* edited by Michael Shinagel
DICKENS *Hard Times* edited by George Ford and Sylvère Monod
John Donne's Poetry selected and edited by A. L. Clements
DOSTOEVSKY *Crime and Punishment* (the Coulson translation) edited by George Gibian *Revised Edition*
DOSTOEVSKY *The Brothers Karamazov* (the Garnett translation revised by Ralph E. Matlaw) edited by Ralph E. Matlaw
DREISER *Sister Carrie* edited by Donald Pizer
ELIOT *Middlemarch* edited by Bert G. Hornback
FIELDING *Tom Jones* edited by Sheridan Baker
FLAUBERT *Madame Bovary* edited with a substantially new translation by Paul de Man
GOETHE *Faust* translated by Walter Arndt and edited by Cyrus Hamlin
HARDY *The Mayor of Casterbridge* edited by James K. Robinson
HARDY *The Return of the Native* edited by James Gindin
HARDY *Tess of the D'Urbervilles* edited by Scott Elledge
HAWTHORNE *The House of the Seven Gables* edited by Seymour Gross
HAWTHORNE *The Scarlet Letter* edited by Sculley Bradley, Richmond Croom Beatty, and E. Hudson Long
HOMER *The Odyssey* translated and edited by Albert Cook
IBSEN *The Wild Duck* translated and edited by Dounia B. Christiani
JAMES *The Ambassadors* edited by S. P. Rosenbaum
JAMES *The Portrait of a Lady* edited by Robert D. Bamberg
JAMES *The Turn of the Screw* edited by Robert Kimbrough
Ben Jonson and the Cavalier Poets selected and edited by Hugh Maclean
MALTHUS *An Essay on the Principle of Population* edited by Philip Appleman
MELVILLE *The Confidence-Man* edited by Hershel Parker
MELVILLE *Moby-Dick* edited by Harrison Hayford and Hershel Parker
MILL *On Liberty* edited by David Spitz
MILTON *Paradise Lost* edited by Scott Elledge
MORE *Utopia* translated and edited by Robert M. Adams

NEWMAN *Apologia Pro Vita Sua* edited by David J. DeLaura
NORRIS *McTeague* edited by Donald Pizer
Adrienne Rich's Poetry selected and edited by Barbara Charlesworth Gelpi and Albert Gelpi
The Writings of St. Paul edited by Wayne A. Meeks
SHAKESPEARE *Hamlet* edited by Cyrus Hoy
SHAKESPEARE *Henry IV, Part I* edited by James J. Sanderson *Revised Edition*
Bernard Shaw's Plays edited by Warren Sylvester Smith
Shelley's Poetry and Prose edited by Donald H. Reiman and Sharon B. Powers
SOPHOCLES *Oedipus Tyrannus* translated and edited by Luci Berkowitz and Theodore F. Brunner
Edmund Spenser's Poetry selected and edited by Hugh Maclean
STENDHAL *Red and Black* translated and edited by Robert M. Adams
SWIFT *Gulliver's Travels* edited by Robert A. Greenberg *Revised Edition*
The Writings of Jonathan Swift edited by Robert A. Greenberg and William B. Piper
TENNYSON *In Memoriam* edited by Robert Ross
Tennyson's Poetry selected and edited by Robert W. Hill, Jr.
THOREAU *Walden and Civil Disobedience* edited by Owen Thomas
TOLSTOY *Anna Karenina* (the Maude translation) edited by George Gibian
TOLSTOY *War and Peace* (the Maude translation) edited by George Gibian
TURGENEV *Fathers and Sons* edited with a substantially new translation by Ralph E. Matlaw
VOLTAIRE *Candide* translated and edited by Robert M. Adams
WHITMAN *Leaves of Grass* edited by Sculley Bradley and Harold W. Blodgett
WOLLSTONECRAFT *A Vindication of the Rights of Woman* edited by Carol H. Poston
Middle English Lyrics selected and edited by Maxwell S. Luria and Richard L. Hoffman
Modern Drama edited by Anthony Caputi
Restoration and Eighteenth-Century Comedy edited by Scott McMillin